The Ba... Mill

by

Terri Nixon

This novel is entirely a work of fiction. The names, characters and incidents portrayed in it are the product of the author's imagination. Any resemblance to actual persons, living or dead, or events or localities is entirely coincidental.

Published by Lynher Mill Publishing
Plymouth. UK

Paperback Edition 01 August 2015
ISBN 978-0-9926956-4-4

Copyright © Terri Nixon 01 August 2015

Terri Nixon asserts the moral right to be identified as the author of this work. All rights reserved in all media. No part of this publication may be reproduced, stored in a retrieval system, or transmitted, in any form, or by any means, electronic, mechanical, photocopying, recording or otherwise, without the prior written permission of the author and/or publisher.

The Battle of Lynher Mill

by

Terri Nixon

Lynher Mill Publishing

About the author

Terri Nixon was born in Plymouth, England in 1965. At the age of 9 she moved with her family to Cornwall, to a small village on the edge of Bodmin Moor, where she discovered a love of writing that has stayed with her ever since. She also discovered apple-scrumping, and how to jump out of a hayloft without breaking any bones, but no-one's ever offered to pay her for doing those.

Terri now lives in Plymouth with her youngest son, and works in the Faculty of Arts and Humanities at Plymouth University, where she is constantly baffled by the number of students who don't possess pens.

Also by Terri Nixon:

The Lynher Mill Chronicles:
The Dust of Ancients (Lynher Mill Publishing, 2013)
The Lightning and the Blade (Lynher Mill Publishing, 2014)
The Oaklands Manor Trilogy:
Maid of Oaklands Manor (published by Piatkus, 2013)
A Rose in Flanders Fields (published by Carina UK, 2014)
Daughter of Dark River Farm (published by Carina UK, 2015)

Writing as T Nixon:
NightRise: horror collection *(Lynher Mill Publishing, 2013)*

This book is dedicated to The Yank and The Brummie.

Let there always be nougat and pasties, and walls with sitting room for 3.

~The Drama Queen ~

Chapter One.

Welsh Coast. Late 1970s

Right up until the moment she fell, she had been certain of escape. So certain in fact, that she had already begun to laugh as the rough grass flew beneath her feet, her hair tugged in all directions in the salt-scented air. She was aware of Lawbryn running beside her, matching her pace but not her humour. Such a fusser, he was! He'd even tried to curtail her harmless little game: full-forming and engaging the mortal fish-finders in lively conversation – after a while she'd revert to her natural form, leaving the men staring at the apparently empty stretch of beach and wondering what had stolen their attention for so long. It had been fun.

Until a few minutes ago.

Lawbryn had been behaving less like her friend, and more like the full-forming teacher she no longer needed. Using his impressive height he'd frowned down at her. 'This cruel streak of yours is a sad surprise, Dafna.'

'I am not cruel, they are not harmed. See?' She'd waved a hand towards the last of the fish-finders. 'They have forgotten me already!'

'Your father will not be pleased to learn of—' His gaze slipped beyond her, and then he managed, in a strangled voice, 'Gwyllgi!'

Dafna's heart faltered, and she turned and strained her eyes through the gathering dusk. If this was Lawbryn's notion of teasing, to teach her a lesson… but it was no jest; a sleek, powerful, and hideously over-sized hound pounded across the beach towards them. Its eyes were glowing red and its mouth hanging open, and although it was too far away to see, Dafna knew from her learnings that it would be showing rows of crooked, dirty teeth.

Frozen in terror, she watched the hound coming closer, kicking up sand, slavering, those eyes fixed on them alone. Neither she nor Lawbryn could move, until it was close enough to hear its rhythmic, grunting growl, and then Lawbryn's paralysis broke.

He grabbed her hand. 'Run!'

They ran for the cliffs, mercifully close since the tide was almost all the way in. The gwyllgi's pace increased, narrowing the gap between them. Its howl cut across the beach, unheard by the mortals, but terrifyingly loud to Dafna and Lawbryn.

'I should not have allowed you to mock the fishermen,' Lawbryn gasped as he dropped her hand, letting her find her own way. They slipped and stumbled, their usually nimble feet alternately sliding into rock-pools, and then finding tenuous purchase on the seaweed strewn rocks. 'The bwca will not stand for it!'

'I wasn't mocking them,' Dafna panted. 'I was just

playing!' But Lawbryn was right; she had risked frightening the fish-finders away, and if they'd left, the bwca would have nothing to eat. The only recourse left to the ancient spirits was to summon their hell-hound... The elements be thanked Lawbryn had seen it while it was still far up the beach. Had they both been distracted they would have been ripped apart by now.

They reached the foot of the cliff and climbed fast, both now finding footholds with ease. Dafna was always just a little way ahead; Lawbryn was older, but heavily built, and he spent far less time out here than Dafna, who knew every part of these cliffs like her own hearth.

Gaining the top, she reached back to pull Lawbryn up, and together they watched in horrified fascination as the gwyllgi struggled on the rocky cliff side. It paced, still snarling, never taking its malevolent red gaze off them, and whenever it appeared to find a likely path, Dafna's limbs turned to water and she prepared to flee again. But eventually, and after a final, frustrated howl, it turned back the way it had come and was soon gone from sight.

Dafna's mood was rarely shaken for long, and she grinned in triumph at her friend and teacher and began to run again, this time towards home. She found a faster pace, running now for the simple joy of it, along the cliff path where the grass had been beaten down by countless mortal feet.

Lawbryn drew alongside and tried to take her

hand again, to draw her further inland. Startled by the sudden contact, she glanced sideways at him and her hair blew across her face. She tried to brush it aside, but stumbled, and the ground beneath her left foot vanished. Her leg buckled and she heard Lawbryn shout in horror, but then all her senses were taken up by breath-halting terror as she tumbled into emptiness.

A numbing impact in her shoulder twisted her in the air, and through the pain that quickly followed there came a flash of realisation that the blow had probably saved her life; entering the water feet-first instead of head-first, she went straight down, her right foot smashing into rock.

She felt her ankle crack, and was only just able to prevent herself from screaming and allowing the sea water to rush down her throat. The pain was huge, white-hot and immediate, but the determination to survive was stronger – she kicked down with her uninjured foot and propelled herself to the surface, gasping as her head broke through, and sucking in a lungful of air before going under again.

Aware she was in danger of panicking herself into a watery end, she searched within herself for calm, and the next time she broke the surface she stayed up, and struggled to the edge of the pool. Shoulder and ankle throbbing, she reached out for the slippery rock and clung on, fighting rising sickness.

Lawbryn's terrified voice cut through the sound of the sea as he slid down the cliff side, and Dafna felt a flash of anger; quite right he should be scared, the whole incident was his fault! But she couldn't bring herself to chastise him when he reached out to help her from the water, and she saw how deathly white and trembling he was.

Once she was beside him on dry ground, he took off his cloak and draped it around her. 'Thank the elements the tide was in.'

'Thank them too that I hit that,' Dafna gestured to the grassy outcropping that had spun her in mid-flight. 'If I had not, I would have gone in the other way up, and broken my head instead of my ankle.'

He drew a worried breath. 'Your ankle is broken?'

'I believe so.' She fought to keep her voice calm. 'Now, please… stop staring and help me.'
He slipped an arm about her waist, and held tightly to her hand as she limped to a flat rock and sat down. She felt increasingly sick and shivery as she looked up at the cliff face that towered above them. 'I need help to get back up.'

'You can't climb!' Lawbryn said, appalled. 'We'll have to take the long way back.'

'But we don't know if the bwcas' hound has really gone. What if it waits farther along the beach?'

They both looked around in renewed alarm. 'I think it's gone,' Lawbryn ventured. 'We will just have to be vigilant. Come on.'

Dafna reluctantly took his proffered arm, and they arrived back at her home well after darkness had descended. Her father was sitting on the rocks, a short distance from where they lived, and, on seeing her, he rose and embraced her, before holding her at arm's length and letting his anger loose in a torrent of half-finished sentences.

Only as he ran out of breath did he realise Dafna had been leaning on Lawbryn through more than tiredness. The walk had almost dried her clothing, but her ankle had swelled inside her boot, and as she tried to put her weight on it she gave an involuntary yelp. Hendrig scooped her up, and she saw him shoot another glowering look at Lawbryn before turning to carry her home.

The moment her father pushed aside the heavy curtain to their home Dafna knew something was different. Her mother was in the cooking room, preparing something of a feast, to judge from the delicious smell. Candles lit the corners, throwing warm, flickering light and creating interesting shadows. Hendrig put Dafna down on the seat by the fire, and her mother came in, drying her hands in her skirt, and began to scold her for her lateness. Then she looked more closely, and her brow creased in sudden alarm.

'What have you done?'

'I fell.' Dafna tried to smile, to lessen her mother's worry, but the warmth and familiarity of her surroundings, and the look of concern on Gethli's face were all too much. She burst into tears.

'Hush!' Gethli said quickly, 'Come with me, I'll help you to change and then you will meet our guest.' She pressed a square of linen to Dafna's eyes to blot the tears, as she had when Dafna was a child.

Dafna sniffed and swallowed another sob. 'I can't walk very well, I think my ankle is broken.'

Gethli flinched, but her voice was matter-of-fact. 'Then we'll splint it. But we can't do anything until we've taken those boots off. Come on.'

They hobbled towards the back room, and it was only then that Gethli's words sank in. Dafna looked around. 'We have a guest?'

'We are honoured by a visit from a traveller. From the Cornish coast.'

'Where is she?'

'Trust you to think it to be female,' Gethli smiled. 'Men can be adventurous also, you know.' She eased Dafna down onto the bed, and knelt down to begin unlacing her boots. 'His name is Talfrid, and he is on his way north, following the coast as far as it will take him. He has stopped to ask a night's rest and a meal.'

Dafna tried not to yelp as Gethli parted the lacings of her boot. She gritted her teeth and concentrated on the conversation instead; anything to take her mind off what she knew must happen next. 'You didn't say where he is,' she prompted.

'He is changing into some of Hendrig's garments so he can wash his own.' Gethli grimaced. 'Your foot has swelled terribly, I am going to have to prepare you a drink before we try to remove this boot.'

Dafna took a deep breath, and hunted for some of the bravery for which she was well known. She wasn't sure if she'd found it, but she found a resolve at least, to have this awful business over as quickly as possible. 'Cut it away, mother, but let's do it quickly.'

'I am not sure our knives are sharp enough—'

'Mine is. Use that.'

The new voice was deeper than her father's, and Dafna's gaze rose from her foot and fixed on the man framed by the crooked doorway, his head almost brushing the top. His hair was dark, his face strong and appealing, and his frown of concern melted under her scrutiny, and became a surprisingly shy smile as he held out his blade, handle first.

'My name is Talfrid. I am quite skilled in healing, if you are in need of any assistance. It's the least I can do, in return for food, and rest under your roof.'

'I expect you have need of such a skill.' Dafna's voice was breathless and uncertain, suddenly. 'Your travels must be dangerous at times.'

Taking her interest as permission to come into the room, Talfrid nodded. 'I have myself broken an ankle. And an arm, and two of my fingers.' His smile widened and became self-deprecatory. 'I am a clumsy oaf, and that is a fact.'

Dafna arched an eyebrow. 'Perhaps then, it's better if you leave the blade-wielding to Mother.'

He laughed, and shrugged. 'Perhaps you're right,' he conceded, and in the midst of the relaxed chuckles that followed, he bent quickly and sliced down the side of Dafna's boot. He had pulled it off her foot with his other hand before they had even realised what he was going to do.

Dafna did yelp, but it was over so quickly, and the relief so great, that she could have wept all over again, this time with gratitude. Between them Gethli and Talfrid bound her ankle and foot, tightly enough to reduce the pain to a manageable throb that matched the one in her shoulder. Talfrid rose and sheathed his knife once more, then he held out his hand, into which Dafna placed hers without thinking twice.

He helped her to stand, and Dafna caught her mother's satisfied smile. 'You deserve second and third helpings for this,' she said to Talfrid, to cover her continuing uncertainty; standing beside him she felt her heartbeat speeding up. She was sure her hand must be clammy with nerves, but he tightened his hold as she wavered slightly on her uneven feet.

'Talfrid,' Gethli put in, still smiling, 'I think Hendrig would enjoy your company, and Dafna must put on clean, dry clothing before she catches a chill.'

'Of course.' Talfrid released Dafna's hand. 'I look forward to hearing the story of how all this came about. I am sure it can have been nothing mundane.'

'Oh, it was.' Dafna shot a guilty glance at her mother. 'But I will tell you while we eat, I promise.'

Alone in her room, Dafna folded her hand over the warm spot left by Talfrid's palm. Then she took a deep breath and shed her wrinkled, still-damp day clothes, wincing at the ache in her shoulder. She shivered in the cool air at the back of the cavern, and pulled on a thick, shapeless shirt that hung almost to her knees. Her hand automatically hovered over her most comfortable and familiar leggings, until she remembered the candles burning in the main room; her parents held this guest in high regard already, and it would not be out of place to dress well for the occasion.

She removed the shirt, and instead chose a plain, cream-coloured shift. She added a subtly decorated green tunic, and released her auburn hair from its binding and brushed it, so it spilled over her shoulders in glossy waves. Her good foot slid into a flat, leather indoor shoe, and, looking in the mirror she took a deep breath and told herself her father would not punish her so severely if she appeared more the woman than the child.

Still she felt a nervous twist inside, and she shook back her hair and straightened her shoulders. Perhaps she should tell a version of the truth that would not anger him too much? *A lie*, her mind instantly fired back at her, worsening the nerves with a thread of guilt; she never lied, and it would be all the more betrayal if she did so now, since her parents would believe her without question. Well, she would just have to see how the mood lay during the meal.

Throughout the evening she could barely keep her eyes from straying to their guest. His stories rolled over her in his low, gruff voice, and his face became more and more animated the deeper he went into his adventures, drawing them out and making the most mild of occurrences sound like the wildest of threats. His exaggerations were so obvious that the little party grew loud with laughter, and with Talfrid's mimicking of the screams of those he had apparently battled and bested.

Now and again one of his stories would have the cold, frightening ring of truth to it, and more than once Dafna saw his eyes take on a faraway look as he remembered. Then he would shake the memory loose, and return to his light-hearted stories.

'But now,' he said at last, accepting more wine from a still-chuckling Hendrig, 'the fair Dafna. How came you to be wearing damp clothing, and with a broken ankle?'

She hesitated and looked at her father, and Talfrid saw that look, and smiled. 'As you have heard,' he said gently, 'I have made my fair share of avoidable mistakes, and suffered from my silly misadventures. So, may we hear your story, just to spare me the embarrassment?'

Dafna blinked, and realised what he had been doing all along. How could her father scold her now? She took a deep breath, and told them almost everything, omitting only the reason for her fall. Justly or not, Hendrig would place the blame squarely on Lawbryn's shoulders, and so she merely told them she had stumbled during their flight from the gwyllgi. She also took pains to point out how Lawbryn had helped pull her from the water – as cross as she had been with him, he did not deserve Hendrig's legendary wrath.

When she had finished, she turned warily to her father, and there was a silence while he looked back at her, his face reflecting the eternal conflict between parental responsibility and deep affection. At last, mellowed by good companionship and wine, he subsided and chose his path.

'I think you have taken your punishment. But let me hear no more talk of you playing with mortals in such a cruel manner. Next time, the gwyllgi might not be so far off when the bwca send for it.'

'I promise,' Dafna said, seized with relief. She met Talfrid's eyes, but looked away quickly; she had thought to offer him gratitude, but there was something altogether warmer in his expression which made her heart race again. She picked at her bread, her appetite waning, but her mother's pointed look ensured she ate something, at least.

'When you are married you had better ensure you pass on that advice to your own children,' Hendrig went on, and Dafna's eyes widened.

'Married?'

'You have been promised to Lawbryn since you were both totterlings, you knew that.'

The mouthful Dafna had just taken stuck in her throat, and her eyes and nose burned. She coughed. 'It was just a notion, surely? A possibility?'

Gethli shot her husband a look of annoyance. 'Tonight is not the time for such talk. We are in company, and Dafna has had a frightening fall. We will discuss it another time.'

'But this is no surprise.' Hendrig appeared genuinely puzzled by the women's responses. 'Gethli, you knew as well as I that the two of them would wed one day. And, Dafna, have we not talked of it before?'

'I thought it was *just* talk,' Dafna managed, not looking at Talfrid. What she dreaded most was his indifference; that she should look up and see no reflection of her own bitter disappointment in his face. 'Lawbryn and I are friends, nothing more. As he and Brythnen are friends. I cannot marry him.' *Not now*, she almost added, but just stopped herself in time; the questions that followed would be unanswerable.

'I will leave you alone,' Talfrid said quietly, into the difficult silence. 'You need to be a family tonight, not a host. The sky is mild, I can sleep anywhere.' He pushed back his chair and stood. 'I am grateful for the meal, Gethli, and I shall spread word of your family's generosity towards honest travellers.' Dafna still could not look at him, but his voice sounded tighter now.

'Stay, Talfrid, please,' Gethli begged. 'You must not feel pushed away, we will talk of family matters another time.'

'Yes, sit down, man,' Hendrig said. 'We can discuss this with Dafna in the morning.'

Dafna dropped her bread back onto her plate. 'There is no discussion to be had. I will not marry Lawbryn.'

'Hush, child,' Gethli chided, not without sympathy. 'The matter is closed until the morning.'

After a pause, Talfrid took his seat again. 'I accept, thank you.'

Dafna at last felt able to look at him, and what she saw made her heart leap fiercely against her ribs;

his smile had gone, and he looked as though his appetite had deserted him despite his appreciation of her mother's cooking skills. As if the light had gone out from behind his eyes. He looked, in fact, exactly as she felt.

But he cleared his throat and kept his tone light, conversational. 'So, you call them bwca? The Cornish too, have their buccas. Only a little difference in our speech, I think, Hendrig?'

While he and Hendrig talked of the spirits that had almost sentenced her and Lawbryn to a messy death on the beach, Dafna found even that horror was fading, in the warmth of the realisation that she had made an impact on such an extraordinary stranger. That something about her had sparked his interest. She sensed he would not find her admiration unwelcome, should she throw caution to the winds and declare it. She bent her head to the last of her meal, feeling a heat in her cheeks that had nothing to do with the wine, nor with the medicinal drink her mother had prepared for her.

The remainder of the evening passed in pleasant enough conversation, but the camaraderie that had been building between Talfrid and Hendrig had faded a little. Dafna was sure her father had not really noticed, he prompted new stories from their guest, and laughed aloud when obliged, but Talfrid seemed to be playing a good part now, nothing more.

Dafna began to feel woozy, and a little nauseated with the wine, and with the shock of the day and its frightening ending. Gethli, ever-vigilant over her only child, noticed, and took her hand to help her to her room,

As soon as they were alone Dafna turned to her. 'Mother, will I really have to marry him?'

'Of course not.' Gethli gathered up Dafna's hair. 'Hendrig has always believed you would, but no-one will force you.'

'Does Lawbryn know of this understanding?'

Gethli finished tying the thong, and let the heavy hair fall down Dafna's back in a long, neat tail. 'He does. He cares deeply for you and will be saddened if you reject him, but that is your choice.' She sat down on the bed and regarded Dafna with understanding eyes. 'This man Talfrid has turned your head, I think.'

Dafna flushed, could feel it, and knew it was pointless to dismiss the truth. 'He has. I feel as if I could listen to him talk forever. He has such wisdom and strength.'

'And an agreeable face,' Gethli added, smiling.

'Very,' Dafna admitted. 'He has lived such a life though! Imagine the stories he could tell. Not the nonsense he was entertaining us with tonight, but real tales, his travels, however dull he might think them… I would give anything to sit by a fire with him and learn all he has done.'

'Well that may yet happen.' Gethli tucked a stray curl behind Dafna's ear, patted her knee, and stood. 'I will talk to your father and ask him to leave talk of Lawbryn alone for the time, and perhaps Talfrid might be persuaded to stay a day or two. What do you think?'

Dafna looked up, startled, but with the beginnings of a thrill deep in the pit of her stomach. 'Do you think he might?'

'Let's see, shall we?'

Before the moon had passed from half to full, Dafna went from promised-bride of one, to bride of another. Lawbryn attended the ceremony but it was plain to everyone that he was rigid with disappointment... and not a little bitterness.

Dafna went to see him on the last morning before she was to leave. She found him on the beach where they had practiced their full-forming, sitting on the rocky headland. She made no secret of her approach, not wanting to startle him, but he still jumped when she sat down next to him.

'Where were your thoughts taking you, just then?' She kept her voice light, playful; she wanted to shed some of the happiness she felt onto his life, but didn't know how, other than to be what she had always been to him. But the look he turned on her was one of betrayal, quickly masked by indifference, and she swallowed hard, unnerved by swift change from confidante to mere acquaintance.

'My thoughts? They were far off, in another time. A happier time.'

After a silence, which neither knew how to fill, Dafna tried another approach. 'Who will you teach to full-form next?'

He shrugged. 'Brythnen, maybe. Or whoever pays me well enough.'

'You never asked me for payment,' Dafna said, and winced when she saw the flash of pain in his eyes.

'Of course not. We were… friends.'

He had to understand now, surely? 'Brythnen is your friend.'

Lawbryn turned away. 'The closest of friends, then.'

'We still are, I hope?' she said quietly.

Another silence, and then he sighed and reached for her hand, still not looking at her. 'Dafna, I will always be your strong right arm. Just because you have another to hold you the way I always wanted to, does not mean *I* am any the less yours.'

The honesty in his reply shook Dafna deeply, and she could think of nothing thing to say. She squeezed his hand, then rose and walked away, not trusting herself to turn back, to look upon the grief she had inflicted. The eager passion waiting for her in Talfrid's arms only heightened her sense of guilt, and she moved through the remainder of her final day with the heady combination of fear and excitement now laced with regret.

But when she and Talfrid took their leave to begin the journey back to the Cornish coast, there gathered such a joyful crowd she was lifted again. Those people she had known all her life, even those whose tempers she had stretched as a child, and again as a young woman, all waving and pressing small, easily carried gifts on them both, all wishing them speed and good fortune. Almost all; Lawbryn was nowhere to be seen.

They travelled slowly, in companionship and a growing affection; the early promise of passion had played out in a first night of deep pleasure for them both, and now they were happy to meander back to Cornwall, to Talfrid's home, in the most relaxed and warmest of glows.

Although the weather had remained friendly, Talfrid had abandoned his notion of travelling further north, so eager was he to begin their new life together. She had teased him, that perhaps he had been worried she might have her head turned by some exotic elemental from a distant shore. When she saw she had partially hit upon the truth she had relented, and assured him he need never waste a moment thinking on such a thing. He had looked at her with such trust and love, she knew she had spoken the truth. He was her life now.

Their arrival at Trethkellis had been late in the evening some two moon-cycles later, and when he took her to his favourite spot on the cliff above his home, she felt his warm, strong hand in hers, and recognised, for the first time, the quickening inside her. She placed a hand over her belly in sudden and secret delight, but it did not remain a secret for long; Talfrid's gaze dropped from her face to her waist, and his own hand covered hers. His sigh stirred her hair, and she felt the contentment flow between them.

Ahead of her the sea rolled and crashed, making her blood sing, and behind her lay the wide, open moorlands, stretching from this coast all the way back to where the royals lived. Lynher Mill. One day she would travel there, she would see the green and grey hills up close, feel the heather and the gorse snapping at her leggings and whipping across her boots. She would touch the rough stone of the chimney stacks, and she would sit and watch the Moorlanders, whose legendary beauty she had longed to one day see for herself. Perhaps she would even make friendships with them.

Life with Talfrid would be one thing to treasure, her children would be another, but the moorlands beckoned her adventurous spirit like a softly calling voice. She would come to know every part of them someday, and she would grow old watching her children do the same. Tonight, that exciting new life had begun.

Chapter Two.

Lynher Mill. September 6th 2012

Laura's eyes were grainy and hot, and her neck barely able to support her aching head, but the thought of leaving, even in search of clean air, had never crossed her mind. The room was silent, the candles dowsed, taking their pungent smell with them, but there was still the combined light of the former Moorlander queen and her servant to see by.

Watching Richard falling into the blackness Kernow's potion had granted him had been both terrifying, and a source of relief. But what if he never woke? What if he went into whatever waited for him, still believing she blamed him for what had happened?

She lowered her head, breathing slowly to calm her thundering heart, but the truth remained; whatever the reason, and however justifiable it had felt at the time, she *had* blamed him. She had sent him off into the night with her furious accusations ringing in his head, and by the time he'd returned it was too late to take back those bitter words. He had taken the Lightning, and was sworn to the land, and nothing could change that now. She would have given anything, at that moment, to be able to hate him again, but just to see him lying there, white and still, was agonising enough punishment for the words she had used against him.

She became vaguely aware of Kernow rising and moving away, and tried to send a look of gratitude towards the old spriggan, but her eyes were drawn back to Richard and she couldn't lift them again. His brow was furrowed slightly, even in sleep, and his breathing was short, his skin clammy to the touch.

She laid a gentle hand on his chest and leaned in, as she had just before he'd slipped under, to press her lips to his jaw. His breath stirred her hair, and her other hand found his where it lay limp on the covers – her fingers twined around it, feeling the raw scrape and now-dried grass still stuck in the cuts.

She sat up and turned his hand over. Kernow had been so concerned with the seriousness of his other injuries that this lesser wound had gone untended.

'Please fetch me some water. And some cloths.' Her voice, unused for hours, was broken and raw-sounding.

A minute later a bowl appeared at her elbow, and she turned, realising with surprise that it was not Kernow who held it, but Deera; they locked eyes for a second, and Laura felt the weight of the woman's grief. She struggled for something to say, but in the end she just said, 'Thank you,' and took the bowl and the cloths Deera proffered. Gently she pulled the blood-stuck grass from Richard's hand, wincing at the deep gouge at the base of his thumb, and began pressing the damp cloth to his palm. It helped to have something to do, to think about, to keep her mind from wandering to Ben, and to those in whom she had placed all her trust to get him back.

When she had finished with Richard's hand, she turned her attention to the graze on his neck. Kernow had done a thorough job of cleaning it, and Laura laid a cool cloth over the blackening bruise, hoping it would help with the swelling. Finally, she peeled away the long strip of linen that Kernow had pressed against the lightning-shaped cut in Richard's chest, preparing to replace it with a fresh one. The wound itself was shallow, and quite clean, but to see this body she knew so well marked forever, with a symbol that meant he would never again be hers, was worse than seeing the much deeper cuts in his hand.

With all these bruises and cuts, then, how strangely sad that it was the unblemished skin that shook her the most; she gently touched his left side, where the scar had once been. He should still have worn that legacy of the bullet that was supposed to have killed him, but it seemed even this life had been turned into a lie now.

'You have done all you can for him.' Deera broke into her thoughts, though her voice was unusually gentle. 'Kernow must tend to him now. Return to your home, and to your business. Maer will find you when he has word of your son.'

'My business is here.' Laura adjusted the cool cloth on Richard's neck. She remembered kneeling at his side after the battle with Loen out by the stones, how she had absently thumbed away a bead of blood beneath his jaw, and Maer's words when he gave her the key ring came back to her: *If you ever doubt Richard's love for you, look at this...* She hadn't even questioned where that blood had come from, but now she knew, and the knowledge threaded cold terror through her at how nearly it had all ended. No, she had never doubted his love for her, the terrible thing was that she had doubted her own for him. And now she had lost him.

She looked up at Deera. 'I'm staying here until your son brings me mine.'

'And what of your friend?' Deera asked. 'Would you leave her alone, even if she is dead? Is that the act of a friend?'

'Shut up!' Laura's voice was tight, but low, she didn't want Richard waking into conflict. 'I sent for help, but there was nothing else I could do. Ben needed me more.'

'And when he comes back he will need his mother healthy, and able to care for him,' Deera pointed out. 'You must go now.'

Laura turned back to Richard. 'You can't make me leave him. Not yet.'

'The very light by which you are seeing the Lord Tir is mine,' Deera reminded her, sounding harder now. 'I could withdraw it, leaving you in darkness and silence.'

'What? *Why?* Why would you do that?'

'Kernow must tend to the king, and your presence forbids it.'

Laura frowned at Kernow. 'Look, you can do anything you have to, surely it doesn't matter if I'm here?'

The old spriggan shook her head. 'You are fully mortal. I cannot practice my art while you remain, it is forbidden.'

'What do you think I'll do, steal your secrets?' Laura couldn't keep the disgust and frustration out of her voice. 'Trust me, I have other things on my mind.'

'Mortals have no place here, you know this. It is for your well-being as much as for ours.' Kernow reached across the bed and touched Laura's arm with real sympathy and tenderness, but withdrew quickly, frowning. She blinked, squeezing her eyes tight shut, and Laura realised how tired she must be.

'Lady Laura, let me treat him,' the spriggan said. 'You will hear soon enough when Maer brings your son back, but in the meantime remember what Tir has said; the boy was happy when he saw him.'

'That was when he was with Jacky.' Laura's throat closed up. 'Who knows where he is now?' She already knew where she was going the minute she felt able to leave Richard's side: home for the car, and then straight to the coast.

'He will be well cared for,' Kernow said.

'How do you *know*?'

'It is as I explained. If they wish to use the boy to

sue for peace, they will not harm him. Prince Maer and his lady will bring him back to you. Go now, see to your mortal affairs, and wait.'

The light dimmed, and Laura's breath caught. 'Alright!' she glared at Deera, and the former queen looked back at her levelly. 'I'll go, but I want to be alone to say goodbye.'

Deera inclined her head in acquiescence. 'I will return soon, for every moment you stay is another moment Tir is without skilled attention. I will leave you my light for a time.' But she sounded faintly unsure – it seemed her own powers were proving a struggle. That was no surprise, after all she'd been through; grief had an insidious way of weakening you. How well Laura knew that.

The two of them left, one tall, regal and beautiful, the other squat and nightmarishly ugly, but Laura knew which of them she trusted the most, and was glad Kernow would be staying with Richard.

The moment the heavy curtain swung shut she saw Richard's eyelids flicker, and a line appear between his dark eyebrows, and then he was looking at her. The fuzziness and confusion of earlier had retreated, although his voice was hardly more than a croak.

'I thought they'd never go.'

Laura lowered her forehead to his, trembling in relief. 'Thank god. Richard, all those things I said—'

'Babe, don't.' He cleared his throat and tried again, sounding stronger now. 'You were right, I screwed up.'

'No! Look, it's hard to explain… it was something else talking. Something wanted to drive us apart.'

'The land, yeah. I've felt it too.'

'But I was so—'

'Don't,' he repeated, and his green eyes were bright with emotion as he raised them to hers and then slid his hand into her hair to draw her closer again. The kiss was chaste and warm, and did not deepen, but his lips were firm against hers. Laura rested her hand on the side of his face, brushing his cheek with her thumb; his skin was starting to roughen with a light stubble and her fingertips came alive with the contact.

Finally she broke the kiss and reluctantly sat upright, but she took his injured hand in hers again. 'Did you know Maer and Nerryn went to find Ben?'

'I think so. Everything was kind of blurry at the end. I didn't even know for sure you were here.'

'Of course I was,' she said, although she understood why he'd think otherwise. 'Kernow says Ben will be alright.' But she spoke with more hope than conviction.

'For what it's worth, I think she's right.' He squeezed her fingers. 'Laura?'

'What?'

'Promise me you won't go after him yourself?'

She looked at him steadily. His eyes burned into hers, and she was reminded of the first time they'd spoken, in the schoolroom a million years ago when he'd caught her out in a lie. He'd read her then, too, and lying now was just as pointless.

'I have to.'

'No, you don't. You can't. Those people are dangerous—'

'All the more reason.'

'They won't hurt Ben, but...' His voice cracked, and he stopped for a second. 'But they'd kill you. They wouldn't think twice.' He brought his free hand up to touch her face. 'Please. *Promise me.*'

Laura saw his raw fear, and did the only thing she could to ease it. 'Alright. I promise.'

He relaxed. 'Thank you.'

'We're just going to have to trust Maer, I suppose.'

Richard squeezed her hand again. 'No-one I'd trust more to do that job,' he whispered. He was growing tired again. Laura knew it was time to leave, but suddenly her promise to wait, to trust, to go back home, seemed like the most stupid, selfish and irresponsible thing she could have said.

Richard must have read the thought even as it flashed across her mind. He released her hand and laid his head back against the pillow. 'You're doing the right thing.'

'You need Kernow's help,' Laura admitted, 'I'm stopping that from happening.'

'Not just because of that,' he mumbled, his eyes half-closed now. 'For Ben. He's going to need you.'

'That's what Deera said.'

He managed a little smile. 'I heard. Kinda scary, me and Deera thinking the same thing.'

'Terrifying,' Laura agreed, with a flicker of her

own smile. Then it faded. 'If I go now, it's not... you know, forever, is it? I mean, I'll be allowed to come back sometimes?'

'Honey, I'm the king. I get to make the rules now.'

'But you can't come home.' She couldn't match his light tone, and he couldn't maintain it.

'No.'

Laura's throat was so tight it hurt. 'How... I'm not...' She shook her head and tried again, 'I don't know how to be without you now.'

'Then come with me.'

Laura was jolted by the longing in his voice, but she shook her head; Kernow's warning had been clear, the old spriggan had known this would have been in their hearts. 'I can't live down here. I can't make light, and the air would be all wrong. I'd be blind, lost—'

'Yeah, I know. I'm sorry,' he said softly. 'I guess I have a selfish streak a mile wide.'

Laura brushed his cheek with a trembling finger. 'No bigger than mine. I'd give anything to be able to stay.' At least he would be close by. He would have his life, and so would she, even if it meant they must spend them apart.

Even as she tried to push that thought aside, the light dimmed, then flickered, and flared surprisingly brightly once more before going out altogether. They both reached out again and, fumbling in the sudden, thick darkness, found each other's hands.

'I love you,' Laura said, fighting to sound calm.

'And I love you. Both of you.' He grasped her

fingers, and his voice shook. 'Don't let him forget about me? Please?'

Laura's tight control slipped, and she let go of his hand and found his face instead. She kissed him, her tears hidden in the darkness but sliding fast down her cheeks now, and she was certain she felt his own mingling with them.

The light came back, sudden and blinding, and Laura wrenched herself away. She stood up and, somehow, managed to leave his side. She shoved her way past Deera and Kernow, who waited outside; if she looked back she'd never leave.

'Tell Maer to bring Ben home,' she threw back over her shoulder in a broken voice.

The loss of Richard was a white-hot slice through her soul, and all she had left now was the knowledge that she would soon have Ben in her arms again. It was the one thing that got her through the cavern, up the tunnel and out into the pitch-black night, and the thing that kept her breathing as she stumbled across the moor back towards the distant pinpricks of light from the village.

As she reached the road and saw Tom's old house, the other events of the night came crashing back: Jane. The drug dealers. Captain. She tried to remember exactly what she'd done, but it was as if it had happened to someone else, some film she'd seen before her world fell apart.

She passed the house where she'd stopped during her flight onto the moors – had they called the paramedics? She remembered hammering on the door and yelling through the letter box, but not whether she'd actually seen any lights on in the house, or any other indication that anyone was home.

The light was starting to creep into the sky, and it had been mid-evening when she'd left home, leaving Jane and Captain at the mercy of Gerai, the rogue Moorlander. At least eleven hours had passed, then. Laura walked up the hill towards Mill Lane Cottage, her legs shaking harder with every step. When she got there she found the house in darkness and the front door wide open. It was unlikely a paramedic team, or the police, would have left it like that, so her cry for help for Jane must have fallen into an empty house. Unless…

Filled with a sudden, wild hope, Laura pushed open the kitchen door. The first thing she saw was that Jane had not miraculously survived after all, she lay facing away from Laura on the floor. The borrowed and torn white nightie was rucked up to her thighs, her skinny legs smeared in vomit and blood. Laura turned away, but when her own nausea rushed up her throat she didn't fight it; she leaned over and retched helplessly, throwing up only a thin yellow bile.

As soon as she could think straight again, she found her mobile phone where she'd left it on the coffee table—back when life had made some kind of sense—and called for an ambulance. It took no effort whatsoever to summon tears. She told them she thought her friend was dead, and gave them the address, then she dug her car keys out of her jeans; she took out the key ring Maer had given her, too, and after a moment's reflection she threaded it onto her own set. She was in her car and twisting the ignition key before she remembered her promise.

She turned off the engine and lowered her head to the steering wheel, trying to breathe calmly, to let her heartbeat settle. She stayed like that for a while, her eyes closed, and eventually sat back and pressed the heels of her hands to her eyes; exhaustion was threatening to stop her thinking properly.

It had been a day and night of dizzying emotional switches, from learning about her father, to losing her son; from hating Richard with a gut-wrenching, unthinking passion, to loving him again with the same ferocity and hopelessness... From all that to now, where, ridiculous though it was, she needed an alibi just so she wouldn't have to answer questions about Ben and Richard. She took her phone from her pocket again and pressed to dial. After a few rings, a sleepy, but worried voice answered.

'Laura?'

'Ann, I need your help... I...' She stopped, breathless and boneless, slumped in her seat, only vaguely aware of Ann's panicked voice buzzing from her lap. Somehow she lifted the phone again. 'Jane's overdosed.'

Silence, and then Ann asked, in a voice that said she already knew the answer, 'Is she alright?'

Laura wanted nothing more than to blurt out the truth. All of it... it was poisoning her. But she couldn't. 'I don't know,' she said, 'I don't think so. I've just found her, and called the ambulance.'

'How do you know she—'

'Listen, I promise I'll explain tomorrow, but I need you to say I've been with you all night, and I left you about an hour ago.'

'Are you at the flat?'

Bless her for not asking about what didn't matter. 'No, Lynher Mill. They're bound to call the police, so...' She hesitated, then said, 'I need you to do something else, too.'

Another silence while Laura waited, her heart hammering. What if she'd already gone too far? Then Ann spoke again. 'What do you need?'

Laura closed her eyes and let out a slow breath. 'Thank you. Okay, you have to tell them you've got Ben as a favour, because Richard and I are moving.' There was a pause. 'Ann?'

'Where *is* Ben?' Ann said at last, sounding much more wary.

'He's with Richard. He's fine, don't worry.' As she said the words, she almost broke down again. 'Will you do this? Please?'

'And where's Richard?'

'Cornwall. Will you?'

'Listen, whatever it is—'

'Please! Trust me? If the police call, I was there all evening after I dropped Ben with you, and I stayed late because he wouldn't settle.'

'You've got me worried,' Ann said, and she sounded almost tearful. 'I'm coming over.'

'Don't be worried,' Laura said, her voice catching. How much could she presume on this friendship? Conversely she knew that if it had been Jane she'd been speaking to, the answer would have been instant *Yes*. No questions asked. Whatever else Jane had been, nothing fazed her. 'Just please, stick to that story. I'll call you tomorrow.'

'No, I'll come over after school. But yes, I'll do it.'

'Thank you,' Laura whispered, and, unable to say anymore, pressed to end the call. She felt queasy and tired, and heard the echo of Richard's voice as he'd said the oath, although she couldn't fathom the words. But Maer had translated, and the words that stuck in her mind were *I will raise up the weak and the weary*.

She had never felt so weary in her life.

The police were duly called, and by the time Jane had been zipped into a thick black bag and driven away, the sun was already beginning to make its appearance. Light crept into the sky from the general direction of Plymouth, making Laura long for her too-small flat, the noise of traffic, and the normality. Most of all, for Ben and Richard.

Back inside the cottage, she looked at the closed kitchen door with conflicted emotions. She wanted to sleep, to put everything out of her head and let her body recover some of the strength it was going to need over the days to come, but the thought of waking to the filth of last night…

She gagged at first, but as she filled a bowl with

hot, soapy water she found her revulsion turning to sorrow; whatever Jane had turned into, she had been Laura's oldest friend. Not the best, but she'd been part of a childhood that had, for the most part, been happy, and now all that was left was the smear of thin vomit, a sticky pool of blood, and a smell that clawed at Laura's throat and made her eyes sting.

She knelt and began the awful business of cleaning away the last remnants of the girl she had known since the age of four; who had both shocked her and made her laugh in equal measures; who had led her into scrapes and, in an oddly touching way, relied on her to get them both out. The girl who had taken Laura's first love, albeit unknowingly… Oh, god. Laura sat back, sponge in hand. Michael should be told. Best to reach him through his parents, if they still lived in St Tourney. One more item to add to the list; things to take her mind off the terrible ache of waiting for Maer and Nerryn to return.

The kitchen cleaned at last, her limbs aching and stiff, Laura said a silent goodbye to her friend and slowly climbed the stairs to her old room. She looked around at the boxes that sat there, waiting for parcel tape and a marker pen. No need to pack any of Richard's things, not now. Her stomach clenched, and she sank down onto the bed and wrapped her arms across her middle, letting out her grief in a long, low groan. Then she twisted her body and brought her knees up to her chest, curling into a tight ball in the middle of the bed, and let the darkness in her heart sweep her away.

Chapter Three

Richard opened his eyes as Laura's parting words filtered through the haze of bizarre dreams that still ricocheted around in his mind. *Tell Maer to bring Ben home...* His thoughts sharpened as his vision adjusted to the candle light in the cavern, and he wondered if she'd meant Maer to take Ben straight to the cottage. As if to bring him into the mine presented a risk to the boy. Did that mean he would never see his son again, even to say goodbye?

Richard's body tensed at the thought, and the pain woke up. His back, pressed against the bed, stung where the skin was broken, but behind his ribs lay a deeper pain, a slow, pulsing ache that throbbed with every heartbeat. His body was recovering, and quicker than he might have hoped for, but it was still too damned slow. He couldn't just lie here.

He braced his hands against the bed and tried to pull himself upright, but the pain flared and he bit back a scream; just lying here suddenly seemed like a good idea after all. He breathed slowly, not liking the tiny sound that escaped on his breath – he sounded like a child – but panic had taken hold, an urgent, physical need to hold his son one last time; his heart raced and the blood rushed around his body, preparing him for motion. The pulses of pain matched the speed of his heart, and it made him light-headed and nauseous. He felt the familiar watering in his mouth.

'Kernow!' he rasped. If he threw up…

A second later a rough, dry hand was at his mouth, pushing a leaf between his lips. He snatched at it with his teeth, remembering the god-awful bitter taste, but also the way it had eased his roiling stomach before. He chewed with frantic relief – he could do with having a supply of these things on hand. He felt Kernow's hand, gentle on his brow, and closed his eyes, letting the juice in the leaf do its work. Gradually the nausea subsided, and his heartbeat slowed again as he accepted that there was no way in hell he was going anywhere. Not for a while, anyway.

'Thank you,' he managed, when the leaf was nothing more than shreds sticking to his tongue, and to the roof of his mouth. Kernow slid a hand beneath his shoulders and eased him up carefully, just enough to enable him to take a sip from the cup she held to his mouth. To his relief it was nothing more than cold, clear water, and he swished it around his mouth, loosening the bits of leaf before swallowing. His throat still ached where the Moorlander's stick had bruised it, but that pain, at least, was fading fast.

When he could speak again, he asked for some of the leaves. 'To keep right here, just in case.'

'I am sorry, My Lord. They are rarely found, and we had only one. I gave you half when you had taken the oath and had need of it, and you have now taken the last piece.'

'Shit,' he muttered. 'Guess I'd better learn some self-control, then.'

'You will.' She smiled gently. 'You are a new king, it is true, but you are also a very, very old one.'

'Now you're messing with my head.' He liked Kernow a great deal, but she reminded him so strongly of Jacky it hurt. Physical appearance aside, they both had that same strange and compelling mixture of servility and superiority; one moment bowing and murmuring their loyalty, the next telling him, in clear and inarguable language, what he must and must not do.

She smiled again now, and rested her hand on his body, just beneath his breastbone. The pain was radiating towards the centre of him from the damage in his back, but where Kernow's hand lay he could have sworn he felt a lessening of it. Whether that was real or imagined he couldn't figure out, but he hoped she'd leave it there. He closed his eyes and drifted, hoping for sleep to claim him before she moved away, but she started to talk again, bringing him back to full wakefulness.

'Learn your strengths, My Lord,' she said quietly. 'You can do more than you think, but if you cannot control it you will bring chaos to your people. You should start with making your own light.'

'How do I learn?'

'When you are well enough, Maer will teach you. But he has limitations of his own to overcome first, and lessons he must be taught.'

'Will you be the one to teach him?'

Her eyes widened. 'It is not my place to instruct the Moorlanders, only to serve them. The task will fall to his mother.'

'That'll be fun for him,' Richard allowed a little smile, surprised to see it mirrored on Kernow's wrinkled face, though hers vanished again quickly and she glanced quickly at the door.

'You must not speak ill of the qu…' But the reprimand fell into silence, as Kernow realised Deera was no-one now. Descended merely from the royal blood of Loen's brother, even if she had caught the two of them chattering like schoolchildren about her she could have done nothing. She was queen no longer. Something occurred to him then, and any other time he might have laughed: Deera was his niece, of sorts, and, yeah… she was his stepmother too. He wondered if Maer figured that out yet, but the thought of Maer brought his half-amused wondering to an abrupt close. *Would* he bring Ben here first?

Kernow must have noted the different emotions that flashed across his face, and she sighed. 'You have a difficult time ahead. Grief and fear will slow your recovery, but sleep will help.' She examined his cuts, and pronounced them healing well. 'I will return, and when I do, you will not thank me. But we must turn you so I can re-dress the wounds in your back.'

He felt himself turning green at the thought, and swallowed hard. 'Wish I hadn't used up your magic leaves now.'

'No magic,' she smiled. 'Just nature.'

'Yeah? Well I think I'm starting to appreciate that a whole lot more than I used to.' He tried not to think about how it would feel to be turned onto his stomach, or even rolled onto his side.

'We will be as gentle as we can be,' she assured him, sympathy on her face. 'Sleep now, My Lord.'

He thanked her, and when she had left she took her light with her, leaving a single candle that sent shadows chasing across the ceiling. He watched them for a while, breathing slowly, trying to let his mind settle along with his body. But a pain that had nothing to do with his injuries cramped his insides as he re-lived Laura's leaving; the plunging into darkness, the frantic grasping of his hands seeking hers, the tears that had flowed between them…

The shadows danced. Richard's eyes closed, but his mind kept moving, searching through the memories that were not tainted with sorrow. They were warm, sweet and perfect, but each one hurt more than the last as he realised he would never experience their like again. The flicker of the candle through his closed eyelids brought him the strongest memory of all, and he stepped back into it, grateful for its clarity. It helped eclipse the knowledge of what their lives had become.

Plymouth, New Year's Eve, 2011.

'Bollocks!' The wrapped cheese rolled across the floor, and Richard paused in the doorway and smiled, remembering the last time that had happened.

'Gesundheit.' He leaned against the jamb, and folded his arms.

Laura looked up, saw him, and laughed. 'Mr Lucas. Do come in.'

'Your language doesn't improve, does it?' He grinned and levered himself off the door frame, and came into the kitchen.

'I hardly ever swear!' she protested, and bent to pick up the cheese. 'Trust you to be loitering in the doorway the one time I do.'

'I spend a lot of my time hanging around out of sight, waiting to hear you talk that way.'

'You're just weird.' She turned to give him a pitying look, and he caught her arm and pulled her close. She was already in her night-wear, ready for the evening, and her white cotton nightie moulded deliciously to her body as he pressed her against him.

Her lips parted beneath his, and he felt a little sigh of pleasure run through her. Her hands, one of them still clutching the runaway cheese, rested at his waist, and he held her face gently as he kissed her, moving from her lips to her jaw, and dipping his head to the warm skin of her throat. He heard her catch her breath.

'Honey, drop the damn cheese,' he whispered, and a second later he heard it hit the floor again, and then her hands were on his back, her fingers tracing his spine and making him shiver. He let his own hands fall to her hips, and he felt her suck in her stomach automatically, but her warm, rounded body felt luxurious beneath his hands; as precious as the arms that held him, the grey eyes that teased him, the heart that beat furiously against his. It was all Laura, and he loved all of her.

'Can we risk it?' he murmured against her neck, and felt her twist towards the door, as if she could see through it to their sleeping son. 'Don't want him to start screaming.'

'*I'll* start screaming if we don't,' she said, 'and then you'll be sorry. Best not use the bedroom though.'

He took her hand and led her into the sitting room, where the Christmas tree lights flickered in the corner of the room. Even when he closed his eyes he could still see them, and it felt magical, somehow. He heard Laura shrugging out of her nightdress, and opened his eyes again. She stood before him, pale-skinned and just a little plumper than she wanted to be, and he stepped forward until she was close enough to touch.

His fingers traced the silvery stretch marks on her lower belly, and when her hand dropped to gently push them away he caught it in his. 'Don't, babe. I love them. I love you.'

'I look awful,' she stammered.

'Are you kidding me? You're amazing.' There was nothing more he could say, he could only show her how deeply she affected him. He put his hands gently on her hips again and drew her against him; this time she did not suck anything in, and instead she smiled and glanced down between them.

'Well you're clearly not fibbing,' she murmured, relaxing into his embrace. Her hands slid beneath his T shirt at the back, and her touch on his bare skin made him gasp, and then give a little growl.

'Ssh!' she whispered against his shoulder, but he could feel her mouth still curved in that beautiful, wide smile as she rested more firmly against him. He lifted her onto the sofa, and less than a minute later he had peeled off his own clothes, and lay next to her, his eyes on hers as he ran his hand gently down her body. She frowned slightly as he reached her belly, but did not try to stop him, and he smiled and kissed away the little line that had appeared on her brow.

Before long she had let go of all her reservations and was straddling him, completely unselfconscious, and as their rhythm grew faster, so did her breathing. He looked up at her in gratitude and wonder, her head thrown back, her soft breasts swinging against her ribs, her lips parted in a silent cry of ecstasy… and when she shuddered at last into loose-limbed abandon, he was only a heartbeat behind.

Lying next to him afterwards, she had smoothed her hand across his ribcage, her thumb brushing the scar there, her hair tickling him where it lay, thick and soft, on his chest. They hadn't spoken much, each was too desperate to keep this peaceful moment and not wake four month-old Ben in the next room. But it seemed fate was smiling on them, and had given them that night alone, to re-discover each other. Their son slept on.

In the kitchen, a little later, they had heard the distant sound of fireworks. Laura looked at the clock. 'It's only ten! Why do people do that?'

'Why not?' Richard said, emptying a packet of snacks into a bowl. 'This enough chips?'

'Crisps,' Laura said, predictably. 'The chips are in the freezer.'

'Sure they are.' He smiled. 'Got any cookies?' The smile turned into a grin as she automatically started to say "biscuits!" before she realised, and rolled her eyes.

He saw the flying chip just in time to dodge aside, and it splintered in the sink. 'What time's that Hootenanny guy on the—okay, *what* are you looking for?' he asked, admiring the sight of her crawling under the table.

'My cheese.'

'Well, don't find it too soon, your ass looks amazing.'

She turned to tell him off, and banged her head on the underside of the table. 'Ow!'

'Ah, honey, I'm sorry!' Richard laughed, and knelt down to help her out. 'Let me.'

'You're bigger than me,' she pointed out, then gave an exclamation and crawled away again. 'There it is!'

'How the hell did it get all the way over there?'

'Don't ask me, you're the one who told me to drop it.'

'Worth it though, right?'

She sighed. 'It's *cheese*, Richard. Food of the gods.'

'And yet you threw it away.' He adopted a tone of startled revelation. 'Wait, does this mean you like me better than cheese?'

'Fishing for compliments now, are we?'

'Babe, cheese is serious stuff. I mean, if I thought you liked me better I'd probably stick around a while.'

She crawled back to where he sat, and carefully peeled the wax wrapping off the cheese. Then, holding the soft white wheel next to Richard's face, she looked from one to the other, a little frown of indecision creasing her brow. He waited, enjoying her closeness, the musky scent of her that wafted over him, and the way her mouth pursed as she considered her two options.

Just when he was about to grab her and kiss her, she beat him to it, throwing the cheese over her shoulder. She wrapped her arms around him, and the laughter between them felt even warmer and more real than the bone-deep thrill of claiming her body with his own. Her hands linked at the back of his neck, and her tongue danced with his, and when the kiss broke she pressed her lips to his jaw instead, but she was still smiling. Her joy was infectious, her relief and happiness was his… that magical, perfect night. The first night of their real lives as a family, the night they had consciously left behind everything that had almost broken them. Or so they had thought.

Richard lay now, in the flickering candlelight of the cavern. He hurt. His heart ached. He was lost. But Laura would have her life, she would have Ben, and she would know some measure of peace away from Lynher Mill. Whatever Richard did now, whoever he became, he hoped she remembered that perfect New Year's Eve the way he did.

***

Lynher Barrow

Daylight was creeping into the barrow through the narrow opening. Jacky Greencoat watched it with heavy eyes, wondering how long he could remain here before he would have to face the outside again. There was food, of sorts, but soon he would have to range farther afield, and find something more substantial than the few nuts and grasses he'd managed to gather. As the light touched the floor he saw a splash of blood. Tir's blood. A little moan found its way out of his throat, and it sounded small and lonely up here, beneath the burial mound.

Anger still flickered and smouldered when he thought of the Moorlanders, but it was no longer burning with the same white heat that had driven him up and away from shelter and warmth, into the exile of the wide open moor. He had been honoured to serve them, hadn't he? He had not forgotten that. They were born to rule over his kind, and could help their dominant nature no more than he could help his meek one.

Yet he should not *be* meek and downtrodden, none of his kind should; Kernow herself had saved Tir's life, Martha had helped her, others worked tirelessly and without complaint, to heal and to provide. The elementals needed the spriggans, but the reverse did not hold true.

But, powerful or not, Jacky remained a tiny being in this great big place, and all the ancient strength in the world could not change what he had done, and what he had failed to do. Perhaps, left alone, he might explore that long-forgotten strength, but for now all he understood was the need to get away from Lynher Mill.

Casta would know, by now, of his part in seeking to place Tir in power over the Moorlanders. Unquestionably treason, punishable by death, and even Casta could not shy away from such a judgement. Gentle he might be, but he was no fool, and no weakling—although skirmishes were no longer commonplace, there had been a time when others had sought to seize the lands, and during those uprisings Casta had fought coldly, and with determination, to protect them all. It seemed now as though those days were returning, and Casta would have need of loyal servants, not traitors.

Jacky Turncoat, Tir had called him. Here, in this very place, when Jacky had made off with Dreis wrapped in Jacky's own jacket. It had been cried out in pain, and in angry betrayal, but that made it no less true in Tir's eyes, and Tir would be sure to tell Casta where to find that turncoat.

But where to go? The forest? Jacky shuddered; those pale, too-lively *trigoryon an goswig* had always terrified him. See how easily they had caught and subdued Martha Horncup. True, she was a timid one, more so after the death of her boy, but she was strong too, as strong as Jacky. The Foresters cared nothing for the spriggans, unless it was to torment them; Martha had not been the first and would not be the last.

The coast, then. It was far enough away to be out of the sight of the Moorlanders, and Casta would never think to look for him there; spriggan clans did not venture so far, and if they did the buccas would never tolerate it, and would drive them back from the coast with any means they could. But a lone spriggan could remain hidden from all until the end of his long, long days, provided he did not seek out company. He would travel now, today, and make his way to the very edge of the dry land, and he wouldn't stop until the water lapped at his boots.

Jacky slithered up through the gap between the granite lintel and the ground outside. Once on his feet again he turned his face to the west. The morning was well on its way, and all past nights were gone and finished with. No sense in keeping them alive in his heart, and to allow his thoughts to dwell on such a night would make his steps heavy.

Unlike the elementals, he possessed no great speed with which to make his way to the waterside. He began his long walk across the tufted moorland, trying not to look down the hill towards the Lynher Mill chimney, lest his bitterness be overcome by the instinct to confess all at Casta's feet. He was Jacky of no-one, Jacky of nowhere. He had no king.

Chapter Four

Trethkellis, Cornwall

Maer and Nerryn approached the top of the cliff as the sky started showing streaks of pink and orange. They stopped above Nerryn's old home and stood, as they had travelled much of the journey, in silence, fighting their own thoughts and fears.

Maer pictured his father. It was no struggle; the tall figure of the wisest, kindest man he'd ever known was always going to be at his shoulder, guiding him. Had Richard really seen him, during that grim battle with his own death? He certainly believed he had, and knew also that, if he hadn't been gently turned back, he would have gone into the unknowable darkness without further struggle. And the facts were irrefutable; Richard had known of Casta's death, and had not been anywhere near the mine when it happened.

In his mortal life Maer had heard much of the 'white tunnel,' and had heard of people claiming to have found their god because of it, but Richard had insisted what he had seen had nothing to do with any mortal religion. Not the preserve of those who worshipped God, whom they proclaimed the only god, but something bigger, more tolerant, more welcoming. It belonged to all, sought neither to rule nor punish, and made no demands. It had no name, nor did it need one. Maer raised his gaze to the lightening sky and his mind reached out, but found nothing. It would come, in time, he was sure of it.

Nerryn's hand crept into his, and he turned to look at her. She seemed as though she were searching for something to say, and he let go of her hand and folded her into his arms instead. She felt so small, and he was reminded of how young she really was, how everything that had happened had swept her helplessly along; her meeting him on the path, their delight in each other and how it had caused her to give up her family life, and the future she had planned.

It had seemed the most difficult and awful thing in their world then, that she had let her father and brothers down, yet how trivial that truly was against the new horrors of the night. Her lord's blade, an incongruously beautiful thing, had stolen the life of a man of such nobility it hurt to remember him, yet her lord he still was.

Maer could feel her taking a deep breath, trying to control herself, and he held her tighter. 'Listen,' he whispered against her hair. 'You needn't come in there with me. They don't have to see you.'

'I don't care if they see me or not,' she said, her voice almost lost in the folds of his shirt. Then she looked up, and her sapphire eyes shone in the dawn's light. 'I will not let you go down there alone, Maer. Arric is… he won't…' she broke off and shook her head. 'I would worry for you.'

His hand dropped to the dagger at his side, but his fingers twitched away from it in sudden revulsion. Could he use it on another elemental? His father had died in anguish, evidenced by the fiercest lightning bolt Maer had ever seen… the thought should have strengthened his resolve, and his hatred for the *trigoryon an arvor* should have driven him down over the cliff with vengeance singing from his blade. But instead it made him feel ill, and that in turn brought a huge wave of self-loathing upon him.

Where was the fury, the powerful need to avenge his father, that had erupted from him in screams of rage when he'd found Casta's body? At that moment he would not have had to think more than once before plunging the blade into the heart of the one who had killed so cruelly. So why now was he shying away from it?

'I think I'm weak,' he said in a low voice.

She caught his face in her hands and made him look at her. 'You are far from weak! You are compassionate, and you are gentle. You are your father's son.'

'But he—'

'There is no weakness in a reluctance to cause pain.'

Maer felt her hand drop away, and then the weight of the blade was gone from his hip and she had stepped back.

'What are you doing?' he breathed in horror. 'This is your family!'

'Cantoc is not my family.' The sudden change in her was startling; her mind was already detaching from his, ready to lead her forward into whatever might come. He could barely reconcile her with the delicate girl he had just tried to comfort; now she was the one giving hope and strength.

'But Arric—'

'Arric will give me the child once Cantoc is gone. I hope I won't have to hurt him, but be assured,' she fixed Maer with a look that told him she was not simply saying the words, 'if he tries to harm Dreis I will end his life.'

'No.' He reached for the dagger again, but she moved further back. 'Nerryn, please. You're right; I am my father's son, and he was a warrior once. Maybe he'd been reluctant too, at first, but he was courageous and strong, and I will be the same.'

'Is this war, then?' Nerryn asked, her voice unsure again now. She frowned at the knife, as if surprised to see she still held it, and handed it back to him. 'Will our people really set against one another to the death?'

'What we do today is not an act of war.' Maer slid the blade back into its sheath. 'It's for Tir, and for Laura, and for their child.'

'And afterwards? When they have lost the one thing that will let them bargain for peace?'

He couldn't help noticing she said *they*, and *them*, and he felt more in awe than ever of what she had given up. 'I will do everything I can to preserve peace between us, but it is for Tir to decide. He is king now.'

He found, to his relief, that there was nothing but pride in his heart when he spoke the words. He had wanted to rule, of course he had; it had been in his blood from the moment of his birth. And he had promised Nerryn she would be queen. But now that Tir had returned and taken the Lightning, and everything was as it should have been, he felt a deep and welcome sense of acceptance.

He would be at Tir's side for the rest of his king's life. If nature had her way it would be a deal shorter than Maer's own, but with the land in this unsettled state, and if war did ensue, who knew if either of them would have the chance to live out the life they'd been promised? In the coming cycles he would act as Tir's right hand, protect him as he had always been meant to. And he would begin by giving him back his son.

He turned back, to look down on the path that led close to the cliff side, and caught his breath, touching Nerryn's arm. She followed his gaze and he felt her stiffen; two men moved down there, swift and sure in their movements. Not mortals. He recognised Arric instantly, and the other took a heartbeat longer but he knew him all the same; tall, slender and broad-shouldered, his hair catching the early morning sunlight in flashes of auburn fire, tied back and falling between his shoulder-blades. He moved with the same easy grace as Tir himself, and in his arms he carried a child, whose black hair peeked above a painfully familiar green covering; Jacky's coat.

'Mylan,' Nerryn whispered, her voice catching. 'I knew there was something—'

'Something that made you take the knife, or something that let you release it?'

She hesitated, troubled. 'I don't know. I felt so strong in that moment, as if I could do anything. But now Mylan's back… Maer, I can't hurt him. Not even for Dreis and Tir.'

'Where are they going?'

The two men had dropped down out of sight, and Maer breathed a sigh of relief; it was clear by the way Dreis was being carried, warmly wrapped and held firmly, his sleeping head cradled against his captor's chest that he was being cared for.

'They were on the path to Cantoc's home,' Nerryn said. Maer sat down on the damp grass, pulling her down to sit beside him. He put an arm around her shoulder and she leaned against him. 'What now?' she asked, in worried tones.

Maer considered. 'We can't battle three men with one blade. Besides, if we burst in on them we'll be putting Dreis at risk.' He closed his eyes, thinking hard. 'Do you think it was Mylan who killed Jacky?' he said at length, and felt her shake her head. 'Then it was either Arric or Gerai.'

'Yes.'

'If it was Gerai, he has given the child to Arric, who has brought him to Cantoc,' Maer said grimly.

'Showing off his prize. I truly do not know how we can get him back without hurting anyone.'

Nerryn grasped his hand. 'I don't care what happens to Cantoc, not now. I had thought him honourable at least, before. But now I would kill him myself.'

'And Arric?'

'It would be harder,' she admitted. 'I might try to reason with him first, but if I had to take the knife to his throat I would do it. For Tir, and his son.'

'But not Mylan.'

'Never Mylan. And nor could I stand by and watch you do it. I love him second only to you.'

'It should not even be second,' he said gently, and kissed her brow. 'He is not only your brother, he is part of you. I couldn't hurt him either.'

'Then what will we do?'

'I don't know.'

They sat in silence. Maer turned all his thoughts onto how they might spirit Dreis away from here without harming anyone, but no solution came to him. After a moment he stood up, and walked closer to the cliff top. He looked out over the sea, the rising sun at his back, its light now paler and losing the blush of early morning.

The waves broke against the rocks, powerful, relentlessly wearing away the fabric of the land, yet still somehow soothing, and he thought of Tir back at Lynher Mill. Helpless himself, Tir had put all his trust in Maer, and now Maer stood, every bit as helpless, while the day marched onward. Closer and closer to the point when he would have to kill, or maim, in order to keep his promise.

A yell sounded below, a child's shout, and Maer's gaze went to the lower path where Mylan and Arric had disappeared with the boy. Nerryn came to stand beside him, roused by Dreis's shout, and put her arm through his. 'Do you suppose they will become angry when he cries, or will they tend to him?'

Her words echoed Maer's fears, but he spoke as reassuringly as he could. 'Mylan was carrying him with great care. You know him better than I, is he as short-tempered as Arric?'

'No, he is more like our father I think,' she said, relaxing a little. 'He knows nothing of children, but he cares deeply for any vulnerable creature. Even mortals.'

'He sounds like a good man,' Maer said, sorrow creeping through him as he realised this man would be his enemy no matter what, and that Nerryn must necessarily be torn away from one of them because of it.

'He is. He is very like you.'

Maer was surprised to find himself smiling amid the tumble of emotions. 'You say the perfect things, at the perfect times.'

'You make it sound as though I'm merely flattering you,' she said. 'But you, the Lord Tir and Mylan – if the three of you were left to bring this awful matter to a close, you would do it in moments.'

'But it isn't so simple, is it?'

'No.' She seemed about to say more, but drew a

quick breath and pointed instead. Mylan had left Cantoc's dwelling and moved back along the path. He held tightly to the bundle he had carried before, but now the black haired boy was held high on his shoulder, exposed to the morning sun, and gazing around him in lively interest, his fist stuffed into his mouth.

'He's taking him to our home,' Nerryn said in sudden excitement. She drew away from Maer and faced him, her expression determined. 'Go back to Lynher Mill, Maer. Tell the Lord Tir and his lady that I will bring their son to them. Soon.'

'How? They will never let him go just for the asking,' Maer said. But hope flowered in him as he saw her jaw set. He had never loved her more than in that moment.

'I will offer to care for the boy, so that when Tir comes to reclaim him he will be healthy and well. Father will know this will help ease things between our people, and will persuade Mylan to let me.'

His heart crashed as he realised he was leaving her at Arric's mercy yet again. 'How will you convince them you have left me? You ran away with me twice, they will not believe you trust in the people who have kil—' his breath stopped, but he somehow got the words out—'killed my father.'

She looked down at the path, and he saw impatience, and longing in her face. What if she fell under the spell of being with the most beloved of her family again, and decided to stay? But when she turned back to him that longing was still there, and now it was directed at him.

'Please, Maer, let me try to gain Arric's trust, with Father's and Mylan's help. If I cannot, I will come to you again.' She stepped into his embrace, and he held tightly to her, breathing in her faint, clean scent for the last time, holding onto the feeling of her slender shoulders beneath his hands, her face pressed into the hollow of his shoulder. He did not doubt her love, but he could already feel her eagerness to be gone.

'I will be as swift as I can in returning Dreis to his mother,' she promised, 'but it may take a while. They will be watching me closely.'

'How long should we wait?'

Nerryn looked to the sky. 'One more moon-cycle. I will come to you when the moon returns to the same as it was last night. The perfect half.'

'Do you really think it might take so long?'

'This cannot be rushed, Maer, it must be done with great care. I need to be certain of them. I will care well for the boy, you can tell Lady Laura that he will be in the best of hands.'

'It might be enough to ease her,' Maer agreed, with deep reluctance. 'Please… take care, and risk nothing.'

'Arric will have his own games to play, and Mylan will not stay long; the traveller's blood will sing him away again soon. It will be just my father and me, and father trusts me.'

'And you will betray that trust,' he said quietly, 'have you thought of that? That you will leave him heart-broken and lost for a third time?' He was reminded of his mother, and the way she had tried to persuade him not to become close to Richard, but their friendship had been just as inevitable as Nerryn's decision to stay here now.

Her words confirmed it. 'Yours is the path I have chosen to walk, and this child is the son of my king. My father's king also. I have to try, Maer. It's our only chance to return the little prince without bloodshed.' She raised her face to his and her hands rose to caress his jaw, as they always did when she longed for his mouth on hers. He dipped his head to kiss her, and she held his face so that he could not break away until she was ready. He would have stayed there the day's length if he could, did she still not understand that?

When she released him she had composed herself, but he saw it had been a struggle to do so. He nearly seized her hand and begged her to change her mind, but Tir's face flashed into his mind again, and he crossed his arms instead. 'If you feel in any way threatened, promise me you will leave. Come home. Without Dreis if you have to, we will find another way.'

She nodded. 'Go now, Maer, before you are seen. Father will be happy to see me, and Mylan will be too. The rest I will manage somehow. Do you trust me?'

'Of course I do.'

'Then go. Tell Tir and his lady their son will be returned to them as soon as I am able to do so.'

She was already walking backwards, away from him, as she spoke, and, with a last sigh she turned and began to run, to reach her home, her father and her much-missed twin before Arric returned to sow his suspicion on everything. It was an echo of a simpler time, when he had watched her go the same way in order to make up her mind whether she loved him. Maer would have given all he possessed to have been able to return to that time, with all its uncertainties and innocent anguish.

Exhaustion was setting in as he began his journey back to Lynher Mill, and he faced the prospect of his mother's grief with rising dismay; if he didn't get some rest he'd never be strong enough to hold her up. He made his way to the edge of the forest, where he picked a patch of shade afforded by the outermost trees, and sat down with his back against one of them. He gave himself to his thoughts, to do with as they would.

Laura had wondered how he could be so calm, and he'd told her he was not calm, but numb. Now that numbness had to be peeled away; he needed to expose himself to the deepest of his hurts before he could begin to heal. The moment he whispered, 'I miss you,' a sharp pain sliced through him, and the tears came. He felt, rather than heard, the low rumble of thunder that came with them, and turned his emotions inward so the sky remained undarkened. He gritted his teeth. There could be no harder way to learn this lesson of control, yet in a way it was still Casta teaching him. Staring upwards, as if he could see what Richard had seen, Maer uttered a short, breathless laugh through his tears. *Thank you, Father. It seems I am still learning from you.*

***

Arric smiled. The mid-morning air was crisp, the sea pounded and roared far below him, the cry of gulls was familiar music and the sky was a glorious pink-gold. But none of these natural pleasures lay behind the smile, instead he let his mind play over the moment when Cantoc had realised what must be done, and that he was as blackly eager to do it as Arric himself.

Raising an army for protection was one thing, but it had been a glorious thing when Cantoc had turned to him, his eyes flashing, his jaw hard, and his shoulders lifted and squared as of old.

'Those killers will sorrow for their former lives.' There had been an edge of granite in his voice. 'They must give up their rule, and if they choose to fight we will meet them, and we will match them. And they *will* fall.'

Sadness had weakened Cantoc over the years, and his regret at the death of the Moorlander king had threatened to turn him into a sack of emotions that had no place in the forthcoming battle. But now his hands were fists again, his words bit hard, and when he had bid Arric farewell there had been a new purpose in him, a new resolve to punish those he believed guilty.

Arric looked out over the sea now, and pulled in a deep, cleansing breath. It had been a long, long night and he was tired, but he could not seek sleep yet; there was too much to be done. An army to raise, a brother to conquer and win over, and a sister to bring back to the family fold. Once Nerryn and Mylan were together, and Nerryn had learned exactly what she was capable of, there would be no question of the Moorlanders standing against them.

He yawned, taken unawares by it, and conceded that perhaps a short sleep might be sensible, after all. He would be good for nothing if he kept dozing, when he should be exhorting the fish-finders all down the coast to rise up, in support of their slain people and their Lord Cantoc.

He turned to go back to his home, then stopped with a groan. Mylan had taken that cursed child back there – There was as much chance of finding peace and sleep at home, as of finding a pearl in a limpet. Even the memory of the boy's piercing yells made him wince, and he glanced up towards the top of the cliff; maybe he could go to the hollow where Gerai had left the boy earlier, and settle down there until the sun had climbed a little. It was sheltered and private... which was presumably what had drawn his sister and her Moorlander prince to it. The thought made him grimace, but the lure of sleep was stronger.

He had taken no more than a few steps in the direction of the hollow before he stopped again, and frowned. Cantoc might well have listened to him, accepted his warnings, and unbent towards him as they'd discussed what must be done, but Arric was thrice damned if he would slumber the day away while the coast lord went to Mylan to make his plans. Sleep would have to wait a little longer.

He pushed aside the door covering, and realised at least one of his problems was solved, perhaps two. Nerryn looked up at him from where she sat on the floor, the boy Dreis propped between her knees.

She gave Arric a cool look from reddened eyes. 'I am back.'

Since that fact was obvious, Arric took it to mean she was not merely visiting. He glanced at Mylan, who sat in their father's chair. He might have felt a surge of anger and jealousy over that—after all, he was the elder brother, and had the right of all that had belonged to their father—but instead he only felt a little inward shudder at the memory of the blood that had flowed and soaked into the back of the chair. Mylan was welcome to it.

He plucked an apple from the dish on the table and addressed Mylan. 'Have you told our dear sister the sad news?'

'I have.'

'And have you told her who committed this terrible deed?'

Nerryn glared at him. 'Do not speak as though I were elsewhere!'

Arric tried not to show his surprise at the strength and fury in her voice. She'd never been a quiet little flower, but she'd never sounded quite so... *there*, as she did now; quite so much a part of what was happening around her. Her head had always been in the clouds, but now her eyes were on his, and they blazed.

'I am sorry,' he said, and was faintly troubled to discover he meant it. Whatever she had done, whoever she had run off with, she had just learned of her father's death. They had been extremely close, her and Talfrid. Now she must try to reconcile the fact of his death with the knowledge that she had left him alone, untended, in order to play at kings and queens with the man who had killed him. No matter what else she learned, she must never know who had truly wielded the digging stick that had ended their father's life.

Mylan rose from Talfrid's chair, and bent to lift Dreis so Nerryn could rise to her feet. She seemed taller too, although that was impossible. She stood straighter, perhaps that was it. She still did not match Arric's own height, nor that of her twin, but her posture said she would not be pushed aside, or otherwise dismissed, any longer.

'Why did you come back?' Arric seated himself at the table to avoid having to meet her eyes. 'The truth, now.'

'I came back to rescue the child, nothing more,' Nerryn said bluntly. Mylan hoisted Dreis higher on his shoulder, and the boy looked around him with calm curiosity.

'Did you, now?' Arric bit into the apple to hide his further surprise. He chewed for a moment, gathering his thoughts. 'And how did you expect to do that?'

'I planned to gain the trust of you, and of f-father,' Nerryn's voice snagged on the word. She took a deep breath and Arric could hear it shaking. 'Maer and I knew it would take time to gain your trust, but I told him I would win you over, and that the first time I was left alone with Dreis I would leave, and take him with me.'

'Maer.'

'Yes.' Nerryn briefly closed her eyes, and reached out to support herself on the corner of the table. 'We meant to take the boy together, thinking only Father to be home. When we saw Mylan was here, and saw him leaving Cantoc's home with Dreis, I was so relieved. I knew it would be easier for me to pretend I was home to stay, if he and Father were the ones I spoke to. You have always despised me.'

'Not you,' Arric said quickly. 'Your choice of betrothed. And it seems I was right.'

She sagged and found her own seat, opposite him. Her eyes were bright with tears, but there was anger and betrayal in her face. 'I cannot believe he could do such a thing,' she whispered. Her knuckles were white where her hands clenched in front of her. Mylan put a hand on her shoulder but she did not acknowledge it.

Arric watched her carefully for signs of duplicity, and found none. 'So you plotted to trick us,' he said, pushing further.

'I did. *We* did.'

'And now you have thought again.'

'Arric, he killed our *father!*' The tears fell, bright drops of diamond that rolled down her smooth cheeks, splashing onto the scrubbed wooden table top. 'He let me pledge myself to him, and to his people. He took all the comfort I could give when *his* father died, and all the while he had slain my own!'

'And he used your digging stick to do it,' Arric said.

At this news Nerryn broke into sobs that shook her slender frame, and although Mylan's hand tightened on her shoulder she still did not seem to notice it. 'Nerryn, do you pledge your loyalty to Cantoc?'

She looked up, red-eyed and gulping. 'To Cantoc?'

'He plans to overthrow the Moorlanders. To rise up against them with all the men at his disposal, and to put an end to the Lightning and the Blade.'

'But he's already killed Casta!'

'In revenge for Talfrid, as you now know. But it is not enough. The Moorlanders and their servants are responsible for the three of us being alone, and for destroying our father's life long before they finally stole it from him.'

'Father told me about Mother's death,' Nerryn said. 'About the spriggans and their darts. But they are mere servants of the Moorlanders, and were not acting in their name.'

Mylan shook his head. 'Father was wrong about that, and he discovered as much before he was killed.' He sat down, still holding Dreis, and Arric shot a suspicious glance at the boy, braced for another of those unthinkably loud shrieks, but he seemed content enough to play with the silver brooch that fastened Mylan's cloak. 'The one who killed Dafna was no spriggan,' Mylan went on, 'it was the queen's own brother, Gilan.'

Nerryn's face paled. She was silent for a long moment, and in her expression Arric saw everything falling into place in her mind.

'Then yes,' she said at last, her voice lowered, but no less bitter for that. 'I pledge my loyalty to Cantoc, and declare my severance from the Moorlanders.'

'Do you swear it?' Arric asked, his heart beginning to thump faster.

She nodded. 'I do. They have played us for fools, they have sought to split us, and they have smashed our family.' She looked at each of her brothers in turn, her hand on Mylan's arm as it encircled Dreis, and for the first time Arric felt the thread that bound all of them tighten. He was moved to reach out and take her free hand, and his other stretched across the table, where he felt it grasped by Mylan.

A shock travelled up both arms, and he almost gasped and ripped his hands away, but neither twin had felt it. Their pain and grief, and their bittersweet joy at seeing one another again, had met and joined in Arric's own body. A dark thrill crept through him; he'd been right about the power these two held but they had no notion of its strength, or of what they might be capable. Now they must learn to understand it and to use it.

'Take the boy away.' Nerryn withdrew her hand from Arric's. 'I do not want to look on him.'

'Why not?' Mylan said, puzzled. 'He's a beautiful child, and innocent.'

'He is Tir's son! He reminds me of those who have taken everything I loved.'

'Nerryn, we will have need of your gentleness,' Mylan said softly. 'The child will be missing his mother. You must learn to see him for what he is, and for what he is not.'

Nerryn shrugged. 'I will tend him, if that is your order. But do not expect me to find any affection for him.'

No, Arric sighed, his thoughts darkening again, *that expectation is reserved for Mylan. Look at him, his face as tender as if he were the boy's father… he defends him at every turn. The sooner we prise the two of them apart, the better for all.*

'How fares the new king?' he said aloud. 'Gerai said he was wounded during the night.'

'He was,' Nerryn said. She appeared troubled, but that was to be expected; Tir was not only their king, he was a story they had all grown with, and a man she had come to know. He was also a man Arric had come to know, and he did not like that knowing one little bit.

'I have heard he has taken the Lightning,' he said. 'Will he live to wield it?'

'So the spriggan says. He cannot move yet, but Kernow is sparing none of her knowledge and skill in helping his body to heal. He is known to be strong, and has beaten death before.'

'And what of his elemental power?'

Nerryn fixed him with a cool look. 'Are you seeking to use my knowledge of the Moorlanders' weaknesses, to further your campaign against them?'

'*Our* campaign. And of course I am.'

In the silence that followed, Arric watched her very closely, and saw her allegiance to Maer's people take one last breath, before dying between them.

'I will tell you everything you have need of knowing,' Nerryn said at last. 'But do not ask me to take you to them.'

'Agreed. Well? What power does Tir have?'

'Maer says he is a strong elemental, though he has not yet learned to control it. But he is also a strong mortal, and that will make him a dangerous enemy.'

'Strong how?' Mylan asked, shifting Dreis to his other shoulder. The boy grunted and tugged at Mylan's hair, but he didn't appear to mind, just lifted the plump hand away and locked it gently in his own fist.

'Maer says—'

'Maer says!' Arric snapped. 'Nerryn, if you must begin every sentence with the name of that nothing little Moorlander, I will lose patience very quickly.'

Nerryn pushed her hair back from her still-red eyes, and leaned across the table towards him. Arric was disconcerted to find himself shifting back slightly, and made himself stop.

Nerryn's voice was hard. 'I saw little of Tir, but

Maer grew up with him. He knows him. They are brothers. Almost all my knowledge of Tir has come from Maer, and I will speak his name as I please.'

Another silence fell, and Arric was aware of Mylan watching them both, reading them, noting their new relationship. He'd been glad of Nerryn's strength, but if he did not take care he would be pushed to the bottom of the pile once again. That could not happen.

His fist came down on the table. 'You will not! Tell me all I need to know, but for the Ocean's sake do *not* begin every sentence with a tribute to the one who passed you the knowledge! I have no need of it!'

'Arric—' Mylan began, but Arric glared at him.

'I am the eldest here, and Father's heir. Do not forget it.' He turned back to Nerryn. 'Now, how do you measure a mortal's strength? What is there to fear from that part of him?'

'He himself fears little. He fights well. And, most dangerous of all, he loves deeply.'

'*Love?* What is there to fear from that?'

Nerryn gave him a pitying half-smile. 'If you do not understand that, you will be dead less than a heartbeat after you meet him again.'

'Nerryn has the right of it,' Mylan said. He looked at the black-haired boy nestled against his shoulder. 'Tir's love for his son, and for his lady, will push him onward. He will do whatever must be done to protect them, and that makes him very dangerous indeed.'

'Then it will also make him reckless,' Arric said thoughtfully, 'and that might be to the good of our cause more than to his.' He sat back. 'What of the others? Maer, Deera, their people?'

'We will see several sunrises before the Moorlanders are able to muster any force against us,' Mylan said. 'Casta was very much loved, and vengeance will urge them on, but they are a people weakened by his sudden death. They will be in confusion.'

'And even when Tir is able to take on a king's duties it will be a long while before he recovers his full strength,' Nerryn added.

Arric looked from one to the other, with narrowed eyes. 'You are sure of this? It is important we know our enemy.'

'Gerai struck him, more than once. Maer even thought...' Arric's mouth tightened, but Nerryn pressed on, with a slightly rebellious tone in her voice, '*Maer thought* Tir had already died, out on the moor. He was lying alone and untended in the rain. The injuries to his back are deep and dangerous, and Kernow has forced him to lie still, to allow his body to recover.'

'He cannot move at all?' Mylan asked, and Nerryn shook her head. 'Then yes, we have some time.' He turned thoughtful. 'Unless we decide to strike now, while he is weak. Any attempt to defend his people would probably kill him. This is something we ought to consider.'

Arric watched Nerryn for some sign of sorrow,

or of disappointment that her beloved twin was speaking so indifferently of the much-lauded Tir. But there was none.

She spoke calmly. 'Maer has agreed to wait the shorter of either a moon's turn, or until I bring Dreis to him, before he moves on Cantoc. He knows it might take a little while to earn your trust.'

'He is right,' Arric said, though privately he was close to being satisfied. There was something about this new coldness in her; Maer's betrayal seemed to have made her into someone new. Someone useful. 'You have earned us some time with your duplicity, and we will use it well.'

'We must speak further with Cantoc,' Mylan cautioned. 'Tell him all you have told us. He alone must decide whether we wait, or take advantage of Tir's injuries.' He shifted Dreis in his arms and held him out to his sister, and Arric winced as he placed a casual kiss on the boy's head before surrendering him. Nerryn too looked startled at the gesture, but took the boy and held him on her lap, stiffening away from any contact other than that dictated by necessity.

Dreis didn't seem to mind. 'Brrrap,' he burbled happily. Mylan tried to hide a smile, but not well enough for Arric's closely watching eyes.

'I will see Cantoc.' Arric rose, eager to be away from this cloying scene.

'No, you stay here,' Mylan said, also standing. 'I will tell him.'

Arric sighed. 'This is foolishness, Mylan. One of

us must stay here and guard Nerryn.'

'Then why don't we bring Cantoc back here to discuss what must be done next?' Mylan suggested.

'And have this one,' Arric gestured at Nerryn, 'carry all our plans back to the Moorlanders?'

'She has told us *their* plans,' Mylan pointed out. 'She has proved that she spares them no love, and owes them no favours.'

'*She!*' Nerryn snapped. 'Why do you both insist on pretending I'm not here?' She lifted Dreis again and placed him on Mylan's now-empty seat, making Mylan grab him before he fell off. 'I will go and see Cantoc myself.'

Before Arric or Mylan could speak, she had pushed aside the door covering, and vanished beyond it into the bright day beyond. The brothers looked at each other, bemused at the speed of her departure, and Arric was astonished to see Mylan's face break into a reluctant grin.

'Welcome back, Nerryn.'

Arric's own mouth lifted in a smile. 'Welcome back, both of you. Just let the Moorlanders see what they have taken on now.'

Chapter Five

Mill Lane Cottage, Lynher Mill

There was laughter in the dream. And cheese, oddly, but it was a dream filled with warmth. Laura floated in its embrace, contented and safe, until the hammering on the front door brought her awake with a jolt. She lay still for a second, her heart thundering while her mind scrambled to find a purchase on where she was; she immediately wished it had failed. She squeezed her eyes shut, but the image of Jane, stiff and unresponsive on the kitchen floor, remained sickeningly clear. Then something else clicked into place: Captain. Why had no-one mentioned him?

'Laura!'

She swung her stiffened legs off the bed and stumbled across to the window. It was Maer. And his arms were empty. A quick glance showed no sign of Nerryn standing nearby, and, hot-eyed and trembling, Laura ran down the narrow stairs, slipping down the last two as she tried to push from her head all the terrifying thoughts that wanted to stop her dead in her tracks.

She dragged open the door, squinting against the

weak midday sunlight. 'Where is he?'

'He's safe,' Maer said quickly, putting a hand over hers where it clutched at the door. 'And he will stay safe, I promise.'

Laura looked at him stupidly for a moment while she absorbed his words. A moment later she was in his arms and sobbing, sixteen all over again and in the embrace of a glamorous boy-stranger she'd met on the moors. She wasn't even aware of him drawing her into the house, but when she could focus once again on the mechanics of living, she was already on the sofa and he was sitting next to her.

Her eyes moved about the room, at the play-gym that sat in the middle of the floor waiting for small hands to hit and squeeze and ring the bells, and then at the lump of misshapen wood with her son's face carved into it.

Maer followed her gaze, and leaned over to pick it up. 'Jacky's work,' he said, a little sadly. 'He could never have taken Dre … Ben, without leaving something in his place.' He looked at it closely, and she saw reluctant admiration for the workmanship. 'He will have used Tir's blade to carve this, it carries his blood. The bond between father and son is so strong, Jacky would have felt he was leaving something of them both here. For you.'

Laura didn't want to think about Richard's blood, he had spilled too much. 'Tell me about Ben,' she said instead.

'He is being cared for by Nerryn.'

'Where? God, Maer, where do they even live?'

'In the cliffs above Trethkellis. We found him there with Nerryn's brother—'

'No!' Laura lurched to her feet. 'Not him!'

'It's alright,' Maer stood too, and caught at her arm. 'It's not Arric, it's Mylan. Nerryn's twin.'

'I didn't know she even…' But it didn't matter. 'So why didn't you just grab him?'

'It will take time for Nerryn to regain her brothers' and her father's trust; if she took up the child and tried to make off with him they would never let either of them go.'

'How long?'

'One month.'

Laura felt the air go out of her. 'A whole month?' she whispered. 'I can't.'

'Ben is happy, well-tended, and safe.' Maer spoke gently. 'Just try to remember that much, it might help.'

Laura forced herself to breathe, slowly and deeply. She hurt all over, and she knew that pain would not go away until she had Ben in her arms again. She would learn to live with it, she had to. She just had no idea how.

'And… and Richard?' she managed.

He drew her back down to sit beside him. 'I know you're angry with him, but—'

'No. Not anymore. Something was working through me when I was out there last night. Trying to make me hate him.'

'And now?'

'Now I have my own feelings back,' she said dully,

'and I wish to God I didn't. Is he alright?'

'I came straight here after I left Nerryn. You have seen him more recently than I.'

Laura sighed. 'Deera made me leave. He was in a bad way, but awake. Kernow was with him.'

'Then he too is in safe hands,' Maer said, with some relief. 'If she hadn't given him that draught last night he'd have killed himself trying to go after Ben.'

'And yet he didn't want me to know,' Laura said, bewildered all over again. 'Did he really think he was going to die?'

'He was told he would, if he stayed. Yes, he believed it. He had to make the oath willingly, in full understanding of what it meant, but he didn't think he would live long enough to have to live by it.'

Laura sat still, struggling to take it all in. How it must have felt to stay, to win Ben's freedom with his own life. 'It's so stupidly ironic,' she said at last, and when Maer raised an eyebrow, she went on, 'All those years when he would accept a challenge, a fight, any kind of confrontation. He's told me about that boy Tanner, and the kids who used to terrorise the neighbourhood where he lived.'

'Tanner was a laugh a minute,' Maer agreed, smiling slightly. 'And yes, if Richard had fought Gerai last night, instead of trying to go after Ben, he'd likely have won.'

But he had chosen not to, for the first time in his life, and that decision had nearly killed him. Laura closed her eyes against the image of Richard, turning away from the stick-wielding Moorlander and being struck down from behind. When she opened them again Maer was watching her. 'It's because of who he is, isn't it?' she said.

'What is?'

'His ...' he couldn't think of the word. Arrogance wasn't right. 'His belief in himself,' she said at last, although that didn't seem quite right either.

'Kings have a way about them,' Maer said. 'True-born royalty will yield only to honour, and neither Gerai nor Tanner have a shred of that in their entire bodies.' He put his hand over hers. 'Laura, you know you must never go to him, don't you?'

She nodded, her throat tightening again. 'At least I'll know he's there, and alive,' she managed. 'It's more than I could have hoped for earlier. More than some people have.' She found herself thinking first of Deera, and then of her old headmistress, the wife of her natural father. They must both have loved just as fiercely, how must they feel now? It didn't bear thinking of, she only had so much grief to spare, and, between them, Richard and Ben had claimed it all.

'What do I tell everyone?' She asked.

Maer looked helpless. 'I suppose you tell them Richard has gone back to his own country. It won't raise any questions, since that's his habit anyway. Later... well, later you must decide what your son should know, and from what he must be protected.'

'Protected?' Laura couldn't suppress the bitterness in her tone. 'You mean, like you protected Richard?'

'Laura—'

Her back was rigid now, her voice cool. 'You probably ought to leave. My friend will be here before long, and I don't feel like having to explain you. Not until I've had the chance to tell her about Ben.'

Maer's eyes widened. 'You're going to tell her the truth?'

'I need someone, Maer! My oldest friend died last night, and you've stolen the one person I could tell everything to. What else have I got?'

'But you can't—'

'She won't believe me at first, but I'm ready for that.'

Maer's expression bordered on panicked. 'All the more reason not to tell her. She's not going to sit by and watch you fall into a black hole of delusion. She'll have Ben's safety at heart, yes, but what good will you be to Ben, locked up in some institution? Drugged to the eyeballs and believed by no-one?'

The picture he painted was bleak and terrifying, and made more so by the knowledge that he was right. His eyes pinned hers, and eventually she nodded, defeated. 'Just go. Do what you can for Ben. And for Richard.' She snatched a quick breath, and felt a single tear spilling onto her cheek. She wiped it away. 'We'll leave Lynher Mill as soon as you bring Ben back to me. Tell Richard that.'

'It's safest,' Maer agreed gently. 'At least until we have avenged Casta's death and the kingdom is settled once more.'

'Will Arric will be killed?'

He didn't answer at first, and she wondered what violent turmoil was going on inside that fair head of his. Eventually he said, 'He will be arrested for his dealings with mortals, and held to account, but there will be no more bloodshed after Cantoc is dead.'

Laura looked at him steadily. 'You're lying, aren't you?'

'I don't—'

'Will there be a war?'

He held his breath a moment, looking unsure. 'I don't know,' he confessed at last. 'But even Cantoc will be safe until Nerryn has brought Ben back. Your son will not be a bargaining tool much longer, I promise.'

At the front door he leaned forward and pressed a kiss to Laura's forehead. She closed her eyes, trying to pretend it was Richard's lips she felt. But they would never touch her skin again.

He drew back, and his gaze lit on the newel post at the foot of the stairs, where Richard's coat still hung. For a moment Laura was certain he was going to ask if he could take it, and she was getting ready with her refusal, but in the end he just gave her a sad smile, and left.

Laura closed the door behind him, and stood staring at it. She tried to convince herself that if she opened it she would see Richard standing there, as he had on that first night; uncertain, hopeful, but with affectionate laughter in his eyes as he'd watched her sucking wine from the sleeve of her dressing gown. The day they'd met. The day she'd drawn him.

The longing to see him again was overwhelming. It might lessen in time, but Laura wasn't ready to fight it yet. She brushed her hand across his coat, resisting the urge to slide her arms into the sleeves, and dropped to her knees beside the sofa. She pulled out the clear plastic drawing box she'd left packing until last, and lifted the lid and slowly drew out the blue folder that sat on the top.

When she saw the drawing of Jacky Greencoat she'd done as a child, a little squeeze of grief surprised her. But it shouldn't have been a surprise; he had died trying to bring Ben to her, and his actions had always had an undeniable nobility about them. He had always had Richard's safety at heart.

Pushing aside the picture of the spriggan, Laura saw the corner of a small wooden frame sticking out of the pile of sketches, and her breath stuck just for a second… then the framed picture went out of her head, and her vision blurred as her gaze fell on the image of Richard.

There had always been something that had stopped it coming to life for her the way Jacky had, and the way her frantic drawings of her mother had, but that did not lessen the pain that struck her as she looked at it. The thick black hair and direct stare were so perfectly him, the strong jawline, a hint of a smile beside the eyes that, although monochrome here, became a clear, vivid green in her mind's eye. Still, there was something not right.

Her hand went into the box again, her eyes still

on the picture, and she grasped the stub of pencil in the corner. When she brought it down towards the paper she realised the tip was going to the open collar of his shirt, and with three swift strokes she drew the shape that wrung a cry of despair from her. The picture came to beautiful, vivid life – she almost saw the welling of Richard's blood in the newly-drawn lightning-bolt shape.

This time she did not put the picture away, but clutched it to her chest and then the tears really came. A great storm of them, washing through her, pulling everything together in a knot of grief until she could barely breathe.

She didn't know how long she sat there on her knees on the sitting room floor, rocking and sobbing, but she jumped as she heard the front door click open, then clunk shut. Surely it couldn't be evening already? No, it was barely mid-day; Ann must be really worried to have left school this early.

She wiped her eyes, placed the picture carefully back on the top of the pile, and took a deep breath, willing herself to calm. The temptation to tell her friend everything was like an itch, but Maer's words had struck home; it was too fantastical to believe. With the best of intentions, and with Ben's safety foremost, Ann would be unable to do anything but report her to the authorities.

Ann came in, and her face was concerned, but taut. She looked as though it was hard to keep her distance, but keep it she did, standing by the door, her car keys in her hand as if she was ready to leave at a second's notice.

'Where's Ben?'

'He's safe.'

'Where?' Ann seemed to realise she sounded sharp, and she came a little closer, her expression melting into indecision. 'Look, you're scaring me,' she admitted. 'I told the police what you wanted me to, but only because it's you and I trust you. Am I wrong?'

Laura shook her head. 'I promise you, Ben is okay. I haven't harmed him, and neither has Richard.'

Ann tensed again. 'Has Richard really got him?'

'Yes.'

After a moment Ann nodded, but she didn't look happy. 'I don't know him that well, but I know you. I'll just have to believe you.'

'Richard would never hurt him,' Laura said. 'Come on, you've seen them together.'

'I do believe you, but I need to know what I've risked jail for. So where are they?'

'We fought,' Laura said. That much was true, but Ann's choice of words made her shiver. 'I think it's over.'

The tension wavered, and Ann's voice softened. 'Oh, Laura...'

'Richard's going back to America to think everything through. He might not be back for quite a while, so I've agreed he could take Ben away for a few days.'

'Are you mad? Isn't he likely to take Ben to America with him?' Ann was on her knees beside

Laura now, and looking at her with worry darkening her brown eyes.

'No. He wouldn't. The fight was bad, but it wasn't...' Laura shrugged. 'It wasn't vicious. And neither is Richard. He'd no more do that to me than I would to him. Or to Ben. He just wanted to say goodbye, you know?' The words tangled in her mouth as the reality of that part sank in.

Ann digested this, then frowned. 'Then why not tell the police that? Lying to them was—'

'Probably stupid, yes. But at the moment, thanks to you, they're not concerned about Richard and Ben, they're concerned about why Jane was left to die alone. In my kitchen. I don't want them going after him over something that was my fault.'

Ann shot a glance towards the closed kitchen door, and shuddered. 'They'd understand,' she said, but in doubtful tones.

'No. If they knew Richard and I had fought they'd want to know what it was about. They'd drag him back here in a heartbeat and haul him over the coals.'

'And what was it about?'

'Jane, in the end,' Laura said, reverting to a part-truth. 'He knew she was doing drugs. He told me she was doing it but I didn't believe him.'

'And?'

'And it came down to trust, and then to choices. He said there was no way we could go on together if Jane was in my life.'

'Shit.'

'Exactly. And what would the police make of a statement like that?'

'But it was an overdose, they said so.'

Laura got heavily to her feet, her knees throbbing from the time she'd spent on the floor. 'At the moment they've got no reason to think otherwise. But if they question Richard, and end up thinking I had some kind of motive—'

'Oh, come on!' Ann stood too. 'You don't know the first thing about drugs. What kind was she even taking?'

'Crack, I think. Thing is, if they search the place they'll probably find all kinds of evidence, from when she was staying here while I was in Plymouth.'

Ann followed her into the kitchen, her nose wrinkling at the lingering smell of disinfectant. 'But they still can't think you'd be able to force her into an overdose, surely?'

'Maybe not, but I can't take the risk.'

'What do you think happened?'

Laura shrugged and took cups off the mug tree. 'She wasn't thinking straight. She was upset she'd caused the row.' She hadn't thought this through at all, yet the lies just fell from her lips with disturbing ease. 'So in a way it was my fault.'

'Don't be silly, of course it wasn't.'

'I left her here in a right state!' Laura went through the motions of filling the kettle and preparing coffee, but it was all automatic, her mind was re-playing last night's horrific scene from this very room. 'She'd already started making the stuff, and she said something about it not being right, but I just washed my hands of her. I left her to it, and drove Richard and Ben down to the coast. And now she's dead.' She remembered something else then, and groaned. 'God, poor Jill.'

'Who?'

'Jane's mum. I suppose she's been told by now. I'll have to go and see her.'

Ann couldn't seem to find any words, she just sat at the table, her face pale and tight-looking while she thought it all through. Eventually she said, 'Okay, I understand why you had to lie, and I'm okay with telling the police what I told them. I believe Ben's with his dad and *they're* okay...' Her eyes fixed on Laura's as she sat down opposite. 'But how are *you* feeling?'

Laura almost caved in then. Words she could never utter were building up, ready to spill and destroy her friendship forever, and she had to clench her jaw tight to stop herself from saying them.

'I'm fine.' She even managed to bend her lips into what she hoped was a smile, of sorts. 'Once Richard's gone back to America it'll be just like before. I'll tell myself—'

The phone rang, and her heart skidded in her chest as she remembered the dealers who'd called the landline looking for Jane. With a shaking hand, and a nervous glance at Ann, she picked it up.

'Hello?'

'Is that Miss Riley?'

'Speaking.'

The voice sounded absurdly, but blessedly, normal amidst the insanity that had twisted Laura's world. 'This is Caroline Webster.'

The tenants in the house she had grown up in. Tom's old house. Laura swallowed a sigh; all she needed now was a complaint about leaky guttering. But she forced a friendly tone into her voice. 'Hello, Caroline. How can I help?'

'I've just had a call from the vet in Liskeard. The charity one. They've got your brother's dog.'

'Captain!' A surge of relief went through her. 'How is he?'

'Oh. I'm so sorry, I should have thought… When I said they've got him, I meant someone found him. On the moors, by the standing stones. The phone number on his chip was still this one, so I said I'd pass the message along. I'm afraid he's gone.'

Laura closed her eyes, and the sting of tears came, tiredly familiar. Caroline's voice dropped. 'Whatever happened to the poor thing, Miss Riley?'

Laura's mind blanked, and she stammered out something vague about probably being hit by a car.

'So sad. And I heard about your friend, too,' Caroline went on. 'Overdose, wasn't it?'

'So they said.' Laura gritted her teeth; that was bloody fast, even by Lynher Mill standards. She wanted to slam down the phone just to stop the questions, but she would have to get used to them. While Ann moved around behind her pouring the coffee, she somehow fielded the flurry of enquiries that Caroline had clearly been storing up, and was about to make her goodbyes, when her tenant spoke again.

'Actually, Miss Riley, there was something else.'

'Yes?'

'We're sorry to do this to you, especially now, but we're going to be giving a month's notice on the cottage. We've found somewhere a bit closer to Liskeard. Better for Col's health, you know.'

'Oh.' More complications. The silence on the line was at once hopeful and expectant, and Laura put the woman at her ease; it wasn't her fault, after all. 'That's quite understandable, thank you for letting me know. Will you put the note through my door, or send it via the agent?'

'Both, if you like.'

'Thank you,' Laura said again. 'Have a good evening, Caroline, and thank you both for being such good tenants.' She put the phone back and rubbed her burning eyes. 'They've found Captain. I think he followed me, but must have been hit on the road.' She tried not to put any emphasis on the fact that the dog had crept to where his master's life had ended, but Ann's gentle words seemed to echo her thoughts.

'So he's back with Tom.'

If you believe that, Laura wanted to say, but didn't. Tom was dead. Jane was dead. Captain was dead. Casta and Jacky too. To think of them all living it up at some huge party in the sky seemed just demeaning and pointless. Yet Captain had made it all the way down the hill, even as far as the standing stones… there was a lot that could never be explained, but perhaps acceptance was almost as good.

Ann raised her coffee cup. 'Here's to the four-legged hero.'

'And all the two-legged ones,' Laura said.

'Heroes everywhere,' Ann said, and they both sipped.

'I'll call the vet tomorrow,' Laura said. 'I have no idea what happens now.'

'They'll probably just ask you to pay for his…' Ann hesitated, 'his funeral. You won't have to go and pick him up or anything, unless you want to.' She pulled open the fridge and found half a dozen eggs and a pint of milk. 'I'm going to scramble these eggs, you make the toast.'

'I'm not hungry,' Laura said, 'I'll have something later.'

'You'll have it now,' Ann said. 'If I need a good dose of carbs before I go running, you're going to need something pretty bloody substantial to get you through the next few days, until Ben comes home. And when he does get home, he's going to need you fit and well.'

'I know. But—'

'Missing Richard isn't going to do you any good either.' Ann's voice dropped its brisk tone. 'He'll come back too, once he's realised what he's walked out on. In the meantime, be glad for the time you had; I've never seen two people so in tune.' She gave Laura a gentle smile. 'You're a lucky woman, Laura, and I know you don't need me to tell you that, but I'm just reminding you. What's the point in building memories if you don't use them when you need them?'

'Why does everyone talk so much more sense than anything I can come up with?' The tears standing out in Laura's eyes made the kitchen glitter. The image brought Ben's first Christmas to mind... No, not Christmas, New Year's Eve. The decorations starting to droop; the chocolates almost all gone; Ben sleeping right the way through; a runaway cheese—a tiny smile found her as she remembered the dream—then later, the two of them sitting on the floor in front of the sofa. Jools Holland was on the TV, and Richard had been singing under his breath when he recognised the songs, his hand looped over her raised knee in a gesture of familiarity and affection. She recalled his faint smile as he'd turned to look at her, as if he was seeing her for the first time.

That room had been glittering too, but there had been no tears. At midnight they hadn't kissed, or counted down, or raised a toast, but they'd shifted closer together at exactly the same moment, on the last stroke of Big Ben, and both let out a gentle sigh in unison.

It had been perfect. And she'd had that. Ann was right; mourning those times now would be as pointless as mourning her childhood. Everything passed, eventually, but the memories were there for a reason.

Ann whistled, jolting her back into the present, and pointed at the toaster. Obediently Laura stood up, and opened the new loaf of bread, and soon the smell of toast and cooking eggs began to permeate the kitchen. She even began to hope that the memory of Jane's stiff body on the floor, and the sight of her own torn nightie caked in stale vomit and blood, might eventually lessen after all, and let her live here in some kind of peace until Ben came home.

Chapter Six

Trethkellis

Cantoc looked at the piece of bread in his hand. It would taste good, it always did, and his appetite was usually strong; he had need of nourishment, and such a powerful frame as his burned through it quickly. But today the very idea of tearing into that crust just made him feel exhausted – he lacked the strength to chew it, and would probably choke. His heart ached, and his head pounded. What had happened? Arric and Mylan between them had managed to find and resurrect the old Cantoc: passionate leader, and seeker of vengeance, but here, alone, his resolve deserted him, leaving only the memory of words spoken in heat and fury. How had everything become draped in this dreadful black shadow?

Not too many days ago he had been going about his business, some of it legitimate, some of it not. His knowledge of Arric's sly little games was nothing new, nor was the pain of Dafna's loss, but that pain had long since settled into a seamless, solid ache that he fought daily, but had learned to live with. Only sleep brought him peace.

And Arric? He had become something altogether different since his father's death. Who would have believed he had it in him to murder anyone, let alone the king? Thank the Ocean the younger brother was back, to temper that impulsive anger and guide Arric towards obedience and calm. They would have need of those qualities if they were to be successful in ending the era of Lightning and Blade.

Cantoc dropped the bread back onto the platter in front of him, and instead took a hefty gulp of wine. He had no sooner replaced the goblet on the table when the rock hammered at his doorpost, and he groaned. No doubt it would be one of Dafna's boys come to complain about the other. Or perhaps both, along with the son of Tir, and arguing as to who should be caring for him. Cantoc sighed and pushed his platter away, not sorry for the excuse to put aside the necessity of eating.

'Declare yourself,' he said, and if he heard the sour, unwelcome note in his own voice, well what of it? He was master here, and his was the right to turn away anyone who displeased him. One scent of squabbling children in these supposedly full-grown men would be enough to make him exercise that right.

When he turned to face the visitor in the doorway his chest tightened painfully. With the sun behind her, touching her auburn hair with flame and casting her face into shadow, Dafna looked real enough to touch. It took only as long as a missed heartbeat to recognise the daughter in the ghost of the mother.

'Nerryn.' He rose from the table, appalled at his own surly manner. What must she think of him? It shouldn't matter, but it did. A great deal. 'I did not know you were visiting... oh, my poor child, your father—'

'I am not visiting.' Her eyes found his, and in their depths he read the pain and grief put there by her prince. His gut clenched in renewed determination; Arric was right, avenging their parents would not bring them back, but it might bring them peace. Then her words penetrated deeper, and he realised she had made her choice.

'You are returned? For good?'

'I am.' She moved further into the room.

Cantoc wondered if he should take her hand; he had no wish to revolt her, or make her withdraw. But she came to him instead, and to his astonishment she put her hand gently on his arm and reached up to kiss his cheek.

The emotions that seized him in that moment had no name in which to tidily wrap themselves. This child he had first seen clutching at her father's legs, her eyes wide, unafraid, curious; this child who had been spared understanding of the unthinkable reason for his visit that day; this child who had no way of knowing she had just saved their family from being forced out of their home. He remembered her fierce glare at her older brother, her tiny pink tongue poking out in rebellion.

She had come to hate Cantoc, he knew that, and who could blame her? Believing his motives to be guided by greed, lust and power, anyone would have felt the same. But now she stood before him, her eyes bright with tears, trust in her touch, and in her closeness. He finally understood the depth of Talfrid's fury at his proposal, the rushing, protective surge that meant a man would kill to protect those he loved. But Talfrid had not killed him... perhaps he should have done.

His breath hitched as he laid his own hand over Nerryn's. 'Does this mean you know the truth now? About my offer?'

'I understand you wanted a companion. A daughter. Cantoc, I have lost my father but I cannot be your daughter, any more than I could have been your wife.'

'I know this. And I am glad you understand I had never wanted that. It would have been your mother's past, revisited upon you. But my affection for you was of the purest kind.' He offered a hopeful smile. 'Will you accept my friendship, at least?'

Nerryn nodded. 'I would be pleased to. Honoured, in fact.'

'You are the very image of your mother,' he told her, his voice cracking slightly. He hadn't meant to say the words aloud, she had no need to hear them; Talfrid would have told her every day.

'I am here to tell you what I know of the Moorlanders,' Nerryn said, moving away. She looked troubled, and would likely have questions about her mother later, but for now she wore the cloak of a messenger, nothing more. At his encouraging nod she told him of Tir's helplessness, his dependence upon the spriggans for his life, and that she and Maer had come back together, with the intention of stealing back Tir's son.

'He stood there with me, on the cliff,' she said, a bitter edge to her voice, 'and he knew I would soon discover my father's death, yet he took my comfort for the loss of his own. If Arric had not seen him running away from our home I would be none the wiser, and would even now be trying to take the child back to his mother.'

'And yet you love him still,' Cantoc said softly. 'I can see it when you speak his name.'

Should she have denied her feelings he might have harboured some suspicion still, or at the very least questioned the stability of her emotions. But it was clear her love for the former prince had not died, even with the knowledge of his hateful act against her family. Maer suffered now, as she did, and that was some small consolation, but Cantoc couldn't help wondering if it simply served to keep the bond between them alive.

'So you have chosen not to take Dreis back after all.' He watched her expression carefully. 'But he is to blame for none of this, nor is his mother. Why should they suffer?'

'It is wrong,' Nerryn agreed. 'But in the end it will help them both. And Tir, too.'

'How so?'

Nerryn arched one perfect eyebrow in a look he knew so well. 'You know this,' she said. 'Are you testing me?'

'Let's say I am. Would you have me do less? Trust everyone?'

She regarded him a little longer, then shrugged. 'Very well. When the Moorlanders are overthrown, as they must be, Tir will no longer rule. He will be free to return to his family. Lady Laura will have her man and her son, and it is of no consequence to them who rules over the moor, the coast and the forest. They can travel far away from this place.'

'And if Tir cannot? Do not forget he is of "this place," and has taken the Lightning.'

'Then he will stay, but his lady may choose to remain nearby also, and with no threat to her family as there is now.'

'All this is true.' Cantoc sighed. 'To be honest it is the only thing that makes me believe we are doing right by keeping the boy, for a time at least.'

Nerryn's expression softened. 'Father told me you are not what they say you are.' She sat down at the table, and he sat opposite her, sensing the questions were about to come. He was right.

'Tell me of my mother,' she said. 'Father often told the story of their meeting, but nothing about when they came back to live here. How she lived, what she loved.' She reached across the table and touched his hand. 'I know you carried a great deal of respect for her. Please… I would hear anything you can tell me.'

Cantoc rose and poured fresh wine, handing her a cup. He did not want to drink, but used the time to order his thoughts. She clearly knew some, but not all, so didn't he owe it to her to give her the truth in its hopeless entirety? Even the tale of Martha Horncup's boy, and the brutal death he'd suffered at Cantoc's own hand?

For a moment he felt the impending relief of unburdening himself, but Nerryn's eyes were still full of trust, and he knew that if he spoke of that day, even though it was the love of her mother that had driven him to commit the murder, that trust would vanish and she would withdraw from him once again.

Still, she deserved at least as much as her brothers knew, and so Cantoc took another huge swig of wine, fixed his eyes on the table, and told her of the night when he had given himself irrevocably into Dafna's hands, and taken her, blissfully oblivious, into his heart.

Dafna and Talfrid had set up home on the cliffs, near a village known by the mortals as Trethkellis, and the first full day after their return Talfrid had visited, alone, to tell Cantoc he would stray no more from his fish-finder duties.

Cantoc wandered idly along the cliff the next morning with Prince Gilan, only mildly curious about the woman Talfrid had described with such passion. He'd planned to visit and introduce himself, but he hadn't yet reached their home before he saw them leaving it, together, and had felt the first true pain of physical longing.

Her beauty was not uncommon next to the other *trigoryon an arvor*, but it was of a subtly different kind; a freedom of dress, of attitude, even from where he stood at the top of the cliff Cantoc could hear her laughter drifting in the air, and could see her leaping with grace and agility over the rocks as she ran down to the beach.

These rocks were not her home, she was not familiar with them, yet she ran as if they were her friends, and their jagged edges were warm, strong hands that held and guided her, rather than stone blades that could strip skin, tear muscle and shatter bone at the slightest slip. Come to think on it though… Cantoc peered more closely, and saw how she favoured her right foot slightly. Perhaps she wasn't oblivious to the dangers after all, merely treated them with contempt instead of cowering away from them.

The young woman turned back to call to Talfrid, who had descended quickly enough, but who lacked the lithe speed of his bride. When he reached her side Cantoc had to turn away, startled and dismayed at the sharp, stabbing jealousy he felt when the girl threw her arms about her husband's neck and kissed him.

'She is a singular creature,' Gilan murmured. Cantoc looked at him sharply, but saw nothing in the Moorlander's expression that said he had read any of Cantoc's thoughts.

'I wish the man well,' he said, meaning it. Talfrid was a good fish-finder, though not someone he knew well, a quiet man but friendly enough. A traveller who had found the reason for his wanderlust, and brought her home. 'He will stay now, I think, and earn his wage.'

'Why did you not stop him from going in the first place?' Gilan wanted to know. 'He has lost you coin and gold through his disappearances. All those days when he should have been working for you, he was away chasing shadows. And women.'

'Not women,' Cantoc corrected, his brow drawing down. Much as he was aware he needed Gilan's goodwill, such as it was, he didn't like to hear the prince dismissing his people in such terms. 'The secret to good leadership, Highness, is to allow the line to play out. Talfrid would have been little use to me had I made him stay, and would have simply cut the line altogether, out of frustration. Then we should never have seen him again.' *Nor his beautiful bride,* his mind finished for him, but he bit the words back. Another glance at Gilan revealed he'd heard them anyway. 'We have things to attend to, do we not? You will be pleased to know I have found a suitable storeroom, higher up the cliff, for your spoils.'

'Our spoils. Do not think to distance yourself.'

'Very well. Our spoils. Would you like to see it?'

From that day onward, Cantoc had found reasons to be walking the cliffs near Talfrid's home whenever he could. He took more time away from his lordly duties than he should, and even more from his extra activities with the crooked little Moorland prince, although he was aware this negligence was giving Gilan the opportunity to stretch the boundaries of their working relationship.

Then one evening a storm had blown up, born of the elements' natural ferocity and, for a rarity, not manipulated by Gilan or himself for personal gain. It was Cantoc's habit to go out walking in such storms, and he stopped to gaze out over the swelling sea; the grey, white-tipped rollers crashing against the rocks, with a roar that made his blood sing with joy to hear it. The *power* of it…

His attention was snagged by movement on the cliff, and he peered through the gloom to see Dafna and Talfrid, their baby son wrapped tightly and held beneath his mother's cloak, hurrying towards their home. Talfrid was carrying wood, and Dafna wore a basket on her back filled with rock samphire and sea-weeds, but she moved lightly and quickly on the wet rocks. The light was disappearing, the sky yellow and swollen-looking, and the rain beat relentlessly on their bared heads, still Cantoc could hear them calling to one another with laughter in their voices.

Envy settled into his heart as he imagined them going into their home, shedding wet clothing and settling down before a crackling fire. They would play with their son, then lay him down to sleep, and then—Cantoc swallowed hard—Talfrid would take his wife's hand and lead her to their own private chamber, where he would have possession of her as a husband would. Her lively, intelligent eyes would turn up to him and her sweet mouth would silently invite his lips... As the wind buffeted him, tugging at his hair and his clothes, Cantoc wondered, just for the space of a heartbeat, if Talfrid truly understood how lucky he was. But of course he did.

He turned away, trying to banish the picture of Dafna, her dark red hair soaking wet and lying thick on her shoulders, her slender body wrapped in a robe, and Talfrid's hands cupping her face. He had taken no more than three steps towards his own empty, dark home when he heard Talfrid shout to Dafna to stop where she was, and he turned back.

His heart lurched as his gaze followed the path they had been on; the cliff directly beneath their home had crumbled away to nothing, the path gone. But even as Cantoc breathed a sigh of relief that they had seen it before running into empty air, there was a thunderous crack, and the cliff side itself, into which their home was firmly set, slid downwards with a terrible kind of grace, until it hit the rocks below.

Dafna held her son more tightly as Talfrid returned to her side, and they both cried out in horror as they watched everything tumbling down into the darkness; all their possessions, clothing, furniture that broke upon the rocks, leaving only so much smashed wood... their life.

Cantoc began to run towards them, calling out, and even in his shock something took control and made him sure to only call Talfrid's name. The young couple saw him and stumbled back over the path to meet him, and with the wind ripping his words away and flinging them into the nothingness beyond the cliff, Cantoc gestured to them to follow him to his own dwelling.

Once inside, he gave them use of his sleeping room to change from their wet clothes, and to borrow something of his to wear while they dried out. Dafna went first, while Talfrid held the baby and Cantoc built up the fire.

When she emerged, Cantoc's breath stuck in his throat; she had put on his own robe, and the picture he had tried so hard to banish from his traitorous mind now stood before him. She shyly proffered her wet clothing and he hung it to dry, then he unpinned the wave-shaped silver brooch from her cloak, and gave it back to her, fighting the urge to lean forward and fasten it to her robe just as an excuse to be close to her.

Instead he poured warmed wine from the pan over the fire, and she accepted it, her eyes distant and unfocused as she struggled to take in the enormity of their loss. He could not think of anything that might ease her mind, so he remained silent, wishing his intentions could somehow pass through the air and make her understand how desperately he wished to help.

She held her son close with one arm, and her other shaking hand gripped Cantoc's finest wine goblet, but after her first few sips she ignored it and seemed to be holding it from politeness only. All her attention was on the blissfully oblivious child cuddled into her shoulder, as if he was the one thing anchoring her to the world.

After a few minutes Talfrid came out of Cantoc's room, wearing clean leggings and a tunic. He and Cantoc were of a similar build, and he looked well in Cantoc's clothing. He and his wife were a handsome and well-matched pair, and Cantoc couldn't help feeling another twinge of envy as Dafna rose and went to him. Talfrid folded her and their child into his arms, and at last she broke down into the sobs she had been battling.

'Where will we live?'

Cantoc could see Talfrid had no answer for her. They had no gold with which to buy land, or to replenish their supplies, they had no family to whom they could turn for help, their friends' homes were small and they too were scratching for means by which to live.

'I do not know, my love, but I will find you and Arric shelter, even if I must sleep under the sky.'

'I will not go where you cannot.' Dafna's voice trembled. 'But I worry for Arric. He's so small. Oh, Talfrid, what will we do?'

'I will find you a home,' Cantoc blurted. They turned to him, astonished but hopeful, and he went on, 'I have knowledge of a dwelling, a little farther up the cliff. It has been set aside for Prince Gilan but I am sure he will be prepared to wait a while until another is found.' Gilan would simply have to wait a little longer for his storeroom.

'Prince Gilan!' Talfrid's eyebrows were almost at

his hairline. 'But we cannot take a Moorlander prince's property.'

'It is not his home, his place is at Lynher Mill,' Cantoc pointed out. 'It would merely have been a shelter for when he visits on business.'

'But... we cannot pay for it,' Talfrid said. He looked at Cantoc over Dafna's head, smoothing down her hair, and even that slight, familiar touch made Cantoc's gut twist with longing. He curled his hand into a fist, almost able to feel the soft, wet hair under his palm, the warmth of her skin beneath it.

'We will discuss terms another time,' he said. 'Sleep here tonight. I will prepare food, if you will tell me what your son will eat, and you may have my bed. Tomorrow I will take you to your new home.'

He wanted to tell them how dreadful he felt for them, how he understood their devastation, how he would do everything he could to help... but his voice stayed business-like, and his words clipped and formal.

The following day he showed them to Gilan's cave, and left them to begin their new life together, without possessions, but with identical expressions of wonder and hope. They would pay what they could, when they could, and Talfrid had agreed to raise the price of his fish and to pay Cantoc the difference.

He would have to work hard to ensure his fish were better, fatter and tastier than everyone else's to justify the higher price, but Dafna had agreed to cure and preserve some stocks, to bake it with sea-weed and take it herself to sell, at least while Arric could still be carried in a pouch on her back.

Life had continued for them, while for Cantoc it seemed to have stood still. From a distance he had watched the little family grow, the birth of the twins was greeted with joy by everyone, and Cantoc saw Dafna regain her spirit of adventure, ranging far over the moors, ever closer to Lynher Mill. Encouraged by Talfrid to explore as far as she wished, assured of her safety with or without his presence, she roamed as far as a day's walk would take her, whenever she could.

'And then, when Gilan told me Dafna was… that she…' Cantoc hadn't realised he was weeping as he told the story, until he came to the most painful part of all and raised his eyes to see if Nerryn understood. As he did so a tear splashed onto his hand, and it seemed to release something inside him. He shook his head, unable to continue, and at last gave in to great, wracking sobs. His hand grasped the stem of the same wine goblet Dafna had held, and he closed his eyes and bowed his head.

A minute later he felt gentle fingers prising the goblet from his grip, and a hand on his head, turning his face so it was buried against Nerryn's midriff. Like a distraught child his hands went around her, and she shushed him, smoothing his hair and making calming noises, until the sobs tailed away into harsh hiccups. Each exhale shook him violently, and was accompanied by a little moan, but finally he quieted and realised what he was doing. He drew back and sat up straight, unable to look at her, and wiped his eyes with the heels of his hands.

'I am sorry.'

'You loved her,' Nerryn said, 'that is nothing for which you need be sorry.'

'I'm, I just …' he waved a hand helplessly. 'She was your mother, I shouldn't have—'

'I'm glad you did,' she said, her voice tight, and he saw then that she was fighting tears too. 'It makes her more real to me, and I better understand what you did for them now.'

'She never looked away from your father,' Cantoc said. He sniffed and found some semblance of control at last. 'Her love for him was as strong, if not stronger, than mine for her. That's how I know you still love your prince. Dafna was a good person but I know that this feeling would not simply go away, even if I learned she had done something terrible.'

'Even murder?'

He looked at her levelly, blinking away the last of his tears, then took her hand. 'Even murder.'

Chapter Seven

Maer left the village and made his way swiftly back to the mine. He ducked under the wire and hurried through the tunnel, his light surrounding him, but his thoughts dark. What if Nerryn couldn't earn her brothers' and her father's trust? What if they were waiting, and waiting, and the day never came that she brought Dreis back to his father? It was well that Tir would have time to recover, but how would they stop him from marching on the coast once he grew stronger, putting Nerryn in danger in his desperation to rescue his son?

The room in which Tir lay was dimly lit and smelled oddly pungent, and Maer noticed the strong-smelling candle burning on a platter on the shelf. Deera was nowhere to be seen, but Kernow and Martha sat in chairs near the king's bed, and Tir himself lay like a stone carving. Maer was reminded of his father's inexplicable and frightening illness, and the relief of his recovery, but how short-lived that relief had been.

'Leave us, please,' he said quietly. The spriggans exchanged a glance, and Kernow nodded.

'Call out if you have need of us. If he wakes, you

must not let him move.'

'I won't.'

The covering fell across the doorway, and Maer took hold of the chair Martha had been using and pulled it closer to Tir's head. He sat down, noting the healthier colour of his friend's skin, the lines of pain smoothed out, and when he put a hand gently on Tir's chest he felt the strong and steady thump of the heart that had been beating so lightly and erratically before. Whatever Kernow had been doing to speed the king's recovery was clearly working.

Maer lowered his head in relief. Tir lived. *Richard* lived. He took a ragged breath, and turned Tir's hand so he could grasp his arm the way of friends and brothers.

His heart leapt as Tir's fingers closed on his wrist. 'Hey.'

Maer smiled. 'Hey yourself.'

Tir licked his lips. 'Ben?'

'He's safe,' Maer said, as he had to Laura. There was a silence, while Tir closed his eyes briefly, and when he opened them and spoke again his voice was stronger.

'He's with Laura?'

'Not yet. But soon.'

He began to explain Nerryn's plan, but Tir's eyes had darkened, and he slid his hand away from Maer's, to rake his hair back from his sweating brow.

'Would you have brought him to me? Before you took him to Laura?'

'Of course I would. How could you think

otherwise?'

'Nerryn swears she'll bring him back?'

'Yes.'

'How can you trust her?'

'How can I not?' Maer said, more sharply than he had intended. 'You would trust Laura.'

After a moment's searching look, Tir nodded.

'Dreis will be cared for,' Maer went on, his voice softening, but Tir's jaw tightened. 'What is it?'

'I've gotten used to calling you Maer,' Tir said, 'and I guess I'll get used to you calling me Tir. But my son's name is Ben. Okay? He doesn't belong here, he doesn't need some stupid new name.'

Maer nodded. 'I'm sorry.' He didn't remind Tir that the child's moorland name meant *displaced one*, and that he was now more displaced than ever. He suspected his friend had no need of such a reminder. Instead he waited a moment, then asked, 'How's the pain?'

'Right now it's just in the background. Flares sometimes, but Kernow won't give me any more of that stuff she gave me out on the moor. Says it only masks it.'

'Spriggans know best,' Maer said, and was rewarded with a faint smile.

Then the smile faded. 'Poor little Jacky, huh?' Tir pressed his fingertips to his forehead, as if to massage away a headache. 'He didn't deserve that.'

'Even though he stole your son?'

'He also gave his life trying to protect him.'

Maer nodded. 'I know. You're right, he didn't

deserve to die.' He had to ask now, couldn't wait any longer. 'Tir, can you remember any more about... about when you saw Casta?'

Tir shook his head, then winced and put a steadying hand to his ribcage. 'Don't move,' Maer said quickly, remembering the elder spriggan's orders. 'Kernow will have my hide.'

Tir gave a short, breathless laugh. 'Trust me, she knows all the best ways to hurt you. Wouldn't want her as an enemy.'

'You're looking better though,' Maer said. 'Listen, I know it'll take a while, but when you're ready I'm going to teach you what you can do, and how to control it.' He leaned over and lifted the edge of the bandage on Tir's neck. 'This is healing well. The bruises are spectacular though.'

'Cool,' Tir said, heavy on the sarcasm, but Maer was glad to see the side of his mouth twitch in a quick, wry grin.

'I spoke to Laura.' Maer replaced the bandage. 'She knows Nerryn will take care of Dre ... Ben. And that she'll bring him as soon as she can.' His voice dropped. 'I know you're not going to want to hear this, but when she has him back she's going to leave Lynher Mill.' He found it hard to hold that steady, green gaze, but he forced himself not to look away. 'She doesn't want to, but it's for the best, she knows that.'

Tir swallowed hard, and his brow creased. 'We talked about her coming back sometime. I guess we both knew it was a lie.'

'Ben won't be truly safe until he gets back to the city.'

'I know.'

'And you're alive. Laura's aware of how lucky you both are.'

'Then why does it feel like the suckiest thing ever?' Tir let out an unsteady breath, and his hand tightened on his ribs. 'Shit. Look, I'm sorry. You've just lost your father. And I know I should just be glad that Laura and Ben are safe, but—'

'I know. It's okay.' Maer didn't like the look of Tir's face, which had gone very white. Sweat was popping out on his brow and he was breathing shallowly again, and kept closing his eyes. 'Let me call Kernow back in.'

'In a minute. I need to ask something first.'

'Ask it.' Maer glanced worriedly towards the door, hoping Kernow might somehow realise she was needed, and come back in anyway.

'We're going to war, right?' Tir said. 'So what happens if we lose?'

Maer shook his head. 'I don't know, Rich. I really don't... why are you smiling?'

Tir closed his eyes, and his voice was faint, but the smile remained. 'You called me Rich,' he said. 'There's hope for you yet, Britboy.'

Maer left Kernow and Martha to tend to Tir, and went back out into the cavern. As Maer watched the people move about, greeting one another and grumbling, as usual, at the amount of work that must be done before winter, he heard muttered speculation about the state of the chimney, and realised with a jolt that they did not yet know about Casta. A few curious eyes settled on him, as the only motionless one in a sea of movement, and he nodded an automatic greeting as he wondered: would it be Deera who must break the news, or was that his terrible duty?

He went back into the private set of chambers, to his mother's room, and stood outside, unsure. At last he raised his hand to tap on the doorpost. 'Mother?'

He heard movement in the room, but it was a long time before she pulled the curtain aside, and Maer was shocked at the sight of her. In the course of that one night and half a day she had aged almost beyond recognition. Her beautiful face was sunken in the cheeks, great dark circles beneath her eyes made her look skeletal, and her hair lay unbrushed and tangled on her shoulders. Her mouth trembled as she saw her son, as did the hand she reached out to him when he had stammered out his question.

'I don't think I can do it,' she said. Her voice was as thin as the rest of her, the imperious tones that had been such a natural part of her had collapsed into a cracked, wavering, aged voice, and fresh tears filled her eyes at the sound of it.

'I will tell them, Mother.' Maer put his hand over hers where it rested on his shoulder. 'You have become ill. You must rest.'

'I will be well again soon,' she promised. 'I will

learn to live without him at my side, I know I will. But, just for now, let me mourn him.'

She drew his head close and kissed his forehead, the dry, papery kiss of an old woman. He withdrew and left her to her sorrow, wondering if she was right; the love she had held for Casta had never been in doubt, but he was only now beginning to understand its depth and its intensity.

Tears came to his own eyes, both for his father, and for his mother's bleak expression of helpless grief. His fists tightened with fury all over again at Cantoc's act of brutality, and even as he called his people together and prepared to break the news, he found part of him was flying back towards the coast, vengeance once again blackening his heart.

***

The room brightened. Richard flinched against the sudden light, and put his hand up to shield his eyes. He blinked a couple of times, recognised Deera's outline in the doorway, and tried not to groan out loud. This was the last thing he needed right now.

Although it could have been worse; turning over to have his dressing changed had, as Kernow had predicted, not been fun. The conversation that followed had been even less so.

When she had presented the clay bowl from under the bed, for him to "make himself comfortable," he'd looked from her to it, wondering how to ask. Eventually he cleared his throat.

'Where does it... you know, go? When you take it away?'

Kernow looked surprised at the question. 'It is removed from here to the surface, do not worry.'

'Yeah, but to where?'

She visibly battled, for a moment, to find the right words. 'My Lord, you usually keep your attention on the ground when you walk on the moor, do you not? So you do not... dirty your boots?'

'Well, sure. But that's just sheep and stuff. This is—' he pulled a face, '—different.'

'Is it?'

'Isn't it?'

Kernow looked uncomfortable; evidently discussing such things with her king was outside the realm of her usual experience. She lowered her voice and leaned closer. 'Have you not noted the change then?'

'Change?'

'In your...' she gestured to the bowl, and Richard felt his eyes widen at the same time as his skin flushed in mingled shock and amusement.

'Are you telling me that every time I've almost stepped in sheep shit, it... might not have been?'

'You must have realised there were not always sheep around.'

'I assumed they'd moved on.'

She shrugged. 'Just as likely, I suppose.'

'Kernow, are we really having this conversation?'

'Meaning no disrespect, My Lord, you asked the question.'

'And I've never regretted one more,' Richard confessed. 'Thanks for clarifying that.'

'Do what must be done, then sleep,' she advised with a little smile. 'You need to regain your strength, and it will take time.'

But despite the draft she gave him, sleep had been a long time coming, and although it was thin, and fraught with dreams, he was pretty sure he hadn't had enough of it yet. Dealing with Deera required a much brighter mind than his, and he wished he'd feigned sleep when she'd come in. Too late now.

'Do not trouble yourself to rise.' The former queen came farther into the room, and Richard almost said, *I wasn't going to,* but bit it back at the last minute. Whatever she had said, and no matter how furious he was at the way she had treated Laura, she was still a woman in the deepest part of her grief. It showed as she crossed to his side, and he heard it, too, in the shaking of her voice.

'I would speak with you, with your permission, of course.'

'Sure.' Despite his determination not to move, the compulsion to be at least on a level with her eyes was impossible to fight. She obligingly looked away while he dragged himself to a sitting position, somehow without swearing, although his teeth were gritted so hard he was half convinced they would splinter in his gums.

When he had settled again he felt more able to take charge of the conversation. 'What is it you want to say?'

Deera studied him for a moment. It unnerved him, but he returned her steady gaze and said nothing further and she cleared her throat.

'I trust you are finding some relief from the pain now, My Lord?'

'Some. Kernow knows her stuff.' He waited a little longer, then said, 'You didn't come here to check on my health, Deera, we both know you don't give a damn about that, so—'

'Of course I do!' Her startled expression told him she was telling the truth. 'You are not only my king, but you are my son's closest friend. And Casta had a deep fondness for you, as you know. Why would I wish you harm, if Maer's life is no longer at risk because of you?'

'I didn't say you wished me harm,' Richard pointed out, 'just that you don't care too much about whether I'm still hurting.'

'You are wrong in that, also,' Deera said. 'You have suffered much, and I have been harsh in my treatment of both you and your lady. But you must understand I have not been myself.'

Richard remembered the day he'd come down here with Maer, when the king and queen had been playful, even affectionate, and although Deera had been a little stiff with him, he had seen a side of her he hadn't expected to see. 'I know,' he said softly.

'I'm sorry, that was unfair. Have you been able to sleep?'

'Not without Kernow's help,' she admitted. 'I lie there in the darkness, and think back over what has been done in the name of Loen, how so much time was wasted in the pursuit of honouring him… If we'd only known we had such little time left.'

'Yeah, I know that feeling.'

'Yes.' She paused, then took a deep breath as if to chase away the darker thoughts. 'You are correct though, Tir, we have much to discuss, and better we begin now.'

'Maer thinks we'll go to war.' His words were bluntly spoken, and he watched her carefully for signs of sudden fear, or shock. There were none, she just nodded.

'He is right. Casta will be avenged, and the Coastals will not take it lightly.'

'What kind of war can it be, though?' Despite the cold feeling that wormed through his belly, Richard's interest was piqued. 'Are we talking about swords and stuff here? Or sneaking around in the dark and looking for a chance to off Cantoc?'

'Off?' Deera looked momentarily bemused, then shook it off as unimportant. She knew what he meant. 'There are likely to be skirmishes, yes. Small bands from both sides will take it upon themselves to win favour with their lords by attempting to take the leader of their enemy.'

'But?'

'Skirmishes of that nature are rarely successful,' Deera said. 'The real victor will be the one who shows true strength.'

'How?'

Deera raised her gaze to the ceiling, as if she was seeing the open sky instead of the high, granite arch. 'The elements. They answer willingly to the strongest of us, you know that.'

'Storms?' Richard frowned. 'I know weather can be pretty dangerous, but I don't see how it could win a kingdom.'

'If a truly powerful elemental were given a chance, and a choice, they could destroy everything they see, and more. Once the storms are done, the land is ruined. Nothing can grow, or survive upon it. Not mortal, not elemental… not even the ancient ones. The strong ones. Like Kernow's clan.'

'And are the Coastals so powerful?'

Deera smiled, it was at once beautiful and ice-cold. 'No, but the Moorlanders are. How else do you suppose we came to be rulers over all?'

He was chilled to the bone, by both her words and her expression. 'And you'd let that happen? You'd destroy where *they* live, to protect this patch of scrubland of yours?' Anger was burning away the ice in his blood now. 'You can't do that. You can't send your people out there to kill the land itself!'

'Your people,' she corrected him calmly. 'It would be you who sent them.'

'No way. Ben's out there.'

'It would not begin until you have brought him home.'

'It wouldn't even begin then.' A sour tone crept into his voice. 'Whoever you have in mind to do this had better come to me, so I can remind them who's in charge here.'

'Are you saying you would never use the powers you have been given by your father?'

'Me?' Richard gave a short laugh; it pulled at him and made him wince. 'Well, there you have it. I can't control anything I may have been *given,* and even if I could, there's no way in hell I'd go down there and cause that kind of destruction.'

Deera was looking at him with an odd light in her eyes. 'Never? Not even if your people demanded it of you?'

'Let them try.'

'And you would not yield, no matter what they said or did?'

'Deera, the coast is as much part of this kingdom as the moors and the forest. To go down there, to destroy even a part of it, to the extent it could never be a home to anyone again... no. I would not *yield.*'

To his utter astonishment she laid a hand over his, and he saw that the strange light in her eyes was a shimmering of emotion. 'Thank you.' She squeezed his hand, and returned her own to her lap, her head lowered.

Richard blinked. 'What just happened here?'

'You have so much to learn,' Deera said, 'but now I feel it's safe for you to do so.' She raised her head again, and her smile was no longer cold, nor was it bright, but it was appealing in its relief. 'I will teach Maer, and he will, in turn, instruct you. We have little time to lose, but first you must ensure you are well enough.'

'You were testing me?' He didn't know whether to be relieved or angry.

Deera lifted one shoulder in an elegant shrug. 'I have just given over the rule of the entire kingdom, and all its subjects, to you. A stranger. When I gave it to Casta I knew he was a wise man…' her voice caught, but she went on, 'I have known him all my life, and had seen his strength, and understood his ability to know when to use it.'

'And when not to.'

She nodded. 'But I do not know you, Tir. I know you have at least some of your ancient father's power, but I needed to be sure you also have the wisdom of your spiritual father.' To Richard's further surprise she reached out and straightened the blanket that lay across his hips. It was a touchingly maternal gesture. 'I am content to relinquish the kingdom into your hands. You will find no quarrel with me.'

Richard didn't know what to say, and even if he had, he wouldn't have been able to speak. This was far from a declaration of friendship, but for now it was enough to know she trusted him, and would teach him. Deera rose to leave, and that gave him the push he needed to ask the next reluctant, but important question.

'What if I'd agreed with you? If I'd said, hell yeah, let me at those Coastals, with a lightning bolt up my sleeve and a hurricane in my hands?'

Deera pursed her lips and thought for a moment. 'Then I would have gone to Maer to persuade you otherwise.'

'And if that hadn't worked?'

There was another pause, and Deera's voice turned hard when she spoke again. 'I would have seen to it that your slow recovery meant you were in no fit state to lead this battle.'

Richard was jolted out of his mellowing state, and his skin crawled as the implication of her words hit him. 'You're serious,' he managed.

'Never doubt my devotion to this land, Tir. It is more vital to me than any single being upon it. Including you.'

'And including Maer?'

'Never doubt,' she repeated, and then she was gone, leaving Richard dizzy with the abrupt shift in mood. What would she have done? Tampered with Kernow's sleeping draughts to turn them into something more sinister? He wrapped his right arm across his waist, immediately regretting the exploratory touch of his fingers on his ribs, and felt a light sweat break out all over his skin. He suddenly felt very vulnerable indeed.

Chapter Eight

'Thank you. Cantoc will hear of your generosity. We will send word when he has need of your support.'

Arric left the peninsula fish-finder's home, with a tight smile of satisfaction, and followed the path up over the cliff. Cantoc would soon recant his words of that morning: *you have a way of raising ire before raising tribute, Arric! Leave it to your brother, for the Ocean's sake!* Simply because of one stupid incident, where his explanations for the reason behind the coming war had fallen flat, and he had lost his temper. True, he should not have struck the man, and perhaps Mylan might have calmed things had he been there, but he had not been.

And whose fault was that? Not Arric's. Mylan was still reluctant to leave Nerryn in sole charge of Dreis, or so he said, and had insisted on remaining behind – in reality his bond with the boy had only deepened over the days since Arric had proudly presented him, and that would doubtless prove a problem. Still, nothing that was insurmountable; few things were, to one of his intelligence.

Take Gerai here. He had failed to retrieve any coin from the dead powder-baker, and Cantoc had blackened his eye for him as a result. He'd even threatened to banish him back to Lynher Mill for good, until Arric had stepped in, and pointed out that they had more need of Gerai's like now than ever before; a Moorlander whose loyalties had wavered and fallen away from his own.

Arric had enlisted Gerai's aid in carrying the news of impending war all down the coast, promising him a place far back in the host, should a march on Lynher Mill become necessary. It would not, of course, but the Moorlander had been grateful and penitent.

Arric's stride lengthened in his eagerness to return to home and comfort. And sleep! Sleep was a fading acquaintance and one he dearly wished to renew. Gerai hurried to catch up, and when he drew level he pointed out to sea.

'There is a boat out there.'

Arric looked at him, incredulous. 'A boat? On the water? Whatever will we see next, some grass in a field?'

'I mean a particular type of boat.' Gerai's voice turned sulky. 'The type that often carries people with more coin than sea-sense.'

Arric turned, his interest reluctantly piqued. 'Are you suggesting we deviate from our business?'

'I'm not suggesting anything.' Gerai shrugged, but his sulkiness dropped away and he gave Arric an encouragingly sly little smile. 'The weather has been very dull of late though, don't you think?'

'It has,' Arric conceded. 'People tend to become

careless when there has been no danger for a while. I've often found a little lesson is valuable, if not well-received.'

'It would be for their own good,' Gerai agreed.

Arric pondered; he had business with Cantoc, but the temptation was too great. 'Do you know, I think we might have missed some strong and able fish-finders down there.' He pointed back towards the headland from which they had just come. 'The type who will be only too glad to help us avenge my parents.'

'Then why wait?' Gerai started down the track, and this time it was Arric who followed. He wondered what Mylan would make of what he was doing, and waited for the twinge of satisfaction at the thought that his brother would be furious, but impotent. It didn't come. Instead he felt the envious acknowledgement that Mylan, should he choose to follow the same dark path, would inevitably do it extremely well. Arric had always been a strong elemental, but while he had worked hard at the subtler points of manipulation, he did not possess anything approaching the raw power he had sensed in Nerryn and Mylan.

Arric and Gerai arrived on the edge of the cliff, and Arric squinted out at the powerful-looking white motor yacht a short distance off the rocky part of the shore. No doubt they had prided themselves on picking this solitary spot, but they would soon wish they'd chosen a noisier, busier place to drop anchor. He cast a quick glance around at the other craft nearby, but they were smaller, business-like boats, and they were moving. This one though, this was a good find, and he nodded approval at Gerai who was hard put to conceal his satisfaction.

Arric turned back to the boat and closed his eyes. His skin came alive with the brushing of the air over it, and within that air he probed, sought and found the first miniscule drops of moisture – always there, but often too small to be of any consequence. Concentrating, he drew the misty drops together and pushed them outward over the sea, gathering pace as they went, taking their own pocket of air that Arric set spinning and twisting. A moment later the water around the motor launch began rippling, lifting, and the smooth swell became sharper, choppier, as the wind picked up.

Figures appeared on the deck, dressed in scraps of clothing that barely covered them, and Arric watched with grim satisfaction as they hurried to pull up the anchor. He sent a strong gust towards the front of the boat, and the water rose; the boat crashed into its trough, shaking loose the hands that had grabbed at the rails. Shouts drew only mildly curious attention from elsewhere; the craft and its passengers were too far around the headland from the beach for anyone to see.

The boat, unable to match its movements to the unexpected swell, danced on the water with increasing violence, and when at last the anchor was ripped free it was too late.

Arric gestured to Gerai to descend the cliff, and

sent one final push towards the side of the boat. It tipped almost completely, spilling screaming figures into the water before crashing back onto its keel; one of those figures didn't come up again, and Arric assumed a submerged rock could claim credit for that.

The others panicked, grasped at the debris that had landed in the water with them, and shouted at the others to do the same. Arric counted eight, including the one who still hadn't… ah, there he was. Face down, arms outstretched, head covered in an ugly crimson that kept washing away and coming back again. The next push sent the expensive yacht right over, and at least two of the survivors were pushed under water by the weight of it. Those two did not re-appear, at least, not while Arric watched.

He turned his attention to Gerai, who had reached the bottom of the cliff and now waited for him to send the spoils shoreward. Arric obliged, and turned the direction of the wind so the contents of the boat, which now speckled the surface of the sea, began drifting towards the rocks. Most of it was inconsequential, but there were purses, clothing and boxes that might hold smaller items of jewellery, the kind that would fetch a price somewhere. It was almost too easy. He sighed, and hoped he hadn't wasted his time and energy, that there would be something to gain from it.

He turned away from the headland and his heart stuttered in shock. A full-grown mortal male stood there, staring straight at him. He tried to remember if he had been practicing his full-forming and somehow forgotten, but he was not good enough for that yet, and besides he did not feel as he did when full-forming.

He glanced down at Gerai, who had cloaked himself in daylight for his foraging expedition, and then back at the mortal; a bearded man, carrying a battered bag over his shoulder, and dressed in rough, shapeless clothing.

The man let his eyes travel over Arric in a very deliberate way, then turned and left, not looking back. Arric felt a lurch of sickness, and a heavy, unsettled sensation in his belly. The stranger had not been surprised, or even alarmed, but he had clearly known exactly what Arric was doing, and his disapproval was almost tangible. Having ensured Arric saw him, he would even now be calling the coastal rescue services. Time and opportunity were slipping away, but that was the very least of Arric's concerns.

He rubbed his hands on his tunic, then wiped at the sweat that had popped out on his upper lip. Was the stranger an envoy of the Moorlanders, seeking evidence to arrest him? His hand dropped to the knife he now carried at his side, and he briefly considered going after the mortal, but Gerai's shout made him turn back.

'See? The boat was a good choice!' Gerai held up a leather bag in one hand and a pouch in the other, which he shook. 'Fine chains in here, by the sounds. This will make up for you hitting that fish-finder…'

he trailed away as he saw the glower on Arric's face. 'I am sorry, I did not mean—'

'Never mind "sorry," bring it to me.' Arric tried to push the watching mortal to back of his mind, but it was fortunate for Gerai that he was unable to do so, and so the Moorlander's thoughtless reference to his failure went unpunished.

'I will take that, and that.' He pointed to two of the bags that Gerai had hooked over his shoulder and that now dripped down his tunic. 'And that.' He snatched the pouch. 'You may keep the rest. Now, I have business at home. I shall tell Cantoc of your help today,' he added, seeing Gerai's face twisted in a scowl as he looked at the small bag left to him. 'And of your generosity. Besides, you never know what might be in there,' he nodded at the bag, 'it might contain the best of it all.'

Leaving Gerai hardly appeased, he turned away from the sea, and moved quickly enough that he soon had the mortal in sight once more. The man had his hand pressed to his ear, and Arric had seen mortals do this all the time; soon there would be a great deal of activity around the stricken motor craft, and the chance of recovering more spoils would be lost. It was safe to assume Gerai had gone back for more, however, so perhaps a visit to him might be worthwhile a little later.

Slowing his pace, Arric followed the mortal at a distance, ensuring he was cloaked from view but still feeling as uncomfortably solid and visible as the cliffs themselves. The closer he drew to his home, the stronger was the feeling of disquiet. The stranger moved easily, but not with any great speed, and with a mortal's clumsy tread; there was no doubt he was fully of that kind. So how had he not only seen Arric, but known right away he was behind the sudden, and very localised, miniature storm?

Nearly home now, Arric hesitated; should he continue to follow this mortal, or should he instead attend to the business he had with Cantoc? He had just made up his mind to follow, and worry about soothing the coast lord's ruffled feathers later, when the decision was taken from his hands. The bearded man sat down on the cliff, right above Cantoc's door. Arric stopped, an unexpected, unfamiliar, and most unwelcome fear uncurling inside him. The man did not turn his head to watch him approach, but he knew Arric was there… he must.

Arric found himself breathing lightly, clenching his hands into fists, and his heart thundered against his ribs. The man looked calmly out over the water, his hands draped loosely over his raised knees, his bag dropped casually on the grass beside him. Arric tried to dismiss his fear – this was foolishness! What could a mortal do against him in any case? He started to move again, walking the path with a firmer step, keeping his attention on the man on the cliff as if he were a snake that might suddenly strike. But the man did not move, nor look at him, even when Arric swung the rock against Cantoc's doorpost to announce his arrival.

Emerging a good while later, and in the worst of

tempers, Arric's gaze went immediately to the cliff, but the man had gone. He let out a breath he had not even realised he'd been holding, and wondered if he had raised a tidal wave from a ripple; surely the man had not really seen him, had only been fascinated by the squall in the bay? He was becoming nervy, jumpy, and even Cantoc had noted it during their meeting.

'It is time you stopped your ranging down the coast,' he'd said as Arric had risen to leave. 'It is making you distant and unreliable.'

'What would you have me do instead?'

'Work. As your father did. Raise coin that way.'

Arric stared at him, aghast. *'Fish?'*

'You are preparing to lead an army,' Cantoc said coolly. 'You will need to be one of the people, not some shadow they do not know. They will follow you if they trust you, and to earn their trust you must work with them. Let them come to know and understand you. To respect you. So yes, Arric, *fish.*'

Outside, with the clifftop thankfully empty of watchful mortals, Arric picked up one of the unsatisfyingly small rocks on the path, and hurled it as far as he could out to sea. The only reward was a wrenching pain in his shoulder, and no lessening of the anger that tightened his chest. Fish! For the Ocean's sake!

It wasn't until he arrived at his own front door that the fury vanished, replaced by a cold, creeping fear; the watcher was back. And this time he waved.

Chapter Nine

Lynher Mill, September 25th

The truth had sunk in now; it all came down to trust. Laura walked the winding road through the village to her late father's home, half her mind wondering at the phone call from Gail, the other half finally accepting, with a sense of relief, the facts she could neither change nor influence. She trusted Maer, and he trusted Nerryn, therefore Laura must trust Nerryn too.

As for Richard… the drawing had gone away into the box again, and this time it had felt as if a piece of Laura's soul had been fastened to the paper and now lived in the dark, with those she had loved and lost. But she would not take the picture out again for a long, long time, maybe never. Ben would be a warm, living reminder, once he was home, and if she told herself Richard had simply gone back to California … no, Chicago, it would become easier in time.

Where had California come from?

A car rumbled past, jolting her out of her lazily turning thoughts, and she noticed its windscreen wipers were going. She looked up at the sky, only now realising a fine rain had begun to fall, and her gaze automatically shifted to the horizon. Would she never again be able to accept weather for the innocent, natural phenomenon it was? She pulled up her hood and walked a little faster.

The house seemed different today, perhaps because she knew now that the man who'd lived here, made his little changes, and tended the tiny garden, had been her father. Laura had been here so often over the years, calling in for coffee and a chat at least once every couple of weeks, but if she missed that, she certainly didn't miss having her name put down for every extra-curricular activity the school came up with. They always meant meetings, coffee, more meetings, and usually advice about her life she could have done without. But the woman was kind, and she had lost her husband, and even before Laura had learned who Graham Edwards was to her, she had felt a strong need to repay that kindness.

The cottage nestled in the middle of the little row that flanked the lower edge of the moor, a fairy-tale tumbledown, with a crooked slate roof. Laura lifted and dropped the brass knocker, readying the story she and Ann had agreed... after two weeks of telling it, it was even starting to feel like the truth. A moment later Gail appeared, her face tired and pale, but breaking into a smile when she saw Laura.

'Come in, love. Kettle's on.'

Laura kissed Gail on the cheek as she passed her and went into the hall. The first thing she noticed was a collection of filled black bin-liners in a muddle by the kitchen door. She was about to ask if it was jumble, when she saw Gail's face and realised what she'd been doing, and why the phone call had come, seemingly out of the blue.

'Do you want some help?' she asked gently.

'Later. Coffee first,' Gail said, gratitude in her face if not in her words. Laura's heart slithered a little as she realised she was going to have to do the same thing with Richard's things. But he was alive, at least there was that. Perhaps she would even be able to give them to him – the perfect excuse to see him, just one more time.

She followed Gail into the kitchen, stepping around the bin-liners and trying to imagine the familiar clothes, not washed, ironed and folded, but instead clothing the tall, burly frame of a living man. Graham. Her father. She frowned, trying to give the word the same meaning it had held for Martin Riley, but, unlike the tearing grief at that man's death fourteen years ago, she felt nothing more for Graham than a general sort of sadness. A nice man had gone to his grave too soon. It seemed important that she mourn him properly but there was too much distance between them, and she had found out the truth far too late.

Gail put a cup of tea down in front of her, and levered the lid off a tin of Family Circle. 'There's one of the jam ones left,' she said with a little smile, and Laura laughed.

'You remembered!'

'Hard to forget. You'd trample all over every single person in the staff room to get those before anyone else.'

Laura took the biscuit, still smiling, and they sat in easy silence for a minute or two, before Gail cleared her throat and answered the question Laura had been unable to ask. 'I've known for quite a long time that Graham was your father, you know.'

Laura nearly dropped the last of her biscuit into her coffee. 'How long?'

'Since your mother, Vivien I mean, died. When word got out that you weren't hers and Martin's child. Vivien's sister seemed the obvious candidate.'

'How did you know about Graham, though? We don't look anything alike.'

'No.' Gail considered. 'It wasn't to do with you, so much as with Sylvia, really. I knew they'd been an item just before he and I got together, but I'd put it from my head until then. I did the sums.'

'And did he know, too?'

'Not until I told him.'

Laura stared at her, wanting to swallow the biscuit but unable to. 'When was that?' she mumbled through the crumbs.

'Just after you lost poor Tom. I told him he should see you. I thought you might have need of him.'

'But he didn't agree?'

Gail sighed. 'He needed time. We both thought he had that time, so why rush it?'

'What caused the heart attack?' Laura realised

she'd never asked. 'Do they know?'

Gail's eyes cut away from her, to the biscuit tin, to the window, to the sink, and when they turned back on Laura they were shadowed. Laura could have kicked herself for asking such a casual-sounding question.

'No,' Gail said. 'He'd been... distracted for a while. Nothing to do with you,' she added quickly. 'He was in the back room sorting through some old things, and I heard a thump.' She let out a shaky breath. 'He was already gone when I got there. Sudden enough for him, thank God, but I haven't been able to go back up there since.'

'Is that why you called me? Would you like me to do that room?'

'Would you?' Gail's relief was obvious.

Laura nodded, glad to have found some small way to help. 'Of course. If there's nothing you want to keep I'll put it all in bags. You needn't put yourself through that.'

'Anything you're not sure of, just leave on the landing,' Gail said, 'I'm sure I'll be able to do it eventually, it's just... well, you know.'

'I understand.' Laura finished her coffee and stood up, and Gail handed her the roll of bin-liners.

'Back room, next to the bathroom. And thank you.'

Laura went upstairs to the little back bedroom. There wasn't much there, just a small single bed, a narrow wardrobe, and a flimsy set of drawers. The kind you buy and assemble yourself, with a single, cross-head screwdriver and a lot of swearing.

The door to the wardrobe stood open, and she could see a jumble of boxes and bags in the bottom of it, and some shirts and jackets on the rail; Graham must have been going through those when he'd died, probably already putting away his summer shirts, thanks to the unseasonably drizzly weather.

Laura turned to the chest of drawers and knelt down, pulling out winter sweaters and thick, fluffy socks, and filled a bin-bag, tying the top securely to make sure Gail wasn't suddenly faced with something that would cause her any more grief. Maybe Ann would do the same for her, when she felt ready to package up Richard's things… if she ever did.

The thought re-surfaced that she might yet see him again, if he wanted to keep some of his clothes, but now it was followed by the bleak realisation that he would be more likely to adopt the style of his own people; she tried not to think about how natural it had seemed to see him dressed like that, and how striking he had looked. How king-like.

The drawers emptied, Laura blinked to clear her blurred eyes and turned her attention to the wardrobe. She opened the door wider, tore another bag from the roll, and began lifting down shirts and jackets and laying them across the bed. Then she pulled out the closest of the small boxes on the floor of the wardrobe, and saw it had been opened; the brown parcel-tape that had sealed it hung loose, and one flap had been lifted and not stuck down again.

She flicked it up with one finger and peered in, but all she saw was dark clothing, wrapped in clear plastic.

She put the box to one side, but as she continued to pack away Graham's things, eager now to finish, and return to the land of the living, she kept finding her eyes going back to it. The shirt on top wasn't Graham's, that much was obvious from the small neckline, so perhaps she shouldn't even be prying. It just seemed odd that it had been packed away so neatly.

'Oh, that's a wonderful help, thank you!'

Gail had appeared in the doorway, smiling, but when she peered in to see how Laura was doing, her face went dead white. Laura climbed quickly to her feet, certain the woman was going to faint, but gradually Gail's colour returned and she released her hold on the door jamb. 'Sorry, it's this room,' she mumbled.

'I found this box in the wardrobe,' Laura said. 'Some old clothes. Can't be Graham's, are they yours?'

'No. They belonged to an old friend. Deceased now.'

'Oh. I'm sorry. Do you want me to do anything with them?'

'No,' Gail said quickly. Perhaps it was a closer friend than she'd hinted at; she sounded almost panicky at the thought of losing the clothes now she'd re-discovered them.

'Well, I should get out from under your feet.'

Laura said, to fill the faintly awkward silence. She lifted the three bin-bags she had filled out onto the landing, having to edge around Gail in the doorway where the woman stood, transfixed by the sight of that one small box. It seemed an old grief had been added to her new one, and Laura regretted her own inquisitiveness.

She had a sudden thought that there might be a secret tragedy here; perhaps there had been a child between Gail and Graham after all. The thought that she might have lost another sibling, even a half-sibling she did not know she'd had, was extraordinarily sad. But she would not ask, and if Gail chose to tell her someday that was up to her.

'It's so kind of you to help,' Gail said, finally tearing her gaze away, and joining Laura at the top of the stairs. 'I can manage the rest, I should think.'

'Well let me know if you need anything else.'

'I will.'

'And thanks for the coffee and biscuits.'

'Most welcome. Where's your boyfriend, by the way? I forgot to ask. Got your boy, has he?'

'No, he's gone back to California. You know how it is. Visa stuff. Ben's with my friend Ann today.' The lie came so easily, but that had several days ago ceased to be worrying, and instead came as a relief.

'I thought he was from Chicago?'

'Yes. What did I say?'

'California.'

'Sorry, no, you're right. He's from Chicago.' Laura shook her head and pulled a face. 'Brain fart.'

For a moment Gail's expression was that of the headmistress again, and Laura told herself she was a grown-up, and if she wanted to say "fart," she would. But some habits die hard. 'Sorry,' she said. 'You know what I mean.'

'Don't apologise. It's an interesting phrase, perhaps I should adopt it.'

Laura laughed, relieved. 'Do it! Drop it into conversation at the next governors' meeting.'

'You're a terrible influence on me, young lady,' Gail said, but the light words were not reflected in her drawn expression. 'Come and visit again soon.'

'I will,' Laura promised.

She hurried across the village and back up the hill, as always halfway to convincing herself that Maer had come back with Ben while she was out.

But no-one was waiting in the garden. Swallowing a now-familiar lump of disappointment, she looked up the lane towards the mill. She'd walked more miles lately than she could count, but good, healing sleep was a distant memory now, and had been for two weeks. Exhaustion was the only answer.

So she turned away from Mill Lane Cottage and carried on walking, up the hill, and then off onto the grass, following the path that led to the old mill. She saw the broken wall, where she and Richard had sat and talked, close and contented, about the possible answer to his horrific and violent dreams. Then she looked at the place where Gilan had stepped out to strike at poor little Jacky Greencoat, from behind the stump of the windmill-tower. She shivered, although the drizzly afternoon was still warm.

She turned away from the stunted, burned tower, and stepped over the low wall, into the square of ground that had housed the Lynher grinding mill during the civil war. The place where she was sure her ancestors had worked and died. She closed her eyes, and, as before, she could almost see how it had unfolded; the Parliamentarians cutting down the unarmed mill-workers, and then the storm.

It had brought down the roof upon the dead, lightning sparking the fire that had destroyed everything except the stone portion of the tower, and the granite wheel that had long since been removed and set up in one of the heritage centres. She remembered Richard's sense of connection with the artefacts in the Bude museum, particularly the armour behind glass, and although that had been different, stronger and more immediate, this feeling she had could not be ignored either.

There was no doubt now, that Richard's part in that scene had been to cause the storm during the battle of Sourton Down, the same storm that had necessitated a further battle down near Bude. His emotions, as a Royalist soldier, would have been running rampant then, and, knowing what they knew now it was easier to accept the truth than to deny its horror; Richard had also burned down the mill, albeit unknowingly and accidentally. But by then the workers were dead, or dying. Her ancestors. It was a strange, unsettling thought.

She followed the broken wall slowly around its

perimeter, letting her mind reach out in search of something she could cling to. There was none of that wonderful sense of revelation Richard had felt, just the frustrating sense of a memory out of reach. And the flicker of an idea.

She reluctantly stepped back out and moved away, but instead of taking the road she chose a new path, down across the grass towards the village. The rough, uneven ground required all Laura's attention, and a vague idea she'd had up by the mill faded, as she concentrated instead on picking her way carefully down across the heath.

There were a few more defunct mines up here, below the mill. Less imposing and picturesque than the ones out beyond the stone circle, on the other side of the valley, but these workings had provided a living too, years ago, and the smaller chimneys rose from the unkempt ground as solid, moss-covered reminders of those days.

None of these were fenced off, there was no need. Most had been filled in, but there were others where the moor itself had crept across like a thick green carpet, and hidden most of the tunnels. Only one still had the hint of an entrance showing, and there was no chance of anyone falling right into it; heaps of stones had been emptied into the wide dip in the landscape, grass and gorse growing amongst them and softening the jagged edges. A careless walker would be more likely to slip on those stones and break their ankle, than fall into the blackness of the open mine below.

She scrambled closer, her hand outstretched to steady herself against the crumbling stonework, and leaned as far into the darkness as she could. The weak sunlight reached no more than a couple of feet, but when she hooted softly, it echoed and bounced off the walls, returning to her as a hollow, and nastily familiar sound.

She withdrew quickly, her heart beating uncomfortably fast; there might be anything down there, or nothing. A group of Moorlanders, spriggans, something bizarre and unknown... or just a vast, empty space. Her hand felt clammy on the stone lintel, and she wiped it on her jeans as she re-joined the narrow half-path.

The ground began to even out, and Laura allowed her idea to creep back up; it had been the saving of Tom when he'd thought of buying the mill and rebuilding it, so why shouldn't she do it instead, in his memory? With the Websters moving out of Tom's cottage it was the perfect time to consider selling it rather than renting it out again. She could use that money to start off with. The mill was on Duchy land, but Tom had been ready to begin enquiries, and it might provide her the same life-line it had handed Tom... however short that had been.

She glanced behind her, suddenly doubtful as she remembered how she'd felt up there. Could she do it, knowing her ancestors had likely died in that spot, or would she be so aware of the tragedy, every time she set foot in the place, that it would sour everything? There was only one way to find out.

The next stage then, was to find out for sure about her family history. She could have called Gail, but it was too soon; her father's widow was obviously still raw. Maybe her own mother would know? She and Graham hadn't been love's young dream, even when they'd been together, still they might have talked.

She called Sylvia as soon as she got in, and they chatted for a couple of minutes before she moved onto the reason for her call. 'What do you know about Graham's family? Were they from around here?'

'Oh, yes. Been here since the year dot as far as I know. Same as mine.'

'Were your side of the family here in the civil war then?'

'Staunch Royalists,' Sylvia said proudly. 'The men were military, and loyal to the last.'

Laura thought of Richard, her own hand over his, clasping the staff, his voice speaking that strange, ancient language in his own accent. Would his people be as loyal? Would they fight for him? Or would they turn their backs on the stranger who had twice rejected them?

She cleared her suddenly tight throat. 'What about Graham's family?'

'I have no idea, why?'

'It's that old story about the mill,' Laura explained. 'I feel quite strongly that I might have history there and I just wanted to know a bit more about it.'

'Oh, right.'

'I can't really ask Gail. I saw her today, and she's only just been able to start going through his things…' she remembered Gail's reaction to the clothing, and broke off, distracted.

'No, I can see that'd be awkward,' Sylvia said, when she didn't finish. 'Look, let me see what I can find out, and I'll give you a ring in a day or two.'

Sylvia called the next morning, in fact, as Laura finished dressing, her eyes grainy from another restless night. 'You got my interest going, so I signed up for a free trial on one of those genealogy sites.'

'Oh?'

'I found Edwards locally, going back to around 1600, and during 1643, when the mill was burned, they were soldiers, not millers.'

'Oh. Oh, well. Never mind. Thanks, anyway.' Laura's disappointment came as a surprise, she'd thought she'd only been curious to see if the feeling she had about the mill was real, she hadn't realised how much she'd wanted it to be.

'They were at the battle of Stamford Hill, at Stratton. Bude.' Sylvia went on, and Laura felt a jolt as she recalled Richard's story… or rather, the story of a man named Stephen Penhaligon. Perhaps they had fought together? It was an oddly warming thought, but a second later it turned to ice. 'But they came down from Okehampton,' Sylvia said. She went on more gently, 'They were Parliamentarians.'

Laura sat down on the sofa, fighting her dismay. 'So you think they were the ones who...' But she couldn't say the words.

'If you really believe you have a strong connection, that might explain it,' Sylvia said. 'I'm so sorry.'

Laura shook her head, feeling queasy. All this time she had carried such hatred for the men who had slain the innocents at the mill, and now it turned out she was, in all likelihood, descended from one of them. In war there would always be casualties, but the millers had not been soldiers. The attack on them had not been an act of war, not part of a battle, and not self-defence. It had been murder, pure and simple. Unnecessary, brutal, unforgiveable.

Sylvia spoke a little while longer, but Laura had all she needed, and when she pressed to end the call her mind was filled with Richard's story of how they'd been devastatingly out-numbered, and how he'd seen his friend blinded just before he himself had been killed—maybe even by her own ancestor, wouldn't *that* be the kicker? But whoever had struck that killing blow, the truth remained, stark and undeniable: between her family and Richard, they had destroyed the Lynher Mill.

Chapter Ten

'Let me help,' Maer said for the third time, but Richard shook his head.

'I've got this.' He straightened carefully, one hand on his body to remind himself to move slowly, and let out the breath he'd been holding. It wasn't too bad at all, as long as he didn't push it, and it felt good to be dressed again, even if the shirt and tunic felt weird.

He'd have to work behind Deera's back to have his jeans washed and returned to him, but in the meantime these soft leather leggings weren't too bad. They made movement easy and comfortable, and they didn't cut into his waist when he bent over to lace his boots, the way his jeans would have done. He buckled his belt across his hip, and finally picked up Ulfed's blade, his blade, now, and sheathed it.

'Okay, I'm ready.'

'Good, I have much to show you.' Maer led the way out into the chamber, and Richard followed, his legs trembling slightly, but, to his relief, stronger than he'd thought they would be; the last thing he wanted to do in front of his new people was fall flat on his face.

While he'd lain in bed, the Moorlanders had been

busy on his behalf, sewing fresh clothing that fit him much better than the ones he'd borrowed from Maer. And now he saw they'd also been making gifts that they had arranged on a long table in the main cavern, and baking delicious-looking food they displayed in between the bowls, goblets and belts.

Richard swallowed past a sudden lump in his throat, and thanked everyone he saw, whether he knew they had contributed or not. His voice shook, and although he tried to hide it at first, he soon gave up; the Moorlanders did not seem to see it as a sign of weakness.

'Do I make a speech or what?' he whispered to Maer.

'Later. It is not expected now, you are merely showing your people you are recovering, and accepting their homage.'

'Homage. Jesus…' He shook his head, bewildered. 'How soon can I go up?'

'Up?'

'Outside.'

'My Lord—'

'Dammit!' Richard turned on Maer, furiously. 'I need *you* now, not some bowing, scraping, damned… *subject!*'

Maer looked at him steadily, and there was sympathy in his eyes. 'I know it's hard, but in front of these people I must be that subject. We'll talk properly in private, but out here things must be seen as they are.' He lowered his voice. 'Rich, these people will be the ones you call on, should Nerryn fail. They need to see you strong and in command, or they will not follow you into battle.'

'They know I'm a mess,' Richard argued. 'I was almost crying back there, for Chrissakes.'

'They can see you are struggling,' Maer said, 'but they do not confuse emotion and physical injury with weakness. However, they will soon see if your resolve crumbles, so *do not* give them cause to doubt you. My Lord.'

Richard saw a few faces turned to them with interest, and recognised the wisdom in Maer's words; Ben's safety might rely on whether Richard fully embraced his new role or not, and so embrace it he must. Seeming to do it would not be enough.

'Then let's go talk,' he said grimly, and turned back towards the private chambers. He didn't stop to see if Maer was following, but knew he would be; it was a disconcertingly satisfying knowledge, and he didn't like it one bit.

On his way to Maer's chamber he passed a half-open door, and glanced into the room out of nothing more than idle curiosity. He stopped short. Deera was unfolding a familiar bed covering, too large for the narrow bed, and smoothing it over the mattress with shaking hands.

'Deera?' Richard took a step forward but stopped in the doorway, not sure how to proceed. 'What are you doing?'

'My Lord.' She drew herself up with evident difficulty. 'I am arranging my room.'

'This isn't your room.' Etiquette be damned,

Richard stepped into the room and looked around. It was small, though not uncomfortable, and nowhere near as luxurious as the rooms she and Casta had shared at the very back of the cavern.

'Things are different now,' Maer reminded him again, following him into the room. 'This used to be Jacky's chamber. The rooms my parents shared are now yours.'

'Jacky's…' Richard noted the various stone bottles and pouches that lay on the shelves, and the old boots in the corner, and his heart clenched with renewed grief at the loss of his strange little friend. 'I'm not taking Casta's bed. I'll have this one.'

'This is no room for a king,' Deera said, and Richard heard a tinge of bitterness in her voice. She spoke the words, but, unlike the other Moorlanders, she clearly did not believe them.

'I'll have this one,' he repeated, and his eyes met hers. 'I don't need anything but a bed and someplace to think. Go back to your rooms, and thank you.'

'But you—'

'Will be fine right here,' he said. 'Please. Go. Take your things. Maer, you help her, and I'll see you back in here when you're done.'

When Maer and his mother had gone, Richard sat carefully down on the bed, taking slow, deep breaths and feeling the ache inside him ease. He was recovering fast, thanks to Kernow and Martha, there was no doubt about that, but now he was pretty much on his own again and had to take things easy or set himself back.

He lay down, surprised at the deep comfort of the bed despite its appearance, and closed his eyes. Laura and Ben were with him in his thoughts, they always were, but now there was little Jacky Greencoat too, his face alternately creased with worry and dark with determination; all he had ever wanted was to restore the Lightning to Tir, son of Loen, and to be accepted back into his own family.

'I'm so sorry, Jacky,' he whispered. 'You were the best of us. The strongest and the smartest. No matter what happened, you didn't deserve this.'

He awoke some time later, with no way of knowing how long he had slept; something else he would have to get used to. Maer touched his shoulder and sat down on the bed, waiting with patience and quiet sympathy as Richard slowly pulled himself into a sitting position.

'I came back earlier, but you needed the rest so I let you sleep.'

Richard ran his hands through his hair and gave him a sideways look. 'Is that how it works? I give the orders in public, and you make up your own mind in private?'

Maer's face creased in a smile. 'Yeah,' he said, slipping easily into his old speech pattern. 'That's pretty much it.'

'Well I'm glad we understand each other,' Richard said, smiling back. For a moment he wondered if it was in some way disrespectful. Uncaring even. But it felt good and, in an odd, but welcome way it made him feel stronger.

'How's the pain?' Maer asked, watching him closely.

'Not too bad.' Right now it thumped and pounded like a fist in a mailed glove, thanks to his inactivity and then sudden movement, but it would soon fade. Maer was clearly about to dispute Richard's words, but Richard held up a hand. 'I mean it. It's still no fun, but compared to the way it was, I'm almost cured.'

'Good. Because we have a task to fulfil and you have to be there for this one.'

'Task?'

Maer took a deep breath. 'It's been a few days. I trust Nerryn with all my heart, but I can't help worrying.'

'You think we should go down to the coast and check things out?' Richard braced himself against the bed, ready to stand, but this time it was Maer who held up his hand.

'No! Almost cured or not, you're not ready for that.'

'What then? If you think Nerryn's not going to be able to get Ben after all, I'm—'

'We should visit the *trigoryon an goswig*.'

'Those guys who live in the woods?'

'If it comes to battle we'll need the Foresters on our side, so we have to get to them before the Coastals do. And besides, you're their king, you need to make yourself known to them.'

'So what do we do?' Richard did stand then, but slowly, and keeping his face away from Maer in case he flinched. His back flared with a bolt of pain, and his ribs seemed to tighten like hard, bony fingers on all his internal organs at once, but when he was on his feet the pain faded some, and he trusted himself to face his friend again. 'We just go there and put our case, and hope they support it? I'm ready when you are.'

'It's not so simple,' Maer said, rising too, and his concerned expression said he'd noted Richard's little act for what it was. 'To go there simply to claim their allegiance in a war that might not even happen, might in fact be a catalyst for that war. You understand what I mean?'

'I guess.' Richard saw the point clearly, in terms of his own former life. 'Getting a gang together in case of trouble usually only starts it.'

'Exactly.'

'So we… what? Just pay them a visit, like me going out there earlier,' Richard waved in the direction of the main cavern, 'and showing those guys I'm up and about?'

'We have a better reason,' Maer said, and his face tightened as if his thoughts hurt him. 'They have offered to host my wedding, remember?'

'Yeah.' Richard's voice softened. 'She'll come back, Maer.'

'Well even so, I cannot count on them honouring that promise now.'

'Why the hell wouldn't they?'

'I am no longer royalty, Richard,' Maer said gently. 'They offered to host the wedding of a prince and his princess, not some *nobody*, descended from a king's brother who should never have held the Lightning.'

'Descended from a king,' Richard reminded him. 'Good old Uncle Borsa was a king in his own right. The first of the Lightning and Blade era. Who better to hold it?'

'But Loen was not properly dead,' Maer pointed out, smiling a little at Richard's description of Loen's brother. 'So Borsa and his line, including my mother, and then me, were royals only in name, not in truth. Even Casta should not have held it.'

'Bullshit!' Richard felt his own smile return as he looked at Maer, at the familiar white-blond hair and light blue eyes, and the lithe grace of a true prince of the Moor. 'It's written through you like tree rings. Besides, we're brothers, right? Half-brothers at least.'

'We are, thanks to Casta.'

'And I'm the king. Which makes you—' the smile broadened into a grin—'still a prince. Or have I got that wrong?'

Maer stared at him, and Richard saw the realisation cross his face in slow waves as the implications became clear. 'And Nerryn would still be a princess.'

'Damn right. So, we just assume those Forester guys will see it that way, and go there to make wedding arrangements, right? And while we're there we happen to mention we'd like to please go get my son back, and would they mind helping out?'

'We'll do it, Rich.' Maer stood straight, with fresh determination. 'We'll get them both. Are you able to walk to the forest? It's a good distance.'

'Sure, when do we leave?' It was strange not even knowing if it was morning, afternoon or evening, but it was also comforting to realise he didn't care; sleep would come when he was tired, just as he would eat when he was hungry. But the Foresters were a night people, and, king or not, he'd get a crappy reception if he showed up while they were sleeping.

'We will go as soon as we have eaten. Ykana and Yventra will rise soon.'

'The way you talk makes me dizzy,' Richard grumbled. 'You've gone all Moorlander on me again.'

'Get used to it,' Maer advised. 'I don't even know how I talk anymore myself. 'But something about even mentioning Ykana makes me remember my manners. You'd do well to copy me.'

'Seriously? What's she like?' Richard began to lead the way out of his room, but Maer stopped him.

'I should go first.'

'Is that polite?'

'No, but it's less dangerous.'

Richard raised an eyebrow. 'Dangerous?'

'Do you accept me as your second-in-command?' Richard was about to reply with a joke until he saw Maer was deadly serious. 'Sure,' he said, frowning. 'I… of course.'

'Then I act as your protector,' Maer said. 'I go first, and if there is danger in our path, I face it in your stead.' He softened his tone, but his eyes were hard as he fixed them on Richard's. 'If this becomes a war, I will protect you with my life.'

'Look—'

'No. You must learn to accept pledges of this nature, Richard. Your people will kneel at your feet and swear their lives to protect yours. You must not stammer, or argue, or look at the sky, or anywhere but at them. You would dishonour them by doing that.'

'I don't mean to.'

'I know,' Maer said, and gave him a little smile. 'I learned how to be a mortal by watching you for all those years, but you must learn from me now. Will you?'

Richard's chest tightened in renewed fear. This was real. Everything was different now, and he must learn how to live this life he had never wanted. 'I will,' he managed at last. 'Maer, I swear I'd never do anything to risk your life, or anyone else's.'

Maer regarded him calmly, seeming suddenly much older. 'Yes, you will,' he said. 'You might wish it otherwise, but you will.'

Before Richard could answer, he turned away and started towards the dining hall. Richard watched him go, feeling a nasty, cool sweat breaking out on his skin, and his heart began to pick up pace. Was that true? Would he put those he loved in danger, in his desperation to find Ben? A fresh pain twisted in his stomach as he heard his son's giggle, and saw the trusting blue eyes, dancing with curiosity and life. *Brrrap!*

'Brrrap yourself, kid,' he whispered. 'If they've so much as *heard* you cry, I'll rip them apart.'

***

The Forest.

'Tir approaches!' Yventra entered the clearing to find her sister crouching beside the fire, feeding it twigs. 'I have seen him from the Tall Tree.'

Ykana looked up. 'At last. He has waited too long. Does he bring any of his people?'

'Prince Maer is with him, of course.'

'But not Maer's near-bride?'

Yventra sat down on the tree stump closest to the fire. 'No. She likely stays behind to comfort Deera.'

'It is the saddest time,' Ykana agreed. 'For such a king as Casta was, to meet such a terrible end is a tragedy and an outrage.'

But for all her regret, even Ykana had grown impatient as the days had passed with no visit from the new king, and Yventra feared her sibling would, in the end, march on Lynher Mill herself and demand an audience. Thank the elements he had finally come, and spared them the conflict the hot-headed leader might have caused.

'The lord Tir walks with reluctance,' Yventra warned. Better Ykana be prepared, in order to curb her temper when she observed it for herself.

Ykana scowled. 'Reluctance?'

'Maer often has to urge him onward with a hand at his arm.' Yventra had watched the king from her tree-top, with rising irritation; the two men could hardly make it more obvious they would rather be elsewhere.

'Perhaps Maer should be ruler then,' Ykana said. 'He has his father's wisdom, and the love of his people. What does Tir have but a violent history? A bed-time tale for totterlings. And those can be conjured from nothing, after all.'

Yventra sighed. 'I know you took kindly to Maer when he was here, and I confess to surprise when you offered to host the marriage ceremony, but order is now restored, and Tir has made his choice.'

'Let us hope then, that he has more self-control than his father,' Ykana said, with an edge to her voice. She rose from the fire and dusted off her hands. 'Are they far off?'

'They have just passed the river. They will be here before the others are fully risen for the night.' Yventra rose too, and took a piece of flat bread proffered by her sibling. 'We should prepare the space.'

By the time the clearing was brushed down, and the fire leaping high enough to boil water, Yventra could hear the approach of the Moorlanders. She watched with approval, as Ykana drew herself upright and fixed a smile of welcome on her face. This was one of the reasons she was a good leader;

it took more than skill at hunting, battle and the providing of sustenance, and few realised it until they were called upon to show wisdom and diplomacy.

The Moorlanders waited on the edge of the clearing, and Yventra stepped forward to welcome them. No matter how highly regarded, Tir was yet a stranger, and as such Yventra would face him before he spoke to her leader. Up close she felt a twinge of remorse as she realised she had misinterpreted Tir's slow movements and that, rather than reluctant, he in fact appeared to be ill. His face was almost as pale as a Forester's, but his smile banished the shadows from his eyes and made him almost handsome.

'I recognise and greet you.' He half bowed, his smile slipping as he straightened, but he copied her open-handed gesture of trust, placing his palm against hers. He would never have the white-skinned, big-eyed beauty of the Foresters, but in the manner of the Moorlanders he had his own rough kind of appeal. He seemed humble enough, and his uncertainty and self-consciousness lent him an odd kind of vulnerability.

Yventra stood back and gestured the visitors towards the centre of the clearing, where Ykana stood waiting. 'The lord Tir, and ...' she hesitated, but Tir spoke up firmly.

'My brother, *Prince* Maer.'

When Maer stepped forward to greet her, Ykana clasped his hand in both of hers, instead of the more formal gesture. 'I am sorry to hear of the terrible loss you have endured,' she said quietly. 'Casta was a great man, and a great king. He has given us a worthy son.'

'Thank you.' Maer's voice cracked as he struggled to keep control of his emotions.

When Tir and Maer were invited to sit, Tir's difficulty confirmed Yventra's suspicion; the king was clearly deeply unwell. She exchanged a glance with Ykana and saw that she too had noted this. Was he a sickly man, after all, despite the stories? Elementals were rarely ill, and it would not bode well for them to accept a king who was less than robust.

Tir lowered himself very carefully to the tree trunk, where Maer had so recently sat and laughed about his father's unfortunate first meeting with the Foresters, and Maer looked at him with concern. Tir gave him a brief smile and shook his head, but his breathing took a moment to return to normal.

'My Lord,' Ykana said, 'Can we do anything to ease you?'

'Thanks,' Tir said, in a tight voice. 'But I'm okay. I mean...' He looked at a loss for a moment. 'Uh, I'm receiving excellent care, and recovering well.'

'I am glad. So, are you here to talk of your joining, Prince Maer?' Ykana turned to the fair-haired man. For a heartbeat Yventra was appalled at her sister's apparent rudeness towards their exalted guest, but when she saw a flicker of gratitude on Tir's face she realised that the change in conversation was Ykana's way of giving him time to recover.

'I understand things are different now,' Maer was

saying, 'I will not be king, and Nerryn cannot be queen, but we would be delighted and grateful if you are still willing and happy to host our ceremony.'

Ykana bowed her head without hesitation. 'A title matters nothing. We would be honoured to provide Casta's son with all he requires to celebrate his love. And we will rejoice in it. Truly.'

'Thank you.' Maer relaxed. 'You must wonder why Nerryn herself is not here to greet you?'

'We presumed she had remained behind to comfort your mother in her grief,' Ykana said, but Maer shook his head.

'No. There is more. Much has happened since my father's death, and we have need of your help.'

'Our help?' Ykana turned now to Tir, who was ready to explain, but Maer went on, clearly fighting a deep anger and not hiding it well.

'While Cantoc was carrying out his... *evil* deed, one of our own people, working for him, attacked the spriggan who had care of Tir's son.' Tir's eyes closed briefly, but he said nothing as Maer went on, 'Cantoc holds the boy prisoner at the coast.'

'But why take a child?' Ykana wanted to know, and now she sounded as much interested as concerned, and she was sitting forward, almost eagerly. Yventra recognised the signs of her sister sniffing danger in the air and becoming intrigued rather than wary. She couldn't help smiling a little despite the seriousness of what Maer was saying.

'He is using Tir's love for the child to prevent a Moorlander attack on the coast. They rightly fear retribution for Casta's death, and have taken Dreis to ensure we do not descend on them or stir the elements against them.'

'Dreis,' Ykana mused. 'A likely name for a missing child.'

'*Ben*,' Tir snapped, coming to life suddenly. 'He's got his own name, he's not one of... one of us. Not anymore. He belongs with his mother in their world.'

There was a pause, heavy with tension. Then Ykana spoke softly. 'Were you ready to say "he's not one of *you*," My Lord?'

Yventra drew a quick breath; no matter what they thought, Ykana should not have questioned him aloud. Maer's face was apprehensive too, as he looked from one to the other.

Tir faced Ykana, and his green eyes were hard as granite. 'Get this straight. I took the Lightning to protect my son. And only for that reason. I don't give a damn if that's not good enough for you.' There was another uneasy silence, and Maer laid a hand on his arm. Tir's eyes met his brother's, and then he shook his head, visibly swallowing his anger as he turned back to the Foresters' leader.

'I'm sorry. Look, whatever's happened I'm still from ... out there.' He waved his free hand to the edge of the clearing, where the forest would eventually give way to wide, open spaces. The land of mortals. 'You're going to have to give me time, okay? I've been king for a few days now, but pretty much that whole time I was out of my head on Kernow's magic drinks.'

'Magic?' Yventra looked to Ykana for help, but she shook her head. It didn't matter. Tir had shown a flash of fierce strength that hadn't been immediately apparent, and once the worry for his son was over he might prove a good king after all. Time would tell, and if he did not, well then that would be something to think on later.

Maer leaned forward, his hands clasped on his knees. His resemblance to his late father was startling, given the difference in their appearance; it was all in the manner, and in the eyes. 'Nerryn is not here with me because she has returned to the coast, to try and find a way to bring Ben home. Should she return without him after one moon-cycle, half that time now, your king will have need of your support. Will you pledge yourself to the cause now?'

'How could there be any question?' Ykana said, and Yventra nodded her agreement.

'You have only to ask, My Lord.' She addressed Tir. 'Our people are yours to command.'

'Thank you.' His voice betrayed his tiredness and worry. 'I hope to god there'll be no need, but it's good to know.'

'But what of the child's safety, were we to attack the coast after the time has passed?' Yventra asked. 'He will be in as much danger then as he is now.'

Tir shook his head. 'All I know is I want to go down there right now, and to hell with everything else, but I've put my trust in Maer, and in Nerryn. If they say they'll bring him back to me, then I'm going to have to accept that.'

'And if she doesn't?'

'In two more weeks I figure I'm going to be well enough to go down there myself.'

'Sensible. You will be no good to your son dead,' Ykana agreed bluntly. 'And you are too sick to consider such a journey now, there is little doubt of that.'

Footsteps scuffled at the edge of the clearing, and they all looked up. Two young Foresters stood there, waiting to be invited in, and Yventra immediately tensed; the newcomers had doubtless been listening from the shadows, typically sly behaviour. But Ykana beckoned them into the circle.

'Prince Maer, you will remember Lyelt and Keityn? They have grown much, and well, have they not?'

The young men looked from Maer to Tir, and although their eyes widened slightly at the sight of their new king, it was Maer who held their attention. Were they hoping he'd forgotten?

'Of course.' Maer rose and offered a gesture of trust to each of them in turn. 'You are fine young men, now. I hope you learned well from your lesson with Martha.'

Tir seemed about to try and rise, but Maer noticed, and put a surreptitious hand on his shoulder, pressing him back down. 'Your king is happy to recognise and greet you,' he said, and stepped back to allow the young men to kneel.

Tir appeared uncomfortable, and Yventra glanced away, not wishing to make it worse for him. She was beginning to warm to him, to his earnest determination to do the right thing, and it was hard not to respond to his fear for his child, born of a love she was just beginning to understand.

Her hand rested on her own lower belly which was yet flat and firm, its life-song still too quiet for others to hear. Yet she heard it, in the darkness of the night, and she wondered which of the Foresters had put it there. Certainly neither of these two; Lyelt and Keityn might think themselves men, but they were boys still, and dared not approach the second-in-command for release.

Her Chosen could not have made this new life either, it must be a male. Yventra smiled at the thought of telling Wydra, when the time was right – they had both been longing to hear such a song, and neither cared which of them heard it first. Her Chosen would smile to shame the moon.

When Tir's greetings were done, and Lyelt and Keityn had risen to their feet once more, Ykana patted the tree trunk at her side, and Lyelt took his place there, his companion at his other side.

'We are just talking of Prince Maer's ceremony,' Ykana said. 'We need music, which I hope you will be pleased to provide?'

Lyelt nodded. 'We would be honoured.'

'Good.' Ykana smiled. 'Prince Maer, Lyelt here plays the whistle to great applause, during gatherings and parties. And Keityn sings well.'

'Perhaps we might even persuade the king himself to sing for us also?' Maer suggested.

'The king?' Keityn looked at Tir, doubtful, and not a little put out.

'Tir has a fine voice,' Maer assured him. He turned to Tir, perhaps to begin cajoling him into agreement, but his good humour abruptly faded. 'I think, perhaps, it is time for us to return to Lynher Mill,' he said quietly.

Tir looked up at him, and Yventra was disturbed to see, in the leaping firelight, the deep bruise on his neck that had been hidden by his torc. Sickness did not usually produce bruises – if he had received his injuries in battle it would be a mark in his favour. But would half a moon's turn give him enough time to become as strong as he would need to be?

'I am glad you have visited tonight,' Ykana was saying to the newcomers. 'Your pledge to your king is timely—'

'Since it might be some nights before he returns,' Yventra put in quickly. She could not place the source of her reluctance to tell these two mid-growns of the troubles at the coast, yet neither could she ignore it.

'It is well that our two strongest men have made themselves known to their king,' she went on, and was rewarded by flattered smiles from the boys. 'Now, he must take his leave, and we thank him for his attendance tonight.'

When the Moorlanders had made their farewells, Lyelt and Keityn went to begin their tasks and Yventra and her sister were alone again. Yventra picked up her blade, and set to work sharpening a stick in preparation for digging roots. After a moment she spoke of what had been troubling her since the visit.

'Ykana, will our people be as happy to pledge for the new king as us? We have answered for them, without consulting any of them but Lyelt and Keityn.'

'They have no choice,' Ykana shrugged. 'Perhaps it would be better if the Moorlanders chose their leaders by merit, the way we do, or even adopt the Coastals' lazy habit of following the strongest and wealthiest. But they have their ways, and while they rule over us all we will follow.'

'And you are our leader, so we follow you.'

'Quite so. For now.'

'Do you suppose the challenge will come soon?'

Ykana pursed her lips and stopped scraping dirt from her boot. 'I think so. And I think it will come from either Lyelt or Keityn.'

'Will you win?'

Ykana looked unsettled. 'I have to. Whichever of them challenges, if they win then the other will be second-in-command. Battle chief. As you are to me. Would you see them with such power?'

Yventra felt a chill wash over her, and she shook her head.

'Then we must be sure they do not,' Ykana said grimly. 'We may well need to ask for the Moorlanders' help before they ask for ours.'

Chapter Eleven

Mill Lane Cottage

Darkening skies, a disappearing landscape, a feeling of creeping exhaustion. Clutching the phone, Laura could hear herself slurring her words, and made an effort to sound bright in case Ann thought she'd been drinking. 'Thanks for checking, but I'm alright, really.'

'You don't sound alright.' The faintness of the phone line did not hide Ann's concern. 'I know you, don't forget. How long is Richard going to be away, anyway?'

'Two more weeks.'

'Bloody hell. That's a long goodbye.' Even as she spoke Ann seemed to realise she sounded heartless. 'I'm sorry, I know it's going to be hard for him. But to be honest I'm more worried about you.'

'I'm fine. I just… well, I didn't sleep too well.'

'Do you need me to come over? Maybe getting it all off your chest will help you sleep.'

Laura hesitated. The temptation was strong, but she was in danger of letting something slip, and Ann was no slouch in picking up on stuff like that; she'd be relentless in digging out the truth, and she was so kind about it, it would be hard not to cave in. Laura was surprised to find herself missing the acerbic tongue that had been Jane's own brand of therapy, at least that way she was usually cured of whatever had delivered the blow that signalled the end of her teenage world.

But this was no case of a too-tight dress, a chin-spot on the day of a party, or a boy who looked right through her, it truly was the end of her world. Her stupid promise to Richard kept her locked in Lynher Mill, and knowing he was right hardly helped; she had to at least *see* Ben soon, or she would go mad.

'I've been thinking,' Ann said, 'have you ever tried hypnotherapy?'

'Hypnosis?' Laura went cold at the thought. 'No. No way.'

'Not hypnosis. Therapy. It's a relaxation technique, to help you sleep.' When Laura didn't answer, Ann went on, more firmly, 'Laura, the last time I saw you, you were wasting away in front of my eyes. Another two weeks, and you'll have dropped two jeans sizes.'

'At last,' Laura tried to smile, but Ann's concern touched too deep for that. Her eyes stung, she was so tired, and her muscles shook with exhaustion. What if she had to fight for Ben after all? In this state she'd be lucky to raise as much as a shout. She took a deep breath. 'What would it involve?'

'Why don't I bring Tonya over?'

'Tonya?'

'You know, the girl I went to when I was getting stressed out by the last school inspection. The American.'

'She did help you,' Laura mused. The therapist came recommended by the school, and Ann's headaches had all but disappeared within a week.

'She was brilliant,' Ann said. 'She teaches you the techniques to use on yourself, to help you sleep, so she'll only have to come out once. By the time Ben gets back you'll be more than ready for him.'

'Would she come out here though, d'you think?'

'I can ask her. We hit it off quite well actually, still meet up now and again for a chinwag. Nothing to lose, right?'

Laura closed her eyes, and hoped she sounded convincing. 'Nope, nothing to lose. Thanks.'

Long after the end of the conversation Laura kept looking at her phone, and eventually she picked it up and scrolled to her calls list, poised to ring Ann back and cancel everything. Her thumb hovered over the green handset icon, but after a moment she exited the screen and went back to just staring at the phone until her eyes blurred.

Even blinking hurt, but she knew if she went upstairs and lay on her bed now she would just be dashed in the face by the icy emptiness where Richard should have been lying. Sleep would dance away out of reach once again, and the tears would come hot, burning her eyelids but not warming her skin. She would lie there, as she always did, refusing to move until a few shallow and irregularly spaced snatches of oblivion had given her enough strength to stand up and begin a new day.

It was an insane way to live, but the herbal sleep preparations she'd tried had not worked, and she was loathe to take something stronger; what if she couldn't be roused when Maer brought Ben back? She needed real, practical help, and Ann's friend Tonya might just be it; she'd never know, if she didn't try… She just had to hope she didn't relax too much and blurt out the truth.

The dark had crept all the way across the moor, shrouding the hills and closing another day forever. Looking out at an emptiness that was nowhere near as empty as her home felt, Laura finally understood the addict's desperate plea: *just one last one before I quit for good*. It didn't matter what it was; drugs, a cigarette, a drink, a pizza… the thought that one more would somehow help was universal. For her, it was to be near Richard. She would have to let him go, eventually, but tonight the craving to be near him, even if she couldn't see him, was too much.

She seized her jacket and went out into the dark, finding her way down the hill, through the village, and along the familiar path towards the mine. There was a faint sliver of moon above her, and the clouds were sparse tonight; even once she was past the village there was just enough light to see by, once her eyes adjusted. The stones loomed grey and ugly away to her right, and she walked faster, not looking, until they had fallen behind her.

She stopped by the chimney, eyeing the slope down to the tunnel, her heartbeat picking up speed. Was there actually any point in this? She'd see nothing, Deera would see to that, and she'd get no closer to Richard than the door of his chamber… but she would be closer than she was out here. Two steps down the slope and she halted again. What if, by being there, she stopped Kernow doing her stuff? The thought that she might unknowingly cause Richard more distress turned her around and pushed her back up onto the flatter ground, where she sat down with her back to the engine-house wall, and closed her eyes.

She felt more peaceful here than she did at home, alone, and there was a strong sense of Richard's presence here that slowly filled her up. She drifted, remembering their first walk out here; his sudden slide into cold stillness, when only her touch had brought him back, confused, mortified, and neither of them guessing what had begun in those few dark moments.

The darkness deepened around her, and she drew her coat tighter, fully aware that the romantic notion of spending the night here had been just that. But still, it had helped a little, and maybe she'd be able to sleep now.

She was about to rise when she heard voices. She stilled, her heart thumping with sudden excitement. She'd recognise both those voices anywhere, even if she couldn't hear the words. Her fingers curled into her palms, and she turned her head to lessen the sound of the night's breeze as she strained to hear better.

He sounded tired. She still couldn't make out his words, but she knew it by the way his voice dropped off at the end of his sentences; it was the same whenever he was hit by jet-lag, or when he'd stayed up late into the night with Ben, to give Laura a chance to sleep.

The voices stopped abruptly, and so did the faint swishing of boots in the grass. Laura waited, breathless, and then Richard spoke again, his voice cracking. 'Laura?'

So, he felt it too. Laura stood up, on shaking legs, and turned to face them. 'I had to see you.' *Just once more.*

Maer spoke gently. 'Laura, you have to go. It's dangerous.'

She ignored him, all her attention was on Richard. The tension in his body was clearly outlined against the sky, but his face was unreadable. 'I'll go if you want me to,' she said softly.

'Christ no,' he breathed, taking a step towards her. 'I don't want you to. But Maer's right, it's getting more dangerous by the hour out here.'

Laura fought the urge to close the gap between them and wrap her arms around him. It was supposed to have been enough just to be near him. But it hadn't been. Then to see him, to hear his voice, but still it wasn't enough. The hopeless truth hit her: however much she was given, in any moment, she would always want more. And more.

Eventually nothing would be enough, until they were locked together, in shared acceptance of the fate that must, *must* keep them that way.

She struggled to find something to say, but had only got as far as opening her mouth before he had taken those remaining few steps. His eyes searched her face, and then he groaned and pulled her to him, pressing her head to his chest, his lips moving against her hair as he spoke her name, over and over, in tones of both relief and despair.

Her own arms had gone around him the instant he'd reached her, and her fingers twined into the fabric at the back of his tunic, with something close to panic in case he moved away again. Beneath her hands she felt the lumpiness of the dressings put there by Kernow, but even that could not make her loosen her grasp, and he wasn't trying to pull away.

They stayed like that, in silent desperation, for what seemed like a long, long time, before relaxing their hold on one another. Richard raised his head from where it had lain on top of hers, and she saw him exchange a glance with Maer, before Maer stepped forwards and touched her arm. Up close, she could see his face properly, and he looked no less tired than Richard had sounded.

'I will leave you,' he said, 'but you must stay for a short time only. Richard has need of rest, it's been a hard evening.'

'Thank you,' Laura said, returning the gentle pressure of his hand with hers.

'This cannot happen again,' he said, but his voice was still soft. 'I know how it must feel, but now you can see he is getting well, and you can let him go.'

Laura snatched her hand away, and saw a flicker of regret cross Maer's face. But he said no more, and turned towards the tunnel entrance. She faced Richard again. '*Are* you getting well? Or just a bit better?'

'I'm good, I guess. Probably pushed things a little hard tonight though.'

'Where have you been?'

He took her hand and led her away from the mine a short way, until he found a lump of granite big enough for them both to sit on. Even side-by-side it felt as though he was half a world away, and Laura inched closer so their thighs pressed together. He hadn't let go of her hand, and raised it to his lips before releasing her, with obvious reluctance.

'We had to go to the forest. To get the support of the guys who live there.'

'They're going to help get Ben back?'

He nodded. 'Let's hope it won't come to that, though. If it does, we're at war with the coast.'

'And what will that mean?'

'Deera paints a pretty nasty picture, but to be honest I have no idea.' He sighed, and touched her face. 'Laura, I can't even begin to tell you what it feels like seeing you—'

'You don't have to.' She leaned into his hand, turning to press her lips to his palm. It was his damaged hand, and she felt the roughness of the healing scars under her lips. 'Are you still in pain?' she asked. 'And don't lie.'

He gave a soft laugh at her suddenly stern tone. 'Some,' he admitted. Her fingers brushed the fabric of his tunic, smoothing it over his ribs as he put his arm around her. The last time she'd seen him he'd have flinched away when she did that, now he just smiled tiredly. 'Maer was right though, I'm getting better fast. It's always been that way, you know that.'

'Thank god. But you're not right yet.'

'Not totally.'

'Have you heard anything about Ben?' Her voice faltered, and she watched his face carefully for any sign he might be hiding anything, to spare her any worry. But he shook his head, and his bleak expression convinced her he was telling her all he knew.

'Nerryn's sensible, she'll wait until she's sure they trust her. He's going to be well cared for, and that's pretty much the only thing that's stopping me from going down there right now.'

'I know,' Laura said, 'but if I'd be in danger down there, think what it'd mean for you.' She tightened her hold on him at the thought, but he tensed and she sat upright again. 'I'm sorry.'

'Don't be.' He touched her face and she turned towards him. He kissed her, softly, where she could feel the frown line crease her brow. 'Never be sorry for holding me. I'll take anything for that.'

Fighting tears, Laura searched for something positive to hold on to. 'I never really got to know

Nerryn, but Maer seems to think she's tougher than she came across.'

'For what it's worth I think he's right.'

As much as she wanted to spend the whole night thinking and talking about Ben, just the thought of him in the care of those creatures made her feel sick and cramped. She had to turn her thoughts away from him, or risk coming unravelled. 'How is Deera?'

Richard shrugged. 'She's getting there. It's hard, you know? She lost everything.'

'She didn't lose her son, which she might have done if it wasn't for you,' Laura pointed out. 'And she still has a glorious home.'

'Casta *was* everything to her,' Richard said quietly. 'I don't know if you ever really saw them together, but they had something pretty special.'

'I did see them,' Laura said, remembering her first time in the mine, dragged down there by Gilan. 'I remember wondering how she could be so cold, having the love of a man like that.'

'She's not cold. She's just frightened. She was then, and she is again now. Only now she's alone, too. Maer can't get close, she won't let him. I guess she knows that when Nerryn comes back he'll be gone too.'

'Poor Deera,' Laura was surprised to hear herself say, and even more surprised to hear Richard's soft laugh.

'I know, I keep finding myself thinking stuff like that, and then wondering where the hell it came from.' His hand found hers again, and their fingers wrapped tightly around each other. 'Babe, I know we talked about this, but... isn't there *any* way we can go on together? I mean, Tom was able to live in the village, right? He had a life, even though Loen was working in him.'

She found herself clutching at his logic for a brief, heart-stopping moment, before acknowledging the difference. 'He was still Tom, mostly,' she said sadly. 'But you're fully their king now. You have this.' She touched his chest where the Lightning was carved beneath his shirt. 'You can't live with me, you'll die. Just like Tom did when Loen took over.'

'His heart gave out,' Richard said. 'It's not the same. He was in shock, he didn't know what was going on.'

Laura's finger traced the shape she could not see. 'You're their king,' she repeated. 'You'll be expected to marry someone who can live underground, and can give you kids. One of your own women.'

'I don't want anyone else.' He sounded as though every word was being forcibly ripped out of him. 'Laura, I love you. *You*. God, I can't believe we have to let each other go.'

His longing was fuelling hers, and she reached across to rest her hand on his face, then slipped it around the back of his head to pull him closer. Her fingers brushed the back of his neck, and she felt him shiver.

His voice was hoarse. 'Letting you go will be...' He gave up, and rested his forehead against hers. He must have realised he had no need to struggle to explain, that she was feeling the same hopeless pain. 'I can't even ask you to come here again, to meet me. Just so I can see you.'

'But I *can* come here,' Laura said urgently. 'We can arrange to meet, just for a few minutes each day—'

'No!' He quietened again, but sounded no less firm. 'Maer wasn't kidding about the danger. I can't let you risk coming out here, you have to stay someplace safe.'

'The Coastals can't hide from me, I can see them. And I can run. Maybe not as fast, but I can hide.'

'You won't see them coming,' Richard told her. His eyes found hers, and in them she saw the reflection of the sliver of moon. 'They're just as likely to hit you from a distance with a bolt of lightning as come at you with a knife.'

Laura's blood turned to ice at the calm certainty in his voice. Reflexively she turned to look around them, realising that even if their new enemies were doing things the human way, the darkness would cover their movements, and they would be silent as shadows on their feet.

'I don't want to frighten you,' Richard went on. 'God knows I don't want that. But you have to realise they know who you are now. Arric does, for sure. They don't need you around screwing things up for them.'

'So this is it, then. The end.'

'More farewells than a Status Quo tour,' Richard said, surprising her into a sort of sobbing laugh. He leaned close and pressed his lips to her forehead again, lingering there, and she felt his fingers tighten on hers. When he pulled back his eyes were bright.

'Maer's going to let me say goodbye to Ben when Nerryn brings him back. But don't worry, he'll be with you soon.'

'I can't believe we can feel like this, and it could still be wrong,' Laura said in a small voice. 'I'm scared for you. Is that stupid? Or should I be?'

He stood, and drew her to her feet too, then he took hold of her shoulders and said, in a solemn voice, 'Honey, I *really* hope you're just stupid.'

Laura shook her head. 'How can you always make me smile, when I feel as if I've just swallowed broken glass?'

'Because I'm awesome.' He shook their linked hands gently. 'Come on, I'll walk you to the village.'

They walked in silence, most of the way. Laura tried to soak up the memory of this last walk, and store it; she'd need it all too soon. The brush of his arm against hers, as they bumped into one another on the uneven ground, was something else she wanted to remember, and the sound of him breathing on the night air. But that part wasn't so warming; he'd said he'd pushed himself too hard tonight, and it seemed he was right. His breath came in shallow bursts, and once or twice she felt him slow almost to a halt, and she wanted to stop, to question him, but she knew he wouldn't answer.

At the edge of the moor, she found herself reluctant to step off the grass and onto the road – to leave him in his world, and return to hers. Now she could see his face properly, in the lights that spilled across the road from the houses and the Miller's Arms. He was pale, but had found a smile for her, and it bathed her in its beloved familiarity.

She tried to return it, but as they let go of each other it faltered, and he wrapped his arms across his chest, tucking his hands beneath his armpits. If he was feeling anything like her, it was an attempt to stop himself reaching out for her again, and she desperately wished for it to fail.

'The real last farewell,' she said quietly. 'No encores. No curtain calls.'

'No.'

'I love you, Richard. Be safe.'

'I love you too. Crazy amounts. Just…' he stepped towards her again, and she felt her heart stop, but he just dropped his hands to his sides, clenched into fists. 'For Christ's sake be careful. As soon as Ben comes back, get the hell out of here.'

'You'll always be with me,' Laura whispered, feeling it so deeply that no words were enough. But it was in the look that passed between them, in the ache echoed in each other's eyes, in the trembling of his fingers on her face. And then it was in the emptiness of the air between them, as he turned and left her alone on the edge of the moor.

Chapter Twelve

Porthcothan Bay, Cornwall

He was beginning to become accustomed to the wind, and to the smell of salt in the air, but the sound... Jacky huddled by his rock, wishing he had his jacket to wrap around himself to ward off the evening chill. Below him the great grey and white water roared and crashed, and his muscles shrivelled as he remembered, with sickening clarity, the moment when he'd realised one more step would have sent him plunging to his death.

He had walked and walked, keeping as far west as he could, but now and again he'd had to alter his path to avoid being seen. He had dismissed the idea of taking cover beneath the trees, lest some gleeful Forester leap out and frighten his heart into stopping, but there were many more villages than he had expected. New ones and old ones, big and small, pretty and ugly. And everywhere there were whooshing carriages like the one Tir rode in when he'd lived in Lynher Mill, only shinier. And much, much faster.

As the evening light began to fade, Jacky had found himself crossing flat farmland, hardly a hedge to hide him, and no trees even if he had wanted them. Did this mean he was close to the edge of the land after all? He looked down; his boots were not wet, and no water lay in his path. Not yet, then.

His feet picked up a faster pace, to find somewhere that offered more shelter, and gradually he began to taste a tang in the air. A little farther, and he heard a hollow, booming sound. Not like the ones he had come to recognise back when the mines had been working; those explosions deep underground that travelled up through the layers until they reached the surface as a low rumble. This was constant. Sometimes louder, sometimes fading a little, but never quietening completely.

Jacky skirted the southern edge of another village, and crossed a small road, the sound drawing him on even as it reached into his heart and laid fingers of fear over it. Fields passed by beneath his weary feet, and now the sound lay to his right so he turned that way. *Why was he so intent on finding its source if it scared him so?* But fear was for the old Jacky. The moor-dwelling Jacky. This Jacky knew it was the water he was hearing, and that meant the end of his journey.

A worn path showed just ahead, a pale line through the heavy dusk, and he crossed it, wiping his suddenly damp fingers on his tunic. The ground sloped away downhill, and he strode with renewed energy. The freshening wind tugged at his clothing, he became aware of taller grasses brushing at his boots, and then some instinct made him stop, mid-step and look down. He shrieked, and his insides twisted into tight knots; the toes of his front foot hung over nothing.

He waved his arms madly, seeking something to catch hold of and finding nothing, and just stopped himself from transferring his weight forward. Instead he dug the heel of his other foot into the ground and flung himself backwards. He sat down, hard enough to bring his blunt back teeth together, and tasted blood where he had nicked the edge of his tongue. His back flared with a spasm of pain, and he pitched onto one elbow, striking a stone and feeling a shuddering numbness flash down into his fingers. None of it mattered. He took a slow breath, and heard it catch, before escaping him again on a trembling moan.

When he was able to move again he crawled forward, putting his hands out in front of him and patting the ground as if it might give way at any moment and send him tumbling into nothing. The ground fell away, almost straight down, and at the bottom there was the water.

Jacky watched the grey mass surge forward, turning white as it rose into peaks and then thundered over the rocks. The boom came when it disappeared into one of the black caves that lined the bottom edge of the fallen ground. Then it ran back out again, frothing, its fury spent against the immovable land.

The water. Had Jacky really believed he would just keep walking until he felt it lap over his boots? That the land would just fade away, and he would know he had reached its end only by having wet feet? He might have laughed if he hadn't still been struggling for a calmer breath. This was no moorland lake, not even the largest of them had been like this; stretching into the distance forever. Night raced towards him, the sun already swallowed in the heaving mass of living horror that writhed as far as Jacky's eyes could see.

The moorlands he loved were just as wide and open; glorious vistas of greens and greys and golds, undulating hills, crumbling ruins, rocks and marshlands. But this…

It was death that waited out there. Choking, suffocating death.

And now night had fallen, hard and cold, and the noise only seemed to grow louder. How did the mortals in the nearby village sleep? How did the coastal elementals live with it? Lynher Mill crept into his thoughts; quiet—almost silent—on the moor, and hardly noisier even in the village. His heart ached with missing it.

From his shelter by the rock, Jacky stared out over the water. Who could bear to set themselves at its mercy? Yet there were shapes out on the water, and he guessed they were boats – although they were quite unlike the ones he'd seen along the rivers at home. They were few and far between, but they travelled both north and south, and the sight of them gave Jacky hope; perhaps the coast wasn't like this all along its length, but safer elsewhere?

He was minded to go south, where it might be warmer. There was no hurry after all, and if it should become apparent that there was no quieter coast that way after all, he would simply turn back. The ledge down to the water was sickeningly high, but he might find a good shelter for the night if he searched for a shallower climb. He would certainly be safe from mortal eyes here. He'd considered travelling by night, but, while walking the path in daylight would put him in danger from the sight of mortals, at night one mis-step and he would never see the dawn. He shuddered, closed his eyes and huddled further down into his own shoulders. Daylight it would be.

By the time the sun was mid-sky, Jacky had reached a mortal town so big it took him most of the rest of the day to travel around its edge. Never had he seen a place with so many people, even this late into the cycle. Many had huge, colourful slabs they carried either on their heads or strapped to the tops of their carriages.

In the fading warmth of the late summer, many still walked about clad in scraps of cloth, or second skins that fit snugly but came only to their knees. Most wore protection for their eyes against the sun, and, though crouching in terror at the sheer numbers of them, Jacky felt a flicker of envy for their carefree manner.

He took the path inland, fighting the temptation to carry on in that direction until he was back home, and scolded himself all the way around for his fears. Several times he had to hide or risk being seen, and when he emerged, shaking with nerves, at the other side of the town, he kept going south instead of heading back towards the coast; with the sound of the water far away, he felt safer putting one foot in front of the other, being reasonably sure the ground would not suddenly disappear from beneath him.

Whenever a town or village offered enough shelter in its streets he took his courage in both hands and went through it. More often he was forced to go around, and in this way he arrived, after many sunsets, at the end of the world.

The Lizard Peninsula, Cornwall.

The sky darkened immediately overhead. Everywhere else it was the slightly unsettled, pale blue of the end of the warm days; cloudy, but with no imminent sign of rain. Directly above Jacky it turned grey, then black, then purple, and a very small portion of the water began swirling, faster and faster, until it was whipped into a fiercely boiling cauldron.

This had happened before, but never when Jacky had been on the beach. He had reluctantly left the small cave he had found, away from the reaching tide, and was foraging for shellfish in the rock pools around the rocky headland. To his immense relief he hadn't seen another living soul here since he'd arrived; mortals and elementals alike were far more interested in the noisy and colourful land a little to the south. It was perfect.

The wind gusted, and Jacky frowned. He knew well the signs of weather-meddling, and this sudden squall felt very familiar. He looked up and, sure enough, on the land above he recognised the lithe form of an elemental, staring out over the water. Jacky followed his gaze, drawn in fascination to the rising peaks as the wind played savage games with the water. A glint of sunlight flashed on something mortal-made, and he realised a boat was out there, caught in the eddies.

He drew a quick breath and squinted upward again; the elemental had been joined by another, considerably shorter, and they stood side by side but looked in no way companionable; both were clearly tense, neither glanced at the other. Jacky peered harder at the shorter man, but he was distracted by the sudden increase in the tiny storm's ferocity. The boat began to make its way out of the circle of devastation in which it had found itself, until the elemental above realised this and widened that circle.

The boat was caught up again immediately, and it was all over in moments. A sudden, sharp gust that nearly blew Jacky off his feet, even from his sheltered spot, and the water surged up against the front of the boat, lifting it high and turning it, urging it towards the waiting rocks that jutted out from the headland.

There was nothing Jacky could do, but watch. As the wind dropped, and sudden squally rain eased, all that was left of the boat were splinters, bags, and broken seating; the rest had plummeted to the depths, weighed down by the useless engine. Three people struggled with the tide, finding their way to safety at last, and climbing, shivering and speechless with shock, over the rocks and away towards the peninsula.

Jacky became aware of voices coming closer. He shrank back into the shadows, his ears straining to hear the words, and he very quickly recognised the sounds of discord.

'Foolish question! Cantoc needs every bit of coin he can reach, that was the *point*!'

'But, Arric, look. Some broken seats. Some clothing. What good is that?'

'We don't know that's all there is. But if you insist upon it, then please, do go and prove me wrong.'

Jacky steeled himself to peer out, and his breath caught in his throat: Gerai! What had he done with Dreis? Perhaps he had already returned the boy to the Moorlanders and claimed his reward, since there was certainly neither sight nor sound of an infant here. Likely he was sharing the reward with the Coastals then. An alliance between the quarrelling elementals was not unheard of; Gilan had been the same, scuttling off to the coast to show off his talents to Cantoc, and now it seemed Gerai was doing the same thing with this younger Coastal.

The Moorlander was wading into the water, and although his face was turned carefully away from Arric's view, from where Jacky stood he could see Gerai's dark expression. So, it seemed the one he'd called Arric was the bringer of the storm, and, although the more powerful elemental, Gerai was simply the brawn – a Moorlander working for a Coastal! No wonder at that set look of anger.

Once the few bags had been dragged in and laid, sopping wet and heavy on the rocks, the elemental named Arric braced his feet and stooped to open one. His brows drew in as he pulled out exactly what Gerai had said he would; piece after piece of useless clothing.

'There will be others,' Gerai ventured. 'Cantoc will tell us when there is something worthwhile to be—'

'Cantoc has had his head turned. Again, and by the same means.'

'But he will still know when the powder boats are expected.'

'How? Those mortals have not returned since Tir confronted them on his doorstep. He *frightened* them, the cowards! Them, with their vile weapons and their brave words.'

'Cantoc has others.'

'*Had* others. It did not help that you took it upon yourself to see that one of the few remaining powder-bringers breathed sand instead of air.' He sighed. 'Besides, Cantoc commands less respect than ever. He has softened over the cycles, and now it is left to me.'

'Arric...' Gerai's voice faltered, then he cleared his throat. 'I must speak of this, I must know. Was it you who killed Casta?'

Jacky's world went black. He swayed, clutching at the rock. Casta? Dead? His whole body clenched painfully tight, and he had to bite the back of his hand to prevent himself from crying out. When he was able to listen again Arric was talking.

'... and his son killed my *father*!'

'But Maer is not Casta! The punishment should have fallen upon the prince, not the king.'

'Are you questioning me? And why does it matter who did the deed, Gerai? You are with us now! You pledged yourself to Cantoc, and to his cause, knowing that blow had been struck against the Moorlanders.'

Jacky shuddered. So much he hadn't known about that terrible night. He remembered seeing the shattered engine-house chimney and wondering what it meant... did that have something to do with Casta's death? The two words did not want to sit together in Jacky's mind, but when they did, their clashing, discordant sound made him clutch at his head with clawed fingers. What else had happened? And again, where was Dreis? Then his blood ran cold as he remembered leaving Tir at the mercy of this evil Moorlander. What if he too had been killed?

'I begged for your understanding that night, Arric,' Gerai said hollowly. 'I tried to make you understand my conflicted feelings; Casta was a just man. An honourable one. He was my king. And yours!'

'Not mine. Never mine. And if you had remained a loyal Moorlander, who would be your leader now?' Arric rose from the useless plunder on the rocks, aiming a kick at the nearest bag. 'You made your choice, and you chose wisely. Tir has no understanding of what it is to be king. He is wounded, lost, and grieving for his family. The Moorlanders will not have the strength they need. You are on the side of victory, for the Ocean's sake enjoy it!'

Jacky dropped his hands from his head. Tir lived... He must have taken the Lightning to protect his son, there could be no other reason. And if he was king, then Jacky had succeeded after all, and his family must welcome him back.

The urge to return to Lynher Mill was a painful thing, but he had to remain here and find the boy, or at least learn what had happened to him. He battled a wave of grief for Casta, and listened with great care to the exchange on the otherwise deserted beach, hoping for an answer.

Arric was now very close to Gerai, and the former Moorlander was backing away, step by stumbling step on the wet rocks, his attention behind him to search for solid purchase. 'You *have* my allegiance,' he said earnestly. 'But you must also have my honesty.'

'Honesty!' Arric barked a short laugh. 'You know nothing of it! You were quite happy to return and kill your own prince on my orders!'

Maer! Jacky sagged in renewed horror, but Gerai spoke again quickly.

'But I did not! And if I had, that should have proved my worth to you!'

'It might, but only if you had given yourself up. Nerryn would have come back to us believing Maer's own had turned against him, and if she had run to us in fear for her own life we could be all the more sure of her.'

'But she *is* here,' Gerai muttered, and Jacky had to strain to hear him. 'And so is her brother. Your plan is falling into place, Arric, their combined powers will surely win you all you have worked for. Nothing can stand against them.'

'She cannot yet be trusted.'

'She has care of the boy, surely you must believe her loyalty, or she would make off with him.'

Jacky's thoughts raced. If the lady Nerryn had Dreis, Jacky's own task must now be to steal him back, and return him to his family. But it seemed it would not be so easy.

'She is still never left alone with him,' Arric was saying. 'While Maer walks the world, there is too much to draw her back to Lynher Mill.'

'If I am discovered, I will die! Then what good would I be to you?'

Arric ignored the question. 'When will you do it?'

'Arric, please—'

'Are you refusing me?'

'I would take such an order from Cantoc.' Gerai drew himself up slightly, as if he had found new courage in his own words. 'But what if Cantoc did not after all wish it? *You* would still order it done, and then I would be cast out by both Moorlanders and Coastals.'

Gerai of no-one. Jacky felt a treacherous twinge of sympathy.

Again Arric paused, looking at the former Moorlander thoughtfully. Then he said, 'As you wish. We will go to Cantoc together and discuss this.' He shifted his gaze over Gerai's shoulder, towards the sea. 'You have missed a bag. It might be the one that makes this trip worthwhile. I will wait while you fetch it.'

Gerai turned, frowning. 'I see no more bags.'

'Out there, wedged in the rocks.' Arric pointed. Jacky couldn't see it himself, but he saw Gerai peer more closely, then shrug.

'*Then* we will go to Cantoc?'

'We will. Hurry, now, before the mortals return for their trinkets.'

Gerai moved out of Jacky's sight, and after a moment Arric followed. Taking his courage in both hands, Jacky leaned out from behind his rock and watched the two elementals; Gerai wading into the water and Arric remaining on the very edge of it, each foot astride a rock.

'I cannot see it!' Gerai shouted.

Arric sighed, Jacky could see it in the exaggerated rise and fall of his shoulders, even though he could not hear it over the rushing tide. 'Right there! Look! Oh, what is the use? I'll show you.'

He went after Gerai, who had gone slowly, feeling his way. The rough heathland was nothing to Moorlander feet, which found their way from tussock to tussock, avoiding the marshes and never faltering in their flight. But here the Coastals moved with the greater ease, over the wet, slimy rocks amongst which they lived; Arric caught up to the stumbling Gerai quickly.

As Jacky watched, he pointed towards a group of rocks near the headland, and Gerai now up to his chest in the water, turned to follow the pointing finger. In less than a heartbeat Arric had seized him by the back of the neck and plunged him face-down into the turbulent sea.

Jacky yelped, mercifully unheard, as Gerai flailed upwards in a desperate panic, and one of his hands made a lucky connection, striking Arric beneath the chin. Arric slipped and disappeared, momentarily, beneath the water, but he recovered quickly, lunging forward and grabbing at the shocked and breathless Gerai, as the Moorlander reached in panic for a hand-hold in the rocks.

Jacky could not hear their words, but he heard their shouts. Gerai's voice rose to a scream of furious terror as Arric's hand found the back of his head, and then cut off abruptly as his face was forced, once more, beneath the waves. This time

Arric kept well away from Gerai's increasingly feeble struggle, and, after a frighteningly short time, the Moorlander went limp.

Jacky's blood was like ice. He watched Arric pull his former accomplice back towards the spray of jagged rocks that served as the beach here, and tried not to moan aloud; was there no end to the killing?

The Moorlander would need to be in contact with the ground in order to return to it, and Arric dropped the lifeless body face-down on the rocks, while he regained enough strength to drag it up to the cliff. A spurt of seawater came out of Gerai's slack mouth with the pressure of the rocks that drove up into his belly. It made Jacky's own gut clench and he swallowed a moan of revulsion.

Arric sat down beside Gerai, breathing hard and wiping his hands through his wet hair. Jacky hoped to see those hands shaking, but they were as steady as the rock on which he sat. He was not new to killing then... Gerai had likely been right to accuse him of Casta's death.

The anger that burned in Jacky at that moment might have driven him out of his hiding place and towards Arric with a sharp rock in his hand, if he had not seen a sudden twitching movement from the drowned Moorlander.

Instead he drew a sharp breath and willed the man to move again. Arric was staring morosely out to sea, but Jacky could not take his eyes from the limp body behind the Coastal, the fingers spasming... he had seen involuntary movement in the dead before, and tried to tell himself that's what this was, but the closer he looked, the more he could see that wasn't true.

Move, Gerai! Rise up, strike!

Gerai's head jerked. It hung down, his hair dripping, and his arms were stretched to hang down below it, his hips awkwardly tipped, and his body lying heavily on the jagged tips of rock—it was a wonder he could breathe, but breathing he was. If Arric had dropped him on his back it would be a different story, but Arric's own carelessness had saved the Moorlander's life.

Move!

Gerai moved. Jacky saw his eyes flicker open, then close again in pain, then open once more and focus on something by his left hand. *A rock, it must be a rock...* The hand moved, and still Arric looked out to sea, his face set and still, emotionless as he waited for his strength to return.

Gerai's hand rose. He twisted his upper body so he could bring the rock around with enough force to do some damage, but the movement made him cry out, and Arric whipped around. The stone, instead of striking the back of his head, caught him across the temple and sent him crashing sideways. Gerai dropped his weapon and, gasping and groaning, tried to wriggle clear of the rocks upon which he lay. But Arric was too quick for him.

Blinking away the blood that dripped into his right eye, the Coastal fixed his clear left one on the struggling Moorlander, and crawled towards him. He planted one knee in the middle of Gerai's back, pinning him, and seized the soaked collar of his coat with one hand, and his hair with the other.

The sound Gerai's head made as it smashed down onto rock was something Jacky would never forget if he lived to be as old as the land itself. A crunch the first time, a splinter the second, and the third time it was a wet, squelching combination of both.

Jacky turned away and retched, as quietly as he could, feeling the hot squirt of tears as he wiped his mouth on his shirt sleeve. Tears of sorrow, not for Gerai himself—although there was no denying that the death of a Moorlander would always feel a little like the death of one of his own—but they were tears of terror, also. And bewilderment; what had happened to this land he loved, and what would happen now? Something flickered deep in his mind, something about Nerryn and her brother, but for now he had to get back up to the land above and try to find Dreis.

When he looked again, Arric had dragged Gerai towards the cliff. The trail of blood, that would disappear as the tide made its twice-daily assault on this place, now glistened slick and red in the daylight. No-one else would ever see it. Jacky closed his eyes briefly and sent a thought towards the spirit of the fallen Moorlander; it was not his place to forgive, but in this time of utter confusion and turmoil across the whole of their land, he at least understood.

It wasn't until he was almost at the top of the steep climb to flat ground, that he remembered his half-thought about Nerryn and her brother, and the realisation that came with it nearly sent him crashing back down to the shore again. He stopped, breathing hard, his heart squeezing with horror, his eyes so wide they burned. Surely even Arric wouldn't use his siblings' power like this?

But he might, if he had no idea how devastating those powers truly were.

Chapter Thirteen

'When will you leave?' Cantoc accepted a warm drink from Nerryn with a smile of thanks, and turned his attention back to her twin.

'As soon as Arric returns.' Mylan's voice drifted, muffled, from the depths of his bag where he was searching for something.

'Yes,' Nerryn said stiffly. 'He must wait for the mighty Arric. I cannot be trusted, you see. Still.'

Cantoc thought it best not to respond, but tried to send a sympathetic glance her way. It was wasted; her attention was once more on the totterling, who held on to the edge of the chair she had vacated, and bounced at the knees. Sturdy boy, so beautiful, always smiling… Cantoc couldn't help smiling himself, and quickly turned away.

'Mylan, when you find Dafna's people you must tell them about Talfrid *before* you ask for their support.

Mylan emerged from his bag, and looked at him with narrowed eyes. 'That was my intention. And before you remind me yet again, I will make it clear they must come straight to you.'

'Indeed. The very last thing we need is for them to go marching on the Moorlanders and showing our strengths. Or worse, getting themselves killed.'

'They have as much right to their vengeance as myself, and my brother and sister,' Mylan pointed out, and Cantoc noted how his own name had been omitted. No matter; his heart held its secrets well.

He glanced again at Nerryn, and this time she was watching him and he saw understanding in her expression. He blinked and looked back at Mylan, who had found what he was seeking; the brooch he always used to fasten his travelling cloak. His mother's brooch, shaped like a curling wave. He laid it on the table, and Cantoc tried hard not to look at it, but his eyes were pulled back to it time and again as he struggled to concentrate on his instructions.

'The food and extra weapons, we will expect a little later, with as many of those of fighting ability that the village can spare.'

'Cantoc, we have been over this.'

'Just make sure Lawbryn and—'

'And Hendrig are among the first, yes!' Mylan sighed. 'It seems you have little faith in me as a messenger.'

'I do have faith in you, I just…' Cantoc shook his head. 'I just wish I could go in your stead, that is all.'

'These people do not know you. They know me. I am their blood.' Mylan's voice softened. 'I will bring them to you, and they will be in no doubt as to who is to blame for the death of their daughter, and that of the man she chose for her husband. They will fight for you, Cantoc, because you are a coast lord, but even more so because of the regard you held for our parents.'

Cantoc blinked hard and nodded, grateful when Mylan picked up the silver brooch and placed it ready with his belongings, but beneath the folds of his cloak. The memory of handing it back to Dafna, that night her home had been lost, was fresh and warm in his mind.

Watching Talfrid fasten it for her the following morning, when her cloak had dried out, had almost driven him to violence on the man; jealousy was a terrible, terrible thing, and almost too strong for him, but he had fought it. Even when Talfrid had kissed his bride—a brief, affectionate press of his lips on her smooth, clear brow as he settled their son into her arms—Cantoc had managed to smile for them. How it had hurt.

'... doing while I'm away?' Mylan was asking.

Cantoc swam back, only guessing at the full question, his mind and heart still entangled in Dafna's memory. 'I shall continue my work as usual, there is much to do to ready ourselves for what lies ahead. Homes to find for Dafna's people—'

'I said Arric,' Mylan said. 'What will *he* be doing?'

'Oh.' This time Cantoc's smile was genuine, and it felt good as it spread across his face. 'He's going to take on your father's trade.'

There was a stunned silence, and then Mylan's own mouth widened in a grin. 'A fish-finder? Arric is going to be a *fish-finder*?'

'A noble calling,' Cantoc pointed out, his tone stern, but he was still smiling.

'It is. And we all need fish, after all. But still... *Arric?*' It had been a long while since Mylan had looked so young. Bright-eyed, his cheeks flushed, blood fired with the adventure that lay ahead, and sorrow pushed to the back of his mind, just for that instant. Nerryn joined him in his laughter, and Cantoc thought he had never heard a sound sweeter. He felt his heart swelling, and he cursed the Moorlanders for giving the twins so much as a moment's grief. They should always be like this.

The totterling's mouth had dropped open at this unexpected explosion of humour, but he was clearly no stranger to it. He too let out a laugh, a surprisingly raucous sound from such a sweet, rounded little face, and that made the others look at each other in surprise and laugh all the harder. Dreis bobbed up and down faster, enjoying the effect he was having on his new people, and when he lost his balance, and plopped down onto his bottom on the floor, he just clapped his hands and beamed around at everyone.

Cantoc was clutched by momentary panic; what if he were forced to hurt the boy in order to destroy the Moorlanders? Could he do it? He threw a glance at Nerryn, who crouched beside Dreis and mimicked his clapping; what would *she* do? Despite her initial revulsion at being near the child, Dreis had quickly found his place in her heart. And Mylan... one look at the traveller, his eyes soft on the boy, told Cantoc all he needed to know; if any harm befell this totterling he, Cantoc, would lose everything. He would lose the twins. Before that happened Cantoc would take Dreis back to his mother himself, under a flag of temporary truce. Neither he, nor Nerryn, nor Mylan would risk the child's safety.

But he could not say the same for Arric.

***

Arric rounded the headland, stepping over seaweed-strewn rocks, half his attention on his footing, the other half scanning the beach ahead for abandoned bags and unguarded belongings. Working this late in the cycle held mixed fortunes for this, the least favourite of his private activities; the beaches were not quite empty, but almost. Most mortals had returned to the places they had come here to escape, and, although the water was only just beginning to warm up, the sun's warmth was weakening. Few people enjoyed emerging from the sea onto a chilly beach.

However, there were still some, taking advantage of uncluttered water, and reluctant to pass up the chance to frolic in the waves together. These would rather risk their treasures than take turns to guard them. Fools, each and every one! It was at times like this Arric actually missed Gerai; the Moorlander had been so much better at this kind of thing, and of course the risk to himself was far less. But Gerai was gone.

Arric stopped beside one of the three-sided, striped enclosures that faced out to sea. He ensured he was not full-formed, and, satisfied that he would be forgotten as soon as he was seen, he knelt on the towels that were littered with bags and boxes, clothing and valuables. Someone had tried to be a little clever, at least, and buried their money pouch in the sand – but then they had evidently been worried they'd forget where it was, and had stuck a small wooden stick there, with a sweet wrapper fastened to it like the sail of a ship.

It was the work of a smiling moment to uncover the leather pouch and slip it into his own pocket. Likewise the various bags that he knew would hold the chains, time-pieces and other things that people would not want salt and water-damaged.

He rose to his feet, watching for the return of the trusting mortals who had left their things unprotected, and the breath stuck in his throat as he came face to face with the bearded stranger. The watcher from the cliff. There was nothing between them but an arm's length, and absolutely no doubt at all that the man was looking right at him.

'Put it back,' the watcher said. 'Now.'

'Who are you?'

'Put it back.'

'I take orders from no *mortal!*'

'It's not an order. It's a warning. Put it back.'

'A warning?' Arric managed a tight laugh, though his heart was pounding uncomfortably fast. 'You dare to think you can warn me?'

'Put it back.'

'Stop saying that!'

'Then do it.'

Arric felt an almost overwhelming urge to do just that, but considered his advantage: no-one could see him, but anyone could see this scruffy, suspicious-looking man hovering next to an unguarded enclosure. He noted that the watcher had folded his arms and was attempting not to look as though he was talking to anyone, but someone would remember him, when the valuables were found to be missing.

He smiled. 'I don't believe I will.' He bowed, and stepped out of the back the enclosure, swinging one leg and then the other over the striped barrier. 'Good afternoon, whoever you are. I'm sure I'll see you again soon.'

'And I'll see you, too.' The watcher smiled suddenly, but it wasn't a friendly smile. 'Interesting that, isn't it? I mean, how do you know I'm the only one who can?' The watcher indicated the others on the beach. 'What if, even now, someone is coming over, having seen you climbing over the *back* of this nice couple's windbreak? However will you explain that?'

Arric couldn't help glancing around, and although he saw no-one approaching, he couldn't deny the curiosity, and the sense of uncertainty that he really was outside everyone else's sight.

'Put it back,' the watcher said, 'and I'll tell you what you want to know.'

Arric hesitated, then withdrew two of the small bags from his pocket and tossed them onto the towel. 'All of it,' the watcher insisted. He waited while Arric re-buried the money pouch and dusted damp sand off his hands. Then he gestured for Arric to lead the way up the beach.

Scowling like a chastened child, Arric swiftly climbed the cliff, and felt a twist of satisfaction as he looked back to see the watcher falling farther and farther behind. To make his point, he sat down and adopted a relaxed attitude, and by the time the watcher appeared again, his anger was under control.

But despite his intentions, he felt uneasy with the stranger standing over him, and stood up, trying not to let the reason show in his manner. 'Now, an explanation.' He phrased it deliberately, avoiding any hint of a request, and the watcher regarded him steadily for a moment.

'I think, for the avoidance of boring you with repetition, it would be better if I spoke to you and your people together.'

Biting back an impatient retort, Arric considered. Would it be, not only folly, but actually dangerous to bring this man into his home? What if he was one of the Moorlanders' go-betweens, working for Tir? But Mylan had not yet left, and even if this mortal were able to take them by surprise and steal the child, he could not move fast enough to leave the place alive.

He nodded. 'You will surrender your blade before you enter my home.'

But the watcher only laughed. 'Blade? What use would I have for one of those?' He spread his hands, indicating he neither carried a weapon, nor had one strapped to his hip. He wore mortal clothing, snug fitting about the torso, with short sleeves, and the same kind of leggings many of them wore in varying shades of blue, with pockets too small and tight to be of any real use.

Arric had to accept the watcher carried no weapon, but kept a careful eye on him as he gestured for him to lead the way. 'You clearly know where to go.'

'I do,' the man smiled again, infuriatingly, and set off towards Arric's home.

Once there, having moved at his irritatingly slow, mortal pace, the watcher stood aside to let Arric enter first. He didn't take his eyes off Arric as the elemental passed by him, and Arric tried to appear unaffected but couldn't help a little shiver as he considered the implications of being involuntarily visible to mortals.

Inside, Mylan looked up with an impatient grunt. 'About time. I want to get as far as I can before it becomes dark. Nerryn is in the…' His voice sharpened. 'Who is this?' He stared beyond Arric, to where the watcher now stood in the doorway. 'Arric, what have you done?'

'Don't blame him.' The watcher came into the room and looked around him with interest, ignoring the fact that Mylan was now on his feet, his hand hovering over his blade. 'I am unarmed, and intend no intrusion,' he went on. His tone had lost that faintly arrogant sound and now sounded sincere.

Mylan did not draw his weapon, but his voice was hard. 'Who are you, mortal, and how is it you can see and remember us?'

'I have travelled from... actually, could I sit down? I'd like to talk properly to you both.'

'Where is Nerryn?' Arric said.

'She is bathing the—' Mylan stopped himself, then went on. 'She is busy.'

'Bathing the child? The one belonging to the Moorlander king?' The Watcher smiled again. 'You people aren't as careful as you think. The boy's mortal too. You ought to bear that in mind next time you go carrying him around outside.' His voice took on a faintly sarcastic tone. 'You're welcome.'

Arric exchanged a glance with his brother, whose face wore a bemused look. What was going on? How long had the watcher been following them?

'Sit, then.' Mylan indicated a seat at the table, and he and Arric drew out their own chairs and sat down to await an explanation. Mylan kept shooting glares Arric's way, but Arric only returned them; the watcher might have approached anyone, and Mylan was the one who had been carrying the totterling, after all.

He shook off the niggling insistence that the watcher had chosen him because of his activities at sea, and took the opportunity, in the silence as they all waited for someone else to speak, to seize control of the conversation. 'What is your name?'

The bearded man shrugged. 'I had a name, but I don't need it now. What would you call me?'

'You would have us choose your name?' Mylan said, surprised. 'Is this an indication that you are looking to *join* us?'

The man's eyes slipped from one to the other, and Arric saw a glimmer of hope there. 'If you'll have me.'

'Why?'

'I've watched you. I've seen the hard work you do, the honest life you have here.'

'Why not go back to the mortal world?' Mylan wanted to know.

'I've seen too much of it. I'll tell you everything, if you'll take me in.' His voice turned eager. 'Let me work for your coast lord. I'll earn my shelter and my food.'

'Tell us all first,' Arric said. '*Then* we decide if you belong with us. You're mortal, for the Ocean's sake! Do you suppose we welcome anyone with open arms?'

'These are turbulent times, as I'm sure you know,' Mylan agreed. 'You are aware of the child Dreis, and his relationship to the Moorlanders, how much else do you know?'

'A name first, if you please?'

Arric nodded. 'Very well. We will call you Hewyl.'

The man thought for a moment, then nodded. 'Watchful? A good choice, I'll take it.'

Mylan laced his hands on the table before him. 'So, Hewyl, it seems it's your turn to give us something back. I will put off my leaving until the morning. Arric, fetch Nerryn.'

Arric almost told him to do it himself, but a glance at the newly-named Hewyl told him it was too late to try and regain control of this; Mylan had, in his quiet way, stolen it yet again. His brother's tone rankled, and Arric sought to make it sound less as if he had received an order.

'A good idea,' he said, forcing approval into his voice. 'It will save me making the explanations again later. When you're gone,' he added pointedly to Mylan as he rose. Leaving the two of them to their silent, speculative contemplation of one another, he went through to the rooms at the back. 'Nerryn! I have returned.'

She pulled back the thick crimson curtain and stepped into the passage. 'Good. Mylan wants to leave, but he still doesn't—' She stopped as her attention travelled past him and lit on the newcomer in the main room. Her eyes widened. 'Who is this mortal you have brought?'

'His name is Hewyl.' Arric made sure his voice travelled well. 'He has a tale to tell us, of spying and begging, and he does not want to tell it twice. Come through and join us.'

'Spying and begging?' Hewyl sat up straight, and his face had darkened. 'Allowing me into your house hardly gives you the right to hurl insults.'

'And what would you call it?' Arric demanded, with disdain. 'By your own confession you have lain in shadow and watched us. Now you have asked us for shelter and food. Spying and begging.'

He stalked back to the table, having taken the situation in hand once again and grateful Mylan had not argued. That the stranger posed a threat there was no doubt, but to bend and bow to him would be a very big mistake.

Arric wanted nothing more than to pour some wine, but if he did so he would be compelled to offer some to their guest. Instead he contented himself with fixing Hewyl with a steady look, and waited for the boring and predictable mortal reaction to Nerryn's beauty.

But Hewyl merely nodded at her when she emerged from the back room. 'I trust you and the child are well?'

Nerryn ignored him and turned, instead, to her brothers. 'Who is this?' she asked again. 'Why has he come into our home?'

The newcomer did not give his hosts a chance to answer. 'My name is Hewyl now, as your brother said. But my tale is not as he described it.' He bowed his head and was quiet for a moment, but just as Arric was about to lose patience, he sat up straight and started to talk again.

'When I was a child I saw something that terrified me. So much so, that I hid it, even from myself. Somehow I pushed it away into a little box in my mind, but as I grew older it began to leak out. I thought I was losing my mind, I had to find out what I'd seen, and to learn what it meant. So I started in Africa.' He saw their blank expressions, and shook his head. 'It doesn't matter, it's a far-off place, and the people there are deeply superstitious. I learned a great deal, enough to know I couldn't live among other mortals again. So, since I came back I've watched you. Not just you, but the Moorlanders, the Foresters… even the spriggans and buccas. Your people are the closest I have seen to the perfect way of life.'

'And how did you find us, and learn *how* to watch us?' Nerryn wanted to know.

'I started with the Moorlanders of course. They are more careless than most. Some of them even move among the mortals in the village. I grew to understand them, to become attuned to the way they cloak themselves in the daylight. Once I knew, I found that, with a little concentration I could see through the ripples, and after a while my eyes found them easily.' He gave a brief, appreciative smile. 'So many! I'd never dreamed… Well anyway, when I came to the coast I saw you, and because I had no barrier of disbelief my mind did not dismiss, or forget you.'

There was a pause while the siblings took this in, and considered what it meant.

Then Arric spoke. 'And why should we take you in?'

'Because I can help you win the war.'

Arric, Mylan and Nerryn looked at one another, and Hewyl smiled. 'It *will be* a war, although the Moorlanders don't know it yet.'

'They will soon enough,' Arric said, ignoring

Mylan's warning glare. 'You might be of use to us after all.'

'Oh, yes,' Nerryn said icily. 'He can watch over me while you two play your power games. Mylan has been waiting for you to return, Arric, so he may leave, to go to our mother's people and secure their support in this *war* you both seem so insistent upon.' She stood up and poured wine into a single goblet, neatly avoiding the necessity of offering any to their guest, by offering none to her brothers either. 'You still treat me as though I am likely to take up Dreis and run back to the murdering Moorlanders!'

'I trust you,' Mylan protested. 'We only remain with you to protect—'

'Stop it!' Nerryn snapped. 'Do not treat me like a fool as well as a traitor. I am as much a child needing care as Tir's son is. Well, now you have allowed this mortal into our lives you're *both* free to run away and play.'

'No decision has been reached,' Mylan pointed out. 'Cantoc is the only one who can accept Hewyl.' He switched his gaze to the newcomer. 'We will go there now, let you make your claims to him about how you will help win the war. Hear your reasons for such an arrogant certainty.'

'And if they ring true, then let Cantoc extend his own offer of shelter and food,' Arric added. 'We have none. We have an extra mouth to feed as it stands.'

He stood, ready to escort Hewyl to Cantoc's home, but Mylan rose too. 'I will take him.'

'Had enough totterling-tending?' Arric sent a thin smile his sister's way. '*Two* children must be such a bother, Mylan.'

Mylan's brow darkened. 'When you mock our sister as a child, are you forgetting I am of an age with her?'

'I think we all know the number of cycles we have seen has little to do with our ability to be trusted alone,' Arric said softly. Before either Mylan or Nerryn could answer he waved a hand. 'Go on, then. I'm tired anyway.'

At least it felt as if he were giving them permission, which took some of the sting out of Mylan's habitual control-taking. He'd have given much to have seen Cantoc's reaction to Hewyl, but for now it would be pleasant enough to remain behind and enjoy some peace and tranquillity. He could always try the beach for more reward tomorrow.

'Pour me some wine,' he said, on a yawn, when they'd gone. Nerryn merely looked at him, her features set in a scowl, and Arric sighed and went to the shelf to pour his own. He settled into the chair opposite his dead father's, and had no sooner raised his goblet to his lips, than a soft thump came from the back room, followed by a rising wail.

'Dreis has fallen from the bed again,' Nerryn said, needlessly. 'No matter, his landing will not have injured him, the bed is low and I have placed cushions all around it.' As if he cared for the child's comfort. She put her wine down on the shelf and crossed the room. 'He will not sleep now, though, so I fear your rest will be disturbed, Arric.'

She turned her face away as she passed him, but before she did, Arric could have sworn he saw her smile.

Chapter Fourteen

Lynher Mill. 8am, September 27th

Dear Miss Riley
Re: Benjamin Dean Lucas.
An appointment has been made for Benjamin's twelve month check-up and vaccinations…

For a moment Laura wished she hadn't asked Ann to forward the post from the flat, but that wouldn't have solved anything; the appointment would still have been made. And even if it hadn't, sooner or later someone was going to get concerned enough to try and contact her anyway.

Just the sight of her son's name on the letter made her heart lurch painfully, and her arms felt emptier than ever. To think of all the times she'd complained about how heavy he was getting… she'd never have guessed she would one day give anything to feel that weight pulling on her shoulders again. So why the hell was she just sitting here, panicking about some stupid doctor's appointment?

Abruptly she shoved her chair back and stood up; when she'd made her promise to Richard they'd both been halfway convinced Maer would turn up before the morning, holding their son. She was finished with waiting. For a moment she thought about his warning, the danger she would be in, but if things were so dangerous then surely that was all the more reason she should go. Instinct was something she had learned to trust, and until she had seen with her own eyes that Ben was unhurt, and unafraid, she would damned well fight for him.

She seized the thick jumper that hung over the back of her chair, and stopped to take another look around the kitchen where Jane had died, and where poor, faithful Captain had given his own life to protect her. She blinked hard to ease the pockets of dry heat her eyes were sitting in, picked up her keys, and left. To hell with promises.

The road to the coast was less busy now the schools had started up again. Even driving through the Glyn Valley towards Bodmin was fast and easy, and once through to the other side, and onto the dual carriageway again, she put her foot down harder still, and arrived at Trethkellis a little more than an hour after leaving Lynher Mill.

She left the car in the deserted clifftop car-park, and walked quickly down towards the cliff's edge. Her heart thumped hard at the thought that Ben was so close, and she looked around, her loose ponytail tugged almost free of its scrunchie by the wind that blew, salty and strong, off the sea.

The tide was in, she could hear it crashing and frothing over the rocks far below, and she tried not to think of the possibility that Ben might have defied hers and Richard's expectation that he'd bypass crawling, and go straight to walking... She took a deep breath. If she didn't find Nerryn's home soon she'd fall apart completely.

The popular tourist village of Trethkellis lay down the hill to her left, so Laura turned right instead and took the cliff path, keeping her eyes on the moving grasses either side of her as she walked. Now and again she shifted her gaze further ahead, but saw nothing to give her any hope that a family of elementals might live nearby.

She finally rounded a headland, puffing with exertion and almost running now, but skidded to a halt as she saw a tall, strongly-built man, climbing the narrow path with the ease of someone born to it. She dropped to a crouch behind a grass-topped dune, her heart in her mouth. Could this be Nerryn's father?

The stranger carried himself with the poise of one in complete control; strength made grace by the smoothness of the walk, the way he held his head, and the long, easy stride. A fierce ache took hold of Laura as she saw echoes of Richard in the man's movements. The place he had emerged from was below the lip of the cliff, so she couldn't see if anyone else was there. She waited a few minutes, but if it was Nerryn's father, he was alone. Perhaps they lived further along the cliff?

She had taken only a few more steps along the coast path when all the strength ran out of her legs, and she pitched to her knees. There he was. Her child, for whose weight her own arms yearned, was twenty feet away in the arms of an impossibly beautiful young man, who bore such a strong resemblance to Nerryn it could only be her twin brother.

As she watched, the young man blew a gentle raspberry against Ben's face, and Laura could feel her son's soft skin on her own lips. Her heart tightened so much she thought she might actually die here, on the clifftop, but Ben's giggle broke the spell, and, through the wash of tears that almost blinded her, Laura saw Nerryn's brother raise the boy towards the sky, and heard him laugh in return. Maer had told the truth, then. She leaned forward until her head rested on her knees, and let her shuddering breath steady before she raised it again.

Nerryn had emerged from what Laura could see now was a cave, cut into the side of the cliff. There was even a doorway... how had she not seen it before? Farther along the cliff she saw another door. And another. All with covered doorways, and the coverings themselves were heavy-looking curtains of... perhaps leather, each decorated differently. A rock hung on a rope on the frames over which the curtains were hung, and each dwelling had a sizeable wooden box, tightly lidded, outside. The more she saw, the more she realised they had always been there but her mind had not allowed them in until now. Until she had seen Ben in their world.

Maer's fiancée reached out to lift Ben from her

brother's grasp, and her words carried as clearly to Laura as Ben's chuckle had. 'I know you will miss him, Mylan, but it's time you started out.'

'I won't miss him,' Mylan replied, a little defensively, then grinned. 'Alright, yes, I will. A little. He's a bonny totterling and he seems to like me.'

'Which is more than can be said for our dear brother. It is no surprise you would rather spend time with Dreis than with Arric.'

'I would rather spend time with a jellyfish than with Arric,' Mylan said drily. 'Better conversation, and infinitely more intelligence.' He smoothed Ben's hair and squeezed the boy's round little shoulder—Laura's fingers mirrored the gesture, in empty air—'I will return soon, Dreis. Feel free to make Arric's life miserable until then.'

Nerryn gave a little laugh, and Laura wanted to run over, to rip her child from between them, and scream that people's lives were being destroyed while they played at happy families. She clenched her fingers into fists on her knees, and made herself stay put. Mylan was going somewhere, and Nerryn would be alone.

She settled herself more comfortably in the grass, keeping out of sight of the twins and Ben, and waited. Before long Mylan came outside again, this time clad in clothing that made Laura gasp and sit upright. They were clearly travelling clothes; leggings, boots laced to the knee to keep brambles and thistles from snagging them, a belt hung with all kinds of implements, and a bag bulging with God only knew what. But it wasn't the fact that Mylan was dressed for travelling that had caught Laura's attention, but that he looked so familiar; if he had been a woman he might have been her drawing, come to life. It must, then, have been Nerryn she'd seen and drawn.

It gave her an odd, faintly dizzy sensation to realise all the seemingly disjointed parts of her life that were in fact intertwined, and with something very like fascination Laura watched him put the finishing touches to his travel attire, fastening a warm cloak with some kind of brooch, and checking the knife that sat on his hip. He spoke to his sister in a voice too low for Laura to hear, and then leaned in and kissed her on the forehead before doing the same to Ben. A moment later he was gone, and Nerryn had taken Ben back into their home. Laura's heart picked up; it was time.

She rose, wincing at the stiffness in her knees from sitting in the same position for too long, and was momentarily swayed by a memory of sitting on dry, dusty ground and feeling the same ache in her bones. She couldn't place it, and brushed it aside as she gave herself a moment to loosen up before approaching the side of the cliff.

Her mind was already working on how she would climb down the short but steep distance to the door, when another thought froze her in her tracks; if that much was going to be difficult, how the hell would she get back up, and with Ben? For a second she hesitated, but her feet moved her forwards again, the pull of her child, so close, giving her no thought of turning back.

When she reached the edge of the cliff she saw a rough track had been hewn into the rock, winding back on itself to create a shallower climb, and she let out a little laugh of relief. Soon she would see him. Hold him. Soon…

A second later she felt hard fingers grab her arm, and before she could draw enough breath to scream, a hand was across her mouth.

***

The edge of the forest loomed dark and threatening just ahead. Jacky stopped, his aching legs trembling, threatening to drop him to the ground should he dwell on their weakness. He raised his gaze to the tops of the closest trees. *Yes, trees! Find your courage, Greencoat. That strength you were so proud of! They're just trees.*

Jacky took a step forward, and stopped. The terror of the woods ran so deep in him, he didn't know if he'd be able to take another breath until he was out at the other side. Surely he could go around instead, the way he had on his way to the coast. But no. Time was too precious; if Tir and Maer were not told of Arric's intentions they would all die.

That Arric and his Coastals would themselves number among the dead gave Jacky no pleasure; the land would be laid to waste from the Lizard right up through Cornwall, and to the larger world beyond.

Who could tell how far? Those who survived the storms would have nothing to sustain them, and the elementals and little folk alike could not leave, unlike the mortals. Their early deaths would be just as sure, if a little longer coming.

He shuddered, and curled his stubby hands into fists. It made him feel stronger, just a little, and he forced himself to take the first steps into the forest. If those fiendish *trigoryon an goswig* were abroad during the day they would likely be sluggish, and, more importantly, up to no good – they would be the ones hiding, and Jacky need have no fear.

He made himself think, instead, about what the Moorlanders might do to stop Arric's deadly plan, to protect themselves and the land, but there seemed nothing for it except to separate Nerryn from her twin forever… the thought brought a rush of sickness and Jacky stopped again, resting a hand on the nearest tree, and breathing deeply.

After a moment the urgency came upon him again and he turned to follow the path that led deeper into the forest. His feet throbbed with the long days' walking, and although he was not hungry he felt weak and shaky.

Exhaustion was creeping over him, draining his strength with every step, but the thought of resting here, in the forest, made him want to run. The sun was already beginning to slide downward in the sky, and once it dipped below the horizon the Foresters would be awake and starting to roam … Jacky's flesh wanted to crawl off his bones.

Martha Horncup had fallen foul of these evil beings, but even before then Jacky had known they were bad through and through. Something about their pale skin; their piercing eyes that seemed to see through, not only the dark, but also the words of their fellow creatures, and right into their hearts; their swift and agile movement, as they ran unerringly through root-strewn pathways and over fallen trees.

They claimed to be allied to the Moorlanders, yet never paid anything more than a cursory respect to the royals, and Jacky had often heard Casta and Deera talking after they had visited the forest, of how they had felt tolerated at best. Could the Foresters be trusted, should they be needed in the fight to come? Or would they retreat into their gloomy lives and let the Moorlanders and the Coastals battle for control between them? They would be likely to bend the knee to whichever was the victor, never suspecting that, if Arric had his way, their home would be smashed to firewood around them.

Jacky had not been walking beneath the canopy of branches for more time than it took to worry through these thoughts, before he realised his heart had gradually slowed to a more peaceful rhythm. The lazy rustle of leaves was curiously calming, and the way the light dappled the path ahead of him, always changing, drew his eyes back from their worried squinting into the shadows.

It gradually crept through his wondering and

newly-understanding mind that the forest, far from a dark den of terror, was truly a place of cool, dimly-lit beauty, and he silently scolded his frightened self for always listening to his fears instead of his natural curiosity. He even managed a smile, as he glimpsed a grey squirrel leaping up the trunk of a nearby oak tree and disappearing into the branches.

Trees gave life, this was something everyone knew, and there was shelter here for all manner of creatures. Maybe even himself, if he found somewhere well away from the known Forester homelands. It would be preferable to the awful, wide-open sea, at least. Some of the trees he passed were twisted and bent, but hollowed out and their floors coated with a thick fall of leaves – comfortable and quiet, and provided he kept to himself he could be safe here, the rest of his days… But such thoughts were for another time.

He picked up his pace again, wondering how long he must walk before he would see open ground once more. He felt a momentary flicker of unease when he thought of presenting himself at Lynher Mill after all that had happened, but surely Maer would not turn him away, not when realised the importance of the news he brought. And although Tir would never forgive him for allowing Dreis to be taken, perhaps his fury would be lessened once Jacky helped him to get the boy back.

'Spriggan!'

He stopped in shock, almost tripping over his own feet, and turned to see two Foresters stepping out of the trees onto the path behind him. They were young, but not children, rather they held themselves with the arrogance of youth but without its tempering innocence. Jacky's blood ran cold.

'What are you doing in the forest?' the taller of the youngsters wanted to know. 'Spriggans never come here anymore.'

'I am bound for Lynher Mill,' Jacky managed. 'To see the king.' He wanted to turn back, to continue his journey, but something about the way they looked at him pinned him, helpless.

'Why would the Moorlander king want to see the likes of you?' the shorter boy said. 'Are you his servant now?'

'I always served the king,' Jacky's voice strengthened. 'I have been pledged since birth to the Lightning, no matter who wields it.'

The taller boy peered closer, and his eyes widened. 'Keityn, this is Greencoat! The one who lost Dreis!'

Jacky's breath caught, and he cursed the pride that had spoken through him. To be recognised by these loathsome creatures was worse than never to be recognised by anyone again. His voice dropped until it was hardly above a whisper. 'Please, I must go, I have important news.'

'Greencoat died,' the one called Keityn protested. 'Gerai killed him. This must be some other spriggan. They all look the same.'

'Ugly, and not worth grieving over,' the taller one agreed. 'But I'm certain of it nevertheless.'

Jacky tried again. 'I have news for the Lord Tir, please—'

'News for Tir?' Keityn glanced at his companion. 'Did you hear that, Lyelt? The spriggan is far too important to stop and talk to the likes of us, even when he treads on Forester lands. Uninvited.' He said this last very clearly as he moved a few steps closer, and Jacky fought against the screaming instinct to turn and run.

'It is a matter of grave importance,' he stammered. 'Of life itself! The Coastals are going to destroy everything!' His voice rose, and Lyelt's eyes narrowed as he too came closer. Jacky pleaded again, 'Arric means to wield powers he does not understand—'

'What powers?' Lyelt demanded.

'That of his brother and sister... he thinks they will win Lynher Mill, but...' His voice trailed away into a whisper, 'they will end all life.'

'End it how?'

'Please, there is no time, I must tell the king!'

'We'll tell him,' Keityn said. 'You wait here like a good spriggan and rest, and we'll go to Lynher Mill in your place. We can move more quickly, after all.'

Jacky sagged in relief, and almost thanked them until he saw a glance flash between them and realised he would be lucky to see open land again, never mind send his message to Tir. He stepped back, they stepped forward. Quick as a dragonfly, Lyelt's hand shot out and grasped one of Jacky's arms, and Keityn moved to seize his other. He wrenched himself backwards, taking them by surprise with his sudden surge of frantic strength, and staggered as he realised he'd actually broken free.

But it was a short-lived freedom; before he had taken more than two steps towards the densely packed trees Lyelt had grabbed him again, and yanked him around. Jacky flailed wildly and, just as Gerai had with Arric, he struck a lucky blow, this time in the boy's midriff. Lyelt grunted but did not let go.

Keityn took a firm hold of Jacky's arm, and twisted it up behind his back. He looked at Lyelt. 'What do we do with him?'

'Why do you ask me?' Lyelt sounded as though he was having trouble breathing, and despite his dry-mouthed terror, Jacky felt a little tingle of satisfaction. He would have dearly loved the chance to hit the Forester again, but Keityn would not be so foolish as to let him escape a second time.

'One of us should go to the coast and ask Mylan what he wants us to do,' Lyelt said. 'He has the charge of Cantoc's affairs. All I know is neither of them would want that news getting to Lynher Mill.'

'I am the faster runner,' Keityn said quickly. 'You are taller, you should be able to guard the spriggan more easily.'

'I am just as fast!'

'You are not! We saw that when we were practicing for the leader challenge.'

'We don't have time to argue,' Lyelt said in a sour voice. 'Very well, I will guard. You go to Mylan.'

Keityn waited until Lyelt had taken Jacky's arm, and then stepped away, eyeing Jacky mistrustfully. 'Keep a tight hold of him,' he warned.

Jacky could hear the scowl in Lyelt's voice, even as the boy shifted his grip. 'What did you think I was going to do? Just go, since you're so fast.'

Keityn seemed to melt back into the trees, and Jacky reluctantly appreciated the lithe, graceful way he wove through the knotted and twisted trunks until he was out of sight.

Lyelt pulled Jacky over to the edge of the path and pushed him against a tree, holding one hand against the spriggan's chest to keep him there.

'If you try to run again I'll catch you,' the Forester promised. 'And by all the elements, I will make you pay for hitting me.'

Jacky wondered if the lie would stick in his throat, but it came surprisingly easily, in the end. 'Jacky is so sorry, sir. Jacky will never again raise a hand against such a noble son of the forest.'

'I should hit you back,' Lyelt went on, 'but the fact that I haven't just proves I'm better than you.'

'Indeed you are.'

Lyelt lifted his hand away, leaving Jacky standing alone and horribly aware of the hugeness of the forest around him, and the way the shadows were lengthening. While there was only one Forester he felt strangely confident he would remain unharmed, but Lyelt seemed the type of mid-grown who would enjoy tormenting him should there suddenly be an audience.

'Beggin' your pardon, sir,' he said, 'but I have walked a long way and my speed is not as swift as an elemental's. I have been journeying many days to get this far. Might I sit?'

'Stand on your head if you must,' Lyelt said. 'Just stay by that tree and do not think to run.' He sat down himself, still looking a little green and nauseous.

Jacky sank gratefully to the foot of the tree, and turned his thoughts towards what must be done. How long would it take a fast-moving elemental like Keityn to reach the coast? If Jacky moved too soon Lyelt would suspect, but if he left it too long the chance would slip away... The time crept by, the sun dipped lower, and finally Jacky's nerves were stretched so thin he knew it had to be now, or lose everything.

His head had been tucked down into his chest for a while now, so he kept it there, and felt a tingle low in his throat as he worked the muscles there in preparation. A tightening here and there, a half-swallow...

'Lyelt!' The voice came out of the trees, and Jacky glanced up to see Lyelt sit up straight and turn towards the sound. 'Leave him! Arric has a fury on him, and he is coming! If he sees us with the spriggan he will kill us!'

'Why?' Lyelt shouted back.

'Just leave him! Come with me!'

Lyelt looked back at Jacky, his eyes wide and fearful, and Jacky saw that the child in him had not yet been conquered by the man after all. Lyelt yelled again, still watching Jacky. 'Wait for me!' He scrambled to his feet, his boots sliding on the loose leaves that carpeted the path, and lurched into a run towards Keityn's voice.

Before the Forester was even out of sight, Jacky was on his feet also. Then, exhausted or not, he too was running. Running to save his own life, and that of the Moorlanders, with relief and savage satisfaction pushing him on. Running home.

Chapter Fifteen

Her first thought was *Arric!* But the voice that spoke, low and rough in her ear, was not his.

'Shut up! They'll hear you!' The hand slackened off a tiny bit and Laura tasted dirt and sweat and was reminded, with a pang of fear, of Gilan. The voice spoke again. 'Now, will you keep quiet?'

She nodded, and the hand fell away. Immediately she twisted to look at her assailant, and saw a tall, lean, bearded man. Undoubtedly as human as she was, his hair was matted into dreadlocks, and his clothing hadn't seen a washing machine, probably forever. Lean he might be, but he was strong, she'd felt that even in the short time he'd gripped her arm.

He was half-turned away from her, checking the pathway down to the house, and Laura would have taken her chance to run, but Ben was down there. This shabby tramp had stopped her going to him…

Her fury erupted. 'Who the hell do you—'

'Shut up, Laura!' The man whipped back, and Laura blinked in astonishment.

'*Michael?*'

'This lot call me Hewyl.'

'What the blue bloody *fuck* are you doing here?'

He raised an eyebrow. 'When did you start swearing? And, by the way, I might ask you the same question.'

This utterly surreal moment was making Laura dizzy, and she shook her head. 'Look, I need your help. They've got my boy.'

'*Your* boy?' Michael studied her closely. 'Dreis is yours?'

'Ben!' She almost screamed it, but at the last moment changed it to a fierce hiss, mindful of his warning they would be heard. 'His name is Ben. They stole him. I'm going to get him back.'

'Not right now you're not.' Michael caught hold of her hand and walked away, dragging her with him. He pulled her up over the slope towards the cliff path. She resisted at first, but he yanked harder and she stumbled after him, her shoulder aching.

'Let go!' She tried to tear her hand free but he held it tighter, grinding her fingers together until she yelped. 'You bastard! I'm going back to get Ben!'

'If you go in there you'll put him in as much danger as you'll put yourself.'

Laura let out a disbelieving bark of laughter. 'Danger? From Nerryn?'

'She's not alone.' Michael stopped, but did not release her; if he had she wouldn't baulk at kicking him where it would hurt most, and running back to the Coastals' home. He clearly knew that; he was eyeing her feet warily. 'Her brother has left now, but they don't trust her. I don't even know if I do.'

'And how do I know to trust *you*? What *are* you

doing here?'

'You can. Trust me, I mean. But it's hard to say whose side Nerryn's on.'

'What? I don't... Michael, please! Help me get Ben back, then you can explain everything. Just...' her throat closed up, and she couldn't continue.

'We can't. I'm sorry. Not yet.' Michael eased up on his grip at last, and Laura slid her hand out from his, but the news about Nerryn had taken the wind from her sails and she didn't even try to run. She saw Michael's set shoulders relax, and his voice softened.

'Sweetheart, listen to me. Ben is safe. Cantoc is with them, and will be until Arric gets back from his latest wrecking spree.'

Laura shook her head. There was too much going on. 'Wrecking? Wrecking what?'

'It doesn't matter. Look, I promise I'll help you,' Michael said. 'But you'll have to let me do it my way.'

'How?'

Michael eyed her carefully. 'I'm almost one of them now. I plan to join them, if they'll have me.'

Laura just stared at him, not sure she had heard properly.

'We have to talk,' he went on quietly, 'but not here. I'll tell you what I know, and then you can tell me how...' he glanced back in the direction they had just come, 'how it came about that *you* have a child with the Moorlander king.'

Laura's heart thumped painfully at that; as if Richard was some distant entity already, just the ruler of some far-off country she had never heard of, and would never visit.

'Come back home with me, then.' She saw his trapped expression, probably before he knew he'd made it, and managed a wry smile. 'Don't worry. I don't mean forever.'

'Why, then?'

Laura looked over at the cliff. 'Because if I stay here any longer, this close to Ben, I'm going to go in there after him,' she said. 'And I'm pretty sure they'll kill us both if I do.'

'Or keep you both captive. And you can bet your ass Arric will make sure Tir finds out you're—'

'Alright!' She closed her eyes against the image of Richard walking into the trap she would have blindly set out for him. 'I get it.'

'Okay.' He looked relieved. 'I'll come back to Lynher Mill with you. And I'll explain all I know. I owe you that, at least.'

It took every scrap of strength Laura possessed to drive away from Trethkellis car park. She couldn't speak, and Michael didn't either, until he rummaged in the glove box and came out with a CD.

'Laura's driving CD,' he read aloud. 'Re-write on pain of death. Oh, yeah.' He gave a soft laugh and the familiarity of it, now she couldn't see his stranger's face, almost made her cry. 'Sorry about that. But I never did it again, did I?' He slotted the CD into the player and Laura immediately ejected it again; the memory of driving to Land's End with Richard, and of listening to him singing absently along to the tracks while he watched the countryside speed by, was something she wouldn't share. Not with anyone.

Michael didn't question her action, he just stared out of his window, and Laura watched the road, and they arrived in Lynher Mill as the sun hit the top of its daily arc. It felt as if she'd been away for days rather than a few short hours.

'You can have a shower,' she said, throwing her keys onto the coffee table. 'Some of Richard's things might fit you, more or less. There are some still in the wardrobe.' She fixed him with a warning look, before he could correct the name. 'In this house his name is Richard, and if you just once call him by any other name you're out.'

'Fair enough.'

'You can use his razor too.'

'I won't need it.'

Laura watched him go up the stairs of the house they had bought together, so long ago. The familiarity of him in these surroundings was an odd, but comforting thing. Michael Hart: childhood friend, teenage crush, adult lover... Abruptly she remembered that sooner or later she would have to tell him about Jane. Would it never end?

A short while later he came downstairs. Her mind filled with Ben, Laura had almost forgotten he was there, and she jumped when he came into the kitchen where she was listlessly stirring baked beans. She'd never felt less like eating, but if her walk along the coast path today had told her anything, it was that she would need to re-build her strength for what lay ahead.

Michael had not shaved, nor washed his dreadlock-matted hair, but he'd found a T shirt; the white one Richard usually wore for travelling. It wasn't a bad fit, but it hung loose on Michael's chest where it had once clung to Richard's, and it was a little too short for Michael's lanky frame. Just the sight of it, with its familiar frayed neckline, made her longing for Richard return with a crashing pain, and she spent the next few minutes looking anywhere but at Michael. At that shirt.

When there was no choice but to sit opposite him, she watched him eat while she pushed beans around her plate, and waited for him to explain everything.

'How's Tom?' Michael asked eventually, around a forkful of food.

For a moment she thought she'd mis-heard, or that he'd said the wrong name. '*How's Tom*?' She shook her head. 'How can you know about everything that's out there,' she waved at the window, 'and about who Richard is, yet not know about Tom?'

He paled, and replaced the fork on his plate. 'Oh, Christ. Tom was... *he* was the one Loen went into?'

She nodded, not trusting herself to speak; Michael's blue eyes, those eyes she'd fallen in love with at the age of thirteen, had filled with unexpected tears, and she knew hers were every bit as bright.

When he was at last able to speak again, his voice was very quiet. 'You said you hadn't done it.'

'Done what?'

'Gone down the mine. When we were kids.'

'You were the one who dared us!'

'But you told me you never did it! You *told* me... you both said you'd been caught out, and weren't allowed any further than the stones.'

'And what were we supposed to say?' Laura couldn't believe what she was hearing. 'Were we meant to tell you we'd seen some crazy goblin bloke down there? Someone who cried, and threw curses at us? For God's sake, Michael, Tom was coming unhinged! Weird things were happening, and he was going out of his mind. All we could do was push it down until it got covered by enough... enough *life* to let us forget it for a while.'

She took a deep breath and spoke again, lowering her voice. 'Why did you, anyway?'

'What?'

'Why did you dare us?' She saw the answer in his face, but she had to hear it. 'Tell me.'

'Because I saw it too.'

She spoke flatly, unsurprised. 'You saw it.'

'Just one. A spriggan, I found out later. I thought I was going mad, I had to know it was real. I needed someone else to see it too.'

'You bastard.' But her voice was bleak.

'I'm sorry.' He reached for her hand. '*So,* so sorry.'

'Why didn't you tell us?'

'Because you'd have thought I was losing it, and

told some grown-up. Or refused to go, or even made some big joke out of it around school... I had to *know*, Laura!'

'So, now you do.' She pulled her hand away and stood up. 'And what about when you left, after we'd bought this place, what was that really about?'

'I had to get away,' he admitted, his eyes following her movements as she pulled a bottle of wine from the fridge. 'Isn't it a bit—'

'If you're going to say *early for that*,' Laura said grimly, 'I'd advise against it. Go on.'

He shrugged and let it go, talking between mouthfuls. 'Over the years, stuff I thought I'd hidden started to slip back out. I was... there were dreams. I kept seeing things.' His voice was shaking now. 'I didn't know you'd have understood, how could I? I wanted to go somewhere far enough away that I could forget this life, and learn about the ones no-one ever sees. So, I went to Africa. Spent some time among the people there.'

'And what did you find out?'

'They're very superstitious. And less bloody-minded about accepting it. I learned more in three years there than twenty in St Tourney, or Lynher Mill. When I left Africa I went to New Zealand, then Japan. The more I learned, the more I saw.'

Laura nodded. 'I can see them now too, whether they want me to or not.'

'They use our blindness, or rather our blinkered vision, as their defence.' Michael relaxed now he was on familiar ground. 'It's easy for the Moorlanders to wrap themselves in daylight, or shadow, and they blend with what's around them in that way.'

He pushed his half-empty plate aside and leaned forwards, linking his hands. 'The Coastals do it differently. Unless they choose otherwise, we'll see them and forget them in the same instant. But once the barrier is down, once we *know* they're there, they can't hide from us. Any more than another human can.'

'But hardly any of us has reached that point.'

'Exactly. They're everywhere, Laura, you know that. The Foresters use almost the same technique as the Moorlanders, but they're not so good with light. Only darkness. That's partly why they could never rule in their own right.'

'How long have you been watching them here?'

'I started in Scotland, nearly two years ago, then came down the west coast.' He shook his head. 'It's amazing. In some parts of Wales they catch what they call gwyllgi. Hell-hounds. Servants of the bwca until the Coastals get hold of them. Coastals can never properly tame them, but the hounds know they'll feed well if they don't turn on their new masters.'

Laura shuddered. 'And if they do?'

'Salt, I'm told, is one of the few things that can kill them. That and iron. They learn quickly, apparently.'

'What do the Coastals want with them?'

'Kind of a power play I suppose. Intimidation. Or maybe it's just a visible defence, like carrying a knife.'

Laura tried, unsuccessfully, to banish the image of Cantoc's blade slicing into Richard's chest. 'So then you came here?'

'After a short while, yes. You and Ti… you and Richard were in Plymouth by then. I arrived last summer, after you'd left.'

'You could still have found me. Why didn't you even visit? I thought we'd parted friends, at least.' She tried not to sound petulant, but she heard her own words as plaintive and needy, although he didn't appear to.

'I'm trying to get out of the human race,' he said quietly. 'It stinks. There are other lives. Better ones. Honest ones.'

'What, and my life isn't honest?' Her voice had an edge now.

'Don't take it personally. I've seen so much of the same crappy stuff, in so many different places. There has to be a better existence, I believe that. But it's not in the mortal world.'

'Oh, for crying out loud!'

He shook his head, his expression grim. 'No, listen to me. This life has so little goodness left, but no-one in their right mind wants to throw it away. Of course we don't. So we stick around, in the hopes that something will change. But it never does, and it never will.'

'You are so full of yourself!' Laura poured a generous glassful of wine, and drank half of it in quick gulps. His words chilled her, the thought that the human race was basically only wandering around in confusion, that fear of death was the only thing that kept it going. Abhorrent. 'What about love?' she demanded. 'Beauty? Art?'

Michael took her hand again, and behind the awful, shaggy beard she glimpsed that heart-breaking smile she had fallen for all those years ago.

'It all matters,' he said. 'It's all that does, in the end. But where do you think those ideas of beauty come from?' She didn't answer, and he went on, 'From glimpses of what remains hidden from us. Things we've seen, and forgotten.'

He regarded her keenly. 'Why do we yearn towards the majestic? Huge, old trees in a dark green forest? Why does the coast draw us so strongly? The rough seas? The cliffs? Why do the wide open spaces of the moors touch us in a way we can't put into words?' His eyes held hers. 'That's where the beauty is. It's where the art is.'

He squeezed her hand, sympathy and understanding on his face. 'And now, that's where the love is, isn't it? Why aren't you with him, Laura?'

She struggled to find the words, and when she did they fell out like rocks. 'Because if we're together, one of us will die.'

Her bluntness only fazed him for a second, then a reluctant smile touched his lips. 'Well you were all ready to go bursting in on Nerryn and Cantoc, and to hell with what they'd do to you.'

'That was different. It was for Ben.' Laura frowned. 'Cantoc was there? He's the one who killed

Casta.'

'No, that wasn't him. He's the one in charge of all the coastal elementals. Their lord.'

'But Maer found his knife by Casta's body. It's the one they used to... to mark Richard, when he became king.'

He shrugged. 'Maybe so, but it wasn't Cantoc who did it. It was Arric.'

Laura searched inside herself for some surprise, but there was none left, only a weary kind of curiosity. 'Why?'

'Because Maer killed Arric's father.'

'*What?*' Laura's mouth fell open, then she shook her head. 'No. He'd never have done that.'

'You know him that well?'

'Well enough to know he'd never kill anyone. Especially not his fiancée's father.'

Michael looked at her thoughtfully for a moment. 'Well, that's what they claim, and on the strength of it Cantoc despatched Arric to take revenge, on behalf of Talfrid and all the Coastals. He found Casta first, and killed him.'

'And this is what they told you?'

He shrugged again. 'I believe them.'

'You don't know Maer, or you wouldn't.'

'I mean, I believe what they've told me. What they think.'

'Is this why you're not sure about Nerryn?' Laura asked. 'You think *she* believes Maer could have done that?'

'She seems to.'

'She's lying.'

Michael pulled his plate back, picked up his fork again and began to load it. 'She's a good liar, then.'

'She went back there to gain their trust. It was planned that way. She was going to win over her father and brother so she could get Ben back, and then she was going to go back to Maer.'

'That was before she knew her father had been killed, and that he's the one who did it,' he pointed out, putting his food down again. He seemed to have lost his appetite. 'That's bound to put a strain on any relationship, don't you think?'

'Is this all just some joke to you?' Laura shoved her chair away from the table and stood, picking up her half-empty wine glass. It sloshed on her as she drank it; she was already feeling light-headed from too little food, not enough sleep, and the first half of the glass drunk too quickly.

He stood up too, and took the glass from her. 'No, of course it's not a joke,' he said gently. 'I'm sorry. You need to rest, Laura. Go on up to bed.'

'I won't sleep.'

'You might.' He waggled the wine glass and gave her the ghost of a smile. 'This probably helped.'

'You'd think. But it never does.'

'Try, anyway. You're exhausted.'

She couldn't put it off any longer. 'There's something else I need to tell you. It's about Jane.'

'There's a name from the past. Is she back from Liverpool then? Be nice to meet up again. Maybe.'

'I'm so sorry, Michael. She's dead.' Laura watched

him carefully. His face went pale, and his lips tightened briefly, then he slumped back into his chair.

'Wouldn't mind betting it was something to do with drugs,' he said at last.

'You knew?'

'I suspected.' He sighed. 'She was always so… I don't know. Needy? No, fragile. And all on her own up there. Easy pickings for someone to get their claws into.'

'I know I should feel bad for her,' Laura said, 'And I do, mostly. But right now all I can think of is how she was supposed to be caring for Ben when Jacky took him, and was just getting wasted instead.' *And trying to seduce Richard…* but there was no sense in mentioning that.

'Then let me help you get him back,' Michael said urgently. 'All you need to do is trust me. Can you do that, at least?'

Laura studied him, still unsure. He'd wanted to join the Coastals, to be accepted by them, yet if he betrayed them for her they would throw him out. Or worse, knowing Arric, throw him off a cliff. Why should he jeopardise his life to save another man's child, even if that child was also hers? His eyes held hers, their shared past reflected in the unchanging blue depths.

At last she nodded. With even Nerryn's loyalty in question now, there was no-one else to turn to.

'Do you want me to stay?' he asked.

'I'd rather you went back down to Trethkellis and

kept an eye on things. You can take the car if you like, I'm not going anywhere.'

'I'll get the train,' he said. 'Last thing you need is to be stranded here without a car.'

'Alright. There's one about two-ish, I think. Always used to be, anyway. I'd offer to drive you to Liskeard station, but...' She indicated the empty wine glass, and he smiled.

'Probably improve your driving, actually.' He held out his arms. She went into them, glad of the comfort but equally glad she felt nothing more for him now than gratitude and nostalgic affection. Everything else was Richard's.

As soon as he was out of sight, she pulled out her drawing box and took out her pad, and five minutes after she'd flipped it open, there was Ben. His rounded cheeks and big eyes, the tiny, snub nose peculiar to all babies, but so dearly familiar to her she could almost feel the warmth of his newly-bathed skin when she touched the paper, tracing the outline with her finger.

She stared at it until her eyes burned, then carefully tore the page from the pad, looking around for somewhere to put it, where it would provide comfort without causing this searing pain at the same time. Maybe she should put it away tonight, and take it out tomorrow when she might be better able to cope. Her gaze fell on the blue folder. *No. Not there...*

Her trembling hand reached out and, although the folder weighed next to nothing, it drained her strength as she opened it and slipped the picture of Ben inside, where it lay next to the drawings of his father and Jacky Greencoat.

'You don't belong there…' The lie reverberated around the room, and the picture remained where it was.

Much later she was awakened from a light doze, by a distant crack of thunder. She lay on the sofa, holding her breath and waiting for another, but it rumbled away into nothing and there were no further sounds. She shivered against the late night chill and sat up, trying not to dwell on who might have caused the rogue thunderclap.

She stood up, stretching her stiff and aching limbs, and saw the art box still pulled out from behind the sofa. Remembering Ben was in there now she opened the box again to test her feelings, and found herself picking up the small, framed drawing of Nerryn instead. Except… she frowned. The elementals aged slowly, but this slowly? The picture was dated 1983. This was a grown woman, even then; it must be Nerryn's mother, the resemblance was too strong for anything less.

In something close to wonder, Laura examined the picture as she had rarely examined it before, and compared it to what she had seen of Mylan as he'd been preparing for travel. The wave-shaped brooch was pinned to the shoulder simply for decoration this time – the woman wore no cloak. Her leggings were laced, as Mylan's had been, but there were no bags hanging at her waist, no tools in her belt, no blade. She had not been travelling, the day six-year old Laura had seen her, just exploring. But Laura had not forgotten her, even though it would be another seven years before the direct encounter that would open her eyes to these people forever; the woman must have possessed a talent for appearing to mortals that far outweighed Arric's.

The leggings Laura had drawn were plain, and the shirt and tunic were too, but the collar was edged with a darker thread, picked out in heavier pencil… Laura peered closer still, and froze. The picture fell from her numb fingers, and she hardly heard the clatter as it bounced off the side of the plastic box, to lie face-down on the carpet. She had seen those clothes recently, hadn't she? In a box. In a wardrobe. In the back bedroom of her father's house.

Chapter Sixteen

Richard frowned at the cloak Maer offered him. 'How far are we going?' It was a still evening, with no wind—the main reason Maer had chosen tonight to begin his teaching—but October was almost on them; he wanted his own coat, but for that he'd have to go back to Mill Lane Cottage where it was probably still hanging over the newel post, unless Laura had already got rid of his stuff. He winced at the thought.

'It's not too far,' Maer said, 'but it's getting dark. You'll need it.' He proffered the cloak again. 'Come on. You'll get used to it, and then you'll realise it's good for a lot more than keeping warm.' Maer himself wore something similar, though he'd never needed it for warmth.

'Okay.' Richard took the cloak and, with Maer's help, fastened it at his shoulder with a bronze brooch shaped like a lightning bolt. He was surprised to find the weight of the garment quite a comforting thing; like pulling a blanket to your chin to sleep, no matter how hot you are. He saw Maer's knowing smirk, and rolled his eyes.

'Right, let's do this.'

'Use your light, it's good practice.'

Maer let his own light disappear at the mouth of the tunnel, and Richard concentrated, drawing in the energy he had learned to feel all around him. A glow gradually lit the tunnel—not as bright as when Maer did it, but pretty good for a beginner—and as he relaxed into the knowledge that it wouldn't fizzle out, it brightened further until he barely had to think about keeping it there. The sense of achievement was undeniable, despite the squirming sensation in his blood as he accepted one more sign that he was where he belonged.

Maer guided them north west, up across the moor. He talked most of the way, telling Richard of the time he'd spent with Deera over the past days, and how much he had learned. Richard had only seen her once since the day she'd tested him; when he'd ordered her out of Jacky's rooms and back to her own. He hoped she wasn't avoiding him, he would need someone with her experience to guide him.

'How's she holding up?'

'Not good, but getting a bit better. I think teaching me has helped her. Given her something to think about.'

'Yeah, she knows how important it is. So, where's school today?'

'Dozmary Pool. It's quite remote, and you can direct everything into the water.'

'Jesus…'

'Relax, you'll be fine.'

They eventually emerged from the rough ground,

onto a narrow path beside a lake. The stretch of water was too big to see the other side, at least in this gathering dusk.

Richard turned to Maer. 'This is it?' He hoped so. He was tired now, and aching from hip to shoulder. 'Didn't you say we were headed for a pool?'

'It's just a name.' Maer led them around the dark expanse, until they stood on its south-eastern edge. 'The only natural lake in the county. And quite famous.' He lowered his voice to sound like a TV documentary expert. 'It's generally believed that this was where King Arthur had a sword lobbed at him...' he paused '...by a watery tart.'

Python fan to the end, Richard couldn't help laughing at that, despite the eerie feel of the place. 'I've gotta say those stories are starting to feel a little less crazy now.'

Out here, with nothing to indicate the modern age, they might have expected to see Arthur himself coming along the thin track on horseback, Merlin at his side and his army of knights following.

Maer moved forward and beckoned to Richard to follow. When they stood on the very edge of the lake Richard glanced at Maer, waiting for him to start. 'Is this where you deliberately get me all pissed at you, so you can teach me how to rein it in?' He could feel himself tightening up already.

'No. I know you've mastered that part yourself. At least, as much as I could have taught you. Now I want to show you how to bring it on purpose.'

'The lightning?'

'Eventually. Let's start with a light shower, shall we?'

The absurdity of the conversation eased Richard's tension, and he shook his head. 'Can you believe we're saying this stuff? I mean, seriously?'

Maer smiled. 'I've learned from you, now you have to behave and let me return the favour.'

'Did you say *behave*?' Richard laughed again. 'Okay, I'll be good. Let's get started before it gets too dark for me to see the embarrassment on your face.'

'Good. Now,' Maer took a deep breath and directed his attention towards the centre of the lake. 'It's always easier near water. Just focus on the air above it.'

Richard did. 'What am I looking for?'

'Droplets. Moisture in the air. But you're not looking for it, you're feeling for it.'

'How does it happen accidentally then?'

'When you're angry? Well, it's the natural turmoil of your thoughts that spins it all together. When you're coldly angry about something very specific, it's harder to do. But when you're confused, feel helpless against something, or angry about everything at once, your mind whirls. It's a dizzy, out of control feeling.'

'Well put.'

'So, that's what you're trying to reproduce, once you've found the elements you're searching for.'

'I once did it when I was angry as hell about one thing,' Richard said, remembering the drug dealers on his doorstep.

'Then that's a good sign you have more control than you think,' Maer said. 'But for now don't try to focus too much. Just think about an idea. Like maybe, I don't know, injustice? That covers so much, from silly little things, right up to...' he trailed away, and Richard knew he was thinking of his father.

'Anyway,' Maer let out a breath. 'No sooner are you starting to think about one injustice than another springs to mind, and before you know it you're so bloody furious you don't know *what* you're thinking.'

'And this is what I'm replicating.' Richard's dry voice lightened the atmosphere again, and Maer nodded and shrugged.

'Easy peasy. Off you go.'

And so began the second-longest night of Richard's life. Hours spent staring into darkness, shivering and glad, after all, for the cloak; Maer's voice, low and encouraging; moments of hope as his questing mind found something he could use; rising frustration as he lost it again the minute he realised it.

When at last he found a gathering momentum in the place above the centre of the pond, one that didn't vanish immediately, he felt such a fierce elation it hurt. Now to hold it all together...

The glass-like surface of the water stirred, ripples across its surface catching the light of the moon. Fragmenting it. Richard felt his hair lifting in a breeze that hadn't existed just a moment ago, and he closed his eyes and pushed, as hard as he could.

Seconds later he heard Maer cry out in alarm.

'Stop! Not yet!'

Richard opened his eyes again, just in time to see a huge wall of water crash back down into the pond, and then he and Maer were drenched by the resulting wave. They both staggered back away from the edge of the pool, Richard stunned, Maer starting to laugh.

'Holy crap,' Richard managed. 'Was that me?'

'Don't close your eyes next time,' Maer spluttered. 'You need to see what you're doing so you can control it.'

Richard pulled his cloak around himself, barely aware he was even doing it. It felt like the most natural thing to do, even though it was as wet as the rest of him. 'I can't believe how fast that happened. Let me try it again.'

'Eyes open,' Maer warned, but he was still laughing. 'I'll keep mine open too; I think you're going to be one to watch.'

Richard felt his own smile returning, along with the surge of jubilation he'd felt before. When he looked out over the water this time it was the easiest thing in the world to reach out, find the moisture that hung above the lake, and draw it all together.. This time he watched it all happen; the already dark sky clouded more, over an area of several feet, and the pressure Richard sent out created a wind that lifted the water into little peaks.

He pushed again, and the peaks rose higher, the droplets grew and fell, splashing into the pool, and one final push, with his eyes wide open, created a wave that raced towards them… and dropped at his silent command.

Breathing hard, but not with effort, Richard turned to Maer, whose face had split into the widest grin. His own sense of achievement was only tempered by his physical exhaustion, and he smiled. 'Can I go home now, teacher?'

'No!' Maer grabbed his arm in excitement. 'This is just the start! We'll go somewhere else, and try the lightning.'

'I'll be too damned tired to do anything if I don't get some sleep soon,' Richard grumbled, but he couldn't deny the rush of euphoria that success had given him.

'Alright,' Maer conceded. 'You'll have duties tomorrow so you should sleep a little, at least. We'll go back now, but we'll stop on the way, and you can have another try. See if it's as easy on dry land.'

It was almost morning by the time Richard coaxed enough water from the air, and with enough strength, to set it spinning into real rain. Now he had the whole of the moor to draw from, the wind that blew up buffeted them both until they had to hang on to one another to remain on their feet. At the same time, unprompted and untaught, he produced his first thunderbolt. It cracked down from a paling sky, to strike at the ground twenty feet away, and as the rumble of thunder died away Maer broke the silence it left in its wake.

'If you can do that when you're exhausted,' he

said in an awed voice, 'then may the elements have mercy on those Coastals when you're rested.'

Richard sank down onto a nearby lump of granite and looked down towards the shattered chimney of the mine below—Casta's final mark upon this land he had loved. He was in danger of letting tiredness take control of his emotions; he had to find another focus.

'I guess I still have to practice a lot more,' he said, 'but when do you think I'll be ready to head for the coast?'

'Rest, Rich,' Maer said gently. 'Come on. We can talk about Ben tomorrow. You're done in.'

'Done in?' Richard couldn't help smiling. 'Don't let your mom hear you talking like that.' He stood up, uneasily aware that his legs were trembling more than they should be. He had walked a long way tonight. Too far, after all the time he'd spent lying still. The distance between here and the mine seemed suddenly impossible, and he sat down again.

'Go ahead,' he said. 'I'll be down soon.'

'I'll wait,' Maer said. 'And we'll take it slowly when we go. Mortal pace.' He looked more closely at Richard. 'Are you hurting?'

'A little,' Richard confessed. 'I'll be better after a sleep. What duties do I have tomor—' he glanced at the sky—'today?'

'They can wait. I shouldn't have pushed you so hard. I'm sorry.'

'Hey, the quicker you push, the sooner I'm getting Ben back.' Richard stood up again, this time more carefully. 'This rock is hurting my ass. Let's go. Slow.'

Back in his room, Richard loosened his tunic and lay down, and breathed a heavy sigh of relief. Not only because he was home, and could sleep, but because now he knew he stood a chance against those sonofabitch Coastals. It took a moment before he realised he'd begun to think of this tatty little underground room as 'home,' but it was only a heartbeat later that he felt the smile on his face.

***

In his own room Maer also lay still, but sleep eluded him. He thought about how quickly Richard had produced the lightning; Maer hadn't even had to explain how it was done. He thought too, about the meeting they'd had with Ykana and her sister, and about the youngsters, Lyelt and Keityn… were they strong enough to take part in the forthcoming battle?

His mind turned things over and over, and in rising frustration he knew he would get no sleep at all if he kept on like this. So instead he turned his thoughts towards Nerryn, but instead of calling to mind her face and form, all he could think was, *what if they have convinced her to stay?*

He grunted and flung himself over in his bed, staring into the blackness until his eyes burned. She loved him. This much he was sure of, at least. She wouldn't stay there a moment longer than necessary. He closed his eyes and let out a long, slow breath, waiting for his body to relax into that sweet, pre-slumber state, but he realised his hands were clenched, and, a second later, that his toes were too. No wonder it wasn't happening.

Giving up any thought of sleep, he rose and went out through the labyrinth of tunnels, through the cavern, and up into the dawn. The sun had not yet risen but the sky was gradually lightening, and it glowed a beautiful, autumnal orange over the village—Casta had always loved to walk early, to watch the day begin. He would have stood here today, and watched in silence until the golden glow was swallowed by the blue of the vast, open sky. Only then would he give his attention over to the mundane matters of ruling a kingdom.

Maer sat down on the dew-damp grass, and leaned back against the mine chimney. It had been half a moon's turn since the night of Casta's death, but the grief had a way of slyly waiting until he felt calmer, not accepting but resigned, and then reaching into his chest and crushing his heart once again in its cold, iron fist.

'Father,' he whispered, 'I miss you.' He closed his eyes. This time, instead of Nerryn, it was Casta's face he sought, and found. Those light blue eyes, so like his, were watching him with grave concern. He lowered his forehead to his raised knees and wrapped his arms around them while he struggled with a tight throat and an aching jaw, clenched against the cries that would have set the sky alight.

Do not grieve me, beloved son, live for me.

The voice sounded so real that Maer jerked upright, but it did not come again. He slumped back once more, wondering at the power of imagination; was his longing for his father really so strong? Still, imagination or not, the words rang in his head; life had been his father's gift, he would not want to see its joys and its triumphs blown away in a storm of grief that could change nothing.

He rose, and was about to go back down to his rooms, to seek sleep once more, when a sound stopped him. A footstep, rustling in long grasses. His hand had dropped to his hip before he realised he had left his blade in his chambers, and he stilled, waiting. His heart beat light and fast, he could feel it in his throat and in his temples, and the image of Casta's twice-stabbed body would not go away.

'Who walks here?'

'Sir... I mean no harm. I have important news.'

Maer's breath halted. It had sounded like...

Jacky?

'Yes, sir.' The spriggan stepped out from behind the chimney, and Maer stared, open-mouthed. He could not speak. But Jacky could.

'Please, Highness... I lost the boy, and I know I must be punished, but first—'

'We thought you to be dead!'

Jacky's eager babble halted, and he returned Maer's stunned gaze. 'N, no, sir. I was struck, it's true. And I lost the babe, but he is safe! He is—'

'Yes, we know he is safe.' Maer stepped towards the spriggan, still unsure whether his imagination had taken leave of his reason. 'I am relieved, indeed happy, to see we were wrong about your fate, but—'

'I must speak to you and Lord Tir together,' Jacky said urgently. 'Evil is taking shape down on the coast, and it will be the ruin of everything. Everything! And Arric even planned to have Gerai take your own life.'

'Come with me,' Maer slipped down the grassy slope and into the tunnel. His mind raced as he strode easily through the widened stone throat; why had the spriggan gone to the coast instead of returning home? Had he tried to retrieve Dreis? What plan could the Coastals possibly have, that threatened so much?

Impatient for answers, he didn't knock at Richard's door but went straight in. Behind him Greencoat muttered, 'But this is *my* room, sir…'

'Not now, it isn't. Tir has taken it for his own.'

Richard slept on, fully-clothed, and Maer had time to note the tiny smile on his brother's face, before he bent and shook Richard's shoulder gently. 'Wake up,' he whispered. 'Someone to see you.'

Richard's eyes blinked open and he focused blearily on Maer, then his gaze slid to Jacky and he snatched a breath and rose onto his elbow. 'Shit! It's really you?'

'Yes, sir,' Jacky said, and he sounded close to tears. 'Jacky is so, so sorry!'

Richard sat up properly, and Maer saw him swallow a grunt of pain, but then his smile lit the room. 'You don't have anything to be sorry for,

Jacky.'

'Your son—'

'Was taken. You didn't give him away.'

Jacky shook his head. 'You called me Jacky Turncoat. You were mistaken in that, but still I do not deserve your understanding.'

'I'm just glad you're alive,' Richard said. 'I'm still mad at what you did, but you didn't deserve to die.'

'I will accept your punishment, but first I must tell you Arric's plans. He must be stopped.'

Richard looked shattered, but his eyes sharpened into grim alertness as Greencoat told his tale. 'The Lady Nerryn has another brother, one with whom she shares life. Within them lies the kind of power that would darken this land forever if it were to be unleashed.'

'What kind of power?'

Jacky's voice was hushed, as if speaking the words would make it all too real to bear. 'Together they could create storms the like of which we have never seen. Storms to bring down every tree in the forest. Lightning to scorch every piece of ground, to split the granite itself. Winds so strong no-one would be able to stand against them, and every mortal's house blown apart or set to burn.' Greencoat wrung his hands, and Maer and Richard exchanged looks of horror.

Richard found his voice first. 'This is just because they're *twins*?'

'And Arric would have them learn to use it, I'm sure. But I am certain he does not realise quite how dangerous they are. I cannot think he knows what he is doing.'

'Then why the hell didn't you tell him?' Richard stood up, his hands clenched, his face set and furious.

'My Lord, I had just watched him… he, he smashed Gerai's head to pieces on the rocks.'

Maer felt sick. 'He killed a Moorlander?'

'Yes. And…' Jacky's voice dropped to barely more than a whisper. 'Highness, I am so sorry… he is the one who stole your father's life.'

'No, that was Cantoc, I have his blade.' Maer showed him.

'Sir, I heard him speak of it himself. It was how I learned that…' he hitched a breath, 'that Casta walked the moors no longer.'

Maer sat down on Richard's bed, his heart thundering. 'The coward hid behind his lord.' He shook his head. 'I understand why you would not want to confront him, you would certainly not have lived to bring us this news of his treachery.'

'There is more, sir.'

'What the hell else?' Richard snapped, and Maer was about to beg him to calm down until he saw anger was giving him strength. Better to use it.

'On my way back to you I was set upon by two Foresters,' Jacky said.

'Are you hurt?'

Jacky looked touched at the sudden concern in his king's voice, and shook his head. 'No, My Lord. But I told them what I had heard of Arric's plan.'

'Good,' Maer said. 'We will need their support.'

But Richard was peering closely at Jacky, and frowning. 'You don't look like it's such a good thing. What happened?'

'Sir, they are allied with the Coastals now.'

Maer shot a glance at Richard, who cursed softly, and Jacky went on, 'I had already told them what I had heard, and it was too late to take the words back. They tried to keep me there while one of them ran to take advice from Arric's brother, and to tell Arric his plotting had not been silenced with the death of Gerai.'

Richard chewed the inside of his lip. 'Figures. Not your fault, you weren't to know. How did you get away?'

'I... tricked them. Lyelt, at least.'

'Lyelt?' Maer said. 'I can only assume the other was Keityn then?'

'Yes.'

'How did you trick him?'

'I used my voice gift. As I did on that day by the stones, when Gilan thought his king was calling to him.'

'And gave me a chance to knock the sonofabitch flying,' Richard mused. 'Pretty cool talent. So who did Lyelt hear?'

'Keityn, My Lord. Telling him to leave me alone, and go with him instead.'

Maer felt a flicker of admiration that quickly melted into a confused feeling of disappointment and affection. 'Jacky, out there earlier, just before I heard you?'

Jacky turned to him, and the truth was written on his ugly-sweet face. 'You seemed so deep in your grief, sir, but you had need of strength, not sorrow.'

'You sounded…' Maer tried to smile but it was a sad, trembling effort. 'You sounded just like him. Thank you.'

Jacky looked relieved and seemed about to speak again, but, as much as he longed to speak more about his father, Maer could afford neither the time nor the emotion. He was ready to leave. 'I must get to Trethkellis before Arric can begin to work his will on Nerryn.'

Richard nodded. 'Can we get some guys together?'

'Better to use stealth than strength,' Maer said. 'I know there will be many who would be willing to come, but they are untrained, and the more of us there are, the greater our chance of being discovered before we have freed Nerryn and Ben.'

'Okay. We'll go now.' Richard reached for his blade, but Maer stayed his hand.

'No. You've exhausted yourself tonight.'

'You're not going alone. I'm fine.'

'I'll rouse someone.'

'Someone you trust with Nerryn's and Ben's lives?'

Maer recognised that tone of old. 'There's no chance you're staying here if I go, is there?'

'You're learning.'

'I am,' Maer said drily. He considered; so far there

had been no indication that the training of the twins had begun, with the luck of the elements they might yet have time to do this properly, and effectively, and with less risk to Richard's health.

'I know you have the command over me,' he said, 'but, as your advisor, I can't let you travel yet. We will give it one more day. Please, just one,' he begged, as Richard opened his mouth to protest. 'There has been no sign of disturbance in the weather yet and you *must* rest today. Besides, you will need to send for Laura. Get her here where she can shelter safely underground.'

'Send for her? I'll go myself.'

'No!' Maer said again, then more gently, 'Richard, you can't see her again. You have to accept that.'

Richard looked at him with narrowed eyes, his jaw tight, and Maer braced himself for an argument but Richard subsided. 'Yeah, I know. It's stupid, but I keep hoping there's a way we haven't thought of.'

Maer remembered all too well how it had felt to leave Nerryn behind at the coast; even knowing she still loved him, and would come to him again. He ached in sympathy with Richard's loss, but it could not be helped.

'Send Jacky for her,' he said, glancing at the spriggan, who had remained silent but was looking from one to the other of them anxiously.

Richard followed his gaze. 'You think you can talk her into it, Jacky?'

'Oh, sir, I will try my very hardest.' Jacky looked both immensely honoured, and quite terrified. 'I will not fail you again, My Lord.'

'He'll be carrying your words,' Maer said to Richard, 'so how can she argue?'

Richard spared him a darkly amused look, and Maer was assaulted by a rush of memories of Laura at her most intense, her most passionately furious. It was truly something to see, from such a sweet-natured person.

He gave Richard a faint smile, and spoke to the spriggan again. 'Jacky, you must go to Lady Laura when Tir and myself leave. Make sure you bring her here. Do you understand?'

'Should I use My Lord's voice?' Jacky asked.

'Christ, no!' Richard looked horrified. 'She'll go nuts if she finds out you've tricked her, you'll never get her to come with you.'

Jacky visibly relaxed. 'I won't trick her.'

'Just be sure you bring her to safety,' Maer said.

'And watch her with Maer's mom,' Richard added, the ghost of his own smile warming his features again. 'Don't let them get into it, okay?'

'Into it?' Jacky asked, puzzled, but Richard just shook his head and patted the shoulder of the spriggan, who looked as though he'd been presented with all the riches in Cornwall.

'Now, we sleep,' Maer said firmly. 'Jacky, you have travelled far. You may bed down in my rooms. I will sleep on my mother's couch.' He held up a hand as he saw Richard getting ready to speak. 'I know what you are going to say, but this is no longer Jacky's room. I will be quite comfortable on that couch.'

Jacky looked about to argue too, but Richard nodded at him. 'Go ahead, do as he says. We've got our orders.'

When the shyly smiling spriggan had left, Maer sat down on Richard's bed, and waited until Richard had sat down too, before he spoke. 'What I said. About not being with her?'

'I get it.'

'I know you do. But do you know why?'

'No. Not really.'

'Think about your mother, your real one, just for a moment,' Maer said gently. 'Think of Magara. Would you wish that on Laura?'

'People don't believe that superstitious crap anymore. They're not going to punish her, or Ben, because of who his father is. Hell, they wouldn't even know.'

'The mortals wouldn't, but what about your own people?'

Richard's voice turned dangerously soft. 'Are you telling me *you* guys would throw her out? Or worse?'

'She couldn't live underground to begin with,' Maer said, suppressing a little shiver at his tone. 'But if you were to visit her in her home, and happened to… to…'

'Get her pregnant?'

'Yes!' Maer stood up and began pacing. 'You would be repeating the worst mistake your father ever made.'

'I've already done that,' Richard pointed out tightly.

'But that was before you knew, and so you could not be blamed for it. Now that your people have pledged to you, you owe them your honesty and your loyalty.'

He struggled to find the words to make Richard understand. 'I grew up learning about how it was after Loen died. The panic and revolt. Wars between us, the Coastals and the Foresters, that lasted so long our people thought they should never see the sun again. Borsa held Lynher Mill by the tips of his fingers, and *his* people knew him well. You, they cannot be sure of yet. Just the fear of it happening again could destroy everything we've managed to build since that time. Moorlanders will flee the land and take up with a stronger ruler, one who protects his people instead of betraying them.'

It was clear that Richard was only now beginning to understand the extent of the turmoil his birth had caused, and he looked both horrified and defiant. 'But Laura's... Maer, they know how I feel about her. It's not the same at all.'

Maer blinked in surprise, and his voice dropped. 'You think your father did not care for your mother?' He shook his head. 'Loen watched her for a long time before he made himself known to her. Long enough to have formed an admiration, and an attachment. If he had cared nothing for her, he would not have left her alone once he realised she carried his child. *He knew*, Richard! He knew how his people would respond, and how it would have destroyed Magara to come with him. Even if she could have.'

'But it all turned to shit anyway.'

'Because of Ulfed, and his people. And their terror for who you were.' Maer kept his voice gentle. 'But mostly because of Loen's love for you, and his pain when your life was threatened.'

Richard's face was set hard, but Maer pressed on; it must all be said now. 'You made your decision to stay, and it will take a long time to move past your love for Laura.' How well he himself knew that. 'But when you are ready you may have your choice of brides. Make a queen of one of your own people, and give us the future we deserve.'

'I don't owe you a fucking heir!' Richard ripped the torc from around his neck. 'You got me, that's all I'm prepared to give you.' He flung the torc into the corner of the room, where it clanged off the granite wall, and Maer winced.

'That is your choice, and I hope you will one day change your mind. But in the meantime you cannot give Laura hope that she might have you after all, it's not fair on—'

'I told you, I get it,' Richard said. 'That doesn't mean I have to like it.'

'Good,' Maer said, and let out a heavy breath. He felt wretched for what he was putting Richard through, but a king had to understand where his first duty lay. 'Now we must both rest.'

He turned at the doorway. Richard's brow was deeply grooved between those straight, dark eyebrows, and Maer had the helpless feeling that it was not physical pain that caused such a tortured expression. This was something even Kernow could not ease. He glanced once more at the discarded torc in the corner, and tried to send an understanding look Richard's way, then turned and went to his mother's chambers.

After a short rummage in the chest there, he found a heavy, ornately beaded blanket. He drew it around himself as he sat on the couch on which he had sat countless times, listening to his mother and father talking, planning, occasionally laughing, more often locked in earnest discussion about some matter of their realm.

He found that, if he closed his eyes again, he could banish the sight of Richard's grief, and see Casta and Deera instead; their beauty familiar enough that he never really appreciated it anymore, but their features so beloved he felt a deep, surprisingly intense, twist of pain. The coming war would take its toll, he knew that, and it would not bring Casta back from the ground. But it might help him find some peace.

He could hope for that, at least.

Chapter Seventeen

Lynher Mill. 7am. September 28th

The door was barely open before Laura spoke. 'Tell me about her.'

Gail's mouth fell open but she just shook her head, her eyebrows raised in mute question.

'You know who I'm talking about,' Laura's voice was hard, barely recognisable even to herself. 'Why do you have her clothes? *How* do you?'

'Clothes?' Gail's voice shook. 'Those ones you found in the back room, you mean?' She was looking past Laura rather than at her, and Laura fought the instinct to turn and look too, but she knew the road was deserted.

'You said they belonged to a deceased friend,' she pressed. '*Was* she a friend? How did she die?'

'I don't know what you want me—'

'Just tell me!' Laura kept a tight rein on her frustration, but it took an effort. 'Those clothes belonged to a… someone special, didn't they? How did you get them?'

Gail's lip started to tremble, and she suddenly looked very old. Laura had to stop herself from moving forward to comfort her. 'Tell me,' she said again, her voice softer but still determined.

Gail sniffed, blinked away sudden tears and nodded. 'Come in and sit down. This is going to be a bit of a while in the telling. I imagine you'll have no trouble believing it, but you won't like it.'

Laura's heart plummeted; beyond the lies, how awful could it be? She followed Gail into the front room and sat down. 'I want to hear all of it.'

So Gail began. And as the story unfolded it seemed this small, neatly-kept sitting room was suddenly populated with beautiful creatures and ugly ones, frightened ones and laughing ones; spirits who had no business being here, but brought to vivid life by this scared woman's spilled secrets.

'When we were first married we used to walk everywhere,' she said. 'Down towards the coast, as far as we could manage in a day. Sometimes we'd go so far we'd have to get the bus back. Then I broke my stupid ankle playing netball, and after that I couldn't walk so far, even when it was healed.'

She had told Graham he mustn't curb his hobby on her behalf, and so weekends regularly saw him setting off, map and water-bottles at hand, and a pair of sturdy boots on his feet.

Gail had tried not to begrudge him that freedom but it had been hard to be left alone. Their relationship had suffered, largely because he had taken her at her word, but also because, on his return, he would often be distant and uncommunicative.

'Of course, now I know why,' she told Laura quietly. 'He'd seen her. That one who liked to play with people's minds. Staying visible, making him think she wanted him. Maybe she did, at that, he wasn't a bad looker.'

'My mother said he was quite a strong man,' Laura offered, her voice low. Fractured.

Gail nodded. 'He worked hard, and he was fairly attractive. I thought so, anyway. But, looks aside, he had a short fuse. A very short fuse.' She cleared her throat and went on, 'It got worse after he started walking alone, but I had no idea why. I just noticed it after his longer walk. It wasn't just his temper, he was becoming flaky, forgetful. He scared me. He wouldn't tell me what was going on, so one day I followed him.'

'And you saw her?'

'Not at first. I kept my distance, and for a time I thought he was losing his mind. He kept calling out a name, like Daphne, but not exactly. And then he would talk to nobody. Laugh, too.' Gail shuddered. 'It was eerie.'

'How long did this go on for?'

'A week, maybe more. Until I saw her come out of nowhere.'

Laura had been expecting this, of course, but she still felt a strange chill racing over her skin as she imagined how it must have been, on a chilly, misty day near Christmas, with the ground wet and dangerously boggy, the hills hidden by low cloud, the wind whipping the grasses about their feet. Gail had crouched by a granite lump, her hands cold on the stone, her socks sodden inside her boots, her hair dripping into her eyes.

'He kept calling out, but no-one had appeared and he was getting angry again, I could see it.'

Laura felt a pang of sympathy for the younger Gail, but said nothing. She needed to hear it all first, to learn how the stolen clothes had ended up in this small house, and if sympathy was deserved. To think her father might have been a thief gave her a nasty taste in her mouth, but the other explanation was that Graham had got what he wanted, and Nerryn's mother had been quick to shed her clothes despite the weather. Laura didn't know which to hope for.

'I thought I saw an outline,' Gail was saying. 'The shape of a person. Small-ish, but definitely adult-sized. It kept fading away though. Graham has always been adamant there are things out here we can never truly understand. I began to wonder then, if he was actually right. All I could do was believe what my eyes told me, and so I let myself do that.

The moment I did, I could see her properly.' She shook her head, remembering. 'So beautiful, with long, dark red hair tied back. She was a madam, though. Teasing him, I could hear her, from where I was hiding. Maybe she was just being playful, but… well,' Gail looked ill, now. 'She didn't understand what she was playing with.'

Laura felt queasy too, and Gail went on, 'Graham never even bothered to ask where I'd been, although I got home after he did. He was twitchy, irritable. He'd already back-handed me once, so I daren't ask him about her. But I followed him every time, after that. For another few weeks at least. She didn't come again though, until the last time. The time the other man came out of the forest.'

'What other man?'

'Thin. Handsome enough, but cold. He was dressed in horrible, bright-coloured—'

'Gilan!'

Gail's eyes narrowed. 'You know him?'

How could Laura even begin to explain Gilan? She should have guessed he was involved. She thought of everything he had done to Richard's loved ones, and her hatred for him swelled. Was there no end to his evil? 'Go on.'

After a pause, Gail continued. 'He was threatening the woman, and Graham was getting angrier and angrier with him. I was getting worried, so I shouted to him, hoping to bring him away. Instead the other man just vanished, and so did the girl. Graham... well, he just went insane. Kept shouting at her to come back. He made for the edge of the forest, but then he stopped and it looked as though he was fighting the mist. For a second I'd have sworn he'd run into a swarm of wasps, but it was still too early in the year.'

'Gilan attacked him.' Laura shuddered, remembering the wiry strength of the man. 'He was a killer when I knew him, so—'

'No. It wasn't that.' Gail sighed, and it was heavy and painful-sounding. 'Graham was still shouting at the woman to show herself, to prove he wasn't mad. Then he stopped. He went to his knees, and that's when I saw the other man appear again. He was nowhere near.'

'So it was *Graham?*' Laura's voice cracked with horror.

'He lost his wits, he… forgot himself. He was weeping, saying over and over that he loved her.'

'He *killed* her!'

'Laura, please…' Gail started to stand up, and Laura reached out and grabbed her wrist.

'Finish it.'

She let go, and Gail subsided again. 'He just sat there, crying. I went over to him. I couldn't see anyone there, but his hands were resting on something, I could see that. He was begging her to show herself.'

'What about Gilan? What was he doing?'

'He… he was smiling. I suppose Graham had saved him a job.'

'Don't say that,' Laura hissed. 'Don't you dare! That girl had three young children!'

Gail let out a sob, and hitched a breath, the back of her hand pressed to her mouth. 'I'm sorry, love. So sorry. If I hadn't shouted out she wouldn't have hidden herself.'

'It wasn't your fault,' Laura said, with reluctance, though part of her couldn't help agreeing. But Gail could never have guessed at the consequences. 'So then what?'

'I went over to Graham. He was still crying, I wasn't scared of him anymore. I just wanted to comfort him. I hadn't realised, at that point, what he'd done. By the time I did, I could see an outline. The more I looked, the more detail there was, and I could see it changing shape. After a couple of minutes though, it was just—'

'Dust and clothes,' Laura said dully. She remembered Casta, and how Maer had gathered up his father's clothing to give back to Deera. 'So by then you believed enough to be able to see what was left of her. Why did you bring the clothes home?'

'The thin man told us to. He told us he would make sure no-one ever found out what we did, provided we paid him. So we did. And we started to forget. Gradually, but it happened. Graham even lost that quick temper, and turned into the man you always knew him to be.'

'He was kind,' Laura mused, feeling tears prickling at the back of her eyes. 'He really was lovely. So I thought.'

'He was, in the end. Anyway, over the past few months I noticed he spent a lot of time staring out of the window at the moors. One day he told me he was going to clear out all the stuff from the back bedroom and turn it into a photography studio. That he planned to start walking again, and learn about where we lived, photographing the area. I suppose deep down in his subconscious he was still looking for that proof that he hadn't lost his mind. He emptied out the wardrobe first.'

'And found the clothes,' Laura guessed.

'His heart just gave up,' Gail said, her voice thickening as she fought tears of her own. 'He screamed out that he'd remembered everything, but I didn't know what he was talking about until you found that box. I thought I would die, too. Just fall down dead right there from the shock of it. But here I am.' She pressed the heels of her hands to her eyes. 'Here I am, and here you are. And you know so much more than I do about what's out there.'

Laura didn't answer, but stood up to leave. Her mind was spinning and her head ached. She just wanted to go home, to think about what this meant, to sleep… oh, god, please, just to sleep…

Seeing Gail's haunted and hopeful expression, she relented. 'I will tell you, soon,' she promised. 'But not yet.'

'Laura, listen,' Gail caught her up at the front door. 'Graham *was* as you knew him. He wasn't a violent man. Not really. He was just… frustrated.'

Laura faced her then, and very gently kissed her on the cheek. 'No,' she whispered, 'he was dangerous. He hit you, and he killed one of the most gentle, kind and noble creatures on the planet.'

The unsaid words echoed around her head as she walked away down the path: *and I carry his genes.*

***

'These plants are limp.' Arric prodded at the food on his plate, and pulled a face. 'What's wrong with them?'

Nerryn shrugged. 'We have had a dry spell. No rainfall. If you don't like it, find your own.'

'No rainfall?' Arric snorted. 'Is that a jest?' He looked up from his gloomy perusal of the late meal Nerryn had prepared, and saw it wasn't. 'Nerryn, you can make your own rain!'

She didn't reply, and Arric put down his knife. 'When was the last time you used your gifts?' For the Ocean's sake... if she couldn't even create a little rainfall to sweeten their food, what chance was there of combining her powers and Mylan's? Arric's confidence in the coming war was beginning to wilt. Almost as much as these pathetic leaves.

'You ought to practice, you know,' he said, struggling to sound calm. 'War is walking our way, and the Moorlanders will not care that you were once promised to their prince. You have betrayed them. You need to be prepared, if only for protection for you and the boy.'

'Protection? How?'

Arric could feel his teeth clench, wanting to grind. 'A small whirlwind to keep attackers at bay? A lightning bolt to fell a tree in their path. Darkness, in which to hide. How should I know!' He waved a hand. 'You are not skilled in hand-to-hand battle, so it is all you have. You must be ready to use it, or lose the boy, and thus the war. You never know how strong you are until you try. You might be pleasantly surprised.'

He watched her carefully to see if his words had hit home, but her expression betrayed nothing. He couldn't help admiring the way she had changed, but at the same time she was far less malleable than he'd hoped. He sensed it was time to retreat from this conversation now the seed of curiosity had been sown.

'How long will Mylan be away?' he asked, making sure he sounded more friendly.

Nerryn's reaction was predictable; at the mention of her twin's name, she lost her sullen look. 'I am starting to feel that sense of him nearing, he will return soon.'

'With Lawbryn, I hope. And Hendrig, if he still walks this world. And there must be many other strong men who knew our mother, and would be honoured to come here and fight for vengeance in her name.'

'Men?' Nerryn's voice had sharpened again. 'I understand Dafna's people are equally fierce, whether they have two legs or three.'

'Nerryn!' Arric's mouth dropped open in genuine shock. Where had she learned such talk?

She looked at him calmly, but with a dangerous glint in her eyes. 'I believe her mother Gethli was particularly strong,' she went on. 'I'm sure she must still be able to wield a blade or a bow.'

'Three legs…' Arric muttered, blinking in disbelief. 'Nerryn, you have changed.'

'For the better,' she said archly. And would not be drawn into any further conversation.

Arric ate his meal with no more complaints, but later, as he sat on the clifftop watching the sun sink into the sea, he wondered how best to use his new and improved sister.

Both she and Mylan were far removed now, from the carefree childhood companions who used to run up and down the cliffs for the sheer fun of racing one another, or stand together on the edge of the water and hold hands while they jumped in the waves.

Gone too, were the days when, as young adults, they had sat and talked, seemingly earnest but always with laughter drifting around them. Now each had been hardened in their own fires, and each hungered for justice for their slain parents.

He was certain they would welcome the knowledge of the capabilities, and be eager to begin training, but the longer Arric delayed, the more gold would be raised – for an army nobody would need. By the time Cantoc was king, and Arric was his first lord of the coast, Arric intended to be very rich indeed.

In the meantime he watched the last of the day's mortal fish-finders dragging their nets up the beach, and scowled. Cantoc's instruction rang loud and discordant in his ears: *Work. As your father did. Raise coin that way.* So, he was to fish, was he? In order to gain the trust and respect of stinking men, who struggled daily to bring their stinking treasure back in their stinking boats? He shot an accusatory look at the salt box outside their home, as if it were personally responsible for his miserable fate, simply by virtue of being necessary to his new work. The only work more demeaning than fish-finding was salt-crushing, he ought to be grateful Cantoc had not suggested that.

Even so it was no life for one with his talents, the limits of which had become obvious since the day he had returned from the peninsula, a few chains richer, but an accomplice light.

He could still feel the shifting, crunching change in the shape of Gerai's head in his hands, the first blow had not made much difference, but the second… he had almost let go in revolted horror, but one more slam had convinced him the job was done; he would as soon not get so close to an enemy again. Hewyl might prove useful after all… where *was* he, anyway? Arric had not seen him all day.

A fizzing flash high in the dark sky distracted him. Glancing down onto the beach he saw the slight figure of his sister, her hands raised. Silly girl. As if her mind was not strong enough to guide the lightning without the use of her fingertips. Still, at least she was trying.

Dreis slept, wrapped and tucked into a woven basket on the beach by her feet, and Arric felt a moment's relief that he needn't admit to letting either of them out of his sight. He kept forgetting he was supposed to be watching her, and Cantoc would be sure to make his displeasure felt if he knew. Arric would never forget that moment when the lord of the coast had held him over the cliff, by nothing more than the front of his tunic and a savage grip on his face.

He shook off the memory, and turned his attention back to the beach. Nerryn's lack of success was irritating. He looked up at the cloud she had made, and reached his mind into it, probing deep to find the electrical charges inside. He tugged hard, separating the positive from the negative and at the same time seeking the path to the ground. There followed a blaze that made Nerryn jump, so violently Arric could see it from all the way up here. He smirked, rose to his feet, and made his way down to where she was still straining towards her pathetic little rain cloud.

She turned as she heard him approach. 'Was that you?'

'It was. You didn't think it was you, did you?'

'I cannot make the path to the ground,' she confessed, turning back to her task.

'You do not make it, you find it.'

'How, though?'

'The ground *wants* the lightning, Nerryn. It sends up a messenger to guide it. This is what you must find.'

Nerryn frowned and lowered her hands. 'I cannot concentrate on the two things at once.'

Arric sighed. 'You can, but you are not thinking of two things, you are thinking of a hundred.'

'What do you mean?'

'You created the cloud. That is good; there was plenty of moisture in there. You separated the charges, also good. Then you thought about Dreis, and wondered whether he was cold. You made a flash, good. You thought, at the same time: now, how do I create the pathway to the ground? And I hope the totterling isn't awake and eating sand while my back is turned.'

He would have gone on, but Nerryn had heard enough. 'You are right; he is my responsibility. Perhaps I should leave the weather-games to you.'

'No!' Arric cleared his throat and calmed his tone. 'No. You are an elemental, and it is not your fault you have been discouraged, all these cycles, from using your gifts. You have care of Tir's son, but you need time to learn your craft, and you cannot while you are listening to his chatter, or wondering if he needs a warmer cloak, or counting the time until he must either be fed or deafen us all with his yells.'

'Are you saying *you* would care for him, while I learn?' Nerryn sounded amused, sceptical even, and Arric knew he must play this line carefully.
Confounded fish-finder talk!

'I have grown fond of him, in my way,' he said, pretending faint embarrassment rather well, he thought. 'And you must practice.' He crouched beside the basket, where the boy slept on, soothed by the sound of the waves, and wondered what was going on in that sleeping mind. Probably nothing good.

He picked up the basket—it was heavier than it looked—and braced himself for a shriek that never came. Perhaps this would not be so hard after all. 'I will take him back up, you stay here awhile. Remember, the pathway exists, you just need to find it.' He turned to walk back up to their home, and called back over his shoulder, 'And put your stupid hands down!'

Hewyl was waiting on the cliff. Arric thrust Dreis's basket at him and led the way inside. 'Where have you been?'

'Lynher Mill.'

Arric frowned. 'Why?'

'None of your business,' Hewyl said. 'But, since you ask so nicely, I found the boy's mother poking around and persuaded her to go home.'

Arric paused in the removal of his cloak. 'How has she found us?'

'I don't know, but she was ready to storm in here and snatch him back,' Hewyl nodded at the child, 'or die in the attempt.'

Arric remembered the mortal woman too well; all wild hair and fury. She had seen him and Gerai clearly, immediately, and with none of the wavering uncertainty of her powder-baking friend. 'How did you persuade her to leave, if she was set to give her own life to save the totterling?'

'I knew her in my old life,' Hewyl said. 'We talked a long time, and I convinced her I'd do my best to get the boy back.'

'And she trusts you?'

'Why wouldn't she?'

Arric raised an eyebrow. 'Why should we, at that?'

'I told you. I can help you win this war.'

'And what if I have no need of your help?'

Hewyl put Dreis's basket down on the rug by the fire. He turned back to Arric, who was disturbed by the sudden gleam in his eyes. 'You? What if *you* have no need?'

'What if *we* have no need,' Arric amended. 'Cantoc is powerful, I am skilled. Mylan has gone for my mother's family, who are known for their fearlessness. How can some scruffy mortal claim to be the answer to a problem we do not have?'

'I think you underestimate the Moorlanders,' Hewyl said. 'They're stronger than you and the Foresters put together. Tir will soon be well enough to lead them, and once he has his son he'll have no reason to hold anything back.'

'And what if he does not get the chance?'

'You're full of questions tonight, Arric, but okay, I'll bite. Why would he not get the chance?'

They were both distracted by a sudden crack of thunder, and a bloom of light through the window. Dreis twitched but did not wake. Arric used the moment to gather his thoughts, at the same time thanking the tides that at last Nerryn seemed to be finding what she sought.

Hewyl turned back to him. 'Well? What could possibly prevent the Moorlanders from unleashing everything on you?'

'Mylan will be here soon, with Dafna's people,' Arric said. 'He is under instruction to bring them directly to Cantoc, but if the tales I have heard of Hendrig and Lawbryn are true, it would not surprise me to learn that they have gone instead to Lynher Mill. If so, Maer's life will undoubtedly end in the same way as his unlamented father: in stealth, on the point of a Coastal's blade.'

'Which would inflame Tir still further,' Hewyl argued.

Arric waved a hand. 'Only if he lives long enough. The likelihood is that both of them will be caught unawares, and soon.'

'Before Tir is properly recovered.'

'Quite. He might possess Loen's power with the elements, but hand-to-hand battle is another matter. No. Tir will be lucky to see another whole moon.'

A loud bang from the rock on the door-post made them both jump, and Arric shot a glance at the sleeping totterling, but there was no movement.

'Declare yourself!'

'I am Keityn,' a voice called back. 'Forester, and loyal servant of Ykana.' He sounded young and scared, and Arric frowned. *Trigoryon an goswig? Here?* Then he remembered Mylan telling them of two youngsters who might be turned to their cause. Still, he could not be certain this was one of them.

'State your business.' He took care not to invite the Forester over the threshold; he knew little about these night-loving creatures, but had heard of other dark beings that should never be invited into a home. Who knew if these were the same?

'Please, sir, I am to see Mylan. Is he here?'

'He is not. I am his older brother, and whatever you wish to say to Mylan you may say to me.'

'You are Arric?' The voice grew even more unsure, and Arric's lips tightened in amusement. His reputation was spreading – this could only be good.

'I am.'

'Might I come in?'

'Oh, for crying out loud!' Hewyl crossed to the door covering and pulled it aside. 'It's a *child*, Arric!'

The young man who came in was no child, but he was mid-grown only. Arric sensed no threat in the way he stood, with his arms crossed, his hands tucked beneath them, and his eyes wide and worried.

'Come on then,' he grunted. 'Speak your piece and get gone.'

'We, that is, Lyelt and myself, rose early tonight,' the Forester began in formal tones. 'It was still light. While ranging in the woods we came upon a lone spriggan, bound for Lynher Mill to tell tales of something he had heard at the coast.'

Arric's eyes narrowed. 'What sort of something?'

'He had somehow… overheard a plan, to combine the elemental powers of your twin siblings and to use them against the Moorlanders.'

Arric saw Hewyl's face turn towards him, but he did not meet it. His blood had chilled at the realisation that, if the spriggan had overheard this, it must also have witnessed the dark act that had followed that conversation.

To deflect any questions he switched direction. 'And the spriggan was carrying this news to the Moorlanders themselves?'

'Yes. He seemed to think the danger was more than you realise.'

'Not to Ykana?'

'Sir?' Keityn looked puzzled, and Arric sighed.

'It was carrying the news of this terrible destruction to the Moorlanders, but not to the Foresters?'

Keityn hesitated, and frowned. 'Uh... Yes.' He hurried on, 'We have him still, in the forest. Lyelt is watching him. What do you want us to do?'

'I want you to question why this spriggan was not planning to alert *you* to this danger. Clearly it was happy to see you destroyed, as long as its precious Moorlanders were ready to defend themselves.'

'Sir—'

'You believed its tale, then. That's what you're telling me?'

'Well—'

'You find a single spriggan, alone in the woods. No doubt you play your bullying pranks on it in the same way as you did with the other one, and when it spins a wild story of important news for the king, you believe it.' Arric watched with a thin smile as the certainty faded from the youngster's face, but his thoughts raced. He could not let the spriggan reach the Moorlanders. 'And after you've questioned its motives for telling you its lies, I want you to kill it.'

Keityn's mouth dropped open, and his face—already Forester-pale—went grey. 'Please,' he mumbled, 'I cannot... he is a favourite of the kings, both old and new. My life would be forfeit.'

Arric's heart jolted. 'A favourite of Tir? Surely you are not telling me this spriggan claims to be *Jacky Greencoat*?'

'I am, sir.'

'You are mistaken. One looks much like another, and Greencoat is dead.'

Keityn's confidence returned. 'No, sir. This is him.'

'Then you must be doubly sure to silence him,' Arric growled. While he had been exasperated at Gerai for striking Greencoat down, he could not deny life had been far less complicated for it. The new king would be certain to believe anything Greencoat told him, without question.

Could this bumbling Forester be trusted to do what must be done? Perhaps Hewyl should be given the task instead. Arric hesitated. It was true Hewyl had returned to the coast after removing Tir's lady, but what if that act of protection had been for her rather than his new people? Then again there had to be some point where trust was earned, perhaps this was it.

He opened his mouth, and then abruptly shut it again; Hewyl was mortal, for the Ocean's sake! A slower, more clumsy race there had never been; it would take him far too long to reach the place where Keityn and his little Forester friend were keeping the spriggan. There was no help for it, the Forester must be the one to end Greencoat's lucky, borrowed life.

He was about to pass this order to Keityn, when Nerryn came in, her hair wet and stuck to her face, her boots making squelching noises on the rocky floor. She had a bright air of triumph about her, and a glance at the mid-grown Forester showed he had noted her charms well, but he wisely said nothing.

Arric nodded an acknowledgement to his sister's achievements; he did not want to paint them too brightly, but she should be encouraged. Hewyl though… Arric was still not entirely sure of him; better he should hear as little as possible of what might be said here.

'Hewyl, take word to Cantoc that we have had a visit from Mylan's spies. Now,' he added, as Hewyl hesitated. 'You do not need to tell him what is being said, but he must have the opportunity to speak with Keityn here if he wishes.

He waited until Hewyl had left, and then turned back to Keityn. 'Mylan tells me you and your companion are to bring other news. So tell me, how fares Tir? Is he recovered?'

'Almost, sir.' Keityn was clearly relieved to be talking of something other than the spriggan. 'He and Prince Maer came to speak with Ykana and Yventra. To ask for their support should there be a war.'

'And do they have it?'

'Well, sir,' Keityn looked a bit sly, and Arric felt himself warming to him slightly.

'Well what?'

'At present yes, they do. But Lyelt is nearly ready to set the challenge at Ykana's feet. When he is leader, we are yours. Cantoc's, I mean.'

Arric's face twitched into a smile. 'You seem very sure of his victory. Ykana is a strong leader, she has beaten back several challenges. What makes you so sure she will not defeat Lyelt?'

'She is growing older.' Keityn shrugged. 'Her sister is second-in-command, and more of a problem than Ykana. But I do not believe she wishes to be leader, she is too wrapped in her Chosen.'

'How soon will Lyelt cast his challenge?'

'Before two more moons have passed, I think.'

'He must cast it tomorrow.'

'But—'

'If he will be ready in two moons, he is ready now. We cannot afford to wait. Now,' Arric dismissed the subject with a wave of his hand, and got back to the important point. 'When you say Tir is almost recovered, how close is he to full strength, would you say?'

Keityn considered, and Arric watched him trying not to stare as Nerryn loosened her coat and removed it. Beneath it she wore rough-made trousers and a tunic, hardly the garb of princesses, but it seemed to make little difference to the mid-grown, whose eyes followed every movement despite his attempts to remain unmoved.

'Tir?' Arric prompted.

'He moves well,' Keityn said, pulling himself out of whatever impossible love story had begun in his head, 'but it is also clear he is trying to do too much too soon. His fear for his son,'—he threw a curious glance at the sleeping totterling—'means he will likely push himself hard.'

'And what plans do they have, him and his so-called prince?'

'Oh, but he *is* a prince,' Keityn said, surprised,

'Tir introduced him as such. And he is Tir's brother after all. They also talked of the choosing... the, uh, joining ceremony of Maer and your sister, sir. Their wedding is... *was*, to be hosted in the forest.'

Arric kept a close eye on Nerryn as these words tumbled out of Keityn's mouth, but she appeared unmoved as she kicked off her wet boots and pulled sodden socks from her dainty feet. He turned back to Keityn. 'Plans, I said, not chatter.'

Keityn cleared his throat, embarrassed. 'They mean to recover the child, and soon. They are aware he is safe, they believe Lady Nerryn to be caring for it...' He broke off, clearly nervous at what he must say next. 'Sir, I'm sorry, but you cannot trust your sister!'

'What?' Nerryn finally looked up from where she was drying her feet. 'What are you saying?'

The boy flushed. 'You c... came here with a false purpose, My Lady. Please do not try to deny it. I have heard from Prince Maer's own lips that you planned to win your family's trust, and then to steal the child away back to his mother.'

There was a silence while Keityn looked from Nerryn to Arric in growing fear, but after a moment Nerryn smiled. 'You have proved your loyalty, at least.' She rose and went over to the young Forester, and laid a gentle hand on his shoulder. 'You needn't fear, you did right to tell my brother. It's true, that is why I came here, and I have admitted as much.'

'But since she learned of her lover's treachery she has come to her senses,' Arric put in. 'She knows she cannot return to the people who slew her parents. She belongs here, and has pledged her loyalty to Cantoc.'

'I… I did not know,' Keityn stammered, fixing Nerryn with miserable eyes. 'Please, forgive me?'

'There is nothing to forgive.' She removed her hand and stepped away, but not before she'd let her fingers brush the smooth cheeks, stained red with mortification. Arric allowed himself a fleeting moment of admiration for his sister's casual exploitation of her own charms.

The long moments passed while they waited for Hewyl to come back. Arric listened, impressed, as Nerryn engaged the young Forester in conversation that probed into the lives of the Foresters, while seeming as casual and frivolous as a girl passing her time with gossip. They almost certainly learned more than they would have had Arric questioned him.

'Will Cantoc come and speak to me?' Keityn asked, at length. He sounded nervous at the thought, and Arric had more pressing matters than keeping him calm, while they waited for a visit that would probably never come.

'Less than likely. Go, do what must be done with the spriggan. And do not make the same mistake as Gerai; see he is properly dead this time.'

From the corner of his eye he saw Nerryn's head jerk around; clearly Greencoat's fate had succeeded where news of Maer had failed, to spark her interest. Another indication that her love had been tried and found wanting after all.

Keityn gave Arric one more worried look, but his eyes avoided Nerryn as he left. On his way out he brushed shoulders with a returning Hewyl, who simply shook his head at Arric and went to stand by the fire.

Arric turned to his sister. 'How are you coming along with your weather-games?'

'Careful,' Hewyl put in mildly, 'or I might believe the spriggan's tale myself.'

Nerryn eyed him as she ran her hands through her soaked hair. 'What tale?'

'The one about me hoping to harness the *almighty power of twins* to throw destruction upon the Moorlanders,' Arric supplied, giving the words a scathing emphasis. He hoped he had anticipated her response accurately.

She gave a short laugh. 'Truly? Mylan might possess great power, but I certainly do not.'

'Indeed,' Arric smiled. 'One day, perhaps, you will come into your strength, but it will not be until this business is long over. No,' he stood up and stretched luxuriously, looking forward to his bed, 'our parents will be avenged in the same way they were taken. They deserve nothing less. Now sleep. Tomorrow will be a long and bloody day, I fear.'

Chapter Eighteen

The Forest. September 29th

Yventra woke early, and immediately knew something was different. The atmosphere was charged, and she was not the only one to notice. All over the forest, *trigoryon an goswig* were twitching awake before it was dark, and as they rose from their beds their silence was quite eerie; no more the happy chatter of busy creatures, eager to begin their tasks and their play. Instead they moved about, wordless and nervy, eyeing each other with curiosity, each trying to find the source of this strange weight that had descended upon their home.
It was not long before Yventra found it.

'Ykana?'

Her sister looked up from where she sat in the central clearing, cross-legged, eyes closed. Her face was taut, her body rigid. 'It will be tonight,' she said in a low voice, and her gaze went to those Foresters who waited on the edge of the clearing.

Yventra sat down beside her. Part of her was relieved the wait was over, but her sister's tension was worrying. 'Are you not prepared?'

'If the challenger is one of those greenstick boys, perhaps. If it comes from somewhere I do not expect, then how can I know?'

'But surely you are strong enough, no matter who it is?'

Ykana had been as fierce as ever on the surface, but since Casta's death she had seemed to fade more every night. Yventra had put it down to sorrow for a great man. But now she was less sure. 'Ykana, what is wrong? You can beat back any challenge, you know this.'

'I am certain enough that our people would not choose to see me ousted,' Ykana said, 'but it is not a choice, is it? I have their respect, but it is what they see, what we are capable of, that must decide it.'

'And you believe you are not capable of winning?' Ykana's lack of fight was deeply concerning. 'You are still strong.'

'Not strong enough.' Ykana sighed and rose, brushing off the bits of dried tree trunk that clung to her leggings. 'I am growing old, Yventra. I have seen many more cycles than you, more than I care to bring to mind. I am as certain as I can be that the challenge will come from Lyelt, and he is young, and growing stronger every day.'

'Lyelt is a child!' Yventra snapped. 'And a dangerous and foolish one, at that. He has proved it. He *cannot* be allowed to lead us.' They heard a rustle of leaves, and a moment later Lyelt stood before them, a large bowl in his hands, and a wide smile of anticipation on his face.

'Ykana, esteemed leader of the *trigoryon an goswig*,' he began. He glanced behind him and Yventra's eyes followed, to see a gathering of shadows; Foresters who'd seen him walking towards this clearing with that bowl of water, and would have known exactly what was happening. 'I, Lyelt, do challenge you that your time is ending. That your strength is waning.'

The sisters moved closer together; they had heard the words before, but after Ykana's admission they seemed to strike harder now. 'When the moon is highest tonight, so will your chance rise, to meet this trial.' Lyelt stepped towards the fire, and made sure everyone was watching, raising his voice so no-one would miss the most important part. 'Until this fire burns again, the *trigoryon an goswig* have no leader.'

He upended the bowl, dousing the flames, then withdrew into the unsettled silence that had fallen over the departing Foresters, leaving Ykana and Yventra alone in the darkness.

Eventually, hesitant light flickered around them, and they settled down for a long night. No-one would be permitted in or out of the clearing until the challenge was under way. All they could do was wait for the moon to rise, and plead with the elements that they had not just witnessed the beginning of the death of the Foresters.

The moon took a painfully long time to creep to its highest point. In two nights it would be full, but who knew what would have happened in those two nights? Yventra shivered and looked at Ykana. Her sister's pale skin was glowing softly, her eyes appeared even bigger than usual. The ashy smell of the dampened fire still hung in the still air, and it served as a chilly reminder of what lay at stake; the next Forester to light that fire would be leader, and the future of the Foresters might well depend on it.

'Perhaps you could challenge Lyelt in turn, should he win,' Ykana ventured. 'You would only have to wait a moon's turn to do it.'

'A moon's turn would be too late.' A smile crept across her face. 'Even Wydra does not know yet, but I am carrying new life.'

Ykana turned to her, open-mouthed in surprise, then flung her arms around her. 'Oh, this is glorious!' she whispered. She drew back and touched Yventra's face. 'Wydra will sing your news out from the treetops, I know it. You have wished for this for so long, both of you.'

'We have,' Yventra admitted, her smile widening. 'But it does mean that soon I will be unable to—'

'Hush!' Ykana waved her words away. 'Of course you must not do anything to risk yourself or this new life. Do you know which of the males claims it?'

Yventra shook her head. 'Many have sought release these past two or three moon-cycles, and I have enjoyed them, but felt no different after each. It might be any one of them.'

'Then let us hope it was a strong, handsome creature who will bless your song with his own charms.'

Yventra found her own smile widening. 'What other male would I allow into my bed?'

Ykana laughed, and for a short, blissful moment they were youngsters again; revelling in their own beauty and high status; sought after, and holding their choices in their own hands. But the problem remained, and as the laughter tailed away they both sighed at once, eliciting further smiles that were, nevertheless, tinged with regret.

'If he wins, I will advise him,' Ykana said, and Yventra could hear the determination in her voice. 'He will be glad of my wisdom, though he might not admit to it.'

'If he wins he will select Keityn as his second,' Yventra reminded her. 'And Lyelt will not want *him* to see he needs guidance.'

'Nevertheless, there are those who realise the danger, I am sure of it.' Ykana straightened her shoulders. 'I will garner support from them, he *must* listen to me, and learn that there is more to being a leader than strutting around telling people what to do.'

They both looked up as they heard footsteps, and Yventra caught at Ykana's arm, her mind made up.

'Name me as your second. I will be your strong right arm. My days are early, the risk is small and there is so much to lose.'

Ykana looked tempted, then subsided. 'It's too dangerous. And Wydra will never allow it.'

'I have told you, Wydra does not yet know,'

Yventra whispered, with real urgency now. '*Please!*'

'No!' Ykana wrenched her arm free and turned to face her challenger. She spared Yventra one last, hopeless glance, and drew herself upright. Yventra saw her slender fingers clench into fists as strong as any she'd seen, and felt her apprehension ease a little. It might yet be well...

'*Trigoryon an goswig,*' Ykana began as the crowd thickened. Voices dropped and her voice carried well, clear and authoritative. 'The challenge is set. Lyelt has put himself forward and will be a...a worthy leader, should he triumph tonight.'

Yventra wondered if she was the only one who'd heard her sister's voice tighten on those words. Still, they must be uttered, no matter how sharp they stuck in the throat. She listened to the familiar speech, with half her attention on the crowd; were they surprised? They did not seem to be. Her gaze moved over the interested faces, and found the one she sought. Wydra's eyes were already on her, and their smiles matched, although Yventra knew hers must look forced.

She turned back to her sister, who was now handing a large leather bag to Keityn. He felt around in it to ensure it was empty, nodded, and tucked it beneath his arm.

Yventra felt into Lyelt's bag, and indicated to the watching crowd that all was as it should be. 'We will meet again when the sun strikes the ground here.' She drew a cross in the dirt with the toe of her boot. 'If both bags are full, there will be a test of strength to follow for both. If Ykana fails, there will be a test for Lyelt, who has not yet proved himself.'

She looked for any dissent among their people, but none was ever voiced; it made sense that, if Lyelt failed this most basic of tests, Ykana—as proven leader— would immediately be restored. That was the best they could hope for, since Lyelt would certainly not fail a strength test.

The watching Foresters moved into the cold and dark clearing, to await the challengers' return under the watchful eyes of Wydra and of Lyelt's father. This way, the challengers would not be able to take food already stored in order to fill their bags. Yventra hugged her sister, and went with Lyelt, and Keityn took his place at Ykana's side as the four of them went into the forest to begin their search, for food and for their future.

***

Mill Lane Cottage.

Home. Where she should have felt safe, comforted, at ease. But as Laura's gaze fell on the picture frame, still face-down on the carpet where it had fallen from her shocked, numbed fingers, a tidal wave of images and words battered her exhausted mind into submission. All she could do was sit, trembling, on the very edge of her sofa, and close her eyes.

Graham's family. Descended from men with a brutal sense of entitlement, and a determination to fulfil it. War or not, the deaths at the mill had been unnecessary and cruel, and had destroyed an entire community.

Graham himself. Anger alight in him, big, strong fingers finding purchase on something he couldn't see. How had it been: crushing? Twisting? No-one would ever know now. Graham's own heart attack had been long in coming, but swift and final; violence with no redemption but death. He'd believed he loved the thing he'd killed, yet he had killed her just the same.

And finally Graham's daughter. Facing down the man *she* claimed to love, wishing him harm at her own hands, wanting to tear and gouge at him, her anger consuming the memory of who he was, turning him into the enemy. He had chosen a path he had never wanted, and she had blamed him for it. Had actually tried to strike him, just before he tore the photo in two… and what if she'd been carrying some kind of weapon?

She opened her eyes and looked at her phone, then picked it up, opened the gallery, and pressed the self-destruct button. Scrolling through the pictures, she wasn't aware of the tears that had gathered, until she couldn't see anymore, then she blinked furiously, sending them rolling down her cheeks and her vision cleared again… only for another picture to squeeze at her heart until she could scarcely breathe.

Back and forth through the photos. Torturing herself by remembering them: Ben's voice; the smell of him; the feel of his solid little form in her arms.

And the sound of Richard's low laughter, his voice lifted in song, and the way his eyes softened whenever he looked at his son. The two of them together. Ben's excitement whenever he knew Richard was around, even if they were in different rooms.

The dark and dreadful thought that she was going to kill them both if she kept them apart began to creep over her, and as hard as she tried to banish it, it continued to grow. Right now neither of them had Ben, and they were united in their desperation, but when he came home she would have to take him far from Lynher Mill for their own safety, and that connection between him and his father would be stretched so thin it would soon snap. And then there would be two more desperately unhappy people in the world instead of just one.

The knocker fell against the door and she jumped, heart thumping... *Maer?* before remembering Ann's hypnotherapist was due. Fighting bitter disappointment she knuckled the last of the tears from her eyes and stood up, wiping her hands dry on her jumper before opening the front door.

When she'd spared a thought for the therapist she had alternately pictured some tall, ethereally distant-looking woman, wearing something floaty and shimmering; and a stern, bespectacled, lie-back-on-the-couch stereotype, with an imposing manner, a smart suit, and a notebook. But Tonya was neither. Instead she turned out to be a petite brunette with a wide smile, and was dressed in jeans and an orange sweatshirt with *Ohio* embroidered on the shoulder.

Ann led her into the sitting room, visibly relieved to be sharing some of the burden of worry. 'Laura, this is Tonya. Otherwise known as the Yank.'

Laura blinked. She thought she'd long since ceased to be surprised by Ann's bluntness, but now and again her friend still caught her unawares.

Tonya was also clearly used to it, and rolled her eyes, still smiling. She held out her hand. 'So nice to meet you, Laura. Don't mind her, she always calls me that.'

'Just get your own back by calling her a Brummie,' Laura advised, surprising herself by smiling back as she shook Tonya's hand. Her eyes still burned, but her breath was no longer hitching.

'Don't you dare,' Ann protested. 'Don't listen to her, I wasn't even *born* in Birmingham!'

Grateful for the light banter, and lack of pointless questions, Laura gave Ann a teasing look. 'She never dared to call Richard a yank, interestingly enough.'

'Where's he from?' Tonya asked.

'California.'

'Oh, cool—'

'Um, Chicago?' Ann said.

Laura gave a little shake of her head. 'Did I say it again? Yes, Chicago. Sorry, I've got some kind of a mental block on that.'

'Is that where he is right now?'

Laura exchanged a quick glance with Ann,

wondering how much she had said already, but Tonya saw it and shook her head. 'Forget it, it's not my business.'

'No, it's okay. He's going back there soon, but at the moment he and Ben are taking a few days away, on the coast.'

'Cool. Where?'

'Down near Trethkellis.'

'Seriously? I love it there!' Tonya smiled again, her blue-grey eyes friendly but keen, and obviously taking in everything despite her easy manner. Laura's own eyes narrowed slightly; did the American suspect something already?

'So,' she said, into the faintly awkward pause. 'Would you like a drink, or do you want to get started right away? I have absolutely no idea how this works, sorry.'

'Thanks, I'd love a cup of tea if you have some. And I usually play it by ear, depending on how the client's feeling. Ann, could you make the tea while I introduce myself properly to Lucy?'

'Laura,' Ann corrected again.

Tonya looked blank for a moment. 'Sorry! Yes, not a good start, huh? Seems we're as bad as each other.'

'It's fine,' Laura said. 'You must see an awful lot of people.'

'Well anyway, Laura, I'm not going to use any kind of technique on you tonight. I just want to talk, and get a feel for what's bothering you. Is that okay?'

But Laura shook her head. 'It was, but now... I

need to know something in particular about myself. Something hidden. Can you do that?'

Tonya's expression sharpened with interest, and she threw a glance at Ann, who just shrugged and shook her head. 'I don't know,' Tonya said, frowning. 'Maybe. What do you need to know?'

Laura hesitated, unsure how to begin, but decided to start with the truth. 'Richard and I argued. Badly.' She cleared her suddenly tight throat. 'I came *this* close to hitting him. Would have, if he hadn't moved away.' She couldn't bring herself to question aloud what might have happened if she'd been holding something sharp, or heavy.

She fixed Tonya with a pleading look. 'Thing is, what if that's me, now? What if it's part of my make-up?'

Ann stared at her, clearly amazed. 'Are you mad? You're the gentlest person I know!'

'Not anymore I'm not. It's been getting worse.'

'Bound to, if you're not sleeping. You just need to be able to relax, and the Yank can help with that.'

'But what if it's not enough? What happens if I can't control it when Ben… when… next time?' She turned back to Tonya. 'I've just found out some things about my past, and I need to know if they affect me. Who I am, and what I might do. Can you help?'

'Sure, I can try.' Tonya caught Ann's eye and nodded towards the open kitchen door. Ann went, casting a worried glance over her shoulder at Laura, who gave her a watery half-smile and perched on the edge of the sofa again. She gestured to the chair opposite.

'Okay,' Tonya said, sitting down. 'I'm going to need a little more. Then we can think about how best to do this. Are you ready to tell me what you've heard that's gotten you scared?'

'My father killed someone,' Laura said bluntly, and heard Tonya's breath snag in shock. 'It was a long time ago but I only found out about it today, and the thing that frightens me most is that he did it in some kind of a blind rage.'

Tonya sat very still for a moment, then, thankfully, she moved past the questions that must have been burning her, and got right to the point. 'And your fight with Richard? What kind of fight was that?'

'Passionate,' Laura admitted. 'For a second all I could think of was how much I hated him. And I told him so.'

'Ann tells me you guys are really close. That can happen when the love's that intense.'

The constant, dull pain that had set up home in Laura's heart flared anew at Tonya's words. 'We are close, and yes, it's intense. But he can't live here anymore. It's a legal thing, he's got to go back to Calif… Chicago.'

She wrapped her arms across her waist and gripped her own jumper tight enough to hurt her fingers, it helped focus her on her words. Her lies. 'We've agreed we can't go on with a long-distance relationship,' she said, as calmly as she could. 'It's not good for us, or for Ben, and I can't just leave my mother and move over there. But the reason we're splitting up isn't the issue, it's the way it happened.'

Tonya had taken no notes, but was watching her closely. 'So you need to look inside yourself for this violent streak you're worried about.'

'Yes. Is it possible?'

Tonya nodded slowly, thoughtfully. 'I think so. Worth a try, at least. But what if you find you have that streak? What then?'

Laura hadn't even thought that far ahead, but either way the truth was the same. 'Then Ben will live with Richard, where he's safe.'

Silence fell between them, so all they could hear was the spoon clinking against cups in the kitchen, and a crow shouting from the tree in the back garden.

'How do we do it?' Laura said at last.

Ann brought in two mugs of tea and put them on the coffee table, and Tonya smiled her thanks, and picked hers up, considering. 'Maybe the original plan will work best to start with. Just to go into a relaxed state, and try to figure out your state of mind.'

'Alright.' Laura sat back, relieved to be getting started, and Ann returned, with her own tea and the biscuit tin, and retreated to the chair by the window.

Tonya opened her notebook and settled into her chair. She asked a few questions about Richard and Laura's relationship, and offered sympathy for the difficulties of two people adjusting to a young family, when they hadn't been together that long themselves. Laura's tea was cooling, but she was too comfortable to lean forward and pick it up. Let it cool a bit more first…

'Laura!' A snapping in front of her eyes, Ann's voice somewhere in the distance, 'Laura! Come on!'

Laura jerked upright, kicking the coffee table, and blinking. 'What the hell?' Her mind was clouded, fuzzy, and it took a moment to identify the snapping sound as fingers, a few inches from her face. 'All right!' She pushed Ann's hand away, and rubbed at her eyes. 'I told you I was tired, I'm sorry.' She gave an embarrassed laugh. 'If only it was that easy to zonk off at night.'

'Honey, you weren't sleeping,' Tonya said, visibly shaken. 'And I don't even think you were all the way under, but… you said some stuff.'

'Stuff?' Laura went cold. 'I was probably dreaming.'

'I told you, you weren't… look, Ann, I'm not okay with this,' Tonya said. 'You told me it was just some break-up issues.'

'It is. She just needs to relax and give herself the chance to sleep properly. And eat,' Ann added, proffering the biscuit tin.

'I don't want a biscuit.' Laura sighed. 'Tonya, what happened? Why are you "not okay" with it?'

'I wasn't ready, and you were *this* close.' Tonya closed her book again and leaned forward, her eyes earnest. 'You started talking about things I wasn't asking you. Who is Stuart?'

Laura frowned and shook her head. 'I... don't know anyone called that.'

'Sounded like not you only *do* know him, but that something about him damn near broke your heart.' Tonya sat back. 'Don't get me wrong, I'm happy to do this, to take you back, or whatever. Explore genetic memory, maybe. But I'm not doing it unless we do it properly.'

'Properly?' Despite her reservations, Laura felt a flicker of hope at the thought of exploring genetic memory.

'We set rules. I put a suggestion in place that'll let me control how it goes. Are you happy with that?'

'Can you really do this? Unlock what I might know of my ancestors?'

'I can try.' Tonya sat back again. 'How far back do you want to go?'

'1643. The civil war. I just...' Laura gestured helplessly, 'I just want to find out what kind of people I'm descended from.'

'All we can do is try,' Tonya said. 'I don't think you'll find out a lot of detail, but let's give it a go.'

'Will I be able to control what I say?'

'Sure. It's a trance-like state, but when we do it properly you won't be totally gone like before. Now, you hear the way I'm talking right now?' Laura nodded; Tonya's voice was fairly brisk-sounding, not loud, but not low-pitched and soothing as it had been before.

'Okay, so we're just going to talk a while, and my

voice will change. You'll relax. Go with it, don't fight it. We'll talk some more, and then, when you start to hear me sounding more like this again, you'll realise it's time you came back. It'll be a steady, calm process. Again, don't fight it. Are you ready?'

'Yes.'

'Okay, so let's talk about your job. You like your job?'

'Yes, I miss it.'

'You plan on going back?'

'I hope to.'

And so the talk continued. After a few more general questions, Tonya began to ask about Laura's family. Laura explained about Sylvia, and her parents. Tonya asked about her grandparents, as she knew them. Laura relaxed. Tonya asked her to go back further, just one generation. Laura stalled.

'Laura, honey? It's easy, just skip back over this barrier, tell me about your great-grandparents. Did you know them?'

'No.'

'What about other family? Uncles?'

'No.'

'Cousins, then. Come forward again, and give me cousins.'

Laura shook her head. 'I don't know.'

'There's a door right there in front of you. Your great-grandparents are in there.'

'Okay.'

'Open the door, Laura.'

'It's already open. A little bit.'

'What's in there?'

'Just black.'

'Push the door wider.'

'It won't move.'

Tonya tried again, and again, and each time all Laura could see was a sliver of dark emptiness. 'It's your family, Laura. They can't hurt you, and you need to see them so we can learn more about you.'

'I'm not scared. It's just black,' Laura heard herself say, in a puzzled and sad voice. She was so relaxed and comfortable, she could feel herself drifting into sleep. But she wanted to do this for Tonya, because Tonya was trying to help her. And Ann wanted to help too. 'I'm sorry,' she murmured.

'Don't be sorry, Lucy,' Tonya said gently. 'Just look in the room again.' She had put a strange emphasis on her name, which was odd because it was the wrong one…

Laura pushed the door wider. And everything changed.

Chapter Nineteen

The moon was a couple of nights short of full, and rode high. Richard leaned his shoulder against the shattered chimney and breathed deeply, letting the chill work its way through him and bring him to full wakefulness. He was feeling stronger by the hour; sleep came more easily now, and it was good, healing sleep, rather than the grateful escape it had been before.

He stretched his left hand around to his back, and tested the soreness in his ribs. The ache of the bruising remained, but he was used to it now and, as long as he held himself straight, he should be pretty good to make it all the way to the coast. He had no idea how he'd cope when he got there, but he had to learn not to be constantly looking around for Kernow or Martha, with their bitter leaves and their stinky candles… it was just him now.

Maer emerged from the tunnel, and squinted up at the sky. 'Are you ready?'

'Yeah.' Richard levered himself off the cool stone, and followed Maer's gaze. 'What is it?'

'It's a clear night. We'll have to be careful.'

'It'd be better if it was crappy weather?'

'Clouds and mist mask a lot,' Maer pointed out. 'Plus, on a good night anyone keeping a watch for us is less likely to be in their sleeping rolls, and more likely to be farther afield.'

'But you guys don't feel the cold, so what difference would it make?'

'We still get wet when it rains.' He gave Richard a look, and a little grin. 'And when people cause mini tidal-waves in large pools.'

Richard laughed. 'Teach you to stand too close.' He settled his cloak square on his shoulders. 'Okay, let's do this. Are we going the long way around?'

'No. This way.' Maer gestured. 'You'll see the path soon enough.'

Richard turned his face to the west and started walking. The sensation was always strange to begin with—as if he was moving three steps for every one he was actually taking—but it wasn't long before he settled into a rhythm, and the ground began to fly beneath him.

The direct path between Lynher Mill and Trethkellis required little in the way of detours around villages. Once Maer pointed out the various landmarks they had passed on previous trips, Richard found his feet were unerring in their choice of direction and he could stop thinking about whether he was going the right way.

To begin with, his eagerness to take Ben back drove him on, but after a while he began to feel the ever-present, dull throb of pain behind his ribs as more than just a familiar, but easily dismissed discomfort; Maer noticed him slowing down, and insisted they stop for a brief rest.

Richard reluctantly agreed, and they sat down in the shelter where two dry stone walls met at the corner of a field. A gust of wind shook the gorse bushes nearby, and the temperature had dropped a noticeable few degrees. The skies were clouding over, the stars only peeking out now and again, where earlier they had dusted the dark blue canopy in their thousands.

Richard's thoughts swerved away from what lay ahead, back to Lynher Mill. 'Did Jacky go to Laura yet?'

'I sent him just before I came out to meet you. He'll persuade her, don't worry.'

'You really think she needs to be underground to be safe?'

Maer shrugged. 'I think it's wise, but who knows? If we are able to bring Nerryn away too, we will only have Arric's powers to worry about.'

'And are they strong?'

'I don't know. Nerryn says he creates storms at sea, but they are small, and very localised. Not the kind of far-reaching danger she and Mylan would be capable of.'

Richard stared out into the darkness of the moorland. How many other mysteries were out there? How many confused spirits, searching for bodies the way Loen had? How many of them would find a wandering mortal one, only to kill it in their desperation to take control?

He took a slow, deep breath, trying to ignore the way it stopped short as a band of pain tightened across his ribs. He *was* breathing, that was the main thing, and Ben was getting closer with every step, no matter how much those steps were starting to hurt. 'Come on,' he said, climbing to his feet again.

Maer looked up at him through narrowed eyes. 'You're not ready. Sit.'

'The wind's getting up,' Richard pointed out. 'And according to your logic we don't have the luxury of time, not anymore. We shouldn't have waited this long.' The wind tugged at his hair and his cloak. Even when it wasn't gusting, the air seemed to have taken on a life of its own. It was as if they were at altitude, and it gave Richard the same unsettled, faintly queasy feeling he got from standing near the edge of a mountain top.

'You weren't ready then. We had no choice.' Maer stood up too, his white-blond hair lifting in the freshening wind. 'I'd have left this morning, if you could be trusted to remain in Lynher Mill.' He looked around, and at the sky. 'Is it much colder?'

'A little.' Richard pulled his cloak tighter and turned onto the elementals' path again. He wondered if mortals could see it the way he could now? Laura, maybe… he cleared his throat to loosen it; just thinking about her hurt. 'Let's go.'

They walked more quickly again now. Conversation fell away, as the urgency took over and Richard's mind turned to Ben once more. The boy was more than likely asleep, yet it didn't take much effort to feel the pull of him, just as he had felt Maer's presence before, and the same way Maer had found him in Plymouth.

Ben was no longer of this place, but he was still part of Richard himself, and Richard would no sooner see him again than he would have to let him go. Could he do it? What would it do to Laura if he couldn't? The thoughts were confusing, tumbling around and taking his mind off what he was doing, so it was with a sharp, breathless shock that he heard a shout up ahead.

He stopped, and Maer almost cannoned into him. He felt a hand on his arm, urging silence. They waited, trying not to breathe as they listened; there were no more shouts, but there were voices. Whoever it was, they were making no effort to be stealthy.

'That's a good sign,' Maer said in a low voice, into Richard's ear. 'If they were Cantoc's people they would not want us to know they were there.'

'So where do we go?' Richard whispered back. There was no shelter close enough to reach; they had left the last of the large woodlands behind them at least twenty minutes ago, and were now crossing open farmland. The voices were too close for comfort, it seemed they were only separated by a hedge a few feet away. Richard heard three different voices, but that meant nothing – there could be fifty men, and forty-seven of them silent.

'Pengenna,' Maer whispered at last. 'The manor is

protected by trees, and there's a small forest.' He started for the stone wall, intending to follow it back the way they had come, but another shout drifted out of the dark, and before Richard had time to think, his blade was in his hand.

He turned to face a blurred shape. The shape halted and Richard blinked, watching it solidify into a tall, bearded man. He held no weapon, and Richard lowered his own, but slowly and keeping it held tightly. 'Who the hell are you?'

'My name is Hendrig.' He studied Richard, who was vaguely aware of a scuffling sound up ahead and dared to hope Maer had got away safely, that this man's absent companion was merely hunting for a shadow now.

'What is your name, mortal? And how is it that you can see me?'

'Let me pass.'

'Name!'

Richard smiled suddenly, a smile that felt cold, even to him, and stepped closer to Hendrig. 'I am Tir,' he said, his heart quickening as he heard the name, spoken in his own voice and with real acceptance at last. 'Now let me pass.'

But Hendrig's expression did not change. 'Go home, false king. Your people will need you soon enough.'

As if in confirmation, the wind gusted again, this time strongly enough to make Richard stagger slightly, and that was all Hendrig needed. His hand shot out and ripped the bronze dagger from

Richard's grip, turning it on its owner, who ducked aside as it tore the air where he had been standing a split second before.

Savage pain flashed through him and, for a heartbeat, Richard wondered if he had escaped after all. When he spared a glance downward he saw no blood, but his insides burned and twisted, and he struggled against a sudden weakness in his legs. The muscles trembled and almost gave out, and he knew if he fell he would die. A memory flared: a young soldier, lying helpless beneath the pike that would kill him…

Hendrig slashed again and Richard lunged to the side, once again spared the edge of the blade by inches. He would not be so lucky a third time. From the corner of his eye he saw Maer, pinned to the wall by a man even taller than Hendrig, and his heart sank. And where was the third man?

'You are injured,' Hendrig observed. 'Go home.'

'I am home,' Richard managed, straightening with an effort, and hoping he hadn't set his recovery back too far; his entire torso was a mass of pain, and his ribs were on fire. But although Hendrig was telling him to leave, he knew they wouldn't be allowed to. The clouds parted to allow a sliver of moonlight, and his own blade glinted in Hendrig's hand as the man cut the air between them in a wide semi-circle.

'Put up your weapon, Hendrig!' Maer shouted, from his pinned position.

'I recognise and despise you, Prince Maer.' Hendrig's voice was hard. 'Stealer of Nerryn, killer of Talfrid.'

'What?' Richard shot another look at Maer. 'Talfrid's dead?'

Hendrig grunted. 'You pretend ignorance, yet your prince here is guilty of the crime.'

Maer was white, shocked. 'No,' he whispered. 'Nerryn is… Talfrid cannot be dead!'

He wriggled away, and his captor was caught unawares and almost let him go, but seized him again from behind. They fell to the ground together, and Richard heard Maer grunt as the breath left his body. A glance at Hendrig showed he was momentarily distracted by the scuffle, and Richard lashed out, knocking the big man's wrist and sending the knife spinning.

They were on equal terms now. Hendrig stepped in and delivered a quick blow to Richard's jaw, but as he stumbled aside, Richard kicked out, catching the side of Hendrig's leg. Hendrig went down and Richard turned towards Maer, only to freeze as the third man finally made his appearance.

In his fist he gripped a leather leash, wrapped around his hand several times, and, straining on the other end of it was the biggest, most ferocious-looking dog Richard had ever seen. The damned thing had its eyes fixed on him, it was like a personal hatred. And this was no ordinary dog; those eyes were a dark, blood-red.

Hendrig rose, dragging his injured leg, and glared at the newcomer. 'Where in the Ocean's name have you been, Lawbryn?'

'Who is this?' Lawbryn jerked back on the leash as the hound tried to lunge towards Richard.

'The much-lauded king of the Moorlanders,' Hendrig said, hunting on the ground for Richard's blade. 'And over there is the killer of my daughter's husband.'

Maer climbed to his feet; it was no longer necessary to restrain him, not with that hell-hound within slobbering distance. 'You are Dafna's father?' he said, sounding suddenly hopeful. 'The leader of the *trigoryon an pell*?'

'You would call us that, but to us *you* are the distant-dwellers.'

'Of course. But if you are Dafna's people, then you must know – I am to wed Nerryn. Please, let me go to her...'

'Nerryn? Marry you?' Hendrig abandoned his search for Richard's blade, and turned furious eyes on Maer. 'Once, maybe. But she knows the truth about you now.'

'I did not harm her father!' Maer cried, despair and anger battling in his face. He took a step forward, and the dog's eyes immediately swivelled away from Richard and onto him. 'Please, she will need me—'

'She will never have to worry about seeing you again,' Hendrig said, with deceptive calm. 'Lawbryn, loose the hound.'

'But Nerryn —'

'Loose the hound!'

A second later Lawbryn had flicked his wrist

over, and the leash slithered from his hand as the enormous beast sprang forward, eerily quiet in its slavering triumph.

'Maer!' Richard threw himself at the creature as it pounded past him, but his frantically grabbing fingers slid off the thick, oily fur without gaining purchase, and he fell heavily. Maer's scream tore through the night, and through Richard's heart, but when it was cut brutally short the silence was even more terrible.

***

Lewiston, California. 1916. Military Hospital.

The ward was quiet; most of the men slept, and those who did not, or could not, sat close to the meagre light of their candles, writing their hearts onto scraps of paper to send to family and girlfriends at home, or to their comrades who still fought overseas.

Nurse Helen Moss glanced at the second-to-last bed, by the door; of all the doughboys who had passed through her care Stuart Sullivan was the one whose company she enjoyed the most. From the moment he'd arrived they'd found a thread that drew them together and she couldn't help liking him a great deal. Not romantically, since, although he was undeniably attractive, he was at least ten years older than her—probably halfway into his thirties—but he seemed to enjoy her company as much as she enjoyed his.

There was something big brother-like about the way he teased her, yet stuck up for her against the stricter of the two nursing sisters. He was quiet, for the most part, but his dry humour was infectious and he'd sing sometimes, too, under his breath while he was moving in and out of bed, as if it focused his mind away from any pain he was feeling. He had a nice voice.

He was one of the wakeful ones tonight, sitting up against his pillows, his brow furrowed as he concentrated on writing, but he seemed to feel the weight of her attention and looked up, catching her eye. She smiled at him. He returned the smile, and went back to his letter. *Lucky girl, whoever she is.*

Helen turned away again and busied herself with collecting up the supper plates, and trying not to sulk about it. As a nurse she'd thought she would be changing dressings, at least, but all she'd been trusted with so far was washing dishes and carrying away dirty laundry to be cleaned.

Even some of the voluntaries were given more care of the patients, and although most of the soldiers were simply convalescing, following surgery in England and France, Helen longed to feel she had made a real difference. She couldn't prevent a sigh from escaping as she watched two experienced nurses begin turning back another patient's sheets, ready to change his dressing before he settled down for the night.

'Nurse?'

She looked around. Stuart was beckoning her over, and she put down the pile of plates and went over, ignoring the curious glances of the two busy nurses. 'Private Sullivan. What can I do for you?'

'Nothing,' he said in a low voice, and his green eyes caught the candlelight and glinted. 'I just thought you looked like you could use some company. I sure could.'

'Happy to oblige, sir,' Helen said with a little laugh. 'How are you feeling tonight?'

'Pretty good,' he said. 'They did a damned good job back in England, but it's good to be home.'

She sobered a little. 'Will they send you back out there?'

'I guess. But not yet.' Stuart touched his left side, high on his ribcage, where the biggest piece of shrapnel had struck him. Sister Judith had said it had punctured dangerously deep, and he'd had a long and difficult operation to remove the metal, but he was mending nicely now.

Helen would be sad to see him leave the hospital, but she'd be glad for him too; he'd been through such a lot, and, like all her boys, he'd been stoic throughout. She wished she'd been there to help him when he'd first needed medical attention; it would have been good to be remembered with real gratitude once he'd gone back to his real life, instead of just as the girl who brought him soup and clean sheets.

She indicated the letter he had put aside when he'd called her over. 'What's her name?'

'Katherine, but I call her Kate. She pretends she hates it, but I don't think she does really.'

'Will you marry?'

'I hope so, if she'll still have me.'

Helen couldn't help responding to his smile, and the fact that his voice had softened when he'd spoken Katherine's name. He probably hadn't even noticed. 'You need to get some sleep,' she told him. 'They're never going to let you go home to her if you don't get better. And you won't get better unless you keep your strength up.'

'Nurse Moss!'

They both looked up at the sharp voice that cut through the ward, and Helen sighed again. 'Here we go,' she murmured. 'More laundry and dishwashing. My punishment for talking to you.'

Stuart chuckled. 'You'll make a really good nurse someday,' he assured her. 'Don't take any notice of what they say to you here. Something tells me you'll go just where you're needed the most.'

'Nurse Moss, are you chatting, or cleaning up supper? Your mother would never have been so idle when she worked here!'

'Private Sullivan just wanted to ask me something,' Helen said quickly. 'I'll get right back to it, Sister Judith.'

'Not her fault,' Stuart said. 'I was just asking what's for supper.'

'Supper!' Sister Judith huffed, and rolled her eyes.

Helen grinned at Stuart and went back to work. Gradually the candles were snuffed, and then all that remained was the softly glowing kerosene lamp by the nurses' station, and the winking moon that glinted through the high windows when the clouds parted. Whenever Helen passed Stuart's bed she sneaked a glance at him, at his tumbled black hair on the pillow, and his face, relaxed in sleep, and even smiling faintly… she wondered what he was dreaming of, and realised it was probably his Kate. She must be a very special lady indeed, to have claimed his heart.

Two nights later she arrived on the ward just as dinner was ending. As always, her first glance was to the second bed from the end, hoping Stuart hadn't left during the day. Despite knowing it was what he wanted, she couldn't help feeling relieved to see him still there, dozing lightly against his pillows. He was a little pale though, and Helen frowned, but had no time to go to him before being called into the sluice room.

Later, she saw he was still sleeping, but now he was lying down, and still too pale. Helen stepped over to the bed and touched a hand lightly to his forehead—her fingers came away damp with sweat and she wiped them quickly on her apron.

'Sister!' she called out. 'Sister, Private Sullivan doesn't seem well.'

'Then tend to him!' the duty sister snapped, hurrying past her. 'I have other patients to see to.' She disappeared into the ward next door, from where Helen heard the harsh cries of a man in distress, and then Helen was alone on the ward but for the patients.

'Stuart?' she whispered, touching his shoulder. He snatched a quick breath and opened his eyes. 'Are you alright?'

He blinked, then focused and relaxed a little. 'Sure I am.' He cleared his throat, and winced. 'I guess I just tried to do a little too much today.'

'Of course, you're eager to be gone,' she said with deep sympathy. 'I'll let you rest, but shout out if you need something.'

'I will,' he promised in a mumble, and closed his eyes again. 'I'll be fine, nurse, thank you.'

'Can I fetch you anything?' He didn't answer, just shook his head, and Helen heard her name wafting under the door from the next ward. 'I'm needed,' she said apologetically, and he nodded, his eyes still closed. Why couldn't she help him? What should she be doing?

For the rest of the night she was kept busy running errands, but whenever she could spare a minute she hurried to his bedside, and bathed his face and neck with cool water, but he didn't seem to notice. She called the duty sister again at around two o'clock in the morning, when Stuart began groaning, and the sister frowned down at him.

'It's probably an infection.'

Helen's heart froze. 'Infection? Then we need to—'

'I'm well aware of what we need to do,' the sister said briskly. She called for two more nurses, and Helen found herself pushed aside as they set to work cutting the bandages from Stuart's chest. The suppurating wound beneath drew gasps from the nurses, and a shout from the sister.

'Nurse Moss! Fetch Doctor Phillips immediately!'

The doctor's reaction was worryingly tense. 'Prepare him for surgery.'

By the time the sun came up Helen was a mass of ragged nerves. Stuart's bed was stripped and cleaned awaiting his return, and she hardly dared to hope she would see him lying there again. She wanted to stay until he came out of surgery, but was sent away at the end of her shift, and spent the day tossing and turning, chasing sleep that never came.

Walking onto the ward that night her heart tripped over itself with relief to see the familiar dark head, on the pillows of the bed second from the end. 'You're back with us, Private!' she said, stepping up to him. But the face that turned to her was barely recognisable. Whiter than white, slick with sweat, and with dark purple smudges beneath the eyes. The dry lips were cracked and sore-looking, parted slightly to allow rasping, too-rapid breath.

'There's little we can do, my dear,' a low voice said in Helen's ear, and she turned to see Sister Judith at her elbow. 'Sister Carter told me the infection's taken a deep hold. But we're fighting it as best we can.'

Helen's throat was almost too dry to speak, but she managed, 'How?'

'Doctor Phillips left instruction to irrigate the wound with antiseptic every few hours. It's a new idea they've developed in France, and it's saving lives already out there. The trouble is it's very easy to get the mixture wrong.'

'Will it work for Stu... Private Sullivan?'

Sister Judith shook her head. 'We don't know.' Her voice was still gentle. 'I wouldn't normally say this, Nurse Moss, but I know you and Private Sullivan have developed a friendship. You may sit with him whenever you find yourself with a quiet moment tonight. I will prepare his family for the worst.'

She touched Helen's arm and left, and Helen sat down next to Stuart, trying not to look at the fiercely racing pulse and the way his eyes moved restlessly beneath their thin lids. His wound had been left open to allow the antiseptic wash, and the smell coming off it was horrific, but Helen breathed through her mouth and stayed.

'I won't let you die,' she told him, trying to sound firm, but her voice sounded like a child's helpless whisper. 'I won't. I'll save you, I promise.' It was the first time she had seen someone this young so close to death. He had been perfectly well; on the road to recovery and looking forward to marriage, children, a life...

He began to shiver violently just under an hour later. The shivers were more like convulsions, and Helen cast about in desperation; surely, *surely* she should be able to help him, or at least ease him? She was trained as a nurse, just like her mother was, it was what she was *for*…

But all she could do was shout, 'Someone help!' and try to hold him still, so he didn't cause himself any further injury as his body twisted on the bed. His breathing became even more laboured and thin, and fresh blood flowed. Too much of it, soaking the sheets and covering Helen's hands so her grip on him became slippery and next to useless.

Nurses came, nurses went. Stuart did not see them. Helen didn't even know if he felt their calmly efficient, practiced hands on him; he didn't even seem to feel any pain when they washed his wound out yet again. He was lost; somewhere in his mind he was fighting a monster he could never beat, and Helen could do nothing for him. Her mother would have known what to do, but her mother wasn't here.

He woke just once more. His eyes seemed clearer, just for a moment, as they fixed on Helen's, and he tried to speak, but the only sound he made was a soft sigh, his last words lost as they dissipated in the air.

Katherine's grief was a terrible thing to see. It was as if she hadn't believed what she'd been told, and when she was given Stuart's pathetic few belongings, and saw the letter he'd been writing to her, she collapsed in dead faint.

Helen sat with her as she came around. She'd pictured some long-legged beauty with huge doe eyes and a glorious mane of hair, but Stuart's beloved was actually rather plain, with a snub nose, and earnest blue eyes that shone with unshed tears as she sat in a state of numbed shock, her hands shaking as they clutching Stuart's infantry jacket with its ragged hole in the side.

As Helen looked desperately for something to say, she realised one thing: she was never going to feel so helpless again. Not ever. This hospital was supposed to care for men who were already almost recovered. Such a tragedy should never have happened. Perhaps if she'd had some knowledge of the way things were dealt with at the sharp end, it might not have done. She remembered Judith saying the irrigation technique had been developed in France—so that was where she would learn.

Holding onto Kate's hand, Helen murmured empty condolences, and turned her thoughts towards the war in Europe, and how soon she could leave America to join it.

***

Mill Lane Cottage. September 2012

Light was pulling her forward, but Laura resisted. She felt heavy in limb, and deeply comfortable; she couldn't have moved if she smelled fire. Her breathing was slow, and her heartbeat steady, so she swam back into the dark, until she found another door.

The American's voice was calling from somewhere behind her, but the door stood ajar and beyond it lay the missing piece of the puzzle. This time the barrier gave way under the merest touch of her fingers, and then she was through, and experiencing everything with the bright intensity of a blind woman gifted with sudden sight.

***

Weaverville, California. 1895.
Lucy Rogers looked at the woman who held Gabe's hand. A brisk and efficient nurse, up to the minute on all the latest cures, but she hadn't been able to save Gabe in the end. No surprise; he had been an old man, and Lucy herself was becoming an old woman, stepping smartly up to her seventieth birthday as she was. The nurse couldn't be blamed for the ravages of time, and it looked just like she was about to have that baby any second; stress should be avoided for sure.

'Can I get you anything, Mrs Rogers?' Nurse Moss asked. Lucy shook her head. The nurse touched her arm. 'The doctor will come and certify the... uh, the death.'

'Sure,' Lucy said, finding a smile to send the young woman on her way. 'You take care of yourself and that baby now. I'm surprised you're even working, so close to your time.'

'Well, we're short-handed again,' Nurse Moss said on a sigh. 'Alright, Mrs Rogers, if there's anything you need, you just send for me again. I'll go wash my hands if I may?'

'Of course. The kitchen's at the end of the hall downstairs. Thank you.'

Left alone with her husband's body, Lucy looked at him and tried to picture him as she'd known him when they were young, but instead she saw a different man. Black-haired, green-eyed... Will Deacon, her first and most beloved husband.

As the world about her shimmered into a hazy memory, she remembered the joy and excitement of riding to California, to this very town, back in '49, Will on the seat beside her. The love that had swelled in her breast as he had laughed with her, and hinted at intimacy the minute they stopped for the night.

She heard his voice so clearly, begging her to put their claim to work the gold someplace safe, before it blew away in the wind. She remembered the satisfying crackle of the paper against her skin, as she relented and tucked it into her bodice… And then the memories turned dark and deadly.

The terrifying sound of thudding hooves alongside them; the sight of Will's hands tightening on the reins and urging the horses faster; the moment of breathless horror as the wagon, with all their worldly belongings, flipped and sent them both flying.

The next memory had been the blackest of all; waking to find Will leaning over her, and the relief that they were both alive. But his face was white, his eyes half-closed, and then she had noticed the blood that covered his shirt.

She had done everything in her power to save him, but the blood was pumping faster as his heart struggled, and she could not staunch it. Then his gaze slipped away from her to stare upwards, as if he was seeing something up there apart from the blazing blue of the California desert sky.

She wept, over him, and into him, her face buried against his neck, feeling the warmth of his skin and refusing to believe she could do nothing to help him. Surely if she held him close enough, her own life would quicken in him, make him strong…

Trying to keep his body off the ground, she had made the promise she could not keep: she wouldn't let him die. She had told him that, and she had believed it. And yet, in the awful dust and the stillness of a place that wasn't his home, Will Deacon had dragged one final, hitching breath, and when it left his lungs it had carried the very last flicker of life with it.

She had held him until it grew dark, until her legs cramped and she screamed in pain even as she welcomed the outlet for her grief, and it wasn't until she was finally able to rest his body back down that she began to shiver. Shock had numbed her, but now she realised she had to find someone to help, or she would die out here herself.

She looked down at Will, his eyes now closed, the thick lashes looking darker than ever against his white skin. She had failed him... he had fought for her honour, and she had lost him to the courage that loving her had given him. And the claim... she put her hand to her cut bodice-strings, and felt fresh tears flooding her eyes. He had died for nothing.

Even as he lay in her arms Will had begged her not to go to his partner. He'd known of the danger that awaited her there, from the men who'd stolen their claim, and so she hadn't tried to find Gabe. Instead he'd come to her; after Will had been laid to rest less than a day, in the little town where they'd been heading with such hope, Gabriel Rogers had knocked at the door of the boarding house and asked to speak with her.

Beaten bloody, bruised, and with a broken wrist and ankle, he was barely recognisable as the adventurous young man she and Will had grown up with. He was a shaken, pale, ghost of that boy. He told her how two men had turned up with his and

Will's claim, and how he'd been helpless against them, physically and legally.

United in grief, their stilted and awkward reunion eventually gave way to something more natural, and they had married five years later, in the same church where they'd said goodbye to the man they'd both loved. They'd lived here ever since, watching the gold rush town rise around them. Without Will.

And now Gabe too was gone. His skin papery-soft and stretched over the prominent bones of his wrists, he had done right for her all their lives, and had died with the peace of knowing that. He'd been a good man, had known her heart had never really been his, and he deserved the full weight of her grief. Why could she not even give him that?

Lucy dragged herself to her feet, wincing at the stiffness that had settled into her hips, and went slowly down the stairs to see the nurse off. She felt a twist of sorrow when she thought of all Gabe's things here in this house. His presence stamped over the last forty-some years of her life. *But oh, Will. If only I could have saved you…*

A cry from the kitchen snatched her attention back to the present. Nurse Moss was bending over as far as her rounded stomach allowed, and a puddle of water lay on the floor between her feet. She groaned, and another splash ran out from beneath her skirts.

Lucy hurried over and put her arm on the younger woman's shoulders, and turned her towards a chair. 'Come sit down, honey. I'll find someone to take care of you.'

'Thank you.' Nurse Moss breathed more easily now. She managed a smile, but her face was tensely drawn. 'The truth is, I haven't felt the baby move for a while.'

'Well, don't they always say that happens, right at the end?' Lucy forced a smile. 'That should have been your clue to rest up, young lady.'

'I guess you're right,' Nurse Moss said, and hissed as another contraction struck. 'Oh my… these are coming thick and—ow—fast now. You'd better hurry.'

Lucy had got as far as the front door, when a shriek ripped through the house. She whirled to see Nurse Moss on her knees on the floor, her face turned towards Lucy in panic. 'It's too late! Stay with me, help me!'

Lucy tried to run, but her hip twanged and she slowed to a fast hobble, reaching Nurse Moss just as another ferocious contraction wrung a cry from the stricken nurse. 'Easy, sweetheart. This is natural.' Was it though? Lucy and Gabe had never had children, was it supposed to happen this fast? 'Just breathe as steady as you can,' she murmured. Her left arm spasmed, and she gasped, in a pain of her own that was eclipsed a second later by Nurse Moss's scream. She knelt beside the younger woman and tried to urge her to lie on her back, but the nurse wanted to stay on all fours.

'It feels better like… like this.'

'Alright, honey, I'll fetch some towels.' Lucy stood up, and the room spun lazily around, making her feel sick. She stopped and bent over with her hands on her thighs, but the sickness did not abate.

A violent, crippling pain came out of nowhere and slammed her in the chest. She gasped, and through a roaring sound heard a long, agonised scream coming from the girl on the floor. She blinked, trying to clear her vision, and saw that the river seeping out from under the nurse's skirts had turned deep red… that poor baby… Lucy fell to her own knees again, ignoring the shooting pain in her hips, and tried to reach out to the girl, but instead clutched at her own chest as the pain there increased. Her vision spun and whirled, and from somewhere she heard the front door crash open against the wall – the neighbours, drawn by the shouts and screams. Thank God…

***

Mill Lane Cottage. 2012

'The old lady…' Laura's words seemed to come from someone else. She sounded muffled and distant, but could feel the vibration on her lips and tongue so she knew it was her own voice.

'Which old lady?' Tonya asked softly.

'In the hospital. When I was born.' Laura tried to focus through the clamouring realisations that kept sliding and clicking into place. 'I was... the baby was dead. They told my mother that. Everyone knew it. But while she was waiting to go through labour she got talking to this old lady. It was the war nurse, Helen.'

'And suddenly the doctors were wrong?' Tonya guessed.

Laura wiped her clammy hands on her jeans and nodded. 'The nurse that Lucy tried to help must have been Helen's mother.' The realisation that she, as Lucy, had simply taken over the stillborn infant, and brought it into the world screaming, instead of blue and silent, made her feel alternately sick and humble.

'I don't know how many times you've been here,' Tonya said, still gentle, 'but one thing I'm pretty sure of is that you and this one guy are connected, way more deeply than you ever knew.'

'I've been trying to save him. This whole time, all I've been here for is to keep that one promise.' Laura didn't know whether to embrace the knowledge or deny it. She bit down on the words that wanted to spill out, it would be too easy to start talking and never stop.

She searched for some semblance of normality, and let out a slow, trembling breath. 'At least I know why I kept saying California instead of Chicago. I've been so tired, I suppose it's all a bit nearer the surface now.'

Tonya nodded. 'Well, you've found him again. Whatever he needs saving from this time, you're here for him.' She was looking at Laura with a fascinated interest, clearly dying to ask more, but Ann wasn't as accepting.

'Are you off your head?' She stood up and began pacing. 'I mean, you're so bloody *calm!* I'd be climbing the walls. This is... it's mad!'

'We already knew Richard was a fresh-born,' Laura said, without thinking.

'A *what* born?'

Laura thought quickly. 'He's had dreams,' she said. 'He wanted to understand them, so we tried therapy then too. He told me about Will, and others. It's so easy to believe now, logical, even.'

'Logical my arse! You're telling me you can *remember* this stuff now? That you used to be a cowgirl, and a nurse—'

'Cowgirl?'

'Well, a wild west... I dunno, gold-digger?'

'Ann, I just—'

'It's real, Ann,' Tonya said. 'It doesn't matter if you believe it, it's real. You can't argue with it. I called her Lucy, but it wasn't until we couldn't get back any further than her birth grandparents that I figured out why that was.'

Ann stared at them in turn, bewildered and angry, and close to tears. 'So, what, then? You're not Laura? You're not this teacher who draws brilliant pictures during meetings, that'd get her fired, and then tears them up in case the head sees them?'

'I didn't know you'd seen those,' Laura said, trying on a smile.

'Stop it! Are you telling me you're not really who I thought you were?'

'Of course I am,' Laura said gently. She stood up and went over to take Ann's hand. 'I just know a little bit more about why things are... as they are.'

'And how are they?'

'Over..' Laura heard the word, and knew it was true. She had fought for Richard's life at least twice, and this time she had finally given him the one he'd been meant to have. There was nothing left to save him from now, except the grief of losing his son. For that she must put herself through that same, endless pain, but she would do it. For both of them.

Chapter Twenty

The noise was getting *louder*, for the Ocean's sake! When would that beast of a totterling stop? Arric pulled his pillow across his face and groaned. It didn't change anything. He cursed. Still the dreadful noise continued. Nerryn should be doing something about it... Arric sat up, his heart tripping over itself suddenly; what if she had gone? Run away while he slept?
No, she would have taken the totterling with her. And listen to it out there. Laughing.

'Nerryn! For the love of all the salt in the seas! I need to *sleep!*'

Nerryn appeared in his doorway, a faintly amused look on her face, despite her tiredness. 'You are not alone in your need for rest,' she pointed out. 'But what can I do? He is excited about something. He cannot tell me what, so I could not take it away even if I wished to. I feel a little of it, to be truthful, I think it's because—'

'Well, I'm exhausted,' Arric grumbled. 'You will have your chance to sleep when the sun comes up, and that ridiculous infant becomes too tired to shriek.' He jerked his blanket up to his chin once more and shut his eyes tightly. 'Now take him off outside somewhere, so that those of us with important tasks will not fail in them by nodding off at the wrong moment.'

'Outside?' Nerryn asked. Arric opened his eyes again to see her mouth twitch. 'Outside, *alone,* do you mean?' She clearly realised he meant nothing of the sort, or she would have just gone without asking. He had the horrible feeling she was laughing at him.

'Of course not,' he grunted. 'Just… amuse him in some quieter way, would you?'

'Who's that?' Nerryn turned as they both heard the doorway covering jerked aside. 'It's Mylan! I knew it. Arric, Mylan's back!' She vanished from the doorway, leaving Arric staring at the ceiling, defeated. He listened for as long as he could bear it, to the excited greetings from the main room, and finally threw back his blanket and stood up.

By the time he'd found his clothing and dragged it over his protesting limbs, and presented himself to his brother and sister, Nerryn had poured wine for herself and Mylan. Hewyl had also arrived.

'What are you doing here?' Arric grumbled at him, holding his goblet out to Nerryn, who put the wine jar down next to him. He glared at her and picked it up to pour. 'How did you know we were all awake?'

'Apart from Dreis's noise?' Hewyl shrugged. 'I was walking outside and I saw your brother return. I wanted to know how he fared with Dafna's people.'

'Well?' Arric turned to Mylan. 'How many *did* you bring back?'

'All who were fit to travel.'

'Which was?'

'Around fifty.'

Arric tried to hide his grimace. 'Where are they?'

Mylan's lips tightened in annoyance. 'Do not speak to me as if you were my chief, Arric!' He emptied his wine in one long pull, and slammed his goblet back down. 'They have found places to sleep for the rest of the night. Tomorrow Cantoc will show them to the caves, and prepare them for what is to come.'

'Surely you have not left *Hendrig* to sleep on the cliff?' Arric couldn't believe it. And, it seemed, he was right not to.

'Hendrig and his second, Lawbryn, are not with their people. Nor is Lawbryn's friend Brythnen.'

'They were unwell?'

'No, they have travelled most of the way with us. But,' Mylan sighed. 'They reached the place where the paths cross, and took the one to Lynher Mill.'

'*What?*' Arric replaced his own goblet on the table carefully, with a shaking hand. Had he not put this very possibility to Hewyl himself? Triumph flickered in his heart, and he caught the mortal's reluctantly impressed expression. But it would not be a good idea for Mylan to know he'd had his suspicions and not warned anyone. Better to lay the blame for these dishonourable war games firmly at his brother's feet from the start.

'Mylan, this is… You have let them go ahead of us? It is our revenge, brother of mine, not theirs!'

Mylan scowled. 'Of course it is theirs! Their blood was up, and they saw the path and took it, it was not planned.'

'Why is it such a bad thing they've gone?' Hewyl wanted to know. 'They'd be doing us a favour, wouldn't they?'

'Cantoc is their leader now,' Arric said. 'This is the choice they made when they chose to come here. The battle host must be united behind him or there will be chaos. People will just go running off all across the land, no-one will know who has deserted and who is off seeking glory!' He turned back to Mylan. 'And have you *told* Cantoc?'

'Not yet.'

'Why did you let them go?'

'How could I stop them?' Mylan countered. 'Lawbryn has a gwyllgi, one of the biggest I have ever seen.'

'A what?' Nerryn picked up Dreis, who was still making excited hooting noises. She bounced him on her hip and shushed him, but her eyes were on Mylan.

'A hound. Mortals call them hell-hounds. The *trigoryon an pell* have learned to use them in battle. Killers, every one.'

Nerryn flinched. 'And they are going to Lynher Mill? What can two men hope to do against so many there, even with their hound?'

'I doubt they will do anything, they just needed to *feel* they were doing something more, I think.' Mylan shrugged. 'Hendrig respected his daughter's chosen husband, and Lawbryn, by all accounts, had been deeply in love with her since they were children. Had thought to marry her until Talf… Nerryn, *what* is bothering that boy?'

'Nothing, he's happy.'

'Brrrap!' Dreis proclaimed, jerking up and down on Nerryn's hip, and reaching his chubby little hands towards the doorway.

The child had begun to crawl since the last sunrise, and although the others had shown an almost parental joy in this simple act, something they had all done at one time or another, Arric couldn't help wishing Dreis would crawl out of that door while Nerryn's back was turned, and find the shortest possible way to the beach.

Blissfully unaware of Arric's dark thoughts, Nerryn smiled at Mylan. 'Do you remember it used to feel like that when you'd been away a while? I told you I could feel you returning, and you admitted, in the end, that you felt like singing when you were almost home, too.'

'I remember,' Mylan said, smiling back. 'Even though I love to travel, it was just a sort of… broken thread, about to re-tied.'

'Exactly!'

Arric glared from one twin to the other, his exasperation replaced with a niggling suspicion. Even as the thought formed, it became a certainty. 'Does neither of you think,' he said, slowly and patiently, 'that perhaps the totterling is telling us something?' His brother and sister looked blank, but the watcher got it.

'Tir is coming!'

'Tir is coming,' Arric agreed grimly. 'And the child knows it. You!' he pointed at Hewyl. 'Go to Cantoc, now! Tell him Tir comes, and we don't know if he has an army with him.'

'Hendrig and the others will meet them on the path,' Hewyl argued. 'I should go and make sure they're safe.'

'I will ensure they are unharmed,' Mylan said. 'It is my fault they have taken the Moorland path.'

'No, you stay here,' Arric said. 'I need you. Both of you,' he added, directing this towards Nerryn. 'Tir is unskilled in battle, he will not defeat a chief like Hendrig.'

'But if he has people with him, he—'

'I said stay here!' Arric would not be pushed around, not now. 'You don't know what has happened in your absence, Mylan. Cantoc has left orders. Strict orders. Go!' he shouted at Hewyl, who nodded and left.

Nerryn was looking at him with a mixture of dismay and dawning admiration, but he couldn't take the time to enjoy either. 'What shall I do with Dreis?'

'Put him in your chamber,' Arric said. 'He can babble at the walls and see if they are as charmed by him as you are. Then you and Mylan sit down, and listen.' He took a deep breath. 'We are going to win this war, the three of us, and we do not need our mother's people to help us do it.'

***

The rains swept down, drenching everything and turning the ground into a sodden mudslide. With Maer's scream still echoing in his ears, Richard raised his head to see the giant hound dragging at the limp, blood-soaked body of the young prince.

Fury and grief collided. A growl erupted from his own throat, and he pulled at everything he could find in the air around him and directed it at the snarling, snuffling animal, sending every ounce of his strength with it. Lightning arced down, striking the beast between the shoulders, and the smell of burning filled the air. The hound dropped Maer and fell into a heap, convulsing and slavering, its shrill yelps sounding far too much like those of a normal, pain-wracked domestic dog; Richard's heart squeezed with a sickening mixture of regret, and cold, savage triumph.

He heard the three far-dwelling elementals calling to one another to stand firm, and braced himself for retribution, for the numbing blow of lightning… he had time to think how fitting it was that he should die like this, by lightning on a muddy ground, just as his father had, before a movement caught his eye. The hound was shaking himself and moving.

'No,' Richard whispered. 'You son of a bitch!' He twisted on the ground to see what the others were doing; they were all standing completely still, shocked by the suddenness and ferocity of the storm—he was mortal, how could *he* have created it? Their reaction might have been darkly comical if he hadn't been so torn apart with grief, and so horrified by the sight of the hound staggering to its feet again.

Then, as if feeling his eyes on him, they moved as one, towards him, their faces telling him all he needed to know about what they planned to do next. He drew on the air again, pulled down, and found the leader that sprang up from the ground as easily as if it were a lit pathway to the lightning. The flash was even more vivid this time, the sharp crack of thunder deafening; he could barely hear the screams over it, but at least one man fell, and the others dropped beside him.

'*Hendrig!*'

Richard tried to find that burst of satisfaction again but could not; there was no honour in what he'd done, and he didn't care what they did to him now, in their revenge. But he would not let their hound tear his friend's body apart. With tears of helpless rage mingling with the rain, he dragged himself to his knees and began to crawl towards Maer.

After only a couple of lurches, his knee struck something and he looked down to see his blade, half-buried in the muddy grass. He grabbed it. The hound had regained its feet properly now, and although it stood with its head low and swaying, it still looked damned strong.

'Hey!' Richard gasped, 'Hey, you bastard. Over here!' The hound turned its head slowly, dizzily. Its fur was plastered to its body, and it was easy to see that, although that fur was thick, it did not account for anything near the animal's true size. Those muscles were twitching back into life, the legs had stopped buckling at the hocks, and now that Richard was this close to it he could see it stood at least four feet at the shoulder. The eyes blazed with recognition, as they had earlier, and the dog began to turn slowly, clumsily, away from Maer.

Richard gripped the leather-wrapped handle of the ancient knife and tried to ignore the grinding pain in his body, but it felt as if something had him in a huge fist and was crushing the life out of him. He swayed on his knees and tried to stand up, but he couldn't do it. He dropped to all fours again, trying to breathe through the agony, to will it away.

Somewhere above him he heard the lumbering sounds of the dog coming closer. He heard sobbing. A man. Lawbryn, no doubt, mourning his master even as the man he'd killed lay just twenty feet away. *If I get out of this, you fucker, you're next…*

His head drooped, the rain pouring off his hair and into his eyes, and, motionless, he waited, waited… the moment he felt the heat of the hound, he gathered himself and lunged. The blade ripped through the animal's throat a split second before those huge teeth would have closed on Richard's head.

Richard drove himself forward, dragging the blade through tough, stringy, muscle until it hit bone. Hot blood washed over him, he tasted it, choked on it. But he held the blade firmly until the animal stopped twitching.

Then he sank back onto his heels, his free hand wrapped across his waist, dragging in breaths that felt like naked flame. He raised his head to see the two living far-dwellers rising to their feet, and braced himself once again for a fight, but they were leaderless and lost, now. He watched them turn and stumble away, back to the coast to take with them the news of Hendrig's death. And Maer's...

Richard turned to his brother and closed the distance between them with deep reluctance. Maer lay face-down in the rain, his left arm a mass of blood and shattered bone from the elbow down. Richard rolled him over, as gently as he could, his throat muscles rigid in anticipation of what he might see.

The hound had mangled Maer's arm, but Richard was startled to see blood still pumping from it. 'Christ... hold on. Just hold on...' He stumbled back to the hound and began to saw at the leather leash, cutting off enough to allow him to tie it around Maer's upper arm and pull it tight. The blood flow slowed.

The hound moved.

'No!' Richard cried again, despair swiftly taking over the relief that Maer might still somehow survive. He dragged Maer's arm upwards over his head, and kept pulling on the leather strap, half his attention on the dog's jerking limbs, the other half on Maer, searching for more injuries; a clear bite mark leaked crimson at the prince's shoulder, and there were deep claw marks at the top of his right thigh.

...The hound moved.

Richard turned to face it, and his hatred exploded into unthinking fury. He flung himself at the animal and plunged Ulfed's ancient blade into the base of its skull. He yanked it free, and the memory of Maer's scream made him drive it down again. For a moment he thought he was done, then he remembered Maer's shattered arm, and with a primal cry of his own, he ripped the blade out and stuck it through the hound's eye.

'Is that thing made of iron?'

Richard fell back, panting, and looked up. A man stood there. A human. Bearded, dreadlocked, carrying a medium-sized, heavy-looking bag. Richard shook his head, and managed to gasp out, 'Bronze.'

'Then you'll need this.' The stranger stooped and opened the neck of his bag...

...The hound moved.

'No you don't, you little shit,' the man said, almost conversationally, and emptied the contents of the bag onto it, spreading white crystals over as much of the animal as he could. The dog's howl echoed across the moor, its flesh sizzled where the white stuff touched, and, finally, it fell still and silent for the last time.

'Salt,' the stranger said eventually, into that silence. He held out a hand. 'Richard, right? I'm Hewyl.'

'Help me with Maer,' Richard said, too stunned to ask how this man not only knew him, but why he had called him by his mortal name. He tore off his cloak and bent to drape it over Maer's still form. 'Please, he's going to die.'

'Get him to the forest,' Hewyl said. 'You're in no fit state, let me carry him.'

'Huh uh.' Richard accepted Hewyl's help to stand, and braced his hands on his thighs until the dizziness passed. 'Not the forest.'

'They can help him there.'

'No,' Richard said. 'We can't trust them.'

'Will you trust me? I just saved your life, after all.'

Richard straightened, swallowing a groan. He swayed, and Hewyl caught him by the shoulders.

'Richard, listen. The Foresters can help him, you know that. And we don't have time to argue.'

'They're working with the Coastals,' Richard mumbled, fighting to stay on his feet. 'We have to get Maer back to—'

'Only two of them are.' Hewyl let go of him, one hand at a time, and only when he was sure he wouldn't fall, did he kneel beside the stricken prince. 'There are spies, yes, but only two out of all the Foresters.' He checked the tourniquet on Maer's arm, and nodded. 'This is a good, strong job, but he needs proper help.'

'You're sure? About the spies?' Richard moved to Maer's other side and lifted the edge of his cloak to check the gouges in Maer's leg. He winced.

'No time,' Hewyl repeated. 'But yes, I'm sure. I

met one of them last night. 'Stand back, you can't lift him.' He got his arm beneath Maer's shoulders, and slid the other hand under his knees, and stood. He was not a heavily-built man, but he was clearly stronger than he seemed. In his arms Maer appeared almost child-like, covered in Richard's cloak, his head back, his face white, his blond hair dripping wet, and Richard felt a fresh twist of fear as he looked at him.

'Okay,' he said, his voice shaking. 'I trust you. Let's go.'

As they walked back towards the woods at Pengenna, Richard felt his breath even out, and the pain receded enough to let him talk. 'How did you know to bring salt?'

'I've learned about these creatures on my travels. Iron or salt will do it. Nothing else, as far as I know.'

'I mean, how did you know we were in trouble?'

Hewyl glanced at him, then returned his attention to the uneven ground. 'I was at the coast. Your boy was—'

'You saw Ben?' Richard's heart stuttered.

'He was wound right up. Excited. Sensed you were on your way, we think. At the same time Mylan told us some of Dafna's people had broken away from the group and were coming to find him,' he nodded down at Maer.

'They think he killed Nerryn's father,' Richard said, but his thoughts were no longer on the reason for Hewyl's arrival. 'Is Ben okay? Is he happy?' His voice cracked, and Hewyl stopped, just for a second, so Richard could look right at him.

'Yes. To both. But he needs you, and he wants you.'

'Ah, Christ…' Richard resumed walking, but all he wanted to do was turn and start running for the coast. 'But we don't know whose side Nerryn is on now, do we? Or who you're for.'

'Why would I save your life, if I was with the Coastals?' Hewyl pointed out. 'I promised Laura I would help get Ben—'

'What?' Richard stopped dead again. 'You spoke with Laura?'

'For god's sake keep walking! And wipe that dog's blood from your face, you'll freak everyone one.' He relented, and explained, 'Look, I've known Laura a long time. We lost touch, but, we were close once.'

In my travels, he'd said, and Richard gave a short, disbelieving laugh as he wiped his sleeve across his face. 'You're Michael. The guy who erases music files.'

'Guilty,' Hewyl said. They could see the edge of the forest now, and as if he was aware of it, Maer stirred and groaned. 'Come on, we have to get him fixed up.'

Richard shook his head to try and re-order his thoughts, but they leapt from one surreal revelation to another, barely touching on one before moving on. Michael. He was back, he was mortal, and he'd been to see Laura. She needn't be alone after all… he belatedly recognised his own, frayed-necked T shirt, and tried not to acknowledge the jealousy that wormed through him.

'Okay,' Hewyl said as they passed under the branches of the first trees. 'Keep your eyes open, they'll be watching, but they won't come forward until they know it's safe. Tell them who you are.'

'You know a hell of a lot about these things,' Richard said. He was aware he sounded mistrustful again, but he didn't care.

'I told you, I've learned a lot.'

'So, at least now I know how you knew my name. Will you go to her? When this is over?'

Hewyl threw him a glance, but didn't reply. Instead he found the driest-looking spot, beneath a huge oak, and gently lay Maer down. Maer immediately hissed a breath, and opened his eyes to stare upwards in terror.

Richard knelt gingerly beside him, and laid a hand on his chest. 'Maer?'

Maer swivelled pain-dark eyes until he found Richard's, and bit his lip against a scream at the movement. 'We're going to help you, buddy,' Richard said, blinking back his own tears at the sight of Maer's bewildered agony.

'Foresters,' Maer said, in a harsh whisper. 'They cannot be trusted. Jacky said.'

Richard's eyes met Hewyl's. 'We have to, Maer. This guy says it's only two of them who've turned. They're gonna help you, I promise.'

'You'll have to call them, Richard,' Hewyl said. 'I can't do it.'

'Nerryn,' Maer mumbled, closing his eyes again. 'She has turned against me. Against us... what will happen to her?'

'Nothing. It's all lies.' Richard had no idea if it was or not, but right now Maer needed calm, not to dwell on what might happen to his former fiancée. He squeezed Maer's uninjured shoulder, and accepted Hewyl's help to stand. He didn't know what he was going to say, but instinct told him to close his eyes, and so he did, and let the words find their own way.

'*Trigoryon an goswig!* Before you lies a prince of this realm, brought down in battle. His life depends on your knowledge and so I command this of you: put aside your private allegiances, and give your aid to this man of courage, who has served you all from the day of his birth.'

He looked at Hewyl, who nodded approval, and Richard felt both hope and fear leap in his heart as he heard the rustle of leaves. What if he'd been wrong to trust, after all? A moment later four hesitant Foresters appeared.

'You have come on a difficult night,' one of them said. 'There is a leadership challenge in the forest. But we will help if we can, My Lord.'

The woman stepped over to Maer and looked down with an expression of sorrow. 'Prince Maer. A wise and sweet-natured child.' She lifted her eyes to Richard, and gave a half-bow before extending the open-handed gesture of trust. 'We will do what we can,' she said. 'We shall take him to the leader's clearing, they will not refuse us.'

'How far is that?' Richard tried to work out how

far they had come, against where he knew Ykana to have made her home.

'We will be swift,' she assured him. 'And it seems, My Lord, that you yourself are still not recovered.'

'I'm fine,' Richard said shortly. 'I'm heading back out to—'

'You're not fine at all,' Hewyl interrupted. 'Look at the state of you. Rest here, just for an hour at least. Don't worry, I'll go with Maer.' He stepped up to Richard and gripped his forearm in a strikingly familiar gesture, and Richard was surprised into returning it. 'Take it easy,' he warned. 'And be aware of this; Arric plans to unleash something terrible, and he doesn't care who's in the way when he does.'

'I'd heard,' Richard said. 'He's admitted it to you?'

'No, I just happened to be there when it was mentioned.' Hewyl gave him a brief smile. 'Although, ironically, I was on their side. For real. But he must have read more in me than I knew myself, because he doesn't trust me an inch.'

'So how do I stop it?'

Hewyl's smile dropped away. His face was unreadable behind the shaggy beard, but his blue eyes were suddenly dull and dark. 'There might be only one way.' He lowered his voice and glanced at Maer, now being lifted by the four Foresters. 'You might have to kill one of them.'

'One of them?'

'Either Nerryn or her brother. Can you do that?'

Richard's memory showed him a carefree, laughing Maer, and his shy, beautiful bride-to-be, their faces alight with happiness. He locked the memory down, and his eyes met Hewyl's. He could feel the hardness in them.

'Yeah. I can do it.'

Chapter Twenty-One

Mill Lane Cottage. September 28th

Jacky waited, watching the shapes move beyond the curtain. Someone was pacing. Someone else kept standing up, then sitting down again, but Jacky had no way of telling who it was. There were three people, he knew that, and he must wait until the lady Laura was alone, no matter how agitated he became.

The weather was turning. Not in the normal way of weather, but in the sinister way that spoke to Jacky's deepest fears; no steady build-up of cloud, rain and wind, but unevenly-spaced bursts, increasingly strong, and accompanied by plummeting temperatures. A rattling sound made him jump, and he turned to see a metal bucket rolling down the path, blown by a sudden gust and pushed along by the strong wind that prevailed even after the gust had died.

Someone else had heard it too, and Jacky flinched away as the curtain was jerked aside and a pale face peered out. It was a pleasant face, as mortal faces go, and looked more used to smiling than to the drawn, fearful expression it now wore. Short light-coloured hair was sticking up as though its owner had been running their hands through it… this was probably the pacer. The curtain fell back into place, and Jacky breathed again.

'Go home, mortals…' he murmured. He had been turning over in his mind how he would persuade Tir's lady away from her own home. Thoughts of trickery came first and most naturally, although he remembered the warning that had met his suggestion that he use Tir's own voice.

He wasn't sure he could, anyway; it was one voice he had never fully become used to; its strange and exotic accent, while similar in some ways to the Cornish, was nevertheless very different in many others. And there were so many different tones.

He tried now, very quietly, in case he should ever need it, but quickly gave up. Tir was a puzzle, in more ways than Jacky had ever met in one person before. One minute he was all flashing green eyes and a taut, powerful presence, the next a confused soul searching for some reason for his existence. Then, as swift to change as the Cornish weather, he would turn into a laughing young man, revelling simply in the nearness of those he loved. Jacky clenched his large hands into knobbly fists. He must convince Tir's lady to come away, keep her safe, not only for her sake, but for Tir's.

At last the front door opened and three figures appeared. Jacky sat upright, his heart thudding, and all three mortal women looked up at the night sky, from the warm shelter of the room on the other side of the door. The same room from which Jacky had stolen Dreis away, and where he had left his carved branch.

The wind ripped at the trees behind the cottage, and some of the saplings there bent almost double. Rain hissed on the path, and in the distance Jacky heard the low growl of thunder. He wished once more for his old green jacket; it had not provided much in the way of warmth and protection from the weather, but it had been comforting and familiar. He hoped Dreis was warm beneath its folds, at least.

The two visitors were finally ready to leave. Jacky could hear them calling back to Lady Laura as they ran down the path, their coats over their heads. One of them had the same unusual accent as Tir.

'Call me if you need to!' this one was yelling out. 'I'll come out right away.'

The other woman, the short-haired one who'd come to the window, stopped, and, heedless of the rain, went back and pulled Laura into a hug. Jacky could not hear what they said, but Laura wiped her eyes when they parted, and the woman re-joined her friend. They pulled open the doors of the carriage that waited at the foot of the path, and a moment later, in a roar and a sweep of dazzling false lights, they were gone.

Laura stood in the doorway, her hands worrying at her hair and her clothes, and her face turned up to the sky. She was getting wet, even inside her doorway, but she didn't seem to care. Tears were spilling down her cheeks and she didn't wipe those away, either.

'You win!' she cried, suddenly, and Jacky gasped, thinking for a moment she was screaming at him. 'You *bloody* win! Okay?' She stepped back and slammed the door shut, leaving Jacky wondering who had won. And what was the prize, that it cost her so much?

He stepped boldly up to the door. There was no need to hide now, Lady Laura knew him of old, after all, she would not be shocked to see him. But in that he was wrong. Her face went utterly white, and her mouth dropped open.

'Please, My Lady,' he began, but stopped as she turned away from him and went back into the room, leaving him to follow, but uninvited. 'I don't mean to frighten you.'

'I'm not frightened. Just… surprised,' she said, turning back to face him again. 'I thought you were dead.'

'As I deserve to be,' he said, remorse pulling at him until it was a real pain. 'Your boy—'

'You stole him.'

'I, I did. And now I must beg you to come with me too.'

She gave a short laugh, but Jacky heard no humour in it. 'You must be joking. I'm waiting here. Michael's going to bring Ben to me since no-one else seems to be able to manage it. You remember Michael?' she went on, her voice turning hard. 'You met him a little while before you met Tom and me.'

'My Lady, I am—'

'Stop looking for sympathy!'

'Looking for...?' he trailed away, confused, and Laura's expression melted into regret, and a sort of aching sadness.

'I'm sorry. I know you don't do attention-seeking.' She sank onto the big seat filled with cushions, and dropped her face into her hands. 'It's been a hell of a day and night, and seeing you has just...' she shook her head. 'I can't do this anymore. I've reached the end.'

A crack of thunder shook the small window panes, and brought Laura's head up. 'That was close.'

'You must come,' Jacky said, with real urgency now.

'Come where?'

'To the mine. It is the only place of safety.'

Lightning bloomed, the accompanying thunder rattled the glass in its frame again, and Laura wrapped her arms across her chest. 'I'm not going out in that.'

'Tir has ordered me to see you safe,' Jacky urged. 'It will be better to go now.'

'Richard is there?' Laura half-rose, but Jacky's relief was short-lived.

'No,' he admitted, and Laura sat back down. 'He has gone to the coast with Prince Maer.'

Laura hesitated, but the next flash of lightning made her flinch. They could hear it, even in here, the hiss and crackle, and then, almost simultaneously, the thunder bellowed. 'It's right over the house,' she said. 'I am *not* going out.'

'Then do you have a cellar? It would be the safest thing, after the mine.'

'No, these houses don't have cellars.' Laura sounded scared now. 'Are you serious about how dangerous this is?'

'My Lady, this is just the beginning,' Jacky pleaded. 'The Coastals have a terrible weapon, and they will use it against us all. Please! Come with me!'

Even as he spoke, they heard the ferocious howl of the wind, and the crash of something falling outside. The howl rose to a shriek, and Laura stared wildly out at the night, as if she expected to see it taking shape and lunging at her through the window.

Before Jacky could say any more she had reached for her coat from the hook by the door. At the last moment she moved to the hook next to it, and instead took down a long black coat that was much too big for her. It was only when she put it on and it almost scraped the floor that Jacky recognised it as Tir's. She kicked off her slippers and pulled on her boots, and Jacky was about to open the door when she shouted, 'Wait!' and ran back across the room.

Jacky watched, bemused, and with rising panic as the wind picked up strength, while Laura pulled out a strange, half see-through box and tore off the lid. She grabbed something blue and shoved it inside her coat, then picked up something from the floor and put that in her pocket.

'Come on, then,' she said, and took a look around her room, as if she knew she would never see it again. Jacky hoped she was wrong.

Together they crossed the road, and stepped onto the moorland itself. Jacky's short legs worked hard, but Laura still had to keep waiting for him. He waved her onward. 'You know where it is!'

Out here, the wind didn't sound so terrible, but its strength was horrific. Several times Jacky stumbled, and felt Laura's hand on his arm helping him back up. Once Laura fell too, but she was up again in an instant. Thunder cracked and bellowed all around them, and lightning flared, dazzling against the night sky as it stepped down time and again.

The ground beneath their feet was soft and dangerously pitted, but somehow they found their way, blown and battered until Laura slid beneath the protective wire fence and into the mouth of the tunnel. Jacky followed, with a trembling utterance of relief. The farther underground they went, the less the outside world mattered, but Jacky knew Laura would be thinking of her loved ones out there. Both in the mortal world and the elemental. Tir, Dreis, the human friends she had wept over such a short time ago… none were safe. Not tonight.

Tonight, Death walked the moor.

***

The Foresters were silent. The bags lay in the centre of the clearing and it needed no official count or assessment to see that there would now be a test of strength. Yventra's heart had sunk long before the end of the food-foraging challenge; holding Lyelt's bag for him and feeling it gain weight as the night went on, she had already begun to wonder how Ykana would feel to know her time as leader was all but over.

'You have done well,' the appointed judge declared, when the formality was done. 'You have both proved you can provide for your people. Now there will be a further test—'

'I would speak!' Yventra stepped forward, not even certain, up until that moment, that she had meant to do it. It was early in the child's forming, perhaps there would be no real risk... if she offered before Ykana had the chance to admit to needing her, then who could argue? It was her right, as second-in-command, to prove her own strength from time to time. 'With your permission?' she looked first to Ykana and then to Lyelt.

'Speak, Yventra,' Lyelt said, smiling at her with an odd kind of warmth. Yventra wondered, for one skin-crawling moment, if he planned to ask her to be his Chosen when he was the leader. She would refuse, of course, but it would cause upset right from the start. All the more reason she claim victory for Ykana. She glanced at Wydra and saw the same suspicion on her own Chosen's face, and she shook her head in quick denial and moved to the front of the group.

'I would take Ykana's place in the strength test,' she said. 'I have been second-in-command for many moons now, perhaps I would challenge her myself one day. But for now I claim my right to prove my worth as my sister's right hand.' She turned to Ykana. 'Do you grant me this?'

'I... I do,' Ykana said, and Yventra hoped she was the only one who could see the gratitude glimmer in her sister's eyes. This had been the easy part, Lyelt would be harder to convince.

'Lyelt, challenger for the honour of leading your people, do you consent?' She held her breath, and could sense Ykana doing the same. Everything was pinned on this. Lyelt took his time before answering, then gave Yventra a small bow.

'I consent. Let the test be set.' He smiled again, that warmth was still there, and Yventra felt some of her animosity melt away. He really had changed.

'Might I first say,' he went on, addressing the assembled Foresters, 'that I am in deep admiration of Yventra's strength. I do not underestimate it at all. Far from it. I have seen her hunting, watched her gather so much wood in one day that we were all kept warm for a moon's turn, by her hand alone.' He nodded to her and she nodded back, smiling graciously, although faintly puzzled at his extravagant generosity.

'Tonight's challenge,' he went on, 'will be all the harder for me, as I am sure it will push us both to the limits of our physical endurance. I am younger, stronger, faster, but Yventra's dedication is formidable; she will stop at nothing, shy away from no danger, and risk everything to ensure her sister is re-instated as leader. And should that be the case, she will once again lead us fearlessly in battle. For we all know there is conflict coming.'

As one, they looked to the treetops which were starting to sway. Then Lyelt smiled round at everyone. 'So, having given my consent, I release Ykana from the challenge, and wish Yventra the success that is deserved. Most of all, I wish her safety in the difficult and dangerous trial to come.'

Yventra frowned as she saw his gaze light on Wydra, and stay there several heartbeats. Longer than on anyone else. Something flashed between the two of them, and Yventra's blood went cold. She knew. Wydra knew, and Yventra knew exactly who had told her. She tried to send a pleading look Wydra's way, but Wydra would not return it, and instead stepped into the clearing.

She faced her former leader. 'I do not give my consent, Ykana. You are not ill, nor are you injured. Yventra should not take this test in your stead.'

'But you do not have the right to refuse,' Ykana said. She was clearly trying to sound authoritative, but her voice shook as she turned to Yventra. 'This is for my sister to decide.'

'Who is carrying a new hope, for all of us,' Wydra said softly. 'How could you suggest she—'

'I have told no-one,' Yventra put in quickly. 'Wydra, please!'

'You must not risk our unborn,' Wydra insisted. 'You cannot do *anything* that might silence this song.' She turned back to Ykana. 'You must complete the trial, or concede defeat.'

Ykana met Yventra's apologetic look, with one of understanding. 'I will continue,' she said quietly, and retreated to darkness while the last part of the challenge was set.

By the time the first rains began to fall, and the distant growl of thunder was heard, Ykana was finished. She and Lyelt had carried boulders from one end of the forest to the other, shouldered huge logs to build a shelter by the river, and dug a hole deep enough to stand up in, but Ykana's strength had run out before she could fill it back in again.

Watched by the Foresters, some of whom even looked quite pleased, Lyelt filled in first his hole, and then Ykana's. He waited until the last piece of now-wet earth was patted back in place by Keityn, and then led everyone back to the clearing, where he bent to create the fire from the flint that lay beside it.

He straightened again, and his smile was less warm than triumphant. 'My people,' he began, and Yventra felt Ykana shudder beside her. 'As you know, we have tonight relieved a very worthy woman of her leadership duties. Ykana led us well, in fairness and in wisdom, but I want you all to know that I am no longer the same boy that Prince

Maer was called upon to discipline. I confess I was foolish then, and cruel. The prince's lesson was humiliating.' His voice sharpened, but when he continued it smoothed out again. 'But it taught me a valuable lesson, and for that I am grateful.'

He continued for a while in this vein, and Yventra looked around to see people relaxing and nodding, even smiling, as Lyelt spun his web of warmth and false humility. When he finally accepted their pledges of loyalty, Ykana was the first to go to him. She knelt at his feet and reached her hand up to take his, and when she spoke the words she sounded almost as if she believed them.

When the ceremony was done, Yventra looked at the sky through the waving branches high above. 'It will soon be getting light,' she began to Ykana, but they both cried out as the sky split with the fiercest thunderclap either of them had ever heard. Seconds later it was as if some giant hand had scooped up the river and thrown it down on them. Panic hit, and the crowd broke up, and Ykana was left alone to pack up her things from the leader's shelter.

A short while later, as the storm eased off a little, people began to make their way back. Yventra and Wydra did likewise, only to stop dead at the sight of four of their friends bearing a limp, blood-soaked body down the path towards the clearing.

Everyone stood still, suddenly heedless of the rain, and the low murmur of voices rose in dismay, as the Foresters laid the body on the ground and it became clear who it was.

'Prince Maer,' Ykana breathed. She pushed Lyelt aside and ran to the prince, pulling aside the cloak that had been draped over him. She cried aloud in horror at the terrible injuries to his arm, and to his deeply-clawed thigh. 'He lives, but he must have help!' She looked up, ready to start shouting orders at those highly trained in healing, but Lyelt had recovered from her hasty shove and held up a hand.

'Ykana is no longer the leader. I am.' His determined glare travelled over everyone present, and finally came to rest on the stricken prince. 'We are now allied with the Coastals, therefore this man is our enemy. Our prisoner.'

Chapter Twenty-Two

Arric stared down the dark cliff path, squinting to lessen the shadows and concentrate. Still no sign of Cantoc. Or of Hewyl. He went back inside, out of the rain. Not normal Cornish rain, this... something had happened, even the totterling had sensed it and they'd finally stopped having to put up with his happy babbling from Nerryn's chamber.

'Nothing?' Mylan said, unnecessarily, as Arric flung the door covering closed, hiding the dark.

Arric glowered. 'Cantoc is right here at my side, do you not see him?' Mylan didn't bother to reply, and Arric sighed and found a friendlier tone. Poke an anemone and it would only close up. 'My apologies, Mylan. I am just concerned.'

'I do not trust him,' Nerryn put in. 'Hewyl, that is. By his own admission he has been following our people for a good while, how do we know how much he has learned, that he can carry to the Moorlanders?'

'She is right,' Mylan said. 'You brought him here, Arric. A mortal, for the Ocean's sake! And you, who do not even trust your own family, have given him the freedom to come and go as he pleases. Why?'

'Because our brother enjoyed the feeling of power,' Nerryn put in, acidly. 'The chance to make someone else do his bidding.'

'He believes in us,' Arric muttered. 'He has promised to help us, you heard him.' He could feel the angry flush staining his skin. Nerryn's words stung, and humiliation was never palatable; at the hands of some mortal, even less so.

'We heard his claim that he could help us win the war,' Mylan agreed. 'But Cantoc has not yet accepted him properly. He has been distracted for a good while now.' He flicked the briefest of glances Nerryn's way, and Arric noted the frown that answered it. 'He thinks of Dafna constantly, and since he learned his vengeance was ill-aimed at the spriggans, all he wants is to destroy Gilan's people in her name.'

'And in our father's,' Arric pointed out quickly.

Mylan shrugged. 'He respected Talfrid, it is true. But he would never have gone to battle over it, he would simply have done exactly as he did, and send someone to take a life for a life. And you…' Mylan stood up, and Arric felt his pulse quicken. 'You took the one life guaranteed to spark a full-blown war!'

'He said a *royal!*' Arric reminded him. 'A royal life, for that of our parents! Well I gave him one, did I not?'

'You gave him the king! And from that moment on we were doomed.'

'Not so,' Arric said, grasping at the chance that Mylan's words offered. 'You and Nerryn can save us!'

'Save us? Or destroy the Moorlanders?'

'It is the same thing now. Listen,' Arric jerked his head at Mylan's seat, and his brother reluctantly sat. Nerryn watched them both, expressionless. Arric could not read her at all, and he frowned; with the twins' faith in the necessity of what they must do shaken, how would he persuade them?

A rising wail from Nerryn's chamber made them all jump, and Arric thumped the table. 'Tumbling Tides! *What* is the matter with him now?'

'He will quieten soon,' Nerryn said. 'He is tired.'

'*I* am tired!' Arric shot an exasperated look at the curtain that led through to the rear chambers, as if glaring at the noise might make it stop.

He drew a deep breath in an effort to calm himself. 'You are both skilled elementals—'

'I am not skilled,' Nerryn said at once.

'You are, you have just not found what you need within yourself to raise and control it.' Arric forced himself to sound friendly; showing his irritation and frustration would get him nowhere now. 'Mylan will be able to help you.'

He searched for the right words. 'You carry a great power, both of you. As twins, your combined strength is beyond anything the strongest of us might do alone, or even together.'

Mylan frowned. 'How can *you* know this, if we do not?'

'If you had spent less time travelling,' Arric said, 'and more time with your own people, you too would know this.'

'I did not travel,' Nerryn pointed out, 'yet I have not heard of any great power.'

'*You* have had your mind among the clouds for too long. Did you not feel it when Mylan first returned, and the three of us held hands? The realisation of what you possess… it made me dizzy!'

'Let us say you are right,' Nerryn said. 'Assuming I learn what must be learned, how will it win any war?'

'How will it…' Arric stared at her, incredulous. Was she really so simple? 'Nerryn, once the two of you show your strength, we can demand the Moorlanders abandon all pretence to the rule of this kingdom! We will have them in our fist! They will not dare claim their royal status back, for fear of unleashing more, and worse. And as you and Mylan mature—'

'But think, Arric!' Nerryn's face was tight. 'All this would do, would be to ensure that some night, someone will creep up and put either Mylan or myself, or both of us, to the blade! I cannot believe you have not considered this.'

'You would be protected,' Arric argued. 'You would be our most revered—'

'Weapon! We would be your *weapon!*' Nerryn rose so fast from the table, her chair fell back and smashed against the floor.

From her chamber another cry came, shredding Arric's nerves further. 'See to him,' he said grimly. 'We will talk on this further, when you have calmed yourself.'

'*You* see to him!' she snapped back. 'He is not just my responsibility.'

'Is he not? Do you truly not plan to steal him away at the first chance, and return him to his father?'

'No!' Nerryn's brow furrowed with frustration. 'I thought you believed that! Am I never to be trusted? What more must I do?'

'I trust you,' Mylan said, though he looked unsure. 'But truly, I cannot think while that noise continues. I will see to him if you will not.'

Nerryn's shoulders slumped. 'Do *you* believe there is merit in what Arric says?'

'Not that we may conquer the Moorlanders with fear. But our own—'

'Cantoc!' The voice from outside, despairing and desperate, was punctuated by the fall of the rock against the doorpost. 'Cantoc, we must speak with you! Mylan? Are you there?'

'Lawbryn!' Mylan went to the doorway and jerked the heavy covering aside.

The two far-dwellers who stumbled into the room were heavily-built men, fully bearded as few of the Cornish elementals were, and, even drenched to the skin, they made Cantoc appear a child.

'Hendrig is dead,' the larger of them, Lawbryn, gasped out. Ignoring Arric, he clasped Mylan's shoulder. 'Slain by the Moorlander king!'

'Tir has killed?' Arric stepped forward, forcing their attention on him. 'He has killed my *grandfather*?' What joyful luck was this? He kept his face solemn, and willed tears into his eyes, but without the help of the gritty sand he had used before it was not so easy. Still, the sympathy that fell over Lawbryn's face was gratifying.

'Oh… my boy. I grieve for your loss,' the fardweller whispered. 'I was forgetting, in my own sorrow.'

'Tell us what happened,' Mylan managed, and Arric saw his own shock was genuine – he had spent time with these people, grown attached during happier times. His grief would be very useful indeed.

Nerryn came back into the room as Lawbryn was about to sit, soothing the red-faced and sobbing child in her arms, pressing her lips to his hair.

Lawbryn jerked upwards again at the sight of her, and his hand went to his chest… 'Daf...'

Arric noted the pain that crossed his face. Again, useful. There was so much sorrow and directionless fury here it was as good as a feast for the triumph-hungry.

'This is my sister Nerryn,' he said. 'The child is the son of Tir. He is our hostage.'

'Son of *Tir*?' Lawbryn's companion, who had remained by the door, took two steps towards

Nerryn, his hand going to his blade, before Mylan stopped him.

'The child is an innocent!' he snapped. 'Be seated, for the Ocean's sake!'

Arric waited to speak, until the newcomers had sat down and were less threatening. 'I am Arric, eldest son of Dafna and Talfrid,' he said. 'In Cantoc's name I welcome you to the home of the *trigoryon an arvor*.'

'I am Lawbryn, second in command of the *trigolion o arfordir Cymru*.'

'Leader,' Arric pointed out. '*Leader* of the Welsh Coast Dwellers.'

Lawbryn looked bemused for a moment, then nodded. 'Yes. I suppose so, until a new chief is chosen.' He indicated his companion, whose eyes were still fixed on the sobbing totterling, but without sympathy. 'This is Brythnen, my oldest friend.'

'And your new second, I assume.

Lawbryn nodded. 'Do not fear, he will not harm the child. Swear it, Brythnen.'

Brythnen shrugged. 'I swear not to harm the child.' But he added coldly, 'Until I am called upon to do so.'

'Why is Dreis still crying?' Arric sighed. 'Nerryn, give him some of Mylan's miraculous milky bread.'

'He is not hungry,' Nerryn said, 'he is sad. I think perhaps Tir has changed his plan and does not come near after all.'

'I should think not,' Lawbryn said, with grim satisfaction. 'It will be some time before he is well enough.'

'Surely he must be recovered a little by now?' Mylan said. 'It has been half a moon's turn already.'

'He was,' Brythnen put in. 'He and Maer had made good progress on their journey here, until they met us. And Lawbryn's gwyllgi.'

Mylan frowned. 'I had forgotten. Where is the hound?'

'Wounded,' Lawbryn ground out, his fist clenched on the table before him. 'Maybe dead, if Tir's blade is iron-made.'

'What happened to it?'

'Hendrig ordered it loosed. The weakling Moorlander prince had been pleading, begging for his life. Squirming in fear and invoking all manner of family ties.'

Arric tried not to look at Nerryn, but his gaze slid onto her anyway. She had gone still, and very pale, and had ceased trying to soothe the crying infant. 'So you released the hound,' he prompted, 'and?'

'Tir was enraged and grief-stricken by the prince's death—'

'What?' The exclamation came from Mylan rather than Nerryn, who had closed her eyes and looked as though someone had gripped her by the throat. 'The prince is *dead*?'

'The hound tore his arm off.' Lawbryn waved the details away. 'Listen, this is important.' He braced his hands on the table and glowered at them from beneath bristling brows. 'Tir is a stronger elemental than we'd been led to believe.' He scowled at Mylan, directing his blame for the misinformation with no room for doubt. 'The lightning was not only immediate, but it was directed exactly as he wished it.' He slapped the table and stood back. 'He has been learning.'

'Of course he has!' Arric said. 'What did we expect? But so have we.'

He was fascinated and distracted by the utter stillness of his sister, it was as if her mind wasn't even in the room with them, that she had been struck mid-swallow, mid-breath, and neither one would ever be completed. Her eyes were still closed, her neck rigid, her hands motionless and keeping her hold on the squirming child only by some kind of instinct.

'We have our own weapon,' Arric said, using Nerryn's word. Still she did not react. 'So,' he went on, 'we will take you to see Cantoc. You will have need of shelter, and he has been finding suitable caves along the shore, for your people. Come,' he stood up, 'I will take you to him.'

'Do not trouble yourself.' Cantoc pushed aside the door covering and strode into the room as if he owned it still. 'You should sleep, Arric, you have work to do when the sun rises.'

'Work? But—'

'People must still eat.'

Arric bit down on a furious retort; Cantoc was not yet in possession of the facts, after all. 'Things have moved on a-pace since last we spoke,' he said evenly. 'Prince Maer is dead, and…' he paused, frowning, as Cantoc visibly flinched, then went on, 'Understand. This is no longer something that may happen in the future, Cantoc, *we are at war* with the Moorlanders.'

Cantoc turned cold grey eyes on him. 'And now we have even more mouths to feed. So you must fish, with the others. Which brings to mind: why is your salt-store open to the rain?'

'Open?'

'The lid was off, and most of the salt gone. Whether by rain or thievery, this is your carelessness, Arric. Now go and chase the last bit of sleep you can before the day begins, we will have need of provisions for our guests.'

Arric had had enough. 'Our *guests* can go home! We have no need of them, we have all we need right here.' He waved at Nerryn and Mylan. Nerryn was still motionless, lost in some distant world where, no doubt, her prince still lived, but Mylan seemed less hostile now.

'We have need of every strong arm we can muster,' Cantoc argued, and his eyes glinted dangerously at Arric's tone. 'It is not your place to question, nor to dismiss.' He looked around. 'I heard there were three who broke away and went to Lynher Mill. I see only two, where is the third?'

'Hendrig is dead. At Tir's hand.'

Cantoc's expression shadowed, and he bowed to the far-dwellers. 'You have my sorrow, and my promise that he will be avenged. Dafna was a shining light on our land, and we were ever grateful to her father for allowing her to come to us.' He looked around. 'Where is Hewyl? I have not had chance to question him, but I must be sure of him before we move into action.'

'You are too late.' Nerryn spoke up at last, her voice dull. 'He has gone.' She turned flat eyes on Cantoc. 'I believe he must be the one who killed our father, not Maer.'

Cantoc touched her hand. 'You need not fear reprisals, Nerryn, but please, the truth now. You never believed Maer to be capable of such an act, did you?'

She closed her eyes and shook her head. 'Never,' she whispered, the thin sound barely audible.

Arric was about to lash her with the words that sprang to his lips, but Cantoc spoke first. 'Hewyl's disappearance leads me to suspect him also.' His hand still on Nerryn's, and raising his voice over the increasingly desolate sobbing of the totterling in her arms, he went on, 'I have long wondered about the reasons Maer might have had, and they do not make as much sense now, with a clear head, as they did. I have long suspected another.'

Arric's heart skipped a couple of beats and he fought a momentary dizziness. Then the only way forward opened up, after all it no longer mattered to him whether or not Nerryn believed Maer to be guilty. 'I also think Nerryn is right,' he said, ready to accept a lesser crime. 'I hold myself to blame, in part, for allowing Hewyl to join us.'

'In part?' Mylan leaned back and folded his arms. 'You are wholly to blame.'

'Our father was killed before Hewyl made himself known to us,' Arric pointed out, keeping his voice calm. 'I am of the mind that, as Nerryn says, the prince did not kill him after all.'

'Yet you saw him running from our home, you say?'

'I did. I suspect he made Hewyl do the work for him. It takes courage to do that to a man,' he went on, 'to stand behind him, close enough to smell him, and to...' he eased off, mindful that he was painting too bright a picture. 'Well, I don't believe the Moorlander prince has... *had*, that kind of courage.'

Cantoc was watching him thoughtfully throughout this speech. 'Perhaps you are right,' he mused. 'You were naive to believe so easily, when Hewyl spun his tale of love for this world, but the fact that he has now disappeared would suggest he has returned to his first non-mortal allegiance.'

'Too late for Maer,' Arric couldn't resist saying, though he daren't look at Nerryn when he said it. 'I have a plan, Cantoc, and I need your permission to allow me to put it into action.'

'What plan?'

'Please, allow me to discuss it with those concerned, in case they are unable to help after all.'

'And who is concerned?'

'My brother and sister.'

Cantoc frowned. 'Your sister is not to be put at risk.'

Arric gave him a faintly mocking look. 'I tell you I have a plan which will help us heap vengeance on Dafna's killer, and you balk at even letting me try? Perhaps your regard for our mother is not as deep as you would have had us believe?' He knew he was pushing hard, but he couldn't stop himself. 'Maybe it even suited you for her to have died, so that you might prove your generosity in front of your people? Earn their adoration?'

'Enough!' Cantoc thundered. 'No matter what you feel you have over me, you will never speak to me in that way again!'

He turned away, arms folded across his chest, hands curled into fists. He seemed to have forgotten the presence of Lawbryn and Brythnen, but when he spoke again it was in a calmer voice, and he was clearly still fighting with his conscience. 'I would see vengeance for Dafna even if it meant my own death, you know this. But Gilan is already dead, and not by our hand.'

'What difference—'

'We are not punishing the true killer, Arric!'

'And *you* are not the one who was killed!' Arric shouted, surprising himself and everyone else. 'Yet *you* would take it on yourself to punish Gilan, if he were alive.'

'Of course—'

'But he is not, and neither is she. So it is left to *her* people to pass judgement, and Gilan's people to suffer it!' Arric's voice quietened, but was no less intense. 'It moves on, Cantoc, equal on both sides. Without hesitation.'

Arric saw Cantoc faltering, and lowered his voice further, deliberately gentling his words. 'I know how it eats away at your heart and your strength; you are a different man when you think of her.' Lawbryn's eyes narrowed, Arric noted, but he pressed on, 'You will have no peace until you exact revenge on those who do not deserve to walk the earth while Dafna lies within it; the dust *they* have made her.'

Cantoc studied him for a long, difficult moment, and Arric wondered if anyone else could hear the way his own heart pounded, or could see it in the tremble of his hand as he curled it casually beneath his chin.

'You are right,' Cantoc said, at last. 'This is all that is left to me.' He reached a decision. 'Very well. Talk to your brother and sister and gain their support. If they agree, I will consider your plan.'

Arric nodded, avoiding Cantoc's eyes. 'Thank you. Now I would speak with Nerryn and Mylan. Alone.'

Lawbryn's frown finally slid away from Cantoc and onto Arric. 'Why alone?'

'Why?' Arric turned a dangerously pleasant smile on him. 'Because I have learned my lesson when discussing matters of war in front of strangers.'

'They are not strangers,' Mylan said. 'They are family!'

'I do not know them,' Arric pointed out. 'And they have already disobeyed orders once. An action which resulted in the death of their leader... Would you have them risk the same happening to ours?'

'It was not our doing!' Brythnen's face was a black cloud. 'We were ill-prepared for the power of that half-mortal, and in any case did not expect to meet him and the prince on the path!'

'And what *were* you hoping for?' Arric demanded. 'To find him unattended on his death-bed at Lynher Mill, and to have your puppy chew on his heart for breakfast?'

'Hendrig simply wanted to see the place we would be expected to attack. To plan ahead.'

'You won't be expected to attack anywhere,' Arric said. 'Now Mylan is home we have everything we need.'

'*I* will decide what we need.' Cantoc pulled the covering away from the door and gestured to the far-dwellers. 'Please. Your people are waiting on the beach for their leader. You will need to bear the sad news to them.' He shot a last look Arric's way. 'Do *nothing* until I have heard your plan.'

Then he was gone, and the three siblings were alone at last. Dreis's cries had finally tapered off to snuffles, and his head was buried against Nerryn's shoulder.

'Put him back to bed,' Arric said.

'No.'

'Do it, Nerryn,' Mylan advised tiredly. 'I have had a long journey, and little to eat. If today marks the first of many more of the same, I will need a short rest, at least, before the sun rises.'

Arric scowled. 'Do I understand this to mean you will not even attempt to control the Moorlanders in the way I have suggested?'

'No, I will not. Nerryn is right, once they know who has destroyed them they will not let us live. Besides, we have too much to learn for this to be effective before Tir marches on us again. We would be better to spend our time training our people to protect themselves. And I must speak with Lyelt and Keityn, it is long past time they showed themselves and proved their allegiance.'

'They have already been here.' Arric began a slow walk around the room, thinking hard. 'Nerryn, I said put the child to bed.' She rose, cast a worried frown between her brothers, and finally took Dreis and his infernal whimpering through to the chambers deep inside the cliff.

Arric waited until she had vanished into her own room, and addressed Mylan again. 'Yes,' he said. 'They came, those Forester mid-growns, and I am sorry to say you have over-stated their importance. They will not be taking our side against the Moorlanders.'

'Why not?'

'How should I know?' Arric's mind was whirring, but he pressed on. 'They did not stay long enough to tell me, presumably they were too frightened to do so. Perhaps they never meant to join us, have you considered that? That they have played to your vanity?'

'They meant to,' Mylan said stubbornly. 'I can read people, Arric, and they hate Prince Maer. Something has changed their minds.'

'Quite,' Arric murmured, checking for the sound of Nerryn returning. 'It matters not, though, does it? What is of importance now is that we are on our own. Fifty *trigoryon an pell,* Mylan? It's pitiful! Do you know how many Moorlanders will be readying themselves right now, to strike against us?'

'No. Do you?' Mylan's voice was hard, but Arric knew he was getting through, by the way his brother's fists were clenched on the table before him, the knuckles bone-white. Mylan was helpless in the face of Arric's supposed knowledge, and he hated it.

'At least four thousand.' The number was plucked from the air, but it made Mylan's face tighten. 'Possibly more. We will be wiped from existence. Our only hope is to hit Lynher Mill hard, and fast, and from the safety of our own lands.'

'And you cannot do this without Nerryn and me.'

It was not a question, Arric was glad to see. 'Not with any great effect, no. Will you save your people, Mylan? Or will you run away on your travels again, and leave us to fend off Tir and his army when he comes?'

They both heard Nerryn's light footsteps approaching, and Arric, standing right beside him now, raised his eyebrow in what he hoped was a meaningful way.

Mylan clearly understood. 'Very well. I will try and persuade her. Leave us alone.'

'No, I will not.'

Nerryn had slipped into the room. She and Mylan were like children again, exchanging secret glances. Disobedient ones, at that, and Arric scowled. 'Will you do it, Nerryn?'

'No, I will not.' she mimicked him, but with a savage bite in her voice.

'Not even to save your people?' Arric tried to keep his voice even, but his impatience was wearing to nothing. 'To save Mylan?' He placed a friendly hand around Mylan's shoulder. Mylan did not pull away, but he shot Arric a look filled with loathing. Arric flexed the fingers on his free hand. He was ready.

'Mylan does not need me to save him,' Nerryn said.

Stupid girl.

A second later Mylan's own blade was out of its sheath and in Arric's hand. He pressed the tip against his brother's neck, just below his ear, while the arm that was already around Mylan's shoulder pulled him closer. Mylan hissed but did not fight; he knew Arric of old, and Arric would be no easy match, not with the advantage already firmly in his fist.

'Leave him!' Nerryn cried. 'What good will it do you to harm him? You need him!'

'I only need him if I have you as well,' Arric said. He could feel his own hand shake, as his brother's rich, dark blood rolled down the shining blade towards the handle. His heart was thundering, torn and aching at the thought of hurting Mylan, but the rest of him was drowning in the terrified knowledge of what would happen if Nerryn did not do his bidding now. It had all gone too far to stop.

'Please,' he heard himself whispering suddenly. 'Please, Nerryn. Your people need you. *We* need you!'

Nerryn's voice trembled. 'You are mad!' Her gaze was fixed on the blade at Mylan's neck, and her eyes were alight with horror and disbelief. 'Very well. You may tell Cantoc we agree.'

Almost dropping his knife with relief, Arric took his arm from around Mylan's shoulder, and seized the nearest coat from a pile by the door. He threw it at his sister; Cantoc's anger would be terrifying enough already, but if his precious Nerryn caught a rain-chill and died, his own life would be worthless.

He renewed his grip on the blade, trying to stop the trembling in his fingers. 'Outside, both of you. If you try to stop, or to run, I will use it.' *Please, don't make me...*

'But Cantoc—'

'He will never approve this, but that is only because he doesn't understand like you do.'

'He will punish you, nevertheless.'

'He will reward me!' He caught Nerryn's look, and corrected himself quickly. 'Us. He will realise this is the only way, and he will be king over us all. He will reward us greatly, you'll see.'

'What about Dreis?' Mylan asked. How typical that the deepest concern should come from him.

'Leave the totterling where he is,' Arric said. 'We no longer need him to protect us against Tir.'

'But he will not stay where we put him,' Mylan said. 'He crawls now, and with no doors…'

Good. Perhaps the beach would beckon after all. 'It matters nothing whether he stays or not.' Arric straightened and took a firmer hold on his knife. 'Come with me. It is time.'

Outside on the clifftop in the faint, early morning light, the rain was still coming down. It was hard to know who was making it, and it might even have been passed off as natural had it not been accompanied by lightning that did not belong in such weather. Arric had an idea that Tir was still battling his grief for his prince.

'Put the coat on, Nerryn,' he said, squinting at the sky.

She gave him a sour look. 'It will not fit, you fool.'

Arric looked more closely, she was right: in his haste he had picked up the spriggan's mucky old green thing. 'Then wrap it around your shoulders. Now hurry.'

He led Mylan up over the cliff on the point of his own blade, but kept more than half his attention on Nerryn. Her admission that she had never believed the story of Maer's violence had given him a moment's white-hot fury, but could not necessarily be taken to mean her loyalties remained with the Moorlanders; she simply had not stopped loving Maer, and would doubtless grieve a long while yet.

In an odd way, it endeared the girl to him as little had done before; the changes he had seen in her were good ones, strong ones, and now she had remembered where she came from, those changes would make her a worthy Coastal once again. Maybe even a queen, once Cantoc had the land. It was Mylan he doubted now.

When they drew close to where he planned to begin, he watched Nerryn even more closely. She closed her eyes for a moment but went down into the hollow meekly enough, though it must have hurt her to remember this place. He recalled his own anger at seeing the crumpled flowers where she had lain with her Moorlander, but an unexpected wash of sympathy stopped him from mocking her with it.

'Sit,' he told her, nodding to the most sheltered end of the deep hollow. She did, spreading Greencoat's jacket on the wet ground.

'Now you.' He pressed his hand to Mylan's back, quite gently, but for a moment Mylan didn't move. Arric bit the inside of his lip, and steeled himself, before pressing the knife harder against his brother's neck. 'Do this, or it will be your sister who will suffer, on your behalf.'

Mylan moved reluctantly to Nerryn's side. Once seated, and with Arric beside him, he lifted his fingers to his neck and wiped some of the blood away. Wordlessly he smeared it on Arric's motionless hand, and only then did he meet Arric's eyes. His own were dark and furious, the usual sapphire turned indigo.

'On *you*,' he said quietly. 'All of us.' He reached out and took Nerryn's hand in his bloodied one, and Arric watched their fingers twine together. He felt the stickiness of Mylan's blood, and saw the hatred rolling off his brother and sister towards him, and for a moment he faltered.

He almost told them to stop, that they were right, but Cantoc was now so stirred up that the only thing that would end this would be to avenge Dafna, and if Arric didn't do it now, like this, they would all be marching on Lynher Mill. Doubtless outnumbered, they would all be slain within minutes.

'That's right. Hate me,' he said, his voice hoarse. 'But push it away.' It was finally happening, and he could feel his heartbeat galloping and tripping. 'You know how to find it, how to build it, so do it, but push it eastwards with everything you have. And do not let go of each other's hands.'

Mylan looked at his sister. 'You have lied to us, Nerryn, I know this. I think I have always known, and I might even have helped, in time. But it is too late now, to take Dreis as you have planned.'

Nerryn looked back at him calmly, but she did not bother to deny it, and Arric bit back a furious retort. After those fond thoughts of a few moments ago... It was he who was at fault, for believing the love between her and her prince could ever be extinguished. She had played her part well, and had fooled them all, except her twin. But Mylan had not shared his suspicions, and that told Arric his own ambitions for the future of their people were wading through roughening waters already. There was no time to waste.

His siblings closed their eyes, and Arric waited in silence. He found he was struggling to breathe, and the energy all around him seemed to press in, drawn towards the oblivious twins. After a moment he grew accustomed to the pressure, and at the same time he heard the sudden surge of the tide booming against the rocks, and the first real shout of thunder; the kind that sounded as though it had cracked the cliff itself.

He closed his eyes and tightened his grip on the handle of his knife. Brother or not, if Mylan let him down now there would not be enough clean places within reach, on which to smear his precious blood.

Chapter Twenty-Three

It must be daylight by now. Laura wondered if the storm had abated; down here there was no way of telling. But her question was answered just moments later, as Jacky came into Richard's room.

'My Lady, I have been to the edge of the tunnel. The sun has risen, but...' he wrung his hands and shook his head, his eyes dark with misery.

'But what?'

'It is dark. The sky still shouts, and I could not raise my head far above the level of the ground, for fear of being struck by flying branches.'

'But there's no forest for miles,' Laura said, in horrified awe. 'Only scrubby little bushes. No trees.'

'The winds are coming from the west, from the coast. They will have passed through those forests as lie in their path. Destroyed them.' Fat tears were rolling down Jacky's cheeks now. 'My Lord Tir and Prince Maer are out there, we can only hope they have found shelter.'

Laura looked around the room. On the bed where she sat was the blanket she had last seen wrapped around Richard, when he'd been in Maer's chamber. She ran a hand over it, as if she could absorb part of him from its touch, but it was just a blanket after all. Even his coat gave her only physical warmth.

'Can't we do anything but wait?' she said at length.

Jacky sniffed, and nodded. 'We can take food to those who have gathered in the cavern.'

'Gathered?'

'Those who do not dwell here, but on the land above. They might have sought shelter elsewhere underground, in the other caverns and tunnels, but many such places are sealed shut, by stupid mort—' he looked aghast at his slip, but Laura nodded for him to continue.

'My Lady, we *do* understand that more of you roam the moorlands than before, and that it is dangerous, but when the tunnels were closed off... well, many died. Trapped.'

Laura stared, horrified. Was there no end to the destruction her family and her people had caused? Her guilty gaze went to Richard's coat; the framed picture of Dafna was still in the pocket, while the folder lay, damp-edged and creased, on the shelf.

'It was long ago, in the minds of your kind.' Jacky said. 'But after the first time, most of us stopped living underground. We made our homes in tree roots and old barrows.'

'And now they've come down here. They must be terrified.'

'They needed shelter. And now they need food.'

'Do you have enough?' Laura reached for the coat; it was cold out there in the cavern.

'We have what we have. Whether it is enough, who knows? Will you help?'

'Of course. Show me where to go.'

She followed him to the door, but something in the corner caught her eye and she went back to have a closer look. It was Richard's torc. She reached down with a trembling hand and picked it up, it hung heavy and smooth from her fingers.

'Wear it, Lady Laura,' Jacky said quietly.

'What? No.' She turned to put it on the shelf, but Jacky came back into the room and looked up at her, his eyes solemn.

'You should. You are Tir's lady. These people know you are mortal. An ancient enemy, and to be feared. But if they see you wearing the Lord Tir's torc they will understand you are his presence among them when he cannot be.'

Laura turned the torc over in her hands, and then swallowed hard and lifted it, hesitating only once more before placing it around her neck. She pushed the ends together to stop it sliding off, and shivered. *Now* she felt him. The warm gold was like the touch of his firm, strong fingers on the back of her neck. Perhaps Jacky was right, such a symbol was more than a trapping of wealth.

Out in the huge chamber, where she had first whooped and laughed at the age of thirteen, she could now have wept. There was barely room to move between the people gathered there, some sleeping, some rocking frightened youngsters, some gathered in small groups and talking earnestly about who should go back up to the surface, to check for friends and belongings or to find food. They seemed more solid, more real, than ever before... how could she have lived so long among them and not been even the slightest bit aware of them?

That the destruction was coming from the coast was her only anchor in sanity; it meant Ben would be behind it, not in its path. But at the same time she wondered how big a part Richard was playing in the devastation above ground, and if he was safe.

Jacky had been right about the torc, too. No-one questioned her presence once they'd seen it; many bowed their heads instinctively, and one spriggan even offered a tentative smile, and asked after the king's health. Seeing her hesitate, Jacky quickly advised her to tell the spriggan what he wished to hear.

'They must remain hopeful,' he murmured.

Laura nodded. 'He is recovered,' she said, stooping to hand down a bowl of hot vegetable stew, from the tray Jacky carried. 'He is even now out fighting to turn back this attack from the coast.'

'Thank you, My Lady,' the elemental said, and Laura found a smile for him. Her own words tickled the back of her mind, however, and when she had finished handing out the food on the tray she sent Jacky back for more, and went in search of Deera. She found the former queen standing alone in her chamber, staring at the plain wall. God knew what she was seeing there.

'Can I talk to you?'

Deera looked around, startled and white-faced. When she saw Laura she frowned. 'I had heard you were here. Tir is gone.'

'I know,' Laura said in a tight voice. 'And Maer has gone with him.'

'Maer,' Deera whispered, turning back to the wall. Her hands twisted together and Laura saw her shoulders jerk as she tried to take a steadying breath.

'Maer will return,' she said, trying to sound positive. 'At least he's healthy, and—'

'I feel…' Deera turned around again and took a step towards Laura. Her hands rose to press against her chest, and she was visibly struggling for words. 'I feel he is hurt. In danger, maybe. I don't… if I lose him too, I am finished.'

Laura was discomfited by the intensity of Deera's expression, and by the hopelessness in her voice. 'You're bound to be worried,' she ventured. 'I'm frightened for my son too.'

'Do you feel him like a physical presence?' Deera wanted to know. Her eagerness to find understanding showed in her face, but Laura shook her head.

'I feel his absence like a real thing,' she said, 'and it hurts like hell, but no. I can't sense him. I wish I could.'

Deera blinked and looked away again. 'I feel Maer slipping away from me. He is always strong in my heart, I can always reach out and find him. But he is fading.'

Laura felt cold at Deera's sad certainty. 'It might be that he's farther away now,' she said. 'With all that's happening out… where are you going?'

'I am going to find my son.'

'You'll be no good to him pinned under a tree,' Laura said. 'Jacky told me the storm's still going strong, but he didn't go out. I'll send someone up the tunnel again.'

'Why did you come to find me?' Deera wanted to know, at last.

'Because we have hundreds of elementals out there. Lost, helpless, and currently useless.'

'I know this. Why—'

'They're *elementals,* Deera! Just like the ones who are doing this! Surely they can band together to turn it back on the coast?'

'And you would risk your son's life like this?'

'Of course not. That's why I came to you. To tell you I'm leaving. Just give me half a day to get Ben away from that place, then you can let rip.'

'Rip?'

'Never mind. Look, your people need a purpose, so get them together. Now.' Laura heard the unfamiliar commanding tone in her own voice, and welcomed it. 'Tell them what we need, make them understand, and…' her mind cast about for the right words, '…when the sun is mid-sky, get them up there,' she jabbed her finger towards the ceiling of the chamber, 'and get them all to push it back. Together they should be able to do it.'

'And this will give you time to bring Dreis to safety?'

For once Laura didn't even argue about the name. 'I hope so.'

'And Maer?' Deera's voice was soft, but her eyes were not. They bored into Laura, testing her loyalty, testing her strength. Testing her honesty.

'I don't know,' Laura said at last. 'Nor do I know about Richard. But we can only do our best, as can your people. Make them do it.'

'I cannot. You must.'

'I'm not—'

'You are more their queen than I am, now.' Deera didn't sound regretful, just matter-of-fact. She reached out and gently touched the end of the torc around Laura's neck. 'This has marked you as such.'

Laura shook her head. 'But I don't know how you do it, with the weather and stuff.'

'You do not have to know. They will do that part.'

Laura could think of nothing that might dissuade Deera, so she nodded. 'But I'll go up the tunnel myself, first. I'll have to be able to tell them something about what's up there if I'm going to send them back out in it.'

'Good.' Deera looked easier in her mind now, but one hand still remained pressed against her heart, and it was as if she was holding the last bit of her son firmly there, trying to stop him from slipping away altogether. Laura went cold at the thought, but understood a little more about Richard and Ben, and their strange connection — how could she even think of parting them?

She left Deera's chamber and went to find Jacky. 'I'm going up to check on things outside. Will you come? I need your...' she gestured helplessly, 'your way of making the tunnel bigger. And I'll need your light.'

His face altered slightly, but she couldn't read it; it was too alien for her to recognise all but the most obvious expressions. 'Of course.'

Laura nodded her thanks, took a deep breath, and crossed her fingers for calm skies as she led Jacky to the tunnel. But they were no more than a few steps in before they heard the bitter howling of wind, the roar of thunder, and the cracking sound of lightning finding its lethal way to the ground... Laura's stomach lurched at the thought of going outside. If last night had seemed frightening, then the dawn had only increased the danger.

She stopped well before she'd reached the mouth of the tunnel; the wind was curling down, shrieking as it whipped past the ruined engine-house nearby. The dark echo of thunder rolled around them, and Laura could have sworn to feeling the pressure of the air against her, quite separate from the tug of the wind. She thought of Ben, and pushed on.

As she emerged into the grey daylight she saw what Jacky meant; it was obviously morning, but the clouds swirled and the rain splattered heavily, blowing into her face and making her flinch and blink away the drops. Then her gaze was drawn upwards, and her breath stopped.

Where the hill rose to meet the dark sky in the distance, a darker cloud was forming. Moving faster than the others, and swirling as it travelled across the moor. Even as she watched, suddenly oblivious to the lightning and the rain, a small, perfect triangle appeared, facing downwards, jutting from this new, sinister cloud as if someone had drawn it there.

The triangle grew, widening and reaching towards the grey-green ground beneath it; lightning bloomed inside the cloud, and the noise grew – a rising, booming sound, a waterfall in the sky that was growing, and growing…

Beneath the tip of the triangle a separate cloud formed, and spun lazily, brushing the ground, taunting its bigger brother ever downwards. The triangle lengthened, became a terrifyingly familiar shape, and Laura cried out as the ground beneath her trembled. Abruptly she snapped out of the numbed fascination of this hideous beauty, and turned to scream at Jacky, 'Get everyone *out of the cavern*! Into the back chambers… *Go!*'

She turned to follow him, her feet slipping on the wet grass, and the tornado swept closer. Lightning found its way through the mass of churning cloud and hit the ground again, and Laura stumbled into the tunnel, dry-mouthed and nauseous. She could feel and smell the danger; the burning air, the leaping electricity that seemed to suck all the strength from her legs.

Then, just as she allowed herself a heartbeat's worth of relief to be out of the storm, she felt as though something had grabbed her head and smashed it into the wall. She struggled for breath as the darkness and terror swept in, and from above her she heard the sounds of falling rock, and the roar of the tornado as it reached the mine. Then screams. From down in the cavern they rose, rushing through the tunnel; screams of people trapped and terrified… and screams of agony.

The tunnel started to fall around her; huge chunks of rock and concrete. Laura wrapped her arms across her head and waited for the pain and then oblivion, but it never came.

The roar of the tornado faded, after what seemed an age, and weak daylight splashed across her raised knees. The wind screamed through the holes in the roof, where the ground above had been split wide open, and rain lashed through, stinging her hands. She slowly lowered her arms, wincing at the lance of pain that shot through her head. 'Jacky! Where are you?'

There was no answer, and Laura looked to the mouth of the tunnel. It was blocked by fallen debris from the shattered chimney, and there was no way of knowing if she could get down to the cavern either– she could see the tunnel had at least partially collapsed along its length, and who knew if it would even be safe to try?

Instead she crawled to the entrance again, and began tearing at the barrier between her and freedom. The chunks of stone were at least three deep, and before long Laura felt the slick sensation of blood between her fingers and the jagged lumps, but finally she saw a sliver of light on the other side.

Grunting in cold triumph, she turned around in the tiny space and kicked outwards, driving her boots against the stones again and again, until they fell with a dull thump onto the grass outside.

Moments later she was out, crawling over the pile. Her head pounded anew with the effort, and she blinked away a trickle of blood that ran into her right eye. Richard's coat was covered with mud and dust, and got in the way of her knees, but eventually she scrambled to her feet and looked fearfully at the sky; the huge, whirling twister was still moving eastwards, towards the village. Could this really be the work of just two people, as Jacky seemed to believe?

Jacky... Laura dropped her gaze to look behind her, and froze in horror. A short distance away a fissure had opened up in the ground. The surface of the land had split down the length of what had been the tunnel she had just crawled from, and at the other end, the gentle grassy swells she'd known all her life had just... fallen away into nothing.

She moved towards it, on legs that didn't want to work, until she reached the edge. Alternately pushed and tugged by the wind, and terrified she would be blown over, she dropped to her knees and stared downwards into the depths of the moor itself.

She had always known the tunnel was long, and steeply angled, but had never realised quite how far underground it went. The old mine workings showed clearly off to one side; vertical shafts sunk into the ground, the different levels going off in the other direction, ladders, pulleys, rotten wooden lift mechanisms ... everything necessary for a once-thriving business.

Laura cast about for the shallowest slope down, and soon she was slipping and sliding to the bottom of the crater, trying not to bring more rocks down on the cracked cavern roof, and the struggling creatures beneath it. The rain made it even harder going than it would have otherwise been, the rocks were slippery, and the freshly revealed earth had turned to mud within seconds. By the time Laura reached the broken edges of the roof she was bruised, filthy, and exhausted beyond sensible thought.

She lay on the edge and peered down, fighting a wave of sickness and despair. Bodies were pinned by rocks, or in little crumpled heaps, and there were splashes of blood that told their own grim stories. Many of the injured were elementals, but there were spriggans there too, and she closed her eyes and prayed to whoever might be listening that Jacky was not one of them.

Then, squinting through the erratically flickering light of hundreds of terrified souls, she saw him. How had she ever thought they all looked the same?

He was suddenly as dearly familiar to her as anyone, and she was hit by a rush of gladness to see him.

She was about to call out to him, when she heard a voice shouting her own name; it startled her so much she felt her neck muscles wrench as she jerked around.

'Michael!' Hope leapt in her heart, and she looked beyond him but only saw three very pale, but exquisite elementals, following him down the slope. 'Where's Ben?'

He shook his head, his face solemn. 'He's okay, but—'

'You promised!' Despair made her voice harsh. She staggered to her feet, and met him as he reached the shallow part of the slope near the roof.

'Where are you going?' He grabbed at her as she moved to push past him.

She yanked her arm away, some distant part of her registering blood on his clothes and his hands. 'Where do you think? I'm not waiting around anymore, that's my *child!*' An echo of the very conversation that had passed between her and Deera... her heart went out to the woman as never before.

'And Tir has gone to get him!' Michael said. 'Laura, it's lethal out there, you won't make it beyond Bodmin!' He thumbed away a fresh bead of blood from her forehead, squinted at the cut and seemed to satisfy himself it was nothing serious.

He looked down through the rubble-strewn roof, as she had done. 'They need your help more. Come on, I'll help you down.'

Laura held firm. 'Jacky was right, wasn't he? This is Nerryn and her brother. They're going to destroy us all.'

'I'm still hoping the other brother will see sense,' Michael said grimly. 'When I left, they hadn't started, but yeah, I'd say this is them.'

'And if Arric doesn't see sense?' As if in answer, a fresh gust of wind knocked one of the other elementals to his knees, and Laura almost tumbled through the hole in the roof.

Michael grabbed her by the coat, and she felt her heart pushing against her ribs. 'It's getting worse, isn't it? There was a bloody *tornado!* Where is it now? What if there are more?'

'There will be,' he said. 'All we can do is hope Cantoc will step in once he realises what's happening here. But Arric's got the man's blood so fired up it'll take a miracle.'

'How can he let it happen? How can anyone think this—' Laura gestured at the ever-darkening sky, and then at the carnage at their feet—'is going to help them? There'll be nothing left for them to be kings *of!*'

Michael shook his head. 'Let me help you down, we can talk later.'

'Wait! I have a right to know why we're all going to die, don't I? Everyone else seems to. Why is Cantoc doing this?'

Michael kicked away some of the loose stones, clearing a spot so he could kneel to study the drop into the cavern. 'He's doing it for vengeance,' he said. 'On those who killed the only woman he's ever loved.'

'What? Who?'

'Nerryn's mother. Dafna. She was—'

'I know,' Laura interrupted. The ground tilted once more, but this time it was only her who felt it. Her voice dropped until she wasn't sure Michael could even hear her. 'She was killed exploring the moors. I heard the story.'

'Well it turns out Cantoc has been under the impression it was the spriggans, all this time, and he'd already taken his revenge on them. Then he found out it was Deera's brother Gilan.'

As he spoke, Laura's thoughts turned faster. She saw again the images Gail had put in her mind. She vaguely heard him saying something about Maer, and Nerryn's father, but his voice faded into the wind and she breathed slow and deep, while ordering her thoughts.

'Laura?'

She blinked. Michael was standing again, and he held out a hand. 'I'll hold you until you're ready to drop. It's not too far down just here.'

Laura looked at his hand. She heard the cries from below, almost imagined she could tell Jacky's voice from the others, and wondered for a split second if Deera was alive. Then she realised she had already decided what to do.

'You go first,' she said, keeping her voice calm with an effort. 'I need to see how to do it. You can catch me.'

'Are you sure?' His companions had already grown tired of waiting, and had made their way down through the roof in another spot. Michael was eager to join them. To help. As ever.

Laura nodded. 'Go on, I'll watch how you do it.'

She waited, her own impatience reaching screaming point before he had knelt and inched backwards into the hole, holding on first with his hooked elbows, and then with only his whitened fingertips. He swung, just for a moment, and Laura made herself wait until he had let go, before she called down, 'I'm sorry! Look after them.'

She turned away and began the scramble back up the slope to solid ground, blinking away the rain that drove into her eyes, and trying to ignore the pain in her bleeding fingers as she scrabbled in the loose stones for hand-holds. Michael's helpless, furious voice faded quickly, and by the time Laura had reached flat, grassy ground again she had put him out of her mind altogether.

She gave herself half a minute to get her breath back, and then set off through the driving rain towards the village, her car, and the only way she knew would end this. While there was still hope of survival.

Chapter Twenty-Four

The trees swayed. Now and again Maer could hear a crack, as one was bent beyond endurance and crashed into those that surrounded it, but he daren't move, daren't even swivel his eyes away from the dark sky above, for fear of re-awakening the feeling in his arm and leg. Drenched and shivering, he swallowed, and opened his mouth to the rain. His skin burned, and his head pounded and spun, but the rest of him was, thankfully, still numb.

He remembered being laid down here by a bearded stranger, and hearing Tir's voice somewhere above him, then even that comfort had faded and he hadn't heard his brother again. A few familiar faces loomed close, Foresters, but he couldn't recall their names. They had hovered over him, pulling at his clothing and making exclamations he couldn't hear properly. Before that had been... what? People, coming at him and Tir across open ground. And the hound.

Maer squeezed his eyes shut tight, but the memory of that huge beast launching itself at him remained fixed; the red eyes, the rows of filthy teeth, and the overpowering, nauseating smell. He had felt the claws in his thigh – ripping fiery furrows that felt as if his leg was being shredded to the bone – but even that agony had been eclipsed the moment the hound had seized his arm in its teeth. The jaws had clamped shut, and, from somewhere far away he heard the scream that had left him all but voiceless.

Part of him wanted to look down now, to see if he had been tended to, but he could not make himself twist his head to see. So he simply lay still and begged the elements for it all to go away. After a while he felt a hand on his forehead and he opened his eyes again. The pale face that looked down at him was familiar, but it wasn't Ykana. He frowned. Her sister, Yventra. She was fighting tears, but Maer did not believe they were for him.

'Wh…' He took a breath and tried again. 'What is it?'

'Oh, Maer, I'm so sorry. There has been terrible news from Lynher Mill.'

Maer jerked in response to her words, and his left arm caught fire, making him gasp and bite back a scream. Unable to speak again, he took shallow breaths and looked pleadingly to her for an explanation.

'We have had a great deal damage done here,' she said in a low, unsteady voice, 'but it seems to be gathering strength as it goes eastwards. We have learned that at Lynher Mill the land itself has shaken so hard, it has split where it is weakest.'

A chill raced through him and he could barely get the words past his lips. 'The mine…'

She nodded, biting her lip, and her tears spilled over. 'The ground has collapsed. A great twisting cloud tore the chimney down, and there is only a deep hole where the underground cave once was. And so many dead…'

'No,' he breathed, and struggled to rise, but Yventra put a gentle hand on his unhurt shoulder.

'You must not move, my prince.'

'I have to go, they're my people!'

'I cannot let you. You have lost much blood. Tir did as well as he could, but you bled a long while before he realised you might yet be saved.'

Maer caught a breath. 'Does my mother live?'

'We do not know. We have sent help, but,' she shook her head, 'we have had to do it in secret. We have a new leader now.'

'Secret? I am a prisoner then?'

Yventra nodded. 'He has declared you the enemy, and you must be treated as such.'

'But you are caring for me.'

'You are a hostage, and no use to our new leader if you are dead.' She sounded bitter, and that gave him hope that this new leader did not yet have the full support of his people.

He frowned, half-remembering things he'd heard, then his mind cleared. 'You are allied with the Coastals now?'

'Not through choice!' Yventra sat back, her expression both angry and helpless. 'We knew if Lyelt won the challenge things would be difficult, but we had no notion he would turn the *trigoryon an goswig* away from the Moorlanders. We would have taken him prisoner before we allowed that, and answered questions later.'

'Lyelt. The one I humiliated,' Maer said dully. 'I have brought this on your heads, Yventra.'

'You have not,' she assured him. 'You made a wise judgement, you were not to know the Coastals would move against us.'

'But that is also my fault.' There was a new ache in his chest that was not put there by any gwyllgi. 'I stole one of their most treasured daughters from them, and now I find they believe I killed her father.' He struggled to piece his thoughts together. 'That is why my own father was slain. If I had not persuaded Nerryn to come with me, Talfrid and Casta would still be with us, and we would all be living in peace.'

'That cannot be foreseen,' she said, but he saw a different belief in her reluctance to look at him. She certainly blamed him, in part at least. 'We have sent those we could trust to stay hidden,' she added. 'Not our best warriors, Lyelt would notice them gone. But skilled people nevertheless. And the mortal who brought you in has slipped away as well. Lyelt is not as vigilant as he believes he is, and his people less inclined to help since he imprisoned you.'

Maer acknowledged the loyalty, but couldn't suppress his worry. 'It is daylight. You cannot hide so well from mortals.'

Yventra managed a tight smile. 'Then it is fortunate that few mortals enjoy the elements in their true fury.' She rose, and spoke now with a sympathy that held little hope. 'They will do all they can for your people, Maer, but I fear it will not be enough. You must prepare for that. I will return soon, with food.'

Maer listened with cold dread as the thunder echoed through the forest. The rain on the leaves, usually a soothing sound, now came hard and brutal, each drop that hit him felt like the prick of a thorn. His arm throbbed and screamed, and his leg and shoulder joined in the cacophony, but the biggest and most savage pain was one that could not be eased with dressings and poultices and medicines. Wide awake, frozen to the bone, all he could do was pray for his people, for his mother, for the land itself. And that Richard would find a way to save them.

***

Trethkellis. The Lovers' Hollow.

Arric lowered his hands, his heart pounding and sliding in his chest. His stomach was roiling; that last lightning bolt had threatened to take the top of his head off… 'The east!' he cried. 'Push eastwards!'

The wind shrieked around them, the sky split time and time again and there was barely time for one crash of thunder to die away before the next one set the day trembling around them. He couldn't even tell if his voice was even carrying as far as the twins. They remained locked together, their hands gripped so tightly Arric could see blood welling from Nerryn's knuckles. Arric had tried, once, to separate them, but, short of maiming them forever, there was nothing he could do.

Both their heads were thrown back, and veins were standing out in their necks. Wordless, they fought on. Whether they were fighting themselves, or each other, or whatever force had them in its grip, Arric could not tell.

He crawled over and grabbed at Mylan's shoulder. 'East!' he yelled again. Water was pouring off his brow and nose, running into his eyes and blinding him. He blinked it away, and shook his head to flick his wet hair away from his face.

Cantoc must soon find them, and Arric could only begin to imagine what fury the coast lord would be in, but if that imagining was thin and incomplete, then the knowledge of where the blame would fall was not: Arric had not taken the time to train them, to teach them how to recall, or properly direct, and, worst of all, he had kept Cantoc ignorant of his plans. He would die for this.

There was a hollow-sounding crack away to his right, towards the sea. He wanted to raise his head above the lip of the hollow, to see what was happening, but the wind was blowing so hard he knew he'd be blown off his feet if he did. A moment later he realised he didn't have to look; the sounds that followed told him clearly enough; the cliff side was falling away into the sea below, taking elementals and their homes with it.

The roar of the rock smashing on the beach made him wince... at least there would be no question now, about what to do with Tir's totterling, but, again, Cantoc's fury would light the sky from the peninsula to the mountains. If he still lived.

Arric shook Mylan's shoulder. 'Enough! Stop! I command you to stop!'

To his amazed relief, Mylan managed to speak. He was barely understandable, but Arric just made out his words. 'Cantoc. Vengeance.'

'I am Cantoc's voice!' Arric shouted. 'And I command you to stop!'

'No. Cantoc.'

Another boom echoed across the top of the hollow, and rolled over them like a monstrously heavy blanket. Arric ducked down, fear and frustration building until he thought he might scream. Very well, Cantoc was the only one who could stop them, but Arric could try and make them focus, at least.

'East!' he shouted, yet again, but now he knew that Mylan could hear him.

'Am! East!' Mylan ground out, before letting out a long cry and squeezing his sister's hands even tighter.

Arric reeled, his mouth dry. If they were already pushing this horrific storm east, how much worse must things be at Lynher Mill? Elation mingled with a creeping horror, and he risked a peek above the top of the hollow.

Through the madly dancing curtain of rain he saw long grasses, flattened first one way and then the other, the debris of a shattered barn from the nearby mortal farm, turning end-over-end and then back in the other direction.

Arric's wet hair was first raked back from his face, then snapped forward into his stinging eyes, and he stumbled back into the hollow, almost losing his feet. He sank back down, looking at his locked and tortured siblings. That power should have been his; he'd have known how to harness it, and to use it…

The last bit of control he'd tried to cling to was slipping away. He had to go. Now. Get away before Cantoc came. Part of him fervently hoped his lord had been at the foot of the cliff when it had broken away, shrinking the land and widening the shore, but a greater part of him shuddered at that thought.

Cantoc had threatened and humiliated him, but he did not deserve such a death as this. Unlike the Moorlanders. The blame for Talfrid's death might have been falsely laid at their feet, but Dafna's death was theirs to avenge, and her children had simply done what her husband had not had the stomach to do.

Arric crawled across to Nerryn and touched her rigid face. She did not flinch, or even seem to feel it. Her eyes were closed. Her long dark lashes swept the smooth skin of her cheeks, and her hair hung in bedraggled rags around her shoulders, her jaw clenched tight. Tears leaked from beneath her eyelids but he was as certain as he could be that she didn't feel those either. Moved by a sudden impulse he kissed her forehead, then turned and kissed his younger brother.

Mylan could no longer speak, his brow was drawn down tight, he looked to be in some kind of agony. Was he fighting to stop, or fighting to win? There was no way of knowing. Arric choked out an apology to them both, and braced himself as he climbed out of the hollow and onto the wind-whipped clifftop.

He turned away from the treacherous coastline, but not towards Lynher Mill. Instead he headed north-east, across land, and towards the shelter of that ravaged farm. He could only hope enough of it remained to shelter him until Cantoc found Mylan and Nerryn, and stopped them. Or until one of them died.

***

Laura fought the urge to push down on the accelerator; with so much surface water on the roads it could mean instant, screaming death. She shivered, and it was more than the sodden clothing and streaming hair that caused it; she was shaking so hard she ached, her hands on the steering wheel were fighting for control, and her body was rigid with fear and cold.

The Bodmin Bypass was clogged with cars, some parked haphazardly across the carriageway, abandoned in terror, no doubt. She had now seen three tornados, including the first, and the last one had stopped the breath in her throat; if the one at Lynher Mill had wreaked such havoc on a stone engine-house, what would this one do? It was huge, horrific, a good distance away to the south, but twisting its way towards Wadebridge. A sob escaped her as she thought of the devastation it would cause there, in that picturesque town where she and Tom had spent so many innocent and joyful summers.

A low throbbing sound from above made her look up through her windscreen. A naval helicopter bobbed, low and erratic, and close enough for her to see a small figure in it waving urgently at her to pull off the road. She ignored the order, and the helicopter veered away to safety. Laura hunched down over her steering wheel, and blinked away the water that dripped into her eyes so she could manoeuvre around the stalled and empty vehicles. Nearly there. *Please, God or whoever's up there, get this car all the way to the coast...*

She made almost it all the way to Trethkellis before she was faced with a complete road blockage: a refrigerated lorry, jack-knifed, and with at least eight more stalled and abandoned cars between her and it. There was no way past. As the engine died, the howl of the wind rose to compensate, and Laura became more aware of the swaying and rocking of the car, and the heavy splatter of rain on the windscreen. It was truly terrifying out there; she might die before she'd taken a single step. What was she thinking? How could she do this?

With a little moan, she shifted in her seat and her right knee brushed against the keys. She plucked them free from the ignition and looked at Dean's blue keyring. Once it had been held in the fearless hand of a man who had died for her once, and had been ready to die for her all over again. How could she think of doing less for him, and for Ben?

She took a deep breath and pushed open the door. The wind was whipping in all directions, and no sooner had the door been ripped out of her hands than it slammed back again, hitting her leg with so much force she almost vomited in shock and pain. She stumbled away from the car and fell to the ground, moaning and swallowing rising sickness.

When she could breathe again she tested her foot on the ground, wincing as she put pressure on it; not broken, thank god, but probably only thanks to the thickness of Richard's coat. She dragged herself as upright as she could against the wind, and half-walked, half-hopped over to where the shattered gate led the way directly across the last few fields between her and the sea.

The ground was mud beneath her feet, and the going was painful and slow, but the sound of the waves, in the ever-decreasing moments between thunderclaps, pulled her onward until she crested her small horizon and saw the land falling away before her.

The man she had seen down here before, with the bearing of a soldier, that had to have been, not Nerryn's father, but Cantoc. The lord of the coast who had power over the lives and deaths of so many. And was using it. The strength of the wind snatched at her breath and left her gasping. A particularly loud crack of thunder was followed by the sinister sizzle and explosion of lightning. She could smell it. Too close. She wrapped the heavy coat around herself and stumbled on, towards the place where she'd seen Cantoc climbing the cliff.

As she neared the edge, she stopped, suddenly unsure if she was in the right place after all; it looked so different. She frowned. The South West Coast Path was supposed to lead right along here, past Trethkellis on one side, and up towards Tintagel on the other…

A huge, roaring, rumbling sound pulled her attention to the south and she cried out in wordless horror as a chunk of the cliff peeled away and crashed downward to the rocks below. Her eyes travelled along the misshapen cliff to where she had seen Nerryn and Mylan outside their home, but there was nothing there now except an empty hole leading back into the cliff; she could glimpse the tattered edges of some kind of cloth — one of those door coverings. Everything else was gone. The twins and Arric must have gone somewhere closer to

Lynher Mill to launch their attack, and taken Ben with them. ... unless he was with Cantoc.

She flinched against a gust of wind and rain, and dropped to one knee to brace herself. Behind her lay the dunes, sand and grass-filled hollows... shelter. Below her was death in the form of jagged rocks, and of a man who would not stop until he had avenged the woman he had loved.

She half-turned thinking she had heard someone shout, but recognised it as simply a desire to justify turning back. Instead she inched closer to the edge of the cliff, and peered down. The path cut into the side of this part of the cliff was still clearly marked, although outside Nerryn's home it was as if there had never been one at all. As if the very tricks the elementals used to protect themselves from mortal eyes had passed to the land on which they had lived.

She stood up, her legs trembling, and, for the first time since she had left Lynher Mill she was aware of the warmth of the torc still around her neck. She alone possessed the knowledge it would take to save Tir's kingdom, and, even if it meant she would never share it with him, she would do what it was in her power to do. She was Tir's queen.

Chapter Twenty-Five

Richard blinked awake, and winced as a thunderclap ripped the day apart. How long had he been here? After Hewyl and Maer had gone with the Foresters he'd decided to hell with waiting, but five minutes later he'd been throwing his aching guts up, and swearing his eternal soul for sight of Kernow and her magic leaves.

'No magic,' she'd said, but he disagreed. Vehemently.

He'd sunk down against one of the trees close to the edge of the forest, telling himself that if he could at least see open ground, he'd want to cross it sooner. Waking now, with rain hammering his skin like pebbles, and a throbbing pain that wouldn't let up, he couldn't imagine crossing anything but his fingers.

'Okay,' he told Ben. 'I'm gonna do this.' He gained his feet, spat between them, and looked around for something to take away the sour taste of vomit. In the end he simply turned his face to the sky and let the torrential rain earn its keep.

The weather alternately eased, and picked up intensity. Right now it was possible to walk upright, and to see farther than six inches in front of his face.

Maybe it was just gathering impetus the farther east it went, kind of like a snowball. If that was the case… he swallowed a fearful moan as he considered what it would be like by the time it hit Lynher Mill. Jacky had better have gotten to Laura and seen her safe underground. If she'd let him.

'Promise me you went with him, honey,' he murmured. It helped, in a strange kind of a way, so he kept talking to her as he walked, although the rain drowned his words, those the wind didn't pick up and whirl away into the gloomy morning air.

He told her stuff he'd told her before, and stuff he hadn't. He reminisced about that perfect New Year's Eve. The love and the laughter. The cheese. He told her Michael was a good guy, but she already knew that. He told her he thought he could probably even bear it if she hooked up with him again, after all he'd saved Richard's life. And Maer's… he hoped. He told her about Maer.

And then he saw her.

For a full minute he stood motionless, watching her. Her hair was plastered as flat as his, which was how he knew she was real and not some image gifted to him by a delirious mind. When he'd pictured her as he talked, he'd seen her as she usually was; her thick hair tied back in its half-assed ponytail, and with those little wispy bits that floated near her beautiful silver-grey eyes. The bits he always wanted to push back, but would miss if they weren't there.

But here she was, stumbling and cursing. Her feet slipping and sliding on mud and wet grass, following the path she shouldn't have been able to see. And wearing his damned coat. He couldn't move, his heart was hammering so hard, and his blood rushing so fast, he should have been able to fly to her... But for that he'd need some control over his limbs, and right now he had none. Had he really thought he could give her up?

She dropped to one knee as she reached the cliff's edge, and stayed there for a moment, staring downwards. He shouted. Not her name, he couldn't even manage that. Just a hoarse, 'Hey!' that he thought for a moment she'd heard, but she hadn't. She crawled closer to the cliff edge.

Then, just when he was convinced she was going to pass out of his life again because of his own inability to function, she stood up, turned, and saw him. She stopped still, as disbelieving as he'd been. He could see her legs were shaking, and she staggered in a gust of wind and pushed her heavy, sodden hair out of her eyes. And then, somehow, she was standing in front of him, looking up at him, her wet eyelashes star-fished, blinking in wonder.

His paralysis finally broke, and he touched her rain-wet cheek with his thumb. Her skin, always so fresh-looking, was pale, not rose-blushed as it usually was. He felt her hands on his chest, then his waist, and then sliding around to the small of his back to pull him close.

They did not kiss; all he could do was cradle her head beneath his chin and wrap his other arm around her shoulders and hold her. Some distant part of him registered that she was wearing a torc now, too. Maybe even his. And that it looked right. But the rest of him simply breathed her existence, felt the warm reality of her, smelled the faint scent of her familiar shampoo… and wanted to weep with the longing to be back with her in their little cottage on Mill Lane.

The rain came down harder and the wind buffeted them, but they remained unmoving until a fierce crack of thunder reminded them of the world that existed beyond their own closeness.

'I've got something to tell you,' Laura said at last, drawing back and looking at him with tear-filled eyes. 'It's awful, and I don't know where to start.'

As Richard listened to her halting account of the tragedy at the mine he felt his body wanting to curl up. He wanted to just sink to the ground and stay there forever; he was just so fucking tired…

'So we don't know how many survived?' he managed, in a hollow voice.

'No. Jacky was alive when I left. But I don't know if… if any more collapsed afterward. There were more tornados, the land is… it's devastated…' her breath hitched, and Richard clutched her hand more tightly.

'Don't,' he said. He wiped a hand over his face, knowing some the water would taste salty if it ran onto his lips. 'God, Laura, I can't believe you made it down here, after all that.'

She opened her mouth to reply, but they both turned as they heard a shout of fury coming from the dunes by the clifftop. 'Arric!'

Cantoc. Had to be. Richard let go of Laura's hand and took off in the direction of the shout, at as close to a run as he could manage. He was aware of Laura keeping pace with him, and for a fleeting moment he was confused as to how she could do it, particularly limping as she was, then he realised he wasn't moving nearly as fast as he thought he was; each footstep that came down on the ground was a hammer blow in his back that travelled right through him, and every step that didn't send him crashing to the ground was a bonus.

They reached the hollow together, it looked faintly familiar; long, very deep, with sandy edges and a couple of angrily blowing gorse bushes. But he had no time to work out when he had seen it before, his attention was taken by the kneeling figure of a powerfully-built man, staring around him with an expression of murderous rage, and by the still forms of Nerryn and her twin brother.

They were holding each other's hands as if to let go would bring death to either of them. Or both. It was hard to know who was gripping the hardest, but Nerryn's skin had broken in several places and blood was smeared over her brother's fingers where they held her. He was bleeding too, from a small nick beneath his ear, the blood thinned by the rain that battered the elemental's unprotected skin.

The man on the ground saw them and rose, reaching for the blade at his hip. Richard's hand had already dropped to his, and the two men faced each other, Richard breathing hard, the older man narrow-eyed and still filled with rage.

'Cantoc,' Laura said, and Richard stiffened; there was something about her voice when she said his name, a kind of relief. But this man didn't look like someone they'd want to see, or who would be pleased to see them. He barely glanced at her, before his eyes were back and fixed on Richard's right hand, closed about the leather-wrapped handle of his dagger.

'You are Tir.' It wasn't a question, and so Richard didn't reply. 'Do you know where Arric is?'

Richard shook his head. 'And I don't care. Stop them.' He gestured to the twins.

'I will not,' Cantoc said, and his eyes were bright. 'I *cannot*. The Moorlanders have to pay for what they did.'

'Do your own people have to pay too?' Laura's voice rose as she went on, 'The cliff has collapsed! People everywhere are dying, not just the Moorlanders. The storms are destroying whole villages, barns have been torn down, trees like bloody… *matchwood!*' She broke off, and Richard reached out his left hand to her, keeping his right hand firmly where it was.

The wind gusted again, and the thunder roared, and Richard looked at the twins; Mylan's head was thrown right back, his mouth open in a silent scream. Nerryn was shaking violently, her chest hitching, her hair in her face as she lowered her head almost to her knees.

'Cantoc! Stop them!' Richard tried to ignore the pain that twisted inside him, but it was making him dizzy and disorientated, and Laura shook off his hand easily and slithered down into the hollow.

Richard could only watch, helpless; the ground seemed to heave and shift beneath him, his vision spun and by the time he had managed to climb down after her she was standing before Cantoc, within easy reach of the Coast Lord's knife.

'Where is my son?' she said, barely audible above the noise of the storm. 'Tell me, and I will tell you the truth about Dafna's death.'

'You will tell me anyway!' Cantoc grabbed her arm, and Richard lunged forward, tearing his blade free from its sheath.

'Stop!' Laura shouted, and he was too stunned to argue, but stopped, close enough to her outstretched hand to feel her fingers brushing his shirt. Another second and he would have driven his blade through Cantoc's throat… but that would have been the biggest mistake he could have made.

'What you believed, about Dafna,' Laura said to Cantoc, her voice trembling, 'it's not true. You are punishing the wrong people.'

'I am punishing those who are left to me,' Cantoc snapped. 'The Moorlanders spawned the demon Gilan, and since he is no longer—'

'It wasn't him!' Laura glanced at Richard and there was utter terror on her face now. What was she doing? She looked back at Cantoc. 'Gilan didn't kill Dafna, any more than the spriggans did.'

His voice was cold, certain. 'You are lying.'

'I am swearing to you on my life, and the life of my *child*!' Laura was openly crying now, and Richard's own heart broke to see it. 'It was not Gilan, nor any Moorlander.'

'Then who?' Cantoc's voice had dropped to a dangerous rasp.

'Tell me where Ben is, and let Richard go for him. Then I'll tell you.'

A second later Cantoc's own blade was hovering over her right eye, and she shrank back. Richard stopped breathing.

'Name the killer, mortal!' Cantoc's hand was steady, the blade moved closer and Laura closed her eyes.

'It was m… my father.'

Richard swayed in shock. 'Christ, Laura, no…'

Cantoc grew very still, but did not lower his knife.

'Gilan saw it happen,' Laura said, struggling to get her words out; terror was apparent in every line of her body but she had opened her eyes again so Cantoc could see the truth in them. 'He agreed to put the word out that it was spriggans, so long as my father paid him. Please,' she gestured at the twins. 'Stop them! Whatever you see happening here, at Lynher Mill it's a hundred times worse!'

Cantoc frowned. 'Is this a trick?'

'No trick,' Laura said, and she sounded stronger now. Resigned and ready. 'The truth. I've only just learned it.'

Richard stepped towards her and his voice was tight with anguish. 'Babe, don't...' But he knew it was too late. The words were out and could not be re-called.

'You know I must take your life.' Cantoc sounded almost regretful. It was somehow worse, more final, than his fury had been. 'Dafna's memory deserves no less.'

'Yes.'

'And you came to tell me anyway.' Cantoc knelt beside the twins, pulling Laura down with him. 'You have earned this much. I will make it safe for Tir to seek your son.'

'Thank you,' she whispered.

'I'm not leaving her,' Richard said, but it was as if his soul were being torn in two.

'For me.' Laura's face was blank now, with hopeless acceptance. 'Please, Richard, for me?' her voice cracked. 'And for Ben.'

'Do not make her sacrifice worthless,' Cantoc threw back over his shoulder.

Richard had to force himself not to rip the sonofabitch open there and then. As he watched through a curtain of rain, Cantoc laid his free hand on the tightly linked hands of the twins, and spoke quietly, undercutting the noise of the storm instead of shouting over it. His voice rumbled, deep and strong, but Richard couldn't hear the words.

He stood, with one foot on the slope and one on the flat ground, searching for that tug he had felt before, that sense of nearness he and Ben had always shared. But he felt nothing now except bleak despair at the sight of Laura on her knees, awaiting Cantoc's blade for her father's sins.

He closed his eyes tightly, trying to block it out, but the image would be with him until death claimed him. Cantoc would feel the weight of his fury—of *Tir's* fury—once Ben was safe. Richard remembered Maer's teaching; there would be no effort required to summon a source of injustice here.

Thunder rolled around them still, bouncing off the headland, off the cliffs, off the air itself. He felt it in his bones and in his blood, and he welcomed the strength it gave him. He would need it. And he would use it. Cantoc's voice continued its forceful commands, and Laura's hands were clenched on her knees; she would be both praying for the storm to end, and dreading it, at the same time. Richard could not remember such an agony of intense love and despair.

The screaming winds abruptly fell away, leaving Richard staggering slightly where he had been braced against them. Mylan and Nerryn collapsed against each other, and Cantoc steadied them, dropping his knife so he could lay them down next to each other. Laura looked at it.

Pick it up... Richard willed her, but she read his mind and shook her head sadly at him. She wouldn't be quick enough, Cantoc would be driven into fury again, and they might never find their son.

'Where is he?' Laura said, her voice quiet now. 'Tell us, so Richard can find him, and then do what you have to do. But please, do it quickly.'

Cantoc picked up his blade again and looked around, as though surprised not to see the boy sleeping peacefully in a corner. 'I do not...' Then he gave a brief shake of his head, remembering, 'Nerryn will have put him down to sleep, in her own room.' His face drained of colour. 'But the cliff is... Oh, by the Ocean's mercy...'

Laura's anguished cry cut through the suddenly still air. 'No!'

Richard's heart stopped; she had been staring down over the cliff, what had she seen?

'Go for him, Richard, hurry!'

'I can't leave you—'

'You have to.' She swallowed hard, and gestured towards the cliff. 'Go, you shouldn't see this.'

'Laura, no...'

'Go, Tir!' Cantoc bellowed suddenly. He stood up, his face twisted with indecision, then he looked down at the exhausted and drained twins, and his voice dropped again. 'Take your lady and go.'

Laura froze. 'What?'

'You have proved you are not your father's daughter,' Cantoc said roughly. He sounded as though he was weeping, but it was difficult to tell in the rain. 'You do not deserve to pay for his crimes. I have been…' he hitched a breath, 'I have been misled, played for a fool. Go, both of you, with my word that you will never be harmed while I draw breath.'

Richard's knees unlocked and he almost fell, but he stepped forward instead and seized Laura's hand. He pulled her to her feet, and her touch gave him the strength to draw her to him, out of the coast lord's reach.

'We will discuss our future, in time,' he promised. 'Take care of them,' he nodded at the twins. 'I think they'll need you.'

He didn't thank Cantoc. The Coast Lord did not deserve thanks for doing what was right. But Laura… as they climbed out of the hollow, both shaking with mingled relief and fear, he glanced down at her dark head and knew no amount of gratitude would ever be enough.

She led him to the edge of the cliff, and when he looked down he realised the reason for hers and Cantoc's dismay. His muscles seized up, and for a second he thought he wouldn't be able to move, but he had to. For Ben.

'The steps are gone,' Laura said. It was the first time she had spoken since her life had been returned to her, and she sounded terrified. Her vulnerability was accentuated by the coat that hung from her shoulders and brushed the ground by her feet, and by the way she pushed her wet hair out of her eyes with fingers that only just peeped from the ends of the sleeves. But, vulnerable or not, terrified or not, she was a mother seeking her child, and her voice found more strength with each word.

'We'll need to climb down to the bit of the path that's left.' She pointed, and he followed her finger to where one of the caves lay exposed now, touched by the sun – a sun neither of them had dared to hope they might see again.

'That's the place where they live. Lived,' she corrected. 'That piece of cloth is a doorway… it, it might be Nerryn's room?' Her voice was at once hopeful and fearful.

'I'll go,' Richard said. 'You're shaking like a leaf, you may fall.'

'I've hurt my leg.' She gestured, and for the first time he saw that her lower leg was swollen against her jeans, and through the mud he saw the glisten of blood.

'Christ, what—'

'I'm okay. Just find him. Please?'

Richard dropped a kiss on her temple, and at the touch of her rain-wet skin he was hit all over again by how close he had come to losing her. Only the thought of Ben was enough to make him let go of her hand, and begin the climb down to what remained of the cliff path below. His back was screaming by the time he got there, and his hands bled in a dozen places, but he had seen deep cuts on

Laura's hands too, and he wondered if he would ever know what she had been through during their time apart.

He edged his way along the cliff towards the ruined home Laura had indicated. His heart was pounding fast and hard, and he was still too terrified to allow his mind to reach out for Ben. The thought that he might not feel him was too much to bear.

He had almost reached the gaping hole that was all that was left of the main room, when the wind gusted—a natural wind this time—and the curtain that covered the room blew upwards. The room was whole, but empty.

Richard moaned aloud and turned to face the sea, away from the evidence that he was too late. He sagged against the cliff edge, and tried not to look down in case he saw a tiny, broken body among the rocks and the debris below; if he saw that, he knew he would soon join it; he had little enough strength left now.

'Richard!'

He looked up. Laura was lying down on the cliff's edge, waving, and pointing away to his right. He followed with his eyes, and his heart leapt. On the remaining part of the grassy path was a small figure on hands and knees, his bottom in the air, rocking back and forth as if trying to work out how he had moved before.

'Jesus, Ben,' Richard whispered, almost choking on the words 'Don't remember. Please... not yet.'

Limbs trembling, he slipped and slithered down the cliff, and over the rocks, until he was able to climb back up, and re-join the path on the other side of the crumbled ruin. The storm had left the sea sparkling, almost dazzling, and the grass wet, but the rocks were drying quickly in the October sun and it was an easy enough climb despite the aches and bruises. He daren't shout, all he could do was grab at the edge of the path and pull himself up, praying he would still see Ben in the same place as before.

'If I don't get a *dah-dee* from you after this, kid, we're gonna have words,' he promised under his breath. His blood was singing as he came within reach, and finally laid his hand on his son's rounded back. 'Hey, Ben. Guess who?'

Ben turned his head, saw him, and his face split into his familiar, sunny smile. 'Brrrap!'

'Gotcha.' Richard plucked him from the path, and as he touched that solid warmth, and felt Ben's sturdy bare legs press against his stomach, he thought he might collapse with the relief that gripped him. He breathed deeply for a moment, content to hold his son and absorb every tiny movement, but thought of Laura waiting pushed him to his feet once more.

From that part of the cliff, the undisturbed part, the steps back up were clearly marked, but steep, and Richard held Ben against his shoulder and tried not to rush it. The boy was happily sucking his fist, and his hard little head bounced companionably against

Richard's jaw. Those bruises were going to be awesome.

'Oh, my god, Ben…' Laura had limped across to meet them, and held her arms out for her son.

'Don't expect any gratitude,' Richard said with a grin, as he handed Ben over.

'Hello, little man!' Laura breathed.

Ben bobbed backwards in her arms, to see who was holding him now. He went very still, and reached out a chubby hand and patted her nose, and then her cheek, his own face solemn, his eyes wide. Then he kicked his legs out straight, in his familiar sign of excitement, and flopped his head down against her shoulder, utterly relaxed.

'Mumma.'

***

Nerryn was the first to stir. Cantoc moved closer to her, so she would not feel alone, but when she opened her eyes and saw him, her disgust cut him to the bone. She tried to sit up, but sagged back against the sloping side of the hollow again.

'Be easy, Nerryn,' Cantoc said, trying not to let his hurt show. 'All is well.'

'Mylan?' she managed.

'He sleeps, still. You have used all your strength and more, both of you.'

'We had no choice,' Nerryn said, finding her voice. 'Arric—'

'Arric has gone.' He would wait until Mylan woke, before he explained about Dafna; the uncomfortable thought had come to him that the matter was not his to decide upon, after all. These were her children, and if they chose to avenge her on Tir's lady, they had the right to do that. But the war itself had been his choice, and the Moorlanders must not suffer any longer for his foolishness.

'Tir and the Lady Laura have gone to find Dreis. Where did you leave him?'

'In my room,' Nerryn said, frowning. 'Why do you look so worried?'

'The cliff is destroyed,' he said grimly. 'At least along much of its length. Your home has gone.' Just like Dafna and Talfrid's, except that this time it had been their three children who, between them, had caused the devastation.

'Oh, please, no…' Nerryn raised bloodied and muddy hands to her face. She made no sound, but Cantoc saw tears leaking between her fingers. From the corner of his eye he noticed Mylan stirring, and left Nerryn's side to go to him. When he had fully woken, Cantoc recounted what Laura had told him.

'So you must decide,' he finished, 'Will you let her live?'

'We cannot,' Mylan said at once. 'Nerryn? Do you agree?'

'She is a courageous woman,' Nerryn ventured, wiping her eyes. 'I have seen her great love for those she calls her own.' She took a deep breath. 'But if the Moorlanders were to pay for our mother's death, then so too should this descendant of her true killer.'

'The war was intended to remove the right to rule,' Cantoc pointed out, a quiet desperation wakening in him. 'It was never for the purpose of killing each and every one. Lady Laura has suffered deeply, and may yet suffer more if her child is found dead.'

'Nevertheless,' Mylan said, 'her father took our mother's life. As Arric said, when people are killed in cold blood, those who are left must both punish and be punished.'

Cantoc considered him for a moment. Mylan was sitting up very straight, and although he lacked the strength to stand yet, it would not be long. Not long enough for Tir to get his lady somewhere safe. 'Very well,' he said, 'your decision is made. However, I have given her my word that no-one shall harm her while I still breathe. So, you must first kill me.'

He rose to his feet and flipped Mylan's own knife in his hand, before throwing it to stick in the ground by the younger man's feet. He reached down and pulled Mylan to his feet. 'Make it quick,' he requested, as Laura had, and stepped away, gesturing to the knife. Mylan glanced down at it, then back up at Cantoc.

'Why?' he asked, and Cantoc's heart contracted at the bewildered, youthful confusion. 'Why did you make such a promise?'

'Because she is, as Nerryn said, a woman of true and selfless courage. I could not stand by and watch her suffer any further.' He studied Mylan carefully as he went on, 'Tir is showing himself to be a good king. I would hate just as much to see him hurt. So,' he repeated, as calmly as he could, 'you must first kill me.'

'Don't, Mylan,' Nerryn begged.

Cantoc blinked in surprise, but his heart picked up pace in hope. 'You no longer agree that she should die?'

'Neither of us thinks *you* should,' Mylan said. He shook his head, the anger flowing out of him. 'And… you are right; Tir's lady deserves it no more than you do.'

Cantoc let out a long, shaking breath, and nodded. Nerryn stood, and went to her brother. She took his hand, and he noticed the bloodied knuckles and winced. She shook her head, dismissing it. Her eyes were shadowed and dull as she looked over the top of the hollow, towards the east where they had sent all the destructive power they had not known they possessed. Cantoc guessed where her thoughts were, or at least, who they were with.

'I am sorry to hear of the prince,' he said softly.

She turned back to him, her eyes shining, tears trembling on her lower lids. 'He was protecting his king, and his land,' she said, but the pain in her voice gave the lie to her stoic words. She put her arms around her brother, and leaned against him, and Cantoc turned away and left them to their moment.

As he did so he saw figures approaching from the seaward end of the hollow. The lord Tir and his lady… Cantoc squinted against the sunlight, and weakened with relief. 'Dreis lives!' He looked back at the twins. 'Tir and the lady Laura are coming. You must be sure you have made the right decision,' he warned. 'I would have them know they are safe. If they are indeed safe?'

'They are,' Mylan said. 'They will have my word, as they have yours.'

'Then let us go to meet them,' Cantoc said. 'We have no more need of this shelter and I would as soon not be here any longer than need be.'

'Nor I,' Nerryn said, and she seemed to have her own reasons, as her eyes fixed on one particular part of the ground. But Cantoc did not ask what those reasons were.

The three of them climbed up the shallow slope, and looked towards the cliff top and the two figures coming across the uneven ground. Laura carried Dreis, who slept on her shoulder, nestled as close as he could get. She was limping, and bedraggled, and tired-looking, and Cantoc saw her hesitate as she saw them.

'It is strange,' Nerryn said quietly, 'the first time I saw her I could not understand why such a glory as Tir would be attracted to her. But now I see.'

'She is dirty, and a mess,' Mylan pointed out.

'She needs a good deal of sleep,' Cantoc added. 'And clothes that fit.'

'She has a beauty that cleanliness cannot enhance,' Nerryn mused. 'She is of the land. She is nature itself. See her properly, Mylan. Cantoc. See her as she is.'

Cantoc couldn't help smiling, but as the little group drew closer he saw what Nerryn meant.

The mortal woman wore the odd clothes he had become accustomed to seeing, as muddy and torn and outsized as they were, but her skin was pure, washed by the rain, fed by it. Her hands were unadorned, strong on her child's back, her grey eyes ringed by lashes as dark as her hair. She looked up at Tir, and after a wordless exchange, he reached out to take Dreis from her and she put her hand in the pocket of her coat.

Cantoc felt Mylan stiffen beside him, but put a calming hand on his arm. 'Wait,' he murmured.

Lady Laura drew something from her pocket, and it was not a weapon. Rather it was a straight-edged object, flattish-looking, and she stared at it for a moment before holding it out to Nerryn. Nerryn gasped as she took it, and Cantoc's eyes blurred.

'What miracle is this?' he whispered, blinking rapidly; Dafna lay in Nerryn's hand, and these stupid tears were stealing her from him again. His vision cleared, and she was still there, her very essence, preserved forever behind this protective layer, and kept firm in its frame.

'Who has done this?' Mylan asked, and his finger shook as he traced his mother's likeness.

'I drew it when I was little,' Laura said. She sounded hesitant. 'Is it very like her?'

Nerryn looked to Cantoc, who nodded and swallowed hard. 'It is… perfect.'

Nerryn passed the likeness to her brother, and wrapped her arms around the startled Laura. Then Laura's own arms came up and she returned the embrace.

Cantoc turned to Tir, then, meaningfully, at Mylan, who nodded and crossed to stand before his king. He offered the open-handed gesture of trust, which Tir accepted while boosting his son higher on his shoulder. The totterling sighed, snuffled, and burrowed his face deeper into his father's neck.

'My lord Tir, I recognise and greet you.' Mylan went to one knee. 'Further, I pledge you my blade, my protection, and my life. I am yours to command.' He looked up, and when he saw Tir was too moved to speak, he grinned. 'If I *had* my blade I would pledge it,' he added, and Tir relaxed and even gave a short, disbelieving laugh. The difficult moment scattered, yet the pledge remained, and Cantoc knew he need have no further concerns.

Tir grasped Cantoc's forearm tight when he echoed Mylan's words. 'Thank you, Cantoc. I will come to you, when I've seen my family home, and we'll talk.'

'I await that with pleasure.' Cantoc felt the power of the king's presence like a warm cloak. Very like the way Casta had been. It was a comforting and hopeful feeling, and his heart hurt a little when he thought about what he had planned for this man. He turned his attention back to the others; Laura was offering her condolences to Nerryn on the loss of her father.

'Thank you,' Nerryn said. She sounded harder, all of a sudden, and Cantoc frowned as she stepped away and back towards the hollow again.

'And now, My Lord,' he said to Tir, 'I must begin to rebuild, where I can.'

'Yeah, me too,' Tir said, the light dying from his eyes. 'I heard things are bad back home.'

Cantoc was about to try and express his sorrow for what had passed, but his attention was now fully taken by Nerryn, who had jumped down into the hollow. She stooped, and plucked Mylan's knife from the ground, and Cantoc flinched as she climbed out, instinct pushing him a step back.

'Do not worry, Cantoc. It is not you who will find themselves on the end of this, either by my hand or my brother's.' She tucked the blade into her belt, at the small of her back, and took several steps before Mylan snapped out of his stunned trance and grabbed her arm.

'Wait! You cannot go to the *trigoryon an pell* alone!'

'I am not going to them.'

'But they are the ones who loosed the gwyllgi. Is that not where your need for vengeance lies now?'

Nerryn shook her arm free; Cantoc had never seen her look so fierce. 'Who is the one who killed our father, and began this?'

'Hewyl? You don't know where he is!'

'I will find him,' she said, softly, dangerously.

'Michael?' Lady Laura put in, disbelieving. 'You think he would kill someone?'

'I do not know his mortal name, but if he calls himself Hewyl then yes.'

'But he's so peaceful, he would never... I lived with him for years! He is a traveller, a scholar, wanting to learn all he can of your kind. He would *never* harm one of you. Never.'

'He saved my life,' Tir said. 'I'd trust him with it again.'

'But Arric said...' Nerryn's face paled. 'Oh, Mylan, do you think it was *Arric?* Could he have done it?' Her voice pleaded with her brother to deny the possibility, but Cantoc knew such a denial would never come.

'He described what happened, in great detail,' Mylan reminded her, his voice hollow with belated realisation. 'He was quick to blame first Maer, then the stranger.'

Cantoc nodded. 'And he was the one who came to me, to tell me what he'd found.'

Mylan sighed. 'Yes, I believe Arric killed our father. But he is long gone now.'

Nerryn took a deep breath and squared her shoulders. 'Then I will find him. And I will do what must be done.'

'Please, don't,' Tir said. 'Maer needs you—'

'What?' Nerryn and Mylan both spoke at once, and Cantoc himself felt his heartbeat pick up.

'Maer needs you,' Tir repeated, frowning, then his expression cleared. 'He didn't die, honey... not yet anyway,' he added quickly. 'He was in a bad way when I left him, but Michael took him to the Foresters. Those guys'll fix him up if anyone will.'

'Lawbryn said his arm was torn off,' Nerryn whispered. She looked about to collapse, and Mylan put his arm around her shoulder.

'It was pretty badly mangled,' Tir said, his eyes bleak as he remembered. 'But I have hopes for him, and if he pulls through he's going to need you.'

'Stop!' Nerryn said, hope still on her face, but now tempered with the realisation, 'The Foresters are against you now. Against Maer.'

'Only two of them.'

'No,' his lady put in. She looked worried again. 'Michael said they've had a change of leader. He's turned his people against the Moorlanders and pledged to the Coastals. To Cantoc.'

'Very well,' Cantoc said grimly. 'Let them greet their newly sworn lord.' He folded his arms. 'Who is coming with me?'

Nerryn stepped forward, and so did Mylan. Tir looked to his lady. 'Will you and Ben be okay? Can you get to your car?'

She nodded and held her son closer. 'Please,' she whispered, her eyes only on Tir. 'Come back safe. And soon. I… I need to talk to you.'

'I will. I swear.' He caught her face gently between his hands and lowered his mouth to hers. When he drew back, Laura was wiping at her eyes and sniffing, and Tir was looking wretched.

'My Lord,' Cantoc said quietly, firmly. 'Your brother needs you.'

Lady Laura left them, then, limping back across the field towards where the road lay, and Tir watched her out of sight. Cantoc wondered if he was even aware of the way his hands were working, as if they felt empty and lost without her or the totterling to touch.

Mylan took his blade back from his sister. 'You will not be allowed anywhere near Maer with this,' he said. 'They think you still blame him for Father's death.' He re-sheathed it.

Tir nodded, coming back to life. 'Good call.' He cleared his throat. 'Okay. Cantoc, you and Nerryn will go in first, since you're not their enemy. Mylan and I will wait outside the forest. Once you've found where they're keeping Maer, one of you stay with him, the other one can make your excuses and come find us. Are we clear?'

The three Coastals glanced at each other, and Cantoc saw the twitch of a smile on Mylan's face. 'We are… clear,' he ventured, and Mylan's smile widened into something real.

'Clear,' he echoed.

'Clear,' Nerryn said, and Cantoc's heart flickered with pleasure to see her looking so determined. He felt the flare of a new hope for his people, a fierce pride he hadn't felt in too long. They would rebuild their coastal home, better, and stronger, and these two would be his family. As he would be theirs.

He eyed their king, this stranger who was now every bit as deeply entrenched in this land as any full elemental. Even as Cantoc watched, the bruised and battered body of the half-mortal straightened, the strong fingers curled around the blood and sweat-stained, leather-wrapped handle of his blade, and Tir turned his face towards the east and his ruined homelands. His dark hair lifted in the light autumn wind, and the frown that had been settling between his brows faded.

'Cool. Let's go.'

Epilogue

The Forest, 15 October 2012

The bride wore green. All eyes moved from the young prince who waited for her, to the winding path down which she approached the clearing. Her auburn hair was twisted back at the sides into two long plaits, and the rest hung free down her back; the slenderness of her waist was accentuated by a sash hung with horse-chestnuts and leaves, and her smooth, strong arms were bare but for a coil of copper around each wrist.

'I hate her,' Laura whispered, and she felt Richard shaking, trying not to laugh.

She looked around them at what was left of the forest, and her thoughts went to the mine. All the survivors of that unthinkable day were here, trying, for now at least, to put their sorrows to one side and celebrate the life and love of their treasured Prince Maer.

Their new home in the mine up by the mill was taking shape, and even Deera had shown her deep gratitude when Laura had told her of it… Laura had almost earned herself a smile with that one. Her eyes sought Deera out now; the former queen's face was still bruised but she looked stronger and more beautiful than ever. She was smiling as she gazed at her son, but even as Laura watched, the smile faltered and she turned her face to the treetops, as if Casta were there.

Despite what Richard had seen, Laura had the feeling Casta was more likely to be in the trees themselves, or in the stones, or in the staff Richard held at his side. She brushed her fingers over it, and it felt warm. Smoother than it appeared. Comforting.

Perhaps Kernow, too, was with them today, and looking at Martha Horncup she felt certain the little spriggan was thinking the same sad, but hopeful thoughts. As for Tom, he had loved this land as deeply as anyone, even before. If he was anywhere he would be here, too. She closed her eyes briefly and sent him a welcome. Just in case.

The ceremony began then, and Laura's attention was taken up by the simple beauty of it. Maer and Nerryn linked hands, and when it was time for them to pledge their love they spoke in low, awed voices, as if neither could believe they were truly standing here together at last.

Then Richard took the guitar Laura had brought him from home, and moved to the centre of the clearing. Everyone else ceased to exist for Laura then. Even, for this one moment, Ben, who sat on Jacky's lap.

Richard strummed a few chords, and then looked straight at Laura. His green eyes caught the last of the day's sunlight and held it, turned it magical. His mouth lifted in the faintest of smiles, and he started to sing. She listened, as completely spellbound as she had always been, transported back to when she had listened at the door of his classroom at Lynher Mill Primary, a million and one years ago.

His voice was strong, but he kept it soft now, its power only apparent in the ease with which it lifted and fell. And all the while his eyes were on her. An ache settled into her heart as she accepted what he did not yet know; that this would be the last time they would be together. He had to move into his new life now, and she must move back into her old one. Her pre-Richard one. Her empty, hopeless one. And she must leave Lynher Mill and all these miraculous creatures to do it.

The song ended, and slowly the entranced gathering came back to life. Sticks banged together, and on the ground and the stones, and hoots and calls of appreciation spread like fire throughout the mass of elementals and others in the clearing.

Richard seemed to come back from some far-off place as well, and he put the guitar aside with a faintly embarrassed smile, as if he'd been caught skipping a chore and playing instead. He remembered his duty though, and stood up to speak.

First he paid tribute to the fallen at Lynher Mill, and the losses were mourned by all who gathered in the shaded, half-lit clearing and beyond. The sorrow in Richard's voice elicited answering sighs, and tears, as he named those he had known, and expressed regret that there were so many more that he would never meet.

'And Kernow,' he said, in quiet awe, 'who gave her life to the service of those she loved… in the end that courage cost her everything. Her bravery and skill will never be forgotten, and I am one of the many who owe their lives to her. I will never forget her. I make this pledge to you all: her people will never be homeless or in need, while the Lightning and the Blade hold Lynher Mill.'

He gradually led them back into the joy of the evening; telling of the great love between his brother and their coastal family, of the courage and generosity of Cantoc, the bride's protector, and of the strength and tenacity of the Moorlanders.

Cantoc and Mylan had been hesitant when Nerryn had begged their attendance, but it was widely known that the blame for the direction the war had taken lay with Arric. The same understanding and forgiveness that had been extended to Nerryn, had not been withheld from these penitent Coastals. The two men bowed in gratitude as they were acknowledged by the gathering, and Laura even saw Cantoc's eyes glisten in the cool evening light.

Finally, Richard spoke, with warmth and gratitude, of the Foresters themselves.

'When we came back here on that day, with Cantoc, you rose up and spoke what was in your hearts, not what your new leader had tried to make you believe. For that, we thank you. You helped

Lyelt understand what being a leader was, and what it wasn't. For that, we thank you. You accepted Ykana back as your leader, but were gracious enough to also accept Lyelt as her second-in-command. For that, we thank you.'

His voice lowered then, and softened, and his breath caught in his throat as he said, 'Most of all, you saved Maer's life. For that, *I* thank you.'

'And I thank you,' Nerryn said, standing up.

'And I thank you,' Deera added, stepping forward.

Maer stood, his arm strapped tightly to his chest, and took his bride's hand. His voice, too, was hoarse with emotion. 'And I thank you.'

Ykana moved into the clearing. 'We share your joy, and to it we add our own that your son is safe and well. There will be time for discussion and the declaring of new alliances tomorrow, but this is a celebration. Dance, sing, feast! Move amongst each other with freedom and friendship, for our people are one once again.'

As soon as the first fascinated elemental picked up Richard's favourite, hand-painted guitar, and plucked experimentally at the strings, the party melted into informality. Laura knew it was time to say what she had to say. Her heart suddenly tight, she turned to Jacky, who was holding Ben on his knee.

'Will you care for him just for a minute longer?'

'Hey, don't trust him,' Richard warned, appearing at her side, 'he gives those things away.' He grinned down at Jacky, who was finally learning to understand his king's humour and smiled back, although still a little shy in front of Laura.

The spriggan brushed down the lapel of his rescued, and newly-washed green jacket. 'Jacky will take good care of Ben,' he promised.

Laura's eyes widened. 'What did you call him?'

'Ben.' Jacky looked up, his head on one side, a tiny, puzzled frown painting his face. 'Why, is that not his name?' He gave Laura a little smile then, and she almost laughed, until Ben saw her and leaned towards her.

'Mum-mum?' He held out his arms, his fingers opening and closing.

Laura touched his face. 'In a minute, sweet-pea.' She turned away, so fast she almost fell over Deera, who had come to speak to her.

'I'm sorry,' Laura muttered. 'I have to talk to Richard, would you excuse me?'

'Wait.' Deera put a hand on her arm. 'Please.'

'I can't. *This* can't. Richard, I'm leaving Ben here with you.'

He froze. 'What?'

'Listen to me,' Deera said urgently. 'You do not need to do this!'

'I do. I can't separate them, it'll kill them both.'

'You can stay with them.'

'Of course I can't, how...' Laura's voice stumbled away into silence, and she stared at the former queen, waiting, hardly daring to breathe.

'I suspected something on that night,' Deera confessed. 'When Tir took the Lightning, you held his hand on the staff. Did you not feel something?'

Laura remembered that feeling vividly, it had been as if something else was holding their two hands, keeping them firmly on the staff as Richard spoke the oath. And there had been that strange, comforting warmth earlier, too. She eyed the staff with a mixture of fear and hope, and nodded.

'And have you not noticed other things?' Deera pressed.

'Other... what things?'

'Your own light comes more easily now. I could not take it away from you in the cavern when I wished to, not without a struggle. Kernow felt something in you also, the day you left Tir behind with us. And you are moving more quickly.' Deera's voice was oddly gentle. 'You are not one of us, My Lady, you can never be. But you are Tir's queen. You may stay with him, if that is what you would wish.'

'If?' Laura managed. *If* it is what I wish?' Her incredulous gaze flew from Deera to Richard, who looked equally stunned. 'Are you serious?'

'Why didn't you say something?' Richard demanded, his hand finding Laura's and gripping it tightly. They were both shaking.

'I did not know for sure,' Deera said. 'It was not until I spoke to Hewyl that I came to understand more. As his name suggests, he is deeply observant of both mortals and elementals, and we talked that day, when he came to help. He also found this, and kept it safe until he left on his travels once again.' She handed Laura the battered blue folder. 'The likenesses of Tir and Greencoat are... I wonder if...' She couldn't quite say the words, but Laura nodded.

'I will,' she promised. 'It will be as like Casta as I can make it.' Her mind was still reeling, and she cast about for somewhere to sit but there was only the ground. She took it.

Richard crouched beside her and turned her face up to his. 'Honey? You were really going to let me keep Ben here?'

She didn't answer but, like Cantoc, he must have read the truth in her eyes because he closed his own, and pressed his lips to her forehead. 'I have never loved you more,' he murmured against her skin, 'and it's just getting worse.'

Her voice shook when she found it. 'It's a good thing I'm allowed to stay then, isn't it?'

He rose and pulled her to her feet, and she leaned into his warmth, wrapping her arms around his waist. Deera sensed their need to be alone, and with a tiny nod of her head she went to speak to her beloved son and her new daughter.

'My Lady,' Jacky said, appearing at Laura's elbow. 'The boy is wantin' his mumma, so he says.' He smiled as he passed Ben into his mother's arms.

'So.' Richard bent to speak directly into Laura's ear, over his son's head. 'You're sure you're ready to give up hot food, soft beds, TV and beer?'

She remembered those words, spoken with no

clue what life held in store, but with utter sincerity, in their brightly-lit Plymouth kitchen. The day he had asked her to marry him.

'What, to live in a cold, damp cave underground?' She pretended to consider. 'I suppose I could be persuaded.'

He gave her his best slow, sexy smile, and lowered his voice. 'Oh yeah? How?'

'Got any cheese?'

He snorted, tried to muffle his mirth by pressing his face to her hair, then gave up trying to maintain an air of dignity, and his laughter turned heads all over the clearing. Ben, delighted with the chance to yell his own raucous laugh, bounced in his mother's arms and joined in.

Laura's gaze swept the wedding guests, grouped in little clusters around the clearing, and saw that everyone was responding to the sound with smiles of their own. All but one of them, who was looking at his king with something more than acceptance, and reflected pleasure.

The spriggan's face was utterly still, but there was real love in his eyes as he stood, with quiet dignity, now the elder of his clan and re-named Kernow.

But he would always be Jacky Greencoat to those who loved him best.

The End.

Author's Note:

I chose not to include a blow-by-blow account of the rescue of Maer, and the 'liberation' of the Foresters, as I felt it would have diluted the ending. Instead I let Richard/Tir tell you how it happened. He is the king, after all.

But what about Arric?
Well, for now we're going to leave him running free, making his mischief (if he hasn't yet learned his lesson) but we'll catch up with him a little later, and that's a promise; I'm not quite ready to say goodbye to these beautiful creatures and the land they call home, and I think there are more adventures to be had and more characters to meet.* Maybe the next book will be a full novel in this series, or maybe it will be a series of novellas, with a self-contained story in each one, downloadable from my website. Whatever it is, I can't wait!

*I have a feeling Nerryn is going to turn into something pretty badass, and she has vengeance on her mind…

Acknowledgements

My thanks, as always, to everyone who's bought or read these stories, and especially those who've taken a moment leave a review or feedback. Thank you all for coming with me as I explored this story I've lived with for nearly twenty years! I hope you have enjoyed reading it even a fraction as much as I have enjoyed writing it.

Particular gratitude goes to the utterly brilliant **Sean Ryan**, for his superb manipulation of my bog-standard photos, and to **Jeanine Henning** for turning them into the gorgeous covers she's made for the whole series. *www.jeaninehenning.com*
I would also like to thank **James Johnston-Laffey**, who brought me firmly into the fantasy genre by creating the gorgeous map you will find at the front of the book. You can find more of his amazing artwork at: *www.facebook.com/artofthefairy*
Thank you to my fabulous beta-readers: **Tonya Rittenhouse, Jane Clements, Johnny Nys** and **Anita Davison**. Expert typo-spotters, all!
Lastly, a special thank you to **Ann Spencer** and **Tonya Rittenhouse**, for volunteering as characters in this book, and I hope Ann isn't too disappointed she didn't get any "action" after all!

Printed in Great Britain
by Amazon